MALDON

2 4 OCT 2019

D0766530

Please return this book on or before the date shown above. To renew go to www.essex.gov.uk/libraries, ring 0345 603 7628 or go to any Essex library.

Essex County C

Essex County Council

3013021664998 7

Sarah J Naughton grew up in Dorset, on a diet of tales of imperilled heroines and wolves in disguise. As an adult her reading matter changed, but those dark fairy tales had deep roots. Her debut children's thriller, *The Hanged Man Rises*, featured a fiend from beyond the grave menacing the streets of Victorian London, and was shortlisted for the 2013 Costa award. Her first adult novel, *Tattletale,* was released in September 2017. *The Other Couple* is her second psychological thriller. Sarah lives in central London with her husband and two sons.

the other couple

Sarah J Naughton

For my sister, whose perfect wedding
I ruthlessly stole and made evil.
Thanks, Flissers.

First published in Great Britain in 2018 by Trapeze.
This paperback edition published in 2018 by Trapeze,
an imprint of The Orion Publishing Group Ltd
Carmelite House, 50 Victoria Embankment
London EC4Y 0DZ

An Hachette UK company

1 3 5 7 9 10 8 6 4 2

Copyright © Sarah J Naughton 2018

The moral right of Sarah J Naughton to be identified as
the author of this work has been asserted in accordance with
the Copyright, Designs and Patents Act of 1988.

All rights reserved. No part of this publication may be reproduced,
stored in a retrieval system, or transmitted in any form or by any means,
electronic, mechanical, photocopying, recording, or otherwise, without
the prior permission of both the copyright owner and the
above publisher of this book.

All the characters in this book are fictitious, and any resemblance
to actual persons, living or dead, is purely coincidental.

A CIP catalogue record for this book is
available from the British Library.

ISBN (Mass Market Paperback) 978 1 4091 6698 6

Typeset by Born Group

Printed and bound in Great Britain by Clays Ltd, Elcograf S.p.A.

MIX
Paper from
responsible sources
FSC
www.fsc.org FSC® C104740

www.orionbooks.co.uk

What a beautiful place. The spread legs and arcing belly of the cave, with its neat sapphire bellybutton open to the sky. The grey walls, shimmering with mica and feldspar, sweeping down to the sand where scattered rocks and pebbles warn that this won't be here for ever, that all beauty must decay. One day, thousands of years from now, this shell of stone will crash down into the sea. Or perhaps it will fall in the next storm.

The sun sparking off the waves blinds me. It has all the glitter of glamour magic: that sleight of hand that has you looking one way, while the real trickery is happening elsewhere, in the dark beneath the surface. When we came here I was afraid of the sharks, the stonefish, the stingrays that could drive a barb into your heart. But it was you I should have been afraid of all along.

In nature, beauty is a warning. The multicoloured bands on a coral snake, the rich pigments of a poison dart frog, the rainbow frills of a cuttlefish that tell you it's death to touch. Why shouldn't it be the same in humans? Your perfect face is nothing but a mask. I thought I could read your thoughts in those blue eyes, but they were just mirrors reflecting my own desires.

It's so peaceful, with the murmur of the sea and the light breeze singing through the skylight. The water laps at my toes, skin-warm. The sun is directly overhead. If it wasn't, if we had tipped over into afternoon, I would see your shadow growing in front of me, dulling the glimmer of the sea. You're coming up behind me. I can hear the whisper of your feet sinking into the wet sand. But I can't get up. You've made sure of that.

I fumble for the opening of the bag, the mouth of it pulsing in my vision, as if it's trying to tell me something. That you are a liar and a killer and I must save myself. All I can do is try, but you have taken so much from me already, and now even my strength is gone, my co-ordination. I cannot tell whether my fingers have closed around the knife or my pen or even the empty water bottle. They are thick and numb: sausages on a butcher's slab. But there's no more time. I have just slipped the thing that might be the knife into the pocket of my shorts when your hand descends on my shoulder.

I turn my head and am just able to make out your familiar shape. My vision may be blurred but my eyes are open. At last.

PART ONE

1

FV Hospital, Ho Chi Minh City, Vietnam

Monday 3 October

I'm underwater. But there's no need to panic. I can breathe normally, like a mermaid. There's a sensation of pressure on my body, as if I really am very deep. And yet it isn't dark. I can see daylight through my eyelids. Perhaps I'm looking up to the surface. It's cold down here. I want to swim back up. I kick my legs.

There's a metallic rattle and a shudder passes down my body.

I'm lying on my back in bed. Not our bed. Ours wouldn't shake like that. So, where? I try to remember last night. My mouth is bone dry and I've got a splitting headache so I must have been very drunk. Why aren't we at home? Has something happened? I experience a sickly sensation of dread. Did we argue again? Did I storm off?

Then I remember. We got married. We must have been out celebrating. Then what?

I frown but only half my face seems to move. The left side feels stiff and bruised, as if someone's punched me. Did I fall over? It wouldn't be the first time, although I haven't been *that* drunk since my early twenties.

'Ollie?'

My voice is a croak, barely audible, and is choked off by a coughing fit that sends lightning bolts of pain across my left temple. How much did I have? Is Ollie in the same state?

I feel for his warm body next to mine but my hand blunders across the cool sheet and slips off the edge of the mattress. He's already up. Hopefully getting me some toast and a strong coffee. The daylight has turned my eyelids crimson. It must be late morning. I should open my eyes but I know it's going to hurt, so I just lie there. It's only a hangover. A coffee and some painkillers will sort me out. Ollie's gone to get them.

And yet, that sensation of dread.

I feel like I've done something bad. What have I done?

I concentrate, trying to remember. Flashes of the wedding come back to me. Ollie and I cutting the cake on the lawn, the cool wood floor under my bare feet as we dance, picking pearls out of my hair one by one. And then other images. Stuffing slippery lingerie into the side pocket of my suitcase. Looking down on cotton-wool clouds.

Our honeymoon. We're on our honeymoon. I'm in a hotel bed.

Wincing, I peel my eyes open a sliver. Daylight blares through the crack. I blink and blink, each clunk of eyelid making my head throb, until my surroundings finally start to take shape.

The room is pure white. There are no ornaments, no detritus of human habitation, just bare white walls, a white lino floor and white ceiling tiles, bisected by a single fluorescent strip. The most minimalist hotel room I've ever seen. Painfully I turn my head. Take in the equipment, the monitors, the dials, the tubes and wires.

It's not a hotel. It's a hospital.

What have I done?

2

Emirates First-Class Lounge, Heathrow Airport

Friday 23 September

Asha watches him charm the waitress, catching the glass she almost upends in her hurry to clear the negligible mess from the bar. She has magenta hair and tired eyes, the pallor of an Eastern European who's working too hard. But now she smiles and her cheeks flush: she thinks she's special. And she is. For that moment she's Ollie's world. He feels for her weariness, the thanklessness of clearing up after arrogant businessmen outraged that the crab is finished and they'll have to have smoked salmon instead. Worse are the men who pretend she's not even there: that she exists in another, entirely irrelevant dimension. But Ollie seems to know exactly how she must feel. As he retrieves a balled napkin that has rolled off the plates stacked on the waitress's arm, affection rolls over Asha in a warm wave.

She wanders to the window and gazes out across the floodlit tarmac where, despite the hour, planes are busily swallowing and disgorging passengers, dancing around each other as they jostle for the next spot on the runway. Theirs was due to take off an hour ago, but they've been delayed by a tropical storm over Pakistan.

She doesn't mind. She's tired, half drunk, and dreamy with visions of the resort she refused to even glance at in the brochure.

5

Apparently it was *Tatler*'s 'Ultimate Honeymoon Retreat' last year. Their three-week sojourn, with first-class flights on top, probably cost more than a normal person's annual salary. Than *her* annual salary, back when *she* was a normal person.

And yet it's not pity or camaraderie that she feels as she turns to watch the waitress retreat back into the harshly lit kitchen: it's gratitude. That she's no longer slaving behind a counter in the Islington McDonald's to get herself through university, or knocking out copy for financial brochures in the evenings, back when she barely earned five figures. No, her Prince Charming eventually turned up, as her mother always promised he would. And the best part is, she loves him.

Ollie lifts two bottles from the chrome bar and waggles them at her: *Chablis or Gavi di Gavi?* She points at the Chablis. He brings it back to the table and refills their glasses.

'Poor cow, having to deal with arsehole bankers all day,' Asha says.

Ollie grins and clinks her glass.

He's the arsehole banker, she's the council estate upstart. That's the joke. It's been the joke for the four years since they met. Since he rang her at the office and said, 'It seems that you don't think much of me, Miss Fadeyi.' She'd brazened it out, sounding far ballsier than she felt – if the establishment decided to close ranks on her it could really screw up her career – as she defended her article, with its phrases like 'Don't mistake affability for saintliness' and 'It's easy to be ethical when you're cushioned from all life's hardships.' The truth was, she'd become truly sick of hearing what a nice bloke Oliver Graveney was. She had bitten and scratched her way to the deputy editorship of this small but respected news magazine., and she was not universally beloved. But Ollie had had everything given to him on a plate, which allowed him to be jolly nice to everyone. It wasn't fair. That was what the article was about really: her, not him. But now she had to stand by her words.

'I meant it,' she had said. 'You have no idea what normal people go through. Your *work* involves finding ways to spend your money. Other people slave for every penny.'

'I accept everything you say,' he had said, infuriatingly charming, 'but aside from giving everything away – and I'm afraid I'm too selfish to do that – I try my best to be a decent person.'

'I'm sure you do,' Asha had said, her sails deflating. 'I was making a point about privilege in general, you were just an example.'

'Unfair.'

'Sorry.'

'You may buy me lunch to apologise.'

'I am not spending half my month's wages on lobster at The Ivy.'

'Only half?'

She laughed and hated herself for it.

'There's a sandwich bar next to St Olav's. Can you stretch to a prawn baguette? I promise you by two o'clock you'll be madly in love with me.'

And she was. She bloody well was.

After finishing the bottle they shower in the ridiculously opulent bathroom. Separately. They've been together long enough that showers are no longer just another opportunity for sex. But still, it is their honeymoon, so it might have been nice. She lingers under the hot flow but Ollie seems to take forever over his shave, so she gets out.

It isn't the first time she's been in a first-class lounge, but she never fails to be impressed: all this wood and glass, vases of orchids, cotton-wool robes, designer toiletries. On the way back she'll pocket a few and hand them out at work.

After Ollie finishes his shower she massages jasmine tea body lotion into his shoulders, working the tension out of his muscles. The fuss around the wedding has taken him away from work, and in his absence a couple of issues have arisen that have resulted in tense phone calls. Nothing major, he's assured her, but clearly enough to stress him out, and she doesn't want that, not on their honeymoon.

His shoulders are smooth and tanned, flawless, like everything else about him. The one minor physical imperfection is a black mole the size of a thumbprint on his chest. The damned thing terrifies her and every holiday she makes him promise to get it removed as soon as they get home. But he never does. She suspects he likes the fact she worries about it. She kisses behind his ear, and gets dressed.

They arrive at sunset, after a nerve-shredding connection from Ho Chi Minh City on a prop plane that coughs and grinds its way through the forty-five-minute journey to the island. The view is stunning as they skim over crimson-flecked waves towards a green island rising from the water, but she's incapable of enjoying it. Ollie laughs at her white-knuckled terror as the plane is buffeted by invisible currents of tropical air. When it banks steeply to make the final turn and seems to slide out of the sky she actually closes her eyes and prays.

'I just want you to know,' Ollie murmurs, 'in case something happens, that I love you.'

She doesn't open them again until the engines have whined to a stop and Ollie is helping her from her seat.

They step out into a wall of heat, and she tilts her head back to let it flow over her.

The airport is tiny. Flags like birthday candles are stuck into the roof of the terminal building: among them the Union Jack, the Stars and Stripes, the gold star of Vietnam, and a few others she doesn't recognise. There's something pathetically proud about the display. They've obviously read the *Tatler* article too.

At the top of the metal staircase she pauses to take in the sunset. The few wisps of pink cloud are edged with gold and the rest of sky morphs from orange in the west to crimson, mauve and the deep blue of night. The bumpy black horizon enclosing them on three sides must be jungle. A few lights, very few, twinkle from the blackness like stars.

Starting down the steps in front of her Ollie misses his footing and she lunges to catch him, pulling him back into her body. They both gasp with the shock of the near miss. A broken leg would have ended the holiday there and then.

It's hardly surprising he's wobbly on his feet. There were drinks on the flight from Dubai, and a 'local speciality' on the prop plane – a cloyingly sweet red liquid that she surreptitiously gave to Ollie when the flight attendant wasn't looking.

They carry on down the steps, slower now, and cross the tarmac to the terminal building hand in hand.

The airport is almost deserted. A grim-faced young man in uniform barely glances at their passports before waving them through to the arrivals area. This is not a place you'd want to get delayed. The single row of cracked plastic seats, and a dog-eared poster of a Vietnamese girl with faded flowers in her hair, gives the terminal a post-apocalyptic air. The only sign of life comes from the glow of a vending machine.

The swish of the sliding doors breaks the silence, and a squat middle-aged man slouches in, bringing with him the smell of stale cigarette smoke.

'Mister and Missus Graveney?'

Ollie shakes his hand and, ignoring his protestations, the man takes both the cases and wheels them back to the doors.

As they follow him outside Asha shivers. The heat is dissipating quickly into the clear night sky, and beyond the glow of the airport the road is dark and silent.

The driver loads their bags into the boot of the incongruously stylish Lexus. His eyes are pouched with tiredness and his skin is dull. They were due three hours ago, and this doesn't look like the type of place to give flight updates. But he offers no word of complaint, merely gets in after them, starts the engine, and pulls smoothly away. Asha settles into the now familiar luxury of leather bucket seats, perfect climate control and the faintly

9

sweet aroma of maplewood. Ollie sinks down beside her with a groan, and the velvety purr of the Lexus's engine is enough to send him instantly to sleep.

Through the window is only unbroken darkness so she takes her phone out of her bag to check the news. No signal. She looks at her watch. It's twenty minutes since they left the airport. They must be halfway by now. A full moon is rising above the tops of the trees, turning their canopies silver.

To think she can be bored of such privilege. What would her mum say?

Francoise lived long enough to witness the promising start to Asha's career but she never got to meet Ollie. When Asha visits her mum's grave in Islington Cemetery, she assures Francoise how much she would like him, and sometimes she whispers how rich he is. Not to boast, just so that her mum, who worked three jobs to keep Asha in food and shelter, knows that her daughter is safe, forever.

Guilty at the thought of reducing her beautiful husband to a meal ticket she turns and runs the back of her hand down Ollie's cheek to reassure him, as if he has heard her graveside secrets, that he's loved for himself alone. The moonlight has turned him into a marble statue, cold and remote. She nuzzles him until he stirs and shifts his head to rest it on hers. His heartbeat under her hand is strong and regular and eventually she drifts off to sleep, only waking when the car stops.

Groaning and yawning they get out.

The road has petered out. They stand in a clearing in the middle of the jungle, a lantern-lit path leading away towards an open-fronted bamboo hut. Its butter-yellow light is warm and welcoming. The driver unloads their cases and wheels them up the path and as Ollie runs ahead to help, a man is already rising from the desk inside.

Asha pauses for a moment by the car, inhaling the scent of jasmine.

Then her breath catches.

10

In the shadows of the trees a woman is sitting cross-legged on the ground, smiling at her.

It takes a heart-stopping few seconds before she realises that the figure is a statue. Taking a step closer she can make out the woman's face. Round pale cheeks and enormously long ears above which her black hair is gathered into a complicated topknot. Her gold shawl is chipped and tarnished but she retains an air of majesty. Stepping into the jungle hush Asha gets down on her knees and reaches for the figure's upturned hand. The wooden fingers are cool and smooth. There's a faint scent of incense coming from a brass dish on the ground, and some puddles of wax which must have once been candles.

Are there such things as female Buddhas? Is she a Hindu goddess? Or a deity from whatever folk religion the Vietnamese follow? Either way she exudes serenity and calm.

Atheist though she is, Asha closes her eyes and offers up a quick prayer. *Let things get back to the way they were.* It's a trivial and selfish plea, but maybe the old Eastern gods are more sympathetic to that sort of thing.

A rustling deeper in the trees makes her head jerk up. The shadows are impenetrable. Scrambling to her feet she hurries back up the path to join her husband.

'Mr and Mrs Graveney,' the slight, effeminate man at the desk says in barely accented English. They shake his hand. 'My name is Bay. I'm the manager here at Mango Tree. We've been looking forward to welcoming you.' Hanging on the wall behind him is a huge painting, all scarlets and yellows and gold leaf, depicting a warrior facing off an entire army with a single hunting bow. The warrior's face is totally devoid of expression.

'You must be very tired. Why don't I get you a drink?'

'Probably shouldn't,' Ollie says, smiling. 'But if you insist.'

Bay gets up and leads them to a lantern-lit wooden walkway that passes through the trees.

The sound of waves close by quickens her heart, and she squeezes Ollie's hand. He grins at her.

The walkway leads to a low, open rush-roofed building. There's a bar along one wall, behind which multi-hued bottles glimmer. Tables and benches are arranged on the decking, up to a wicker partition separating bar from beach. Soft music is playing, presumably just for them, as it's past one now and the bar is deserted. A tiny young woman appears to take their order, but Asha's attention is entirely occupied by the view beyond the partition. Bay stands quietly with his hands clasped while they take it in. The lighting has been kept low, just a few hanging lanterns, so as not to interfere with the moonlight. The sea is a sheet of silver, dotted by a few black masses that must be tiny islands. It meets the sky at a horizon so broad and clear she is sure she can make out the curvature of the earth. Leading down to the murmuring surf is a beach that stretches a hundred metres in both directions, bounded at each end by a spur of jungle. The sand is an ethereal, luminescent white. Her toes ache to bury themselves in it. Of all the beautiful, exotic paradises Ollie has taken her to, this is the loveliest.

She turns to him and smiles. He smiles back, but he looks tired. Tired and stressed, still. Her heart sinks a little. Not tonight, then.

Bay mutters something to the woman and she hurries away, then he pulls out a chair for Asha and they all sit.

'First, may I congratulate you on your marriage.'

They thank him. Asha automatically twists her new ring. It's tighter than usual because of the heat and the flight.

'I hope the Mango Tree Resort will be all you dream of for your honeymoon.'

The woman reappears with a tray of finger food and two tacky-looking pink cocktails. Ollie and Asha exchange glances. The place is slick but not *that* slick.

'We have a few other guests staying with us at the moment, but I've placed you in my personal favourite bungalow, at the far edge of the retreat, for privacy.'

By privacy Bay clearly means, *so that you don't disturb the other guests with your rampant newly-wed sex*. Asha sincerely hopes this might be a prescient decision.

12

'In here is everything you need to know: our spa menu, dining options, laundry service, et cetera.' He slides the brochure across the table. On the front cover a woman's legs dangle into an infinity pool. Asha's heart skips again.

'We have a fully equipped gym and a spa. We can organise tours of the area, hikes, treks up the holy mountain, diving and fishing trips, and boat trips to local beauty spots such as the So Den Caves or the old colonial prison at the other end of the island. I'm afraid the only thing we cannot offer you, and we take pride in this,' he smiles, 'is internet access. You are of course welcome to use any of the facilities at the desk, but in the bungalows themselves you will be completely internet-and phone-free. An oasis of calm away from the modern world.'

'Sounds wonderful,' Ollie says.

Asha sighs inwardly. Sometimes these beach idylls can start to pall and it would have been nice to go on Twitter occasionally.

'These,' Bay says, gesturing to the drinks, 'are our signature Mango Tree cocktail made with local rice wine, coconut milk and our own mangoes and lychees from the trees you passed on your way in. Please.'

They sip dutifully. It tastes like a very sweet smoothie. Asha picks up a spring roll and bites off a corner. It's unbearably hot and she hiccups and puts the rest down. Ollie puts a whole one straight into his mouth. Asha sniggers at his attempts to maintain his dignity as his eyes stream and his cheeks burn, until he gives in and gulps down the rest of his cocktail and hers.

'We serve a buffet breakfast here from seven, but of course you can order food to your bungalow whatever time you like.'

'It would be lovely to eat looking out over the sea,' she says.

'Wait until you see your bungalow.' Bay smiles and raises an eyebrow. She likes him. Gets the feeling that however rudely he is treated – and he must have his fair share of bankers and celebrities – he would maintain this air of friendly calm.

Ollie is gazing silently towards the horizon. His eyelids are drooping.

'You must be tired,' Bay goes on. 'Why don't I show you to your bungalow?'

They all stand. Ollie reaches into his pocket for the handful of coins he's changed up especially and lays them on the table for the waitress.

'Could you give this to the driver for me?' He holds out a few notes to Bay, who smiles indulgently.

'This isn't Saigon, Mr Graveney. There is no need to tip here.'

Of course there isn't, Asha thinks, *at the prices you charge*.

'Call me Ollie.'

They follow Bay through the opening in the partition that leads to the beach. Another walkway leads off to the right, and as they set off they begin to see, nestled against the trees, down their own private pathways, the bungalows.

Despite the breadth of the frontage – all glass, looking out across the sea – the only structural supports seem to be two slim posts, which pass diagonally down into the limestone base of the building. In front of this base is the promised infinity pool, just big enough for two, a couple of sunbeds upholstered in beige, a gas barbecue and a patio heater.

Presumably the silver lanterns marking the way are lit for their benefit and will be extinguished as soon as they are safely in their beds, but it's a fire risk nevertheless. Always so practical, like her mother. That's the way it is when you grow up just about managing, as long as nothing bad happens: an accident, an illness, a job loss. If her mum had died ten years earlier, Asha would have been put into care, and then where would she be now? Not here, certainly. A sudden prick of insecurity makes her grip Ollie's arm. He kisses her head lazily. He really is very drunk.

Apart from their quiet footsteps the only sounds are the lapping of the waves and an occasional rustle in the undergrowth beyond the bungalows. She doesn't like the proximity of the trees, which dwarf the fragile wooden buildings, but this time it's not for any practical reason. Though they are still and quiet, she feels their presence at the edge of her vision, watching her.

As if he feels the same, Ollie says suddenly, 'What are the trees?'

'Banyans.'

'With all those raggedy bits hanging down they look a bit like mummies.'

'Those are the roots,' Bay says. 'The banyan seed germinates in the body of another tree then sends them out. When they touch the ground and root there the tree gets stronger and stronger until it kills its host.'

'That's gratitude for you.'

A sharp noise from the edge of the jungle. The other two are laughing so don't hear it but Asha's head snaps round. She stares into the darkness. Ollie's right. With their dangling roots, the trees look like corpses. It should be funny but it isn't.

The noise again, further off, as if the creature is retreating into the jungle.

A big cat? A wolf? She has no idea what animals are native to Vietnam, whether they should worry about snakes or sharks or stonefish. She doesn't even bother to read up on their holiday destinations any more. With other boyfriends, by the time they travelled she would be an expert on local restaurants and attractions. She'd have learned a few words, printed out bus and train timetables. Now she just follows Ollie in a daze. Sometimes she yearns for the sweaty anxiety of a local boneshaker bus ride to an uncertain destination.

Each bungalow is separated from its neighbour by a screen of trees, so that once inside you'd think you had the beach to yourselves. A single light is on in the one they're passing and Asha peers in. There's nothing to see but the ghost of a pale sofa and the black screen of a TV. There may be no internet here but at least there'll be CNN. She hasn't dared to tell Ollie that after a while these island-paradise holidays can start to drag. He seems to think that three weeks on a sun-drenched beach, with plenty of cocktails and manicures and facials, is every woman's dream. It's probably her fault. She's regaled him with horror

15

stories of past holidays, like the time she and a boyfriend were robbed in a remote Malaysian hostel. When they couldn't pay their bar bill they were kicked out and spent a terrified night on the edge of the jungle, taking it in turns to stay awake. Another time the Mumbai police planted drugs in her friend's rucksack and arrested them when they refused to pay a bribe. As they were being hauled away she and the friend managed to slip out of their jackets and flee through the streets, laughing hysterically. She told Ollie these stories to make him feel good about being able to provide for her properly, but they've just made him think all she wants now is peace and luxury. What he doesn't know is that those chaotic trips are some of her best memories.

The walkway is coming to an end. The last bungalow glows softly, lantern light glimmering on the infinity pool.

Bay goes to the door and opens it with a key card, then steps back to let them pass through ahead of him.

Asha's first impression is the smell. A sickly-sweet perfume that reminds her of the hundred-quid candles she's given by Ollie's relatives at Christmas.

It becomes stronger as she steps inside. As Ollie follows, his toe catches on the threshold, sending him stumbling into one of the large white sofas that dominate the room. Righting himself he slumps down into it, lets his head fall back and groans. It looks like she will have to do the tour.

Ceiling spots gradually illuminate to reveal the room.

It seems to be entirely decorated in white, teak and chrome. A low coffee table is scattered with the inevitable photography books and in the centre is a huge glass vase of white lilies. Close up the smell is overpowering. It reminds her of her mother's funeral.

The walls and glass shelves contain pieces of abstract, vaguely Eastern art. The rug has such a deep pile that her flip-flops sink until she can feel the soft cream wool tickling her toes.

Bay points out the remote controls for the blinds and the lights, the air con, the stereo system, the TV.

At the other end of the room is a small kitchen area with a gas hob, an island and a large, American-style fridge. (Asha has no intention of cooking while they're here. She liked the sound of the 'fresh local ingredients prepared by our Michelin-starred chef' from the brochure). A bottle of Cristal champagne sits at the centre of a hamper filled with jars and packets, including something called Kopi Luwak, which looks like balls of clumped-together coffee beans, and a tub of seaweed-green liquid labelled *cleansing broth*. Presumably the signature on the label is supposed to mean something to her. Some clean-eating guru maybe.

'If you want to cook anything at home,' Bay smiles, 'just give us a shopping list and it will all be delivered to you.'

Opposite the kitchen is the bathroom. The bath and sink are blocks of hollowed-out limestone that match the floor, and the pile of white towels stacked by the sink must be two feet tall. The sink is filled and white flower heads bob on the surface of the water. Asha grimaces: the place is starting to make her toes curl.

Bay shows her how to operate the power-shower and gushes about the ingredients of the little bottles of lotions and gels: they are all organic, with proven antioxidant properties, and essential oils filtered for twice as long as normal. She tries to look interested. As soon as he's gone she'll have a bath. Tired as she is, a holiday doesn't really start until you've washed away the sweat and grime of the journey.

. Bay leads her to the bedroom. The first thing she notices, with a nasty jag, is that the large window beside the bed looks out over the jungle. The blind is up and the trees mass darkly, their individual shapes indistinguishable now the moon has gone behind a cloud. Bay is saying something about the sheets but she can't concentrate on his words. She can feel the chill of night seeping between the slats. The window catch looks so flimsy.

'This one's for the air con, this is for the blind.'

With a gentle hum, a band of white descends over the black window and the air in the room becomes breathable again.

She's being stupid. What exactly does she imagine is going to climb in and get them? Now she can give the room her full attention.

The bed is a huge four-poster draped with a mosquito net. Besides a carved wooden wardrobe, an antique or clever repro, the room is spartan. Their cases are stashed neatly by the door.

'Do you want me to send Hao to unpack for you?'

'I think we'll manage.'

'Okay then. If I haven't explained something properly, just pick up the phone. I'll be on duty all night.'

'Thanks.'

Back in the living room Ollie stirs long enough to thank Bay and wish him goodnight, then slumps back down, his blurry gaze fixed on a Vietnamese news channel. 'Couldn't find CNN.'

She finds it for him, then runs herself a bath.

The water is so soft it feels like warm silk against her skin. She can't be bothered to do her hair, it'll take too much drying, so she has to keep towelling off the sweat that dribbles down her temples. Ollie is bumping around the bedroom humming, then he goes quiet. Perhaps he's waiting for her out on the terrace with a beer. It must be nearly dawn but what the hell. Her body clock is shot to pieces by the flight, and they're here for three weeks so it doesn't matter if they miss a morning.

She gets out and dries off. After draining the sink and arranging the poor decapitated flowers in a pile she cleans her teeth, then wraps herself in the tasteful blue sarong hanging on the back of the door.

Ollie is asleep on his back with his mouth open. He's managed to take off his trousers but apparently gave up after the first three shirt buttons.

In the half-light, she is struck by the clean lines of his face. Beauty: another thing that's easy for the rich. Ollie's mother was Deb of the Year in 1975. His father came first in his year at Sandhurst. Letting the sarong drop to the floor she climbs on top of him, squeezing the last drops of water from her hair onto his chest to wake him.

'No, no, no,' he groans. 'I'm too pissed.'

'This is the first night of our honeymoon.' She pulls up his shirt. 'And we are fucking, Oliver De Montfort Graveney, or I'm getting a divorce.'

He peels open one eye and takes in her body, grunts, then closes it again.

She tries her hardest but it's no good. This feeling of disappointment is becoming familiar. When eventually she gives up, Ollie mumbles an apology and turns over.

Still wide awake, she pads naked through the living room and out onto the terrace. The night air is clean and cool on her flushed skin. Her head is so clear. Even her hearing feels sharper. She could go for a dip. The glimmering breakers whisper enticingly. But isn't this shark-feeding time?

The moon is hidden by cloud, but something else has lit up the waves breaking on the shore. A ribbon of bioluminescence stipples the whole length of the beach.

It's magical. She stands very still, as if any movement will break the spell.

Two shapes are outlined in the silver. Buoys perhaps? Or posts to tie up boats? Then they move and the swirl of bioluminescence reveals them to be the legs of a figure, its head and torso lost in darkness. Someone is standing in the sea, looking out across the water.

She should go inside before she is noticed. But before she can, the figure moves again. At first she thinks it must be walking backwards towards the beach, then she realises that the silhouette was deceptive. The figure wasn't looking out across the water, its attention was focused on the bungalows. On their bungalow. On her.

She hurries back inside and fumbles with the remote control for the lights. The bungalow is plunged into darkness, but by the time her eyes have accustomed to the sudden gloom, the figure is gone.

19

3

FV Hospital, Ho Chi Minh City, Vietnam

Monday 3 October

It takes a good fifteen minutes for me to lever myself into a sitting position, then I have to close my eyes and grip the metal bar under the mattress until the world stops rolling. I think I'm going to be sick. I need to get to the bathroom. It seems like miles away, across that expanse of white lino.

Gingerly I feel for solid ground with my toes. I'm afraid to stand. It doesn't feel possible that my legs will support the huge weight of my head.

Lowering the other foot I sit there for more long minutes as the bathroom recedes away from me. But it seems I'm not going to get any stronger or less dizzy so I guess it's just a question of summoning the will.

Taking a deep breath I throw myself forward and up. I'm standing. Swaying slightly, but secure. The sensation is novel, as if I've never been up on two legs before.

I take a step, then another, feeling the floor pressing through my heels and leg bones, all the way to my spine. Then the momentum runs away from me and I stagger forwards, striking the wall with a juddering impact that makes me cry out in pain.

Breathing heavily I manage to lean, panting, dizzy but grimly satisfied. As if my body is my enemy and I've vanquished it.

The bathroom is close. I can smell the disinfectant.

Gripping the doorframe I drag myself along the wall. My legs are definitely becoming stronger but the throbbing in my head isn't getting any better. It's making the room shimmer.

Over my laboured breathing and the scrape of my heart I can hear traffic noise rumbling through the walls. We must be in London. Did we ever make it to Vietnam? Was there a bomb at the airport?

I'm through the doorway, lurching for the sink. Hunkering down, I grip the cold enamel edge, panting like an antelope in the jaws of a lion.

Then I vomit clear liquid into the basin.

'Fuck,' I croak. My voice sounds like someone else's.

The nausea eventually subsides and even the pain in my head seems to ease. I'm ready to stand, to look in the mirror that currently reflects the white veil of the shower curtain.

This isn't a hangover. There's obviously something badly wrong with me. A brain tumour? Aneurysm? A stroke?

Where the fuck is Ollie? I take a moment to curse him viciously, then I grit my teeth. The bulge of my jaw sends a slash of pain through my head, but I don't care. Haven't I always managed on my own? And then, later I managed for Mum too. I don't need Ollie. If he isn't here, fuck him. I can do this.

I stand up.

A few minutes later I vomit again, but this time nothing comes up. My abdomen convulses, as if something monstrous is trying to get out. Once the retching has subsided I lean heavily on the basin, letting my tears plink against the enamel.

A monster looked back at me from the mirror, its scalp hideously distended, half bald and padded with bandages. The black pupils of its eyes swam in lakes of blood. Only the mouth was my own. My full lips, parted with horror, in a face pulped and black.

Go back to bed. Go to sleep. Pray that it's all a bad dream. You'll wake up beautiful again, next to your beautiful husband.

I turn and straighten, transferring my grip to the doorframe, then lurch to the threshold.

A scraping noise from the bedroom makes me look up. Too quickly. My vision rolls. When it clears I see that the door has opened on a featureless white corridor and a woman is slipping through the gap. She looks in her forties, but perhaps the weight she's carrying makes her seem older. Her hair is highlighted, though not for a while judging by the dark roots, her square face haggard: the heavy flesh weighing down her jowls and the pouches under her eyes. I wonder if she's the consultant, but her clothes are casual and she's not wearing any kind of ID.

When she catches sight of me in the doorway she gasps, but I think only because I've startled her. The lack of shock in her expression suggests she's seen me in this state, though I have no memory of her. Then her face crumples.

'Oh my God, Asha. I'm so, so . . .'

I stare at her as her voice cracks and her hand stretches towards me.

4

Mango Tree Resort, Con Son Island

Saturday 24 September

She lies beside him, watching him sleep. His body is pale and flawlessly smooth in the soft light filtering through the blinds. He will tan quickly, his skin remembering what it's supposed to do from a lifetime of skiing trips and Caribbean holidays.

She runs her finger down the line of his spine. Circles a bruise under his rib cage he got from playing squash, then bends to kiss his shoulder blade. He groans and rolls away from her, without waking, apparently. His penis is flaccid under the sheet. She sighs and gets up.

After she's washed and dressed she open the blinds in the living room.

It's perfect. Of course it is, Ollie booked it. In the late morning sunshine the sea is azure, the jungles that enclose the bay are emerald green, and the infinity pool sparkles.

'We could order breakfast in,' Ollie says, wandering out of the bedroom, hair sticking up, eyes puffy, obviously hungover.

'We don't know what they've got yet. Let's go to the buffet.'

As he puts his arms around her and kisses the tip of her nose, the slight sense of unease she's been feeling melts away. Ollie must be exhausted from the stress of what's been going on at work. That's why they haven't been having sex. Give it a few days and he'll be back to normal.

They walk barefoot, hand in hand, up the wooden walkway towards the restaurant. There's a low buzz of conversation and the clink of crockery. More exciting for Asha is the savoury tang of smoked meat. Could it be – wonder of wonders – *bacon*?

Within seconds of them taking their seats the waitress from last night is beside them, smiling and dipping her head, asking what they would like to drink. In the daylight it's clear she's older than Asha had thought – in her forties perhaps. Her hair is a rich dark brown with just one or two coarse greys pinging out from the ponytail.

'Jasmine tea for me please and coffee for my husband. Nice and strong.'

Ollie hasn't taken off his sunglasses and his face has a sheen of sweat. No wonder he didn't feel like it this morning. This perfectly reasonable explanation brings a new sense of relief.

As they wait for the drinks, Asha studies the other guests.

At the table behind Ollie is a fairly ordinary-looking white couple. The wife overweight with highlighted hair; the balding husband in a polo shirt and red twill shorts. She knows this type from banking dos and Graveney family parties. Knows she will have nothing in common with them. Her gaze moves on.

Behind this table is a man sitting alone, presumably waiting for his wife. Maybe she's hungover like Ollie. His muscular back is towards Asha so she can only make out his cropped dark hair, and that he's wearing a t-shirt and jeans. A tattoo creeps from the sleeve of the t-shirt. A footballer?

Two tables away from him, at the far end of the restaurant, is another couple: a grizzled middle-aged man and, with her back to the restaurant, his much younger blonde wife. Asha wouldn't want to sit at that table. Behind the man the dark jungle masses, stretching the odd tendril towards his shoulder.

To her discomfort she sees he has noticed her attention and is watching her steadily, a half smile on his lips. His face is a mess of crags and creases. There's something almost demonic about him: the arched eyebrows, emphasised by hair receding at each temple to give the impression of horns. His shirt is open a little too far, revealing a body gone to seed, with fleshy, drooping breasts. And yet his smile suggests he's in on the joke. That he knows there's something repellent about him; that he's amused by it. His nostrils are flared, as if permanently scenting the air. His mouth is wide and the lifted corner reveals a flash of very straight, very white teeth. American, perhaps. An American fat cat with his trophy bride. She realises she still hasn't looked away, and now his eyes are narrowed sardonically, his head cocked, piqued by her curiosity.

Her head jerks down and she manages to knock her knife onto the floor.

Ollie winces at the clatter. 'Butterfingers.' He's smiling, but something about his eyes makes Asha think he's anxious about something.

'You're not still worried about that work thing, are you?'

'What?' His face is blank. 'Oh, Christ no. I couldn't give a shit.'

'You never really said what happened?'

'Didn't I?'

'No.'

'Oh, just merger talks with a small hedge fund place.'

'Who?'

'Oh, er . . . Hadsley-Kirkwood they're called. You won't have heard of them. Tiny. And they've messed us around so much we probably won't even bother. Where's my bloody coffee? Jesus.'

She watches him craning his neck to get the waitress's attention. He looks self-conscious, as if it's a ploy to avoid catching his wife's eye. Eventually he can't avoid it.

'What?' He's blushing. Not the cute flush of their first dates, but livid splotches in the centre of his cheeks.

'You okay?'

'No. I feel crap.'

'It's just that back in London it seemed to be really worrying you, and now you say you don't give a shit.'

'I don't. Fuck 'em.' He shrugs.

25

'Isn't that what you and Milo were talking about, when I came home early that day?'

He blinks at her and his lips part. Suddenly her heart is beating faster. As if he's about to admit some terrible dark secret.

'Unless you're having an affair, of course?' She says it like it's a joke. Like she *knows* it's a joke, but her heart is lodged in her throat until he gives a snort of laughter.

'You got me. It's Maria. The way she flicks that feather duster: it's irresistible.'

She holds his gaze for a second more, picks up on the effort it takes him to lower his shoulders and smooth his brow.

'Okay, well I'm going to get some juice.'

The American's wife is at the bar. She's so thin, straight up and down in linen fisherman's trousers and a loose, wide-necked t-shirt.

She steps back and treads on Asha's foot. It doesn't hurt, the woman is so light, but at Asha's gasp of surprise she turns and apologises profusely.

Asha stares.

Unable to help herself, her eyes flick down. To the flat chest, the slight bulge in the crotch of the trousers. Back up to the square chin, the broad eyebrows, the ghost of pale stubble.

'It's fine,' she murmurs.

'And you're in flip-flops. I'm such an asshole.'

He's soft voiced, feminine in his mannerisms but not camp.

'You'd be in a lot more pain if it was the other way round,' Asha says.

He gives a sweet laugh and Asha's insides melt. He's flawlessly beautiful: the cute one from a boy band before grizzly adulthood kicks in. How could he let that horrible man paw him? She glances at their table. Unless it's his father?

The American is smirking at her.

'I'm Caspar,' he says, holding out a baby-soft hand.

When she gets back to the table their drinks have arrived and Ollie is sipping his coffee reluctantly, like medicine. She feels

26

sorry then, to have pushed him. He's tired, he's stressed and he just needs her to love him and let him be. When she squeezes his hand he smiles up at her almost gratefully.

As she pours herself a cup of tea, her attention is caught by the couple on the table behind Ollie. She suspects, from their odd, hushed tones and dipped heads, that they're talking about them. Is it a nasty surprise for them, to find a mixed race couple in their little slice of paradise? Suddenly the woman cranes her neck to peer over her husband's shoulder. Catching Asha's eye she looks away quickly.

Asha studies her more closely. The frumpy culottes and baggy t-shirt she's wearing to hide her figure, the red knuckles gripping her teacup. She looks worn down. Asha turns her attention to the husband. The conventional banker uniform means he could be anywhere from twenty to seventy. There's already a smear of sweat down his meaty back. Ollie must have spotted her grimace because he leans across the table and murmurs, 'Come on then, nosy.'

'Oh you'll love them. They're proper PLUs. Tenner they're called Alice and Charlie and live in Barnes with a lab called Toby.'

Ollie had to explain PLUs to her when she first heard it at a party, from one of his odious schoolfriends. It stood for *People Like Us*. White, upper-middle class, public school. Asha was as far from PLU as Ollie could possibly have got. Sometimes she wonders if that was the attraction, but then she feels guilty. His friends might be shallow but Ollie isn't.

Pretending to stretch, Ollie glances round.

'You're on,' he mutters, turning back. 'My money's on James and Sophie.'

After they shake Asha keeps hold of his hand, running her thumb across his knuckles. Sometimes it scares her how close she came to walking away after what happened in July. The hormones and grief had sent her mad enough to do it but she managed to step back from the brink just in time. The thought of it now, of being without him, sends a shiver down her spine despite the heat.

'What?'

'Just thinking how much I love you.' She emphasises the word *love*, flicking it off her teeth almost mockingly. She's always found it so hard to say. They never mentioned such things at home, and before Ollie she'd never even said it. Just added a 'me too' to whoever happened to have uttered it to her.

'Good,' he smiled. 'You can prove it by getting me some scrambled eggs.'

Rolling her eyes she makes her way back to the buffet.

The man who was sitting alone is there. Moving past him her heart sinks when she sees that the tables are heaving with fruit, yoghurt, granola and other *clean eating* delicacies. The bacony smell is coming from a pot of lapsang souchong. The only remotely appealing option is a basket of bread and croissants beside a conveyor-belt toaster. There are leaf-shaped pats of butter and, joy of joys, tiny punnets of Marmite. She selects a seed bread for Ollie and a plain white for herself, then slides them onto the toaster's slow-moving griddle.

As the man reaches past her for the butter she catches a glimpse of his profile. He's handsome, but not like the blond man. There's something rugged about him: something down-and-dirty that immediately makes her wonder what he would look like naked. As his hand brushes hers she flinches guiltily and with a pretence at casualness leans on the table and takes a great interest in the layout of the room. If she doesn't get laid soon she'll be drooling over anything with a pulse.

Apart from the man in the twill shorts.

He has turned now and is openly staring at Ollie's back. Asha feels a ripple of distaste for his fleshy red face, like a slab of meat: the greedy porcine eyes, coarse sandy hair and broad cleft chin. Why on earth is that supposed to be an attractive characteristic? It just looks like squashed buttocks. She smiles at the thought, then raises her head and catches the eye of the man at the toaster. He smiles back and their eyes lock just a beat too long, then, of all things, she blushes.

In flustered haste she snatches up the first slice of toast. It's too hot and with a cry she drops it. He lunges forward and catches it then, wrapping it in a napkin for her, hands it back. For a moment their heads are almost touching and she catches his scent, musky and overtly masculine, quite different from Ollie's fresh, clean one.

'My hero,' she says. 'Thank you.'

'Pleasure.'

His voice is deeper than Ollie's, with a smoker's rasp.

'I'm Asha and that's my husband Ollie.' They shake hands. His is rough and cool.

'Sean. Nice to meet you. And your toast.'

He walks back to his table.

Asha's armpits prickle. When she gets back to the table Ollie is grinning at her.

'Who was Heathcliff?'

'His name's Sean and I said I'd meet him round the back later.'

'Do. I'll be no use to you today.'

She grins, as if it's just casual banter, then plonks the plate of toast down in front of him. 'Sorry, no eggs. And no fucking bacon. Why did you bring me here?'

'To lose weight.'

She kicks him.

After the toast she tucks into a croissant with honey and, finally, some granola with fruit and yoghurt. The food brings some colour back to Ollie's cheeks and he stops sweating.

'I was thinking of trekking up the holy mountain today,' she says. 'Fancy it?'

'Ask Sean.'

'Come on then, you pisshead, let's hit the beach.'

Getting up from the table, her napkin falls off her lap and she bends to pick it up. As she does so there's a momentary lull in the hum of conversation and the hairs on the back of her neck start to prickle. Is she being watched again?

She stands quickly and turns to face the room, eyes flashing, ready for a confrontation. But no one pays her any attention. The eyes of the PLUs and the Americans are fixed not on her, but on Ollie, now stepping unsteadily down from the deck onto the beach. A moment later, the conversation resumes.

Feeling oddly protective, Asha hurries after him and, slipping an arm around his waist, steers him away down the path.

The day is deliciously, enervatingly hot. A small number of sun loungers are scattered over the white sand – at least she supposes that's what they're called. They don't much resemble the brittle plastic contraptions normal hotels provide. They're wide enough to seat two comfortably. The frames are teak – again – and the thick mattresses are covered in a beige fabric that looks spotlessly clean despite the lashings of sweat and lotion that have presumably soaked into them.

But as soon as she's comfortably settled she spots, a few hundred metres up the beach, a large wicker chrysalis draped with white curtains. Not only does it look more comfortable, it's a long way from the bungalows so would be perfectly private. She can't think of a nicer place to make love. To the lullaby of the sea, with the frisson of doing it al fresco, and the possibility of people walking past outside the curtains.

It occurs to her that she's becoming obsessed. The last time they had sex was the night before the wedding, and that was a fairly rushed affair that she initiated. That's, what, three weeks? Is that too long? It feels like it, but with other long-term boyfriends months would sometimes go by. It's just that Ollie's usually pretty highly sexed. They've always been a good match in that sense. And they have just got married.

Perhaps a day of doing nothing will help. She's pretty sure that behind those billowing curtains she could coax him out of whatever funk he's in.

But now Ollie has sunk down beside her with a groan and pulled his cap over his eyes. Stifling a sigh, she sits down beside him and waits for the ache of arousal to ebb away.

While he sleeps off his hangover she spends the morning reading and paddling. The beach shelves so gently that near the shore the water's bath-warm, only cooling off at the ledge a few metres out. The sand is speckled with pretty white stones with grey spirals at their centre. She collects a few, dropping them, still wet, onto Ollie's stomach to try and wake him. She wonders about having one of the Thai massages from the spa menu, then falls asleep instead. When she wakes again she sees Ollie's chest is already red. Opening the large beige umbrella she angles it to shade him, then goes in search of a drink.

After the dazzling brightness of the beach, the restaurant's gloom leaves her momentarily blind. Pushing up her sunglasses she blinks until her vision returns.

The PLUs are eating lunch in silence at one of the tables beside the bamboo fence. Giant prawns or crevettes, by the look of the carnage on their plates. Spicy enough that both of them are sweating. She smiles as she passes them. The waitress standing in the shadows steps forward dutifully and Asha asks for a couple of Cokes to be brought out to the beach.

On the way back, the man is blocking her path. She gasps, almost walking into him.

'David Peters,' he says, holding out a large hand, greasy with prawns.

'Asha,' she stammers, shaking it. 'Asha—'

'Graveney, right?'

'Er, yes.'

'Your husband's Oliver Graveney.'

The wife, still sitting at the table, huffs and gives Asha an apologetic look.

'Are you stalking us?' Asha laughs.

'No no no. Ha. Your husband and I know the same people. McKinley Gordon, early noughties. TG had just bought LLH. We were handling the equity derivative sales.'

Asha smiles and nods. The Cokes pass her on their way to the beach.

'Nice to meet you. I'm sure my husband will want to say hello.'

'Let's have a drink later!' David bellows. 'I'd love to hear how he's getting on with the Hadsley-Kirkwood deal.'

She manages a tight smile. The last thing she wants is for this man to get Ollie all worked up about the merger again.

His wife comes to the rescue. 'Well, the rest of us wouldn't.' She gets up and pushes her husband out of Asha's path.

'Sorry about David. You can't take him anywhere. I'm Sophie and I promise if you were to venture to the bar this evening he will *not* be bringing up mergers or any other boring bank nonsense.'

The roots of her hair are dark with moisture and there's a slash of sunburn across her chest where she hasn't applied lotion evenly. Asha suspects the couple would feel far more at home in a Courchevel ski lodge.

'Thanks,' she says. 'We might.' Then she walks quickly down the path, feeling her back prickle all the way.

Ollie's awake and finishing his Coke. The ice cubes in hers have already melted.

'Got collared by the PLUs,' she says grimly. 'He's David something or other, and you were right about her: Sophie.'

Ollie licks a finger and chalks up the point.

'Takes one to know one,' she grumbles and climbs back on the bed.

'Might go for a swim. I like the look of that island out there.'

She squints at it, a grey rock marooned in the blue. A mile away? Half? It's hard to judge.

'Are you sure? You had a lot to drink last night.'

'Are you questioning my prowess?'

'It looks a bit far, that's all. What if you get cramp?'

'Then you'll be a rich widow.'

'Go for it, then.' She flicks her glasses down off her head and lies back, but while he gets up and walks down the beach she curls onto her side and continues to watch anxiously as he enters the sea and strikes out for the island.

After a few minutes his head is lost in the glitter. She forces herself to pick up her book and not think about sharks and box jellyfish.

It feels like fifteen or twenty minutes before she can make out a dark shape hauling itself up onto the rock. A moment later he's standing on the peak, waving his arms in boyish pride. She waves back, relieved, then returns to her book.

A regular tapping pulls her out of the world of medieval fantasy that a colleague insisted she would adore.

The American couple has arrived on the beach and are batting a small ball between them. Shirt-free, the older man's breasts jiggle while his boyfriend's ponytail bounces like a cheerleader's. Back and forth they go, every now and then dropping the ball into the water: at which point the blond calls out the score. Asha can't imagine what pleasure this activity could bring, other than that of grating everybody else's nerves. She feels like saying something. Ollie always stops her making a fuss but he's not here now and the noise is putting her off her book, just as the hero is about to be decapitated.

But then the sound is drowned out by a louder one. The motor of a little boat coming around the headland.

It's a traditional wooden fishing boat, a shallow elongated hull painted picturesque colours and trailing flags from its stern. The only modern touches are the outboard motor and the headphones on the young man perched beside it. The boat is travelling at some speed, the prow lifted right out of the water, blocking his view of the direction in which he is travelling. Presumably he'll slow down as he gets nearer to the shore, where there may be swimmers.

But there's one swimmer further out.

33

Ollie is back in the water, heading for shore, and his powerful front crawl will bring him directly into the path of the speeding vessel.

She jumps up from the lounger, upturning it and the Coke glass, and runs down to the water's edge.

'Ollie!'

But with his head submerged he can't hear her or the boat's engine. The boy isn't even facing forward now, just fiddling with whatever device he's listening to.

'OLLIE!'

It's hopeless. Ollie keeps swimming and the boatman doesn't even raise his head. She runs into the water and is about to dive off the ledge to try and reach him but there's a flurry of splashing behind her and she finds herself being dragged back to shore.

'Get off me! *OLLIE!*'

The boat is twenty metres from him. Fifteen.

'LOOK UP, YOU STUPID FUCKER!'

Ten.

Others have joined her now, frantically waving and shouting. And then Bay is running down the beach. He plunges fully dressed into the water, arms waving, roaring in Vietnamese. Finally the sound or sight of a fellow countryman gets the boy's attention.

Five.

Ollie stops swimming, turns his head in the direction of the boat. Asha sees the sudden jerk of his shoulders as he registers what is about to happen. Then he's gone.

The boat crashes over the spot where she last saw him, and a split second later the boy kills the engine. The vessel glides to a bobbing halt and the streamers settle.

There's absolute silence as the ripples reach the shore.

5

Burney Castle, Hampshire

Saturday 3 September

Asha stands by the window while Zainab twines pearls into her hair. In the corner is a spider's web jewelled with water droplets that glint as the web quivers in the wind.

It's been raining since last night, but not hard, and they've got a marquee so it doesn't matter. In fact, somehow, it's better. A sunny day would have been too much – saccharine perfection. It ought to have a flaw, this day, to make everything else shine by comparison.

A tiny silver moth bumps against the window pane, hungry for the bright light Zainab has trained on Asha's head. Eventually it blunders against the web, sending out a shower of raindrops as it tries frantically to free itself.

The spider clambers unhurriedly down towards its prey. She wonders why they use those furry bird-eating spiders to try and rid people of their phobias when this gristly spindly thing is far more repulsive.

A sudden rattle of heavier rain against the glass makes her start back, knocking the box of pearls from Zainab's hands. They laugh as they crawl about on hands and knees retrieving them and Asha is soon out of breath. She has yet to lose all the weight she put on in the spring and the bodice crushes her chest.

Soon the box is full again, but making a final sweep on her hands and knees Asha catches sight of one last pearl, under the heavy chest of drawers, gleaming dully, like an eyeball.

She slides her hand past the lion's-paw feet and right to the back. But before she can grasp it her hand catches on a carpet tack. Snatching it back, she's rubbed it on the dress before she's had time to think.

A bright red blotch on the silk skirt.

'Oh no!'

'It's alright,' Zainab says. 'Don't panic.'

As she blots the stain with a tissue Asha sucks the cut, just in the crease at the base of her ring finger. 'Let me run it under the tap.' She pulls away and hurries to the bathroom. 'It'll stop bleeding in a minute.

'Run the dress under the cold – only cold – that should get the worst of it out.'

She'd scoffed at Zainab's insistence that they would need three hours to get her ready. Envisaged them lying on her bed sipping buck's fizz until her uncle came for her. Not standing by the sink, shivering, as cold water seeps up the skirt and into the bodice. They'll need to dry it out with the hairdryer or it will leave a tide-mark.

Half an hour later and the dress is dry. The blotch has faded to pale brown, like chocolate or gravy. That's what she'll say it was. Blood feels loaded with meaning. An omen. Like the curse from a bad fairy: *on your wedding day you will prick your finger and* . . .

Not for the first time she wishes her mum was there to calm her down. It's a real, physical ache not to be able to lean her head on the tiny woman's shoulder, and listen to her words of comfort, always so practical and filled with good sense, right up until the end, when she was instructing Asha to make sure there were halal options at her funeral for the newsagent and his family.

An uncharacteristically serious Zainab makes the finishing touches to her hair, then positions her in front of the full-length mirror by the window. It was a big ask for her friend to take on such an important task, but they've been doing one another's hair and makeup since they were teenagers and somehow it felt right. Now Asha regards her reflection critically. Her hair and make-up are not the problem.

'I look like a whale.'

She's bursting out of the bodice like some hussy from a period drama. The dress was supposed to be an elegant empire-line cut, but the first fitting happened last year. There's nothing elegant about it now. All the old men will spend the day leering at her boobs. Ollie professes to like her new 'curves' but she doesn't. Her clothes all fit badly, and each time she strains to do up her jeans is an unpleasant reminder of what happened. They did think about postponing the wedding but Ollie's parents vetoed it – people had already bought plane tickets – and as she was pretty sure they didn't want him to marry her in the first place, Asha agreed to let it go. Besides, Uncle Thomas probably *had* bought his ticket.

She turns to look from another angle and the green waistband clamps her rib cage like iron.

'It's no good, I'm going to have to unzip it under the arm.'

'Let me unpick the stitches a bit.'

'God, Vera Wang would have kittens.'

This takes another half an hour and having to stand perfectly still for that long, arms raised, under the spotlight, makes her sweat.

Great. That's all she needs. To walk down the aisle sticky and smelly. Again she feels like crying. If only her mum was here. Zainab's great but definitely not a hugger and Asha opted for no other bridesmaids. Far too many precious little princesses on Ollie's side who would take offence at being left out.

'Better?'

'Not really.'

'No cake for you then, hun.'

Asha forces a smile, and immediately the tension starts to drain out of her. This is going to be the best day of her life.

And not because of the setting or the dress or the food or any of the other shit she's spent the past six months stressing about. It doesn't matter if it pours with rain, or the dress splits right in the middle of the vows, or even if some crusty old bag thinks she isn't good enough for her precious son. Today Asha is marrying the man she loves; he is going to tell the world that he wants to spend the rest of his life with her.

Finally she bursts into tears and Zainab folds her arms until she's stopped, then does her makeup all over again.

By ten the rain has cleared and the sky is a cloudless blue, as if the storm never happened. Maybe the weather had last-minute nerves too.

There's just time for a buck's fizz before Zainab has to go and get ready. She's fully expecting to get off with the best man, even though Asha has told her he's taken.

'That's never stopped me before.'

'Wait till you see Liberty.'

'Fuck Liberty.' Zainab knocks back the dregs of her drink and gets up from the bed.

'Right. See you soon, babe. I'd kiss you if it wasn't for all the manky foundation.'

Asha smiles, glad to be alone now, for this last half hour until her life changes for ever. This last *before*, when she is still Miss Asha Fadeyi. A name that speaks, even now, of hardship and prejudice and, by extension, the courage and determination it took to get where she is today. She could have kept it, but she knows it means something to Ollie that she should take his name, so she will be Mrs Graveney. Her mum wouldn't mind.

As Zainab opens the door to the corridor there's a blast of cool air, laden with the heavy scent of the roses on a nearby table.

Asha leans against the doorframe and breathes as deeply as the dress will allow.

'Isn't it bad luck to let anyone see you?' Zainab says.

'Only the groom, you div. Otherwise the driver would have to wear a blindfold.'

'Oh yeah.'

'Anyway, I just want to cool down.'

Zainab waves once, then walks away down the corridor that leads to the clattering old-fashioned lifts with their black cage doors.

Intending to stay out here until her armpits have dried, Asha catches the door as it swings shut. But as she does so there's a soft rustle from the other side.

She looks around the edge of the door.

A bunch of flowers is tied to the handle. But the smile that is about to form on her lips – Ollie – doesn't quite make it.

The flowers are dead.

Brown and so limp they hang from the door handle like a corpse. And they stink of rot.

Someone's cruel idea of a joke?

Jamming her foot in the door so it won't close on her, she sets about trying to pull them off. The knot is too tight and the ribbon is a cheap plastic one that cuts into her fingers as she tries to tear it. Panic rises in her chest, making the dress squeeze tighter. She doesn't want anyone to see this horrible gift. The investigation by the hotel that Ollie would insist on, the checking of CCTV, the discovery of the culprit. One of the spurned bridesmaids? Ollie's mother? It's almost Victorian in its melodrama. Like a curse. Or a warning.

For a moment, standing there in the gloomy corridor, with the weight of all those centuries pressing down on the beams above her head, she feels frightened. As if the ancient walls are infecting her with the superstitions of their time. The rain and the blood and now this. Is the marriage ill-starred from the start?

From down the corridor she hears the grinding shudder of the lift's approach. Someone's coming.

She runs back into the room and rifles through her spongebag for some kind of blade.

The lift's cage door screeches open, clatters shut.

Nail clippers. They'll have to do. She runs back to the door.

Now there are halting footsteps approaching. The floorboards of the place must be specially treated to creak theatrically.

She clamps the clippers onto the ribbon and yanks. They're too blunt. The ribbon just twists.

The footsteps are almost at the corner now. Again that ripple of fear. Is whoever left the flowers coming back? What do they want?

The footsteps stumble – there's also a definite list to the floor – and at that moment the clippers bite the ribbon.

Finally it tears and the flowers are freed, just as a shadow appears at the end of the corridor. Letting the door slam behind her she runs with them, slimy and shedding brown petals, and stuffs them into the bin under the bathroom sink, then wads a fistful of toilet paper on top, in case Ollie uses it later. Finally she rinses the stinking sludge from her hands.

Could it be a mistake? Were they just the remains of fresh flowers that were left on the door and forgotten about before she arrived? Of course not. Someone meant this deliberately: to hurt and discomfort her. Why?

There's a knock at the door.

'Hello?' she says, stepping softly back into the room.

'Hello, my darling!' the Nigerian voice quavers. 'Are you all ready?'

Uncle Thomas!

Arranging her face into a happy grin she opens the door to him.

As she walks down the gloomy corridor, her arm clamped under his elbow, she finds that she can't engage with Thomas's happy chatter, can't tear her thoughts away from those dead and rotting flowers. She feels guilty and afraid, as if she's left a corpse lying there on the bathroom floor.

What has she done so wrong that someone could wish her ill on her wedding day?

6

Mango Tree Resort, Con Son Island

Saturday 24 September

'Can you see him?' Bay asks.

'He dived,' says the man who pulled her out. 'The boat must be light: maybe he got deep enough.'

The boy leans out, peering down into the water. It remains a crystal-clear turquoise, no billow of blood, but if the blow was a glancing one Ollie might have simply been knocked out. He might be drowning as they watch.

Asha stares, not breathing.

A bird swoops low over the water, catching a beakful of insects. A distant aeroplane glints in the sun and burns briefly like an exploding star. Without these it would seem as if time had stopped.

Then, from the far side of the boat, there is an explosion of water and a white arm flings itself over the gunwale.

She screams.

Bay falls to his knees in the surf as the boy hauls Ollie onto the boat, restarts the engine and, at a far more sedate pace, chugs towards the shore.

'Shit shit shit,' Asha sobs.

The man beside her mutters, 'Fuck me, that was close.' It's Sean. She gives a shaky laugh. But the shock subsides quickly and as the boat nears the shore she's overwhelmed with fury.

'You almost hit my husband, you fucking idiot!'

The boatman chooses not to see her, keeping his eyes fixed on the path of the lowered prow.

'Hey! Hey, you moron!'

Ollie is smiling and waving and calling out that he's perfectly alright. As if to prove it, when they come within striking distance of land he dives off the boat and begins a leisurely breaststroke back to shore.

The boatboy puts on a burst of speed, and when he's past the ledge he kills the engine and lets the vessel drift through the shallows, coming to rest on the sand. Clearly over the shock of his near miss, he climbs lazily out and starts unloading lobster pots. He's young. Perhaps not even twenty.

She runs up to him and slams a palm into his shoulder.

'Didn't you see him? You could have killed him!'

'Ash, darling,' Ollie calls from the water. 'It's fine. It was my own fault for not paying attention.'

'No it wasn't! He should have been looking where he was fucking going!'

The boatman's expression is unreadable.

'Mrs Graveney . . .' Bay puts a hand on her arm. 'Let me—'

She shakes it off. 'Tell him! Tell him to watch where he's fucking going!'

Bay says something quickly to the boatboy, his curt tone unrecognisable from the affable servility his guests receive. The boatboy makes no response, just continues unloading the pots.

Bay says something else and the boy looks up sharply.

Now he speaks, his voice high as a child's.

Bay continues, gesticulating towards the lobster pots. The boy starts throwing them, lobsters and all, back into the boat. Bay speaks again and with black hatred the boy hurls them back onto the sand. Then he opens his hand and Bay puts some notes into it. Pocketing them with an expression of disgust, the boy climbs into the boat and roars away at such speed the prow is at a forty-five-degree angle by the time he disappears around the headland.

Ollie walks out of the water grinning. As he comes up to her, seawater dripping off his fringe, she's not sure whether to hug him or slap him. She hugs him, pressing his cold wet body against hers.

'Look where you're going next time.'

'It was all an elaborate set-up to find out if you really loved me.'

She sits down at the edge of the water as Bay comes over to apologise.

'I told him no bonus. Normally he gets a bonus for delivering the lobsters before five o'clock. He is upset. It won't happen again.'

Her anger subsiding, Asha feels a pang of regret for bringing this punishment down on the boy. No wonder he was angry. God knows how much this has cost him. The difference between enough to eat and going hungry?

'They're a local family we've used for many years but I will ask that he does not come to the hotel for the duration of your stay.'

'Thanks, but it's fine, really,' Ollie says. 'My own fault.'

Sean's sitting in the surf a few metres away, tattooed biceps wrapped round his knees, head hanging.

'Thanks,' she calls over to him. 'For stopping me going in.'

He raises his head. 'No problem.'

'Calm down, everyone,' Ollie says, his cheeks pink with self-consciousness at the drama he has caused. 'Drinks on me. Bay, a bottle of champagne and . . .' he counts the figures on the beach, 'six glasses – one for you.'

As Bay walks back up the beach Ollie sits down behind her and wraps his arms around her. Whatever he claims, she can feel his heart pounding against her back.

The drinking goes on all afternoon.

The other people yelling at the boatman from the beach turned out to be Sophie and David, and she finds herself warming to them, to their righteous anger. David starts off by ranting that a hotel like this should have proper, reputable suppliers, not a

43

mickey-mouse *family* operation that probably grows the prawns they had for lunch by the local sewage outlet. But by the second bottle he's mellowed and his wife deftly steers the conversation towards a less inflammatory topic.

'Tell them about the flight.'

'The flight. Jesus. We thought we were goners, seriously.'

'We were over the Urals and the plane hit a pocket of hot air or something. Dropped like a stone. Two thousand feet.'

Ollie laughs. 'I think Asha would have died from a heart attack. Fortunately her blood/Dom Perignon level was about fifty fifty throughout our flight, so she was pretty mellow.'

'Dom Perignon?' Sophie says. 'Lucky you. In business we got some bloody own-brand fizz.'

'We usually travel first,' David cuts in, 'but to be honest we haven't noticed much difference.'

'True,' Ollie says diplomatically. 'There isn't much. So, how about you, Sean? How was your flight?'

He smiles. 'Hate flying. I always drop a pill the moment we leave the runway.'

Asha had suggested this once to combat her own nerves but Ollie wouldn't have it.

'Did you come out with anyone or are you meeting them later?' Sophie asks.

'Nope, just me on my lonesome.' He turns to Asha. 'You're on your honeymoon, right?'

She nods, smiling.

'Ditto,' Sean says.

As they clink glasses Asha can almost see the cogs in Sophie's brain working. Sure enough she blunders in. 'Where's your wife?'

A beat of silence, then Sean speaks quietly. 'She died.'

'Oh.'

A longer silence.

Poor, crass Sophie has turned scarlet. To help her out Asha says, 'I'm so sorry, Sean. Was it very recent?'

44

'Five months next week.'

Ollie pats Sean's back, looking genuinely choked up himself, and David harrumphs his commiserations.

Reaching into his back pocket Sean pulls out a battered wallet and slides a photograph from it.

'Emily.'

Sean stands with his arm around a young woman with long mouse-brown hair and a thin, hard face, heavily made up. He looks ten years younger: the bags gone from under his eyes, a little more weight around his torso, a grin that suits him.

They all gaze at the photo in a silence that might simply be awkwardness, or perhaps, if Asha is being generous, consideration. They're giving Sean the chance to speak more if he wants to.

'She's beautiful,' Sophie says, after a moment, and Asha's heart warms towards her a little more. She herself cannot think of anything to say about the girl. Cannot repress the cheap thought that Sean could have done better. But then, looked at in those terms, so could Ollie.

'What a lovely smile,' she says.

'The week before our wedding she'd had her three-month check-up and they'd found nothing. We were so happy.'

The smiles stiffen.

'I don't blame them. I'm glad in a way that they didn't spot it. We had a couple of months of thinking she was going to be fine. For that time at least we could be . . . carefree, you know?' He glances up at Ollie, who nods sadly.

The others look pained, barely managing to keep the horror from their faces, but Asha understands what it's like to nurse someone through the final stages of cancer. The hope, however misplaced, is what gets you through each day, each hour. The tiny signs that things might be looking up: the extra spoonful of porridge, the extra lap of the park, even when you know it's terminal. Even when *they* know.

'That's when we booked this. We thought we'd wait until she'd got all her strength back and could really enjoy it. Stupid.

We could have spent the money eating out every night, staying in posh hotels in the country or something. Don't get me wrong, this is amazing.' He sighs and swills his drink around his glass. 'But I don't know that it's *us* really.'

'Tell me about it,' Asha murmurs and Ollie looks sharply at her.

'When we found out she was . . .' – he pauses, breathes slowly and deeply, like they teach you in grief counselling – '. . . terminal. When we found out . . . Emily made me promise to come anyway. To lie on the beach and drink cocktails as if she was beside me and she'd do her best to be there.' He looks away.

A hush descends. Each person cannot help but listen to the murmur of the sea and the whisper of the wind in the palm trees.

'Emily,' David says then, 'if you're here, cheers, lovely lady.' Asha watches him raise his glass to the darkening beach, impressed and a little moved.

'To Emily,' she says and drinks with the others.

As Sean raises his drink Asha notices, or thinks she does, a ridged area underneath his tattoos. Could they be . . . could they be track marks? She's seen them plenty of times before, back on the estate, but it still shocks her a little. Lifting her gaze to his face she meets his dark blue eyes. She blushes and looks away. He really is incredibly sexy. It's nearing her period and Ollie should know full well what that means. She recrosses her legs, angling herself away from him to avoid the temptation of ogling, but the sensation of pressure this causes ruins all her good intentions and the flush becomes a full-body tingle. She hopes Sean hasn't noticed, but isn't optimistic. He's probably used to having that effect on women.

'So, what do you do, Sean?' David asks. Asha stops herself rolling her eyes. In all those long minutes that's the best he could find to change the subject.

'I run a bar, in the City.'

'Which one?' Ollie says. 'My friends and I have probably, ahem, frequented your establishment a number of times . . .'

He means it as a joke but the contrived comment makes him sound like a twat.

Sean's smile doesn't waver. 'It's near Tower Hill but I'm sure I'd have remembered you. I never forget a face.'

They move on to the subject of the best pubs in the Square Mile.

The drinking goes on well into the evening and Sophie and Asha have to dissuade their husbands from a swimming race out to the island and back. Sean sits quietly, smiling to himself, and Asha is embarrassed by the ridiculous dick-swinging of the two bankers. This is the part of Ollie's personality she likes least. These posh boys pick it up at public school, like headlice – the competitive alpha-male bollocks – and never seem to shake it off.

After a voluble meal in the restaurant they adjourn to the bar and it's well past two when they finish their last drinks and say goodnight. She really should rehydrate before she goes to bed to avoid writing off tomorrow with a hangover. She pours herself a glass of water and sips it on the sofa, looking out across the rose-tinted sea. The maid has changed the flowers. These new yellow lilies are just as pungent as the last lot.

Ollie comes out of the bath wrapped in a towel, holding his toothbrush.

'What did you mean when you said this wasn't your scene?'

She looks up at him in surprise. It's not like Ollie to pick a fight.

'I said it wasn't really me, that's all. Well, it isn't. Not David and Sophie anyway. But *you're* alright.' She gets up and wraps her arms around him. 'I'll keep you.'

'And the champagne and the first-class travel?'

Her smile freezes. Her arms slip from his waist.

She waits for him to apologise but he turns away and starts brushing his teeth.

'Plus,' her voice is louder, indignant, 'I wanted to make Sean feel less out of place, like he had an ally amongst all the bankers.'

Ollie turns and looks at her coldly. 'Blacks and Irish sticking together?'

She stares at him. 'He's not Irish.'

'You know what I mean.'

'Oh, fuck off.'

He goes back into the bathroom and she stares after him, her heart pounding, wondering whether to follow and continue the argument. She's always been the outsider wherever they go, and now that she's met someone more like herself, someone not born with a silver spoon and a trust fund, Ollie seems to feel threatened. Does he want her to be dependent on him? Would an insecure wife boost his ego? Like a swimming race or a fat cigar?

Her hands are cold and she shakes them to get the blood flowing. She needs to calm down. They hardly ever row, and to do so on their honeymoon seems fateful somehow. Is he *jealous*? Was it so obvious that she found Sean attractive? Another first for Ollie the Adonis: sexual jealousy. She'll have to keep out of Sean's way from now on.

In bed they exchange chaste kisses before Ollie turns his back and falls almost instantly asleep.

Asha lies on her back and gazes at the moving shadows made by the ceiling fan – there for effect as the air con works perfectly.

The blacks and Irish comment was pretty unforgivable. And if she thought about it enough she might find the implications very disturbing indeed.

He's been weird ever since the wedding and not just because of the sex. More possessive than usual, casually asking where she's going or who's been texting her. She used to think jealousy was at least in some part a sign of love, but Ollie himself once told her this was bullshit: that it's a sign of insecurity and weakness.

What's he feeling insecure about? The relationship? Is he starting to think that all this – the wedding, the honeymoon – has been a huge, expensive mistake?

She'll drive herself mad thinking this way.

Maybe she's imagining things. Her hormones still haven't gone back to normal, maybe she's just being paranoid. But then she remembers what he was like at the wedding.

There was definitely something wrong then. Something more than work-stress over a company merger. She's tempted to wake him here and now and demand to know what's going on, but the time isn't right, not straight after a row. To stop herself she gets up and walks out onto the terrace, detouring for a sarong in case someone's having another moonlight paddle.

The night is mild and perfectly still, the moon hidden behind milky cloud.

She stops dead. Sean is walking in the water. As the decking creaks under her feet he turns sharply. Was he hoping it was Emily's spirit coming to embrace him under the moonlight? Or does he just have insomnia? He's perfectly still. She can feel the weight of his gaze.

The moon comes out from behind a cloud, outlining his body in graphic light and shadow. He raises a hand and she waves back, then he turns and walks away down the beach.

She goes back to bed.

Ollie's lying on his back on top of the bunched-up sheet, his pelvis twisted away from her. She wants to touch his naked hip, to turn him gently over, but it seems his body no longer belongs to her.

This time there's no way to distract herself from the ache in her groin.

Half hoping the rustling of the sheets and her laboured breathing will wake him, she masturbates, the usual images scrolling through her head: herself bent backwards over the bed at home as Ollie crouches above her, his head between her thighs. Sure enough, that delicious fuzzy warmth is soon coursing through her bloodstream. Her fingers probe harder, her breath quickens.

In her mind's eye she makes him straighten up. She wants to see his hard cock.

But it's not Ollie's smooth body that unfurls above her: it's Sean's, his flesh a cold orange in the light from the streetlamps, the tattoos crawling over him like snakes.

There's no tenderness in his expression, only hunger. And now he's fucking her, harder than Ollie ever did, his hands gripping her flesh like claws.

The thought tips her over.

Afterwards she gets up and goes to the bathroom, washing herself furtively in the sink in case the shower wakes him. She doesn't want to smell of sex when he wakes.

For the first time since she's been with Ollie she's thought about someone else as she touched herself.

Whatever's wrong with him, they need to sort it out soon.

7

FV Hospital, Ho Chi Minh City

Monday 3 October

Her name is Sophie. Sophie *Peters*, she adds, as if a surname will jog my memory. It doesn't. Once I've extricated myself from her snuffling embrace I politely offer her the blue plastic chair in the corner. As if this is a perfectly normal meeting and I'm not swaying in front of her with a head like an orc and a gown flapping around my naked buttocks.

'Darling, you shouldn't be out of bed.'

'Shouldn't I?'

A look of alarm crosses her face. 'Hasn't the doctor spoken to you?'

'I've only just woken up.'

She swallows and her eyes slide to the door. Should she get the doctor before she lets something slip that she shouldn't?

'But I feel fine,' I say quickly, to forestall this, and lower myself gently onto the bed. Even the tiny jolt as my backside hits the mattress is enough to set my head yammering. I lower it, blinking as unobtrusively as possible to try to clear my vision, then look up and smile. My cheeks nudge at my wound but I don't let the smile slip. I need to hear the unvarnished truth, not a doctor's platitudes.

'I'm really sorry, but you'll have to remind me how we know each other. Did you help me when I had the, er . . . accident?'

She stares at me. 'You can't remember?'

'I can remember a . . . a bang . . .' I pause slyly, like a fraudulent clairvoyant, waiting for her to jump on the suggestion.

'A bang?' She frowns. 'I think I should get the doctor.'

'Maybe not a bang. More a sound of impact?'

'You remember him hitting you?'

The world stops spinning and my eyes snap into focus. She's staring at me, eyes wide, all thoughts of summoning the doctor forgotten.

Who hitting me? *Ollie?*

'What else can you remember?'

'Nothing. Please. At least tell me where I am.'

There's a long beat of silence. Our eyes are locked and the colour is seeping from her face.

'I should—' She goes to get up but my hand shoots out and grips her top. I can feel the damp flesh of her belly through the linen. She must be able to tell from my expression that I will not let her leave this room without a fight because she sinks back into the chair.

'You're in a private hospital in Saigon.'

Saigon. So we did go away. We were only supposed to be transferring at Saigon so why would we have left the airport?

'David and I were staying at the same resort as you, on Con Son Island.'

I blink. The name triggers something in my belly. A smell of lilies.

'There was a gay couple there too. And a man on his own. Sean. Do you remember?'

I shake my head.

'We'd been there about a week when you arrived. You and I used to sit together on the beach while the boys went swimming. We had a massage and you said it was more painful than passing a kidney stone.' She gives a wan smile, rambling now, taking a circuitous route to the part she doesn't want to say.

'Tell me what happened.'

The smile fades. She inhales. 'There were caves. Nearby. You could take a boat trip or walk through the jungle. You wanted to go. I don't think Ollie did.'

My husband's name spilling from her lips is all wrong. He's mine. I want to keep him to myself, keep him safe and warm inside me for this last snatch of time, until he's torn away from me. I think I know what's coming.

Her intake of breath sounds like a gasp. 'A Burmese guy dropped you at the caves. They're a local beauty spot. They're supposed to be very beautiful. You were very unlucky.' She has a desperate look, as if she's hanging by her fingertips from a cliff edge and slowly losing her grip. 'As soon as the police found you they got you airlifted here, to this hospital. David's looked it up online. It's a good one. Angelina Jolie was treated here.'

I stare at her. There's a big black hole in her story, like the crater in my head. The way my heart is clanging I wonder that it hasn't broken apart, cogs flying. I almost wish I'd let her call for the doctor. He'd be checking me over now, answering all my questions with a deflecting murmur. I wouldn't have to know.

Sophie is as white as the bathroom tiles, sweat beading her forehead and upper lip, oiling the roots of her hair.

'Where's Ollie?'

There. I've said his name. I've made it real. I've opened the door to the monsters.

'Where's my husband?' My voice is lost in the bleeps of the machines and the roar of the traffic and the rustle of Sophie's clothes as she writhes on the chair.

'Asha, please, let me . . .' Her words sound wet and fat as her throat closes up.

I rear up on the bed. '*TELL ME!*' My vision washes red. My heart tears itself apart. Sophie presses herself back into the chair, her lips peeled back from her teeth.

'Oh my love, I'm so sorry,' she whispers. 'Ollie's dead.'

8

Burney Castle Chapel, Hampshire

Saturday 3 September, 11 a.m.

Everyone else will have walked. The car journey is ridiculously short: half a mile down a lane at the back of the castle that leads to a chapel nestling in a stand of firs. It was the family chapel, back when the castle was still owned by the descendants of William the Conqueror's cronies. After all four scions of the dynasty were wiped out in the First World War and the estate was bought by a hotel consortium the chapel fell out of use – until the wedding venue craze kicked off.

When Ollie first suggested Burney (he'd gone to school with the son of the hoteliers), Asha's heart had leapt at the diminutive sounding 'family' chapel. But of course this was *old money*, and there had to be room for the servants. The place could easily seat a hundred and forty.

It only sounds bad, Asha thinks as the car purrs down the rain-slick tarmac: in reality a hundred and forty isn't so many. It could have been far worse.

They pass the bench she and Ollie fell asleep on last night, the fountain they tossed coins into – wishing for sun and short speeches and decent canapés – and a moment later the chapel comes into view. The chauffeur pulls in by the lychgate and comes round to open her door. She climbs out, careful not to let her skirt brush against the mud that spatters the Rolls's flank.

From the chapel comes the low murmur of conversation and the occasional laugh. Her chest tightens under the bodice.

Uncle Thomas hobbles round and takes her arm, but as they're about to pass through the gate he holds her back.

A latecomer is just going into the church. A stocky, bald man in an ill-fitting suit – one of Ollie's rugger chums no doubt. They'll give him a moment to settle down before making their grand entrance.

Under the overcast sky the bloodstain on the dress is barely visible, though her hand is still tender and she hopes the cut won't open up when Ollie slides the ring on.

It's raining again, thin and cold as iron filings on her shoulders. She politely refused her mother-in-law's ermine stole for *something borrowed* as it swamped the dress's delicate lace sleeves, but of course, with hindsight, she should have said yes and then just discarded it for the photos. It would have smoothed things over after the awkward moment when they told Victoria and Mackensie they were getting engaged.

'Darling,' Victoria had blurted to her son. 'Are you sure?'

With a bit of luck things will improve when the grandchildren start arriving. If.

The chapel is hushed now, candlelight dancing in its diamond-paned windows. The gravestone angels bow their heads, rain dripping from their aquiline noses.

Thomas waits while she swallows and blinks back the tears, raindrops collecting like jewels in the whorls of his hair.

'Right,' she says finally. 'Let's do it.'

They walk hand in hand through the gate. When he spots them, one of the ushers – Ollie's banker friend Seb – rushes to meet them with an umbrella.

'You look gorgeous.' He grins.

'Thank you.' She kisses him. Today she can even like hedge fund managers.

They step into the porch, her heels echoing on the flagstones. Now they must wait while Seb goes to whisper to the organist.

In the chill darkness she is glad of Thomas's warmth beside her, as if he's brought a little bit of West Africa to this drab corner of the English countryside. She could never tell Ollie she finds any of this drab: his parents' sprawling pile known simply by its first name, Lambton. The endless fucking dog walks, the fuss over the wine, the obligatory tour of the garden with its rare *dwarf mulberry* and *elephant ear*. Victoria has spent so many years weeding and pinching off and propagating she's already into her second batch of knee replacements.

They'll be expected to get their own rural retreat when the kids arrive (if), but as long as they keep a *flat in town* Asha will survive. She's quite happy for Victoria to be as interfering a grandmother as she wishes if it means that she and Ollie can have date nights in London.

The music starts up. Seb opens the door and, painfully self-conscious, she lets Thomas lead her into the nave. To the tuneless honking of the organ she trip-traps down the aisle in her unfamiliar heels, like the goat over the troll's bridge. Her skin prickles as she feels the eyes focused on her. Not all of them benign.

The occupants of the pews are smears of colour as she passes, her gaze focused on the male figure standing at the end of the aisle.

Turn round. Turn round.

She wants to see the look on his face. She's never been vain, never worn much makeup, prefers understated elegance to out-and-out glamour, but despite the heaving bosom (or perhaps because of it) she knows that today she looks beautiful. Proper, fairytale, Disney beautiful.

Turn round, Ollie.

But he doesn't. Milo does. His white face grinning.

Milo. On their second date he was there – *just a quick one to say hello before we head to the theatre* – and he's still here on their wedding day. The brother Ollie never had. The Graveneys certainly seem to think so. Their warmest smiles and most natural embraces are reserved for him while Asha is hugged stiffly and fobbed off with platitudes. He will, no doubt, become a godparent. This is a battle she has already lost.

She smiles at him, but falteringly. Why won't Ollie turn? Is there some upper-class rule she doesn't know about, like not saying *haitch* or holding your knife like a pen? *Don't look at the bride, for God's sake, or you'll never be welcome in polite society again.*

Is she imagining the twist at the corners of Milo's smile? Has he finally done what he's been trying to do for years with his oh-so-innocent insinuations? Has he put Ollie off her?

Someone to her left sniffs. People always cry at weddings, even those with the most tenuous links to the happy couple. She always cries herself and wonders now if Ollie took that as a sign she was sad not to have been proposed to already. Did that push him into it sooner than he would have wished?

He's stiff-backed, staring straight ahead, shoulders high. His ears are bright red. She almost laughs, until she remembers that his ears only go red when he's hyper-stressed. He didn't seem stressed last night.

They dined on the terrace at the back of the castle, looking out across the rolling countryside. It was a beautiful sunset, bands of crimson, gold and mauve streaming across the horizon. They'd got through two bottles of Krug and a half bottle of muscat, then they'd wandered down the steps to the garden and fallen asleep on a bench in each other's arms. After the maître d' woke them and sent them, rather unsteadily, back to their rooms, they lingered on the landing, unwilling to part. She hadn't needed to ask then if he was sure. She knew. Even after what happened in July, how angry she was, how unreasonable, he still adored her.

Uncle Thomas helps her up the steps to the altar, then melts back.

The last sighs and rustles die away and the chapel falls silent.

Ollie is still looking straight ahead, his chest rising and falling rapidly.

She squeezes his hand and he starts, then finally, as if waking from a dream, looks at her. He blinks rapidly and his shoulders drop. Finally he smiles. Mouths *you look gorgeous.*

The ceremony begins and she says all the right things in all the right places, but the occasional glances she sneaks in Ollie's direction do little to quell the disquiet that has crept over her.

His ears are no longer red. In fact they are, like the rest of his face, deathly pale. His forehead glistens with sweat. Is he sick?

He seems distracted while the vicar is speaking, and when they list his entire name, with its silly De Montfort part, he doesn't even smile.

She delivers her section perfectly but though he knew the declaration off by heart at the run-through yesterday, today he forgets *to love and to cherish.*

At the end everyone claps and now, finally, Ollie smiles, taking her face in his hands and kissing her tenderly, before turning to the congregation and yanking both their hands into the air, as if he's just won a race.

She smiles and smiles and smiles as the photographer ducks and crouches to get every angle, until finally it's time to go and sign the register. In the chill grey anteroom she shivers and Ollie gives her his jacket, while the vicar shakes the fountain pen to get the cold ink flowing.

She breathes in the scent of him, clutching his warm, damp back, pulling him against her body, not letting him go even as the vicar waits expectantly.

Eventually she takes the pen and self-consciously traces the shape of her new name, like a child forming her first letters over the dotted lines of an exercise book. Then it's Ollie's turn. Over his shoulder Asha frowns. The signature is odd: cramped and stuttering, barely legible. Then she sees why. His hand is shaking, and when he takes it away, her own new name is smeared across the page like a bloodstain.

9

Mango Tree Resort, Con Son Island

Sunday 25 September

There's a spot on her chin, one of those big ones under the skin that feel more like bruises. Past experience has taught her to leave well alone, she'll just have to suffer an unsightly lump until it goes down in a few days. She always gets spots before her period.

'How did you sleep?' he calls through the door.

'Good. You?'

'Fine.'

He sounds perfectly normal. As if the fight never happened. Maybe it was just jealousy. She'll give it a few days then start teasing him about it, so he knows the idea is ridiculous. It *is* ridiculous. Whatever happened when she was half pissed, it was no worse than fantasising about James Bond, or Poldark. Sean's the archetypal sex-starved housewife's choice: muscular, brooding, tragic. And if *she* hadn't put out for weeks Ollie would probably be having the odd secret wank.

When she comes out he's lying on the sofa flicking through the hotel brochure.

'Anything good?'

'The usual. Tours round *authentic family-run paddy fields*, boat trips to snorkel around a rock with five hundred other tourists. That kind of crap.' He tosses it onto the table. 'I'd rather just catch some rays, man.'

'Sure,' she says. Ollie works harder than her, he deserves a break. But she would like to get some idea of the culture, however sanitised.

'Maybe we could do something later in the week,' she says as he picks up his sunglasses and his tablet.

'Oh wait, do *you* want to do something?'

Good old considerate Ollie. She softens at once. 'Not today. Let's just relax. You've been working hard.'

She crosses the room and runs her palm over his chest. His skin is cool and dry in the air con and he smells of the lime and basil shower gel from the bathroom.

'Come on,' he says. 'Or we'll miss breakfast.

The beach is crowded, relatively speaking. All the other guests are there. Asha wonders if the others have deliberately saved them the chrysalis sunbed, though she can't imagine Sophie and David snuggling up on it – there probably wouldn't be enough room – and the Americans never seem to sit down. At the moment they are shamelessly doing tai chi on the wet sand while Sophie paddles in the shallows and David slouches like a lumpy potato, his sunbed at a stiff right-angle, looking bored. Only Sean seems properly relaxed, lying asleep a little away from the others, earphones on, one muscular arm draped over the edge of his sunbed, a tear-shaped black yin tattoo across his bicep. It brings back memories of the lads she used to get off with as a teenager in Islington – the Dans and Jasons and Robbies. The way they would fuck her like their bodies were two parts of a machine. A piston going into a cylinder.

As they've missed breakfast Asha stands by the sunbed looking pointedly towards the restaurant, and sure enough the waitress – Hao? Hai? – appears to take their order.

Ollie orders curried goat and Asha has quinoa porridge with coconut yoghurt and passion fruit.

Afterwards, having massaged factor fifty into that damn mole and extracted a promise that he will put a t-shirt on at midday, she leans back against the cushions to get on with the swords and dragons. Ollie curls up beside her, his head tucked into her neck, his breath tickling her chest. Occasionally she runs her fingers through his curls. Already they're turning baby-blond in the sun.

A few minutes later a shadow falls across the bed.

'I do hope you're not poofing out on me, sir.'

David's face is red and glistening with sweat and his fingers wriggle in the pockets of his shorts.

'Hmm?' Ollie raises his head sleepily.

'Our little race.'

'You're not at school any more,' Asha says with a humourless smile. She was right about him the first time. He's a tosser. *Poofing out.*

Ollie sits up.

She looks at him in disbelief. 'You've just had curry. You'll get cramp.'

'Yeah, but it was very light.'

She lays her book on her knees. 'Goat. Curry.'

'The portions are smaller out here.' He grins and stands.

She wonders then if he would have been happier skiing or on some other action-packed adventure. He's clever, there's no doubt about that, but sometimes he bounds around like a dozy puppy.

'Right. Shall we race there, stop for a breather, then race back?'

He's jogging on the spot, a jokey warm-up that's only half joking.

David does some half-hearted stretches, his eyes moving nervously over Ollie's rippling muscles. David is solid rather than fat. She gets the feeling that punching his concrete gut would hurt your hand just as much as Ollie's six pack.

Then she remembers. 'Wait. The boat.'

'I checked with Bay,' Ollie says. 'They've already been.'

He checked with Bay? He intended to do this all along?

Kissing her, he jogs down to the surf and dives straight off the ledge while David huffs after him.

61

'Be careful,' she calls after him, hating the whining tone in her voice.

'Be as long as you like,' Sophie calls from her bed.

She's smoking a cigarette, pulling on it hard enough to pucker her whole mouth and chin. Asha thinks about going over and scrounging one now that Ollie's safely occupied, but he'd be bound to smell it on her. And smoking's supposed to affect your fertility.

She picks up her book.

But whatever Bay said about the boat she can't concentrate and has to keep looking up to check on Ollie. His scything front crawl (taught by an Olympic gold medallist) has taken him halfway to the rock before a thrashing, gasping David has swum a quarter of the way. That's something. If Asha were a shark she'd definitely go for the slower, meatier option.

The next time she looks up Ollie is on the rock, calling out encouragement to his rival who has slowed so much he's almost stationary.

'Is he alright?' she calls over to Sophie.

'Just fat and unfit. Hope they've got a good shuttle helicopter to the local hospital.'

Asha laughs but secretly thinks there's a distinct possibility David could have a heart attack.

The next time she looks up, Ollie is pulling David up onto the rock where he lies, motionless: although presumably not dead or Ollie would be making more commotion. A moment later David rolls into a sitting position and Ollie sits down beside him. Their backs are to the beach, as if they're discussing a secret. She feels a rush of irritation. It's their honeymoon and he'd prefer to spend his time with some banker twat than his new wife. Well, she'll show him.

Sean is standing in the water gazing out towards the horizon. She walks down to join him.

'What's it like?'

He smiles. 'Warm tea.'

'Yum.' She goes to stand beside him. The hair on his arms has burned gold. Sweat glistens at the base of his spine.

'He won then. What's his prize?'

'David has to be his fag for the rest of the holiday.'

'He looks the type to enjoy a good caning.'

She suppresses a snort of laughter, hoping Sophie hasn't heard, then lowers her voice. 'The English upper classes, eh? All those suppressed urges.'

'I was far too common for Em's family. Screwed from the moment they saw the tats.'

He flexes his left arm and the design ripples. Again that prick of arousal. Hot fucking is what you'd get from Sean, none of the tender lovemaking Ollie is so good at: the slow climax, the lingering embrace afterwards. Sean would come, scratch his arse and go get a beer. She almost giggles.

'What is it?'

'It's a bulldog. Shut up. I had it done when I was still boxing.'

Boxing. For goodness' sake. Images of flying beads of sweat awash with rampant male hormones, of a bloodied Sean, legs astride his vanquished foe, fists aloft.

'You boxed?' she says, and her voice sounds prissy and high.

'For a bit. In my teens. I was shit though.' He wrinkles his nose.

It feels good to flirt again. The office is so female heavy and Ollie's friends are a bunch of awful, entitled boors. That's why she took an immediate dislike to David but perhaps she's being unfair. Not everyone can be neatly tucked into their stereotype box. Like tough-guy Sean. Shit at boxing and not ashamed to admit it. She should be careful. He's charming and intelligent as well as fit.

'Whereabouts in London are you from? I'm Islington but your accent's more east end, right?'

'Romford. Ever been?'

She shakes her head.

'Don't. It's a dump.'

He asks if she wants a drink and since Ollie's making no move to return she says yes. When he gets back from the restaurant,

63

carrying them himself, it seems perfectly sensible for them to sit on the chrysalis lounger.

Though she's acutely careful to maintain a good foot of space between them, she still responds to the smell of him, her hormones reacting to his pheromones. She is hyper-alert and twitchy as she sips her gin and tonic quickly, wondering if this is perhaps a little inappropriate after all.

Fortunately Ollie's deep in conversation with David, so before he has the chance to glance round she gulps the last of the drink and slides off the other side of the lounger. 'Think I might go for a swim.'

But Sean's not listening. She follows his gaze. Two figures stand at the very end of the beach, where the land starts to curve into jungle. One is shorter than the other but they're too far away for her to make out more. She picks up her camera and zooms in as far as the lens will go. Even then the figures are a grey blur. Something about the way they just stand there – perfectly still, side by side but perpendicular to the sea, as if they're not really interested in the beautiful view but in what's going on further up the beach – makes the hair rise on the back of her neck. They're looking in the direction of the resort and suddenly she thinks of the slaughter on that Tunisian beach. What's the terrorist group out here? The Khmer Rouge? Christ, the name brings up images of gun-toting children and drug-addled torturers. She takes the shot. But now when she zooms in they pixelate completely, dissolving into the sand and sea like ghosts.

She's overreacting. They're only looking. Not scoping the place for an attack.

And yet Sean must feel the threat too because he stands up. 'It's not that boy?' she says, suddenly afraid. 'From the boat?'
'I can't see.'

He starts to walk, purposefully, arms raised from his sides in that thuggish, apelike parody of masculinity she normally hates. Now she's grateful, as before he can get more than ten paces the figures melt away over the ridge.

She's feeling guilty enough about the minor flirtation that she doesn't have a go at Ollie when he returns to the beach, climbing out of the sea with barely a hair out of place, while David labours the last few metres, red-faced and panting.

'Cramp,' the older man gasps, crawling up the sand and massaging his thigh.

'Oh, bad luck,' Ollie says gamely.

'You were lucky,' David says.

'A rematch later in the week then.' Ollie smiles and flops down on the bed.

To Asha's irritation David pulls a bed across to them and the two men discuss the distance they've swum and the increased choppiness as they passed the line of the headland, like two dinner party guests comparing traffic on the M25. When he finally goes back to Sophie and Ollie lies down, Asha becomes acutely aware of Sean's glass on the table beside the bed

'Did you see those people?' she says to keep Ollie's attention. 'Just appeared at the end of the beach. Seemed to be watching us. And then they just vanished.'

Ollie looks at her sharply. She'd only said it to make conversation, assumed he would dismiss it, but his expression is strange.

'What did they look like?'

'I couldn't really tell. It might have been those Americans. Look, I took a picture but it's hard to tell really. That blob of pink could be a sarong, or maybe they were just naked. I wouldn't put it past— Oh.'

She taps a few buttons on the camera but it makes no difference. The picture is gone.

10

FV Hospital, Ho Chi Minh City

Wednesday 5 October

After two days of sedation I tell them to stop the medication. It was only delaying the inevitable. I have to face the truth sometime so it might as well be now.

Ollie and I were attacked by the boatman who took us to the caves. He probably hit Ollie first, to disable him, then me. The blow to Ollie's head was immediately fatal. Mine was a glancing one, causing the skull to fracture but not depress, so there was very little brain swelling. Lucky me.

Oddly, he was the one who called the emergency services and when they arrived he was arrested immediately and transferred to a jail in Saigon to await trial. He's denying any part in the attack. The legal process is bound to be long, but the case against him is strong because a) he was one of the only people who knew we were going to the caves, b) at his home in Con Dao the police found my jewellery and c) the weapon used to attack us was a boat hook.

This is what Sophie told me. Afterwards she called the doctor, Sanjay, who called two nurses who managed to restrain me from going down to the basement of the hospital to view my dead husband's body.

Now I lie in my bed gazing up at the ceiling tiles. The drugs can't have left my system yet because I feel oddly detached. I must have sounded cold and callous in the phonecall to Ollie's parents, answering their questions with listless *I can't remember*s and *I don't know*s. Eventually Victoria became exasperated and Mackensie took the phone. I could hear her weeping as he informed me that he had arranged for his son's dead body to be airlifted back to the UK. But not my living body. Victoria's weeping got louder and then she started hurling accusations. *What kind of world had I brought their son into?* Mackensie terminated the call.

I should be upset but I'm not. I don't feel anything.

Apart from the desire – no, the *need* – to see my husband's body. There's a part of me that's still certain it's all been a mistake: that it won't be him down there.

I wait for the shifts to change, then, when the nurses are preoccupied, I get out of bed.

The room revolves. I think it's the residue of the drugs, because the wound itself seems to be healing rapidly. It doesn't ache to move my jaw any more.

I shuffle to the door and ease it open, careful to lift it over the section of floor it usually catches on. The nurses' station is up ahead, directly opposite the lift. If they see me they'll make me go back to bed. Probably with a forcibly administered sedative. They told me I didn't need to identify the body because they'd had Ollie's dental records sent over from the UK. I try not to imagine what sort of state his face must have been in for that to be necessary.

Three heads are bowed over a computer screen.

I skid across the corridor and press my back against the wall. Now at least I'm out of sight. But that doesn't help me. Perhaps I should have changed into my normal clothes, though even then anyone walking past the station would attract their attention.

Through the half-open blinds I glimpse the patient in the room beside mine. He lies motionless in his bed, tubes and lines scrawled across his distended abdomen. His skin is yellow and even though his belly is huge his skin seems to pull tight across his clavicles. Close to death, surely.

Beside him is a metal trolley carrying various metal implements and dishes.

The idea has barely flitted into my mind before I'm across the corridor and slipping through his door.

I close it silently behind me and pull down the blinds.

The room smells like my mother's in those last few weeks in the hospice. There are no sounds but for the slow bleeps of the monitors, not even the rustle of a sheet as a chest rises and falls. No death rattle yet. I don't think I could have stayed if he'd started that. I could barely stand it with Mum.

The bloated figure on the bed seems hardly to be breathing, although presumably alarms would sound if his heart rate slowed. He must be Asian I suppose, but all those near death look the same. Noses hook, eyes sink back into skulls, mouths slacken and gape. In this way death from disease is kind to those it leaves behind. Our loved ones are already strangers to us.

A few minutes later I'm back out in the corridor, crouching against the wall, still invisible to the workstation, panting and dizzy from the exertion. Leaving the room was nerve-wracking as the nurses had raised their heads from the computer and were chatting, all the important information having been communicated to the new shift. I had to pause in plain sight long enough to softly close the door behind me.

Though they're speaking Vietnamese I can still tell that the conversation is coming to a conclusion. This is my chance. I grip the strand of cotton I pulled from his sheet, praying that it's strong enough, praying that the knots I used to triple its length will hold.

The nurses laugh, then sigh. They're ready to move off.

I yank. The cotton goes taut and the trolley crashes to the floor with a sound fit to wake the dead.

There are exclamations from the nurses' station. If the man has fallen out of bed it will take the three of them to lift him back in.

Footsteps slapping down the lino.

Three figures appear and, oblivious to the strand of cotton snaking across the floor to me, barge through the door to the dying man's room.

I spring up and stagger to the lift. Pressing myself against the doors while I wait for it to arrive means I'm virtually invisible from the dying man's room. I wonder if they will find the thread knotted to the rail of the trolley and make the connection? If so they'll soon work out where I'm headed.

The lift arrives silently and I dive in, slamming my hand on the door-close button, then hitting the lowermost one. Aren't mortuaries always in the basement?

The doors close and the lift begins to thrum.

I've been so busy trying to make this happen that I haven't had time to think about what I'm about to face. Now I close my eyes and picture Ollie: in the kitchen stirring pasta, in the bath, sleeping on the sofa, at a party, laughing. The images are crystal clear. I could reach out and touch him. I know the texture and temperature of his skin, the smell of him, the rhythm of his breath. He can't be dead. I would feel it in my viscera. It must be someone else down there on the slab. The widower from the resort perhaps. Ollie doesn't like sightseeing much so perhaps I went with Sean: the head injury has made him unrecognisable. Ollie is elsewhere. Lost: injured perhaps, but not dead. Not dead. Not dead.

The lift shudders to a halt and the doors slide open on a different view entirely.

The low-ceilinged corridor leads in only one direction. The concrete walls are bare and there's a foetid smell of heat and damp. The lighting is low and tinged with red. Stepping out barefoot into a wall of heat I hesitate: perhaps I should have made them bring him up to one of the viewing rooms, then they could have prepared the body, dimmed the light to make the moment as bearable as it could be. But I get the feeling they wouldn't have allowed it. Whatever is left of my husband they needed dental records to identify.

Doubt assails me with such force I reach out to steady myself against the wall.

The lift doors close behind me and there's a whoosh as it goes back up. The decision has been made for me.

I follow the pipes and wires that snake across the ceiling of the corridor. There's a constant roar and yammer, like factory machinery, and it's sauna-hot. I guess all the air con units that make the rest of the hospital so temperate vent down here. Sweat dribbles down my spine and between my buttocks.

Turning a corner the corridor widens and doors open to the left and right. I see through the small windows that they lead to laboratories and store rooms.

Another corner. Up ahead is a dead end, blocked by a door. Closed and, unlike the others, windowless. My steps falter but I keep moving, my body so numb I feel as if I'm floating.

The air starts to change. At first it seems fresher, as if I'm about to emerge into the outside world, then the freshness takes on the sharp tang of chemicals.

I reach the door. Push it open. Walk in.

The room is blindingly white. As if I've passed through the tunnel and entered heaven. But heaven wouldn't smell like this. Disorientated I stagger against a wall. The air is ice cold.

I'm leaning against a metal cabinet that runs floor to ceiling. The room is lined with them, fluorescent lights bouncing off the polished steel. Each cabinet is made up of drawers, and each drawer is wide and high enough to accommodate a cadaver.

I push myself upright and breathe slowly, deeply. My feet are so firmly planted on the lino I can't imagine being able to cross the floor and pull open one of the drawers. Each is labelled with a pixelated QR code, as if it contained nothing more than groceries. For a moment my muscles unclench. I won't be able to tell which contains his body. I may as well turn round and go back to my room.

No, I will just have to open them all.

By the time I'm halfway round the room my revulsion at viewing grey corpse after grey corpse is waning. I've learned that if I unzip the body bag a little I can read the label attached to the ankle without having to look at distended stomachs or blackened fingers.

I open the bottom drawer of the next cabinet almost mechanically. The cadaver bag is grey, thicker than the others, and as I unzip it a hand flops out. It looks like all the others: whitish grey, yellow nails already drawing back from the cuticles. And then I see, almost imperceptible against the grey flesh, the tanline around the ring finger.

The zip snarls as I draw it back, all the way down past the muscular thigh, to the knee with the mauve scar, the ankle, the foot. The label.

I tumble off my haunches and land against the next cabinet, making the metal ring dully.

It's wrong.

This isn't him. The wrong dental records were sent. This is someone else.

My abdomen cramps, as if I'm being sliced open.

Ollie, Ollie, my Ollie.

I think of the way his hair smells after he's washed it. The way he looks in his glasses – so sweet and studious. The way he bites his lower lip when he's trying not to laugh. The quiff he waxes into his hair when we're going out and how it always tumbles over when he's had one too many. His voice. His laugh. Oh God oh God. How can I survive this? How is my heart still beating?

Someone comes into the room. A sharp exclamation in Vietnamese, then hands on my arm, trying to pull me up.

I want to shout *no* but it comes out as a long, broken howl.

She lets me go, starts babbling into a mobile phone. A tiny woman in a lab coat and thick glasses. She is clearly calling the orderlies or the doctors to come and take me away.

But I have to know for sure.

Grasping the edge of the body bag I throw it back.

All the air leaves the room as I gaze down at the thing that lies on the shelf.

Giving up trying to make sense of what must be the face, I pass my eyes down over the body. The sallow pallor of frozen flesh is broken only by a dark patch of pubic hair and, on the chest, a black mole as big as a thumbprint.

My mind blanks.

11

Grounds of Burney Castle, Hampshire

Saturday 3 September, 12 p.m.

It was nerves. That's all. They laughed about it in the car back to the castle when she said she thought he might have changed his mind. And then Ollie cried and said this was the best day of his life. He kissed her cut hand and she held his head against her breasts, his breath warm on her bare skin. By the time they got out of the car in front of the cheering, confetti-tossing guests, she was just as serene and radiant as she should be.

At the pre-dinner drinks in the rose gardens, Uncle Thomas has a story about her mother.

'She always used to come stay with us for the summer. It was good to have the family back together, even if your grandmother had to stay in England.'

'She used to love coming to see you,' Asha says smiling. 'It sounded magical.'

'Sometimes the boys would be off playing football, and then she would lie out in a hammock, reading her schoolbooks. She was a clever girl, your ma. She knew what she wanted out of life. She was going to make something of herself.'

Asha's smile faltered. Pregnant by seventeen, all that promise turned to drudgery and worry.

He's looking at her, his dark eyes still bright in his crumpled face. 'Look at you, girl,' he says softly. 'She made you.' He nods towards their surroundings. 'And look what you made.'

For a moment all the happy faces around them recede until there's just her and Thomas. Two strangers in this rarefied world.

'That's all Ollie,' she murmurs. 'Not me.'

He takes her hand and rubs a papery thumb across the back of her fingers.

'He loves you because you're something special. That's all money and success is. Is people giving you something because you're worth it. You worth it to Ollie. He knew he betta get you before someone else did. Don't you forget that. You worth it. This is all you deserve.'

'Hear hear,' says a drunk girl, some posh friend of Ollie's. 'He's a bloody lucky boy!' The spell is broken. Thomas takes a step back and starts addressing the crowd again.

'So, one day Francoise she finds this pretty little white egg in a hollow of one of the trees. Now, this little girl left Nairobi when she was eight months old. As far as she concerned, things that come out of eggs is ducks and blackbirds and blue tits.'

He says it like a foreigner. Blue. Tits. There's laughter, and he winks at Asha. He's playing them.

'So it must be a bird's egg, right? She thinking maybe it's a parrot or a bird of paradise. She runs back into the house and gets one of her socks (that she don't need in a Nigerian summer but that her momma packed because she's spent so long in the cold and rain she forgotten what real heat is), then real careful she tucks the egg inside the sock to keep warm. Day after day she keeps this egg nice and warm in its sock nest and don't say nothing to no one in case we tell her she gotta put it back.'

He takes a sip of his champagne, glancing round at the rapt faces. Asha wishes Ollie was here to listen.

'Then one morning, we can't find her. At lunchtime we call her and call her, but she don't come and we can see from the kitchen window that she ain't in the hammock. Clara she's scared by now. A few years back a sick hyena came into the village and damn near killed a farmer. We send out the boys to look for her, and five minutes later Stephen comes in laughing so hard he can hardly talk. When I ask him what's so damned funny he says *you better go see for yourself.*'

Asha knows this story but Thomas tells it so well she can barely keep a straight face as he describes them tramping around the garden calling her mother's name, then finally hearing a pathetic squeak from the upper branches of an acacia tree.

'That egg had hatched on her belly, but it weren't no parrot that came out, nor even a blue tit. It was a white-bellied carpet viper.'

Gasps from the drunk girls.

'To get her through those cold wet English winters Evelyn had read all about the flora and fauna of her homeland and she knew full well that the carpet viper is the most deadly snake in the whole wide world.

'I look about and eventually I see the snake. It's about so long.' He makes a two-inch gap between his thumb and forefinger. 'Can't even get isself off the hammock!'

More laughter.

'"Missy!" I call up to her. "You know snakes can climb trees, right?" For a moment there's a silence, then a crazy rustling of the leaves above my head, then before I can do anything more than stretch out my arms and brace myself, she done fallen straight out of that tree like a coconut. A big scared crying coconut clinging to my neck!'

Asha laughs and laughs at the image of her indomitable mother terrified out of her wits by a two-inch baby snake. Even Thomas is laughing so hard there are tears in his eyes, as if he's never heard the story before either. When the laughter ebbs and Thomas sighs and wipes his eyes Asha sees that the photographer is there.

'Got some good ones,' she says, grinning.

Attracted by the laughter perhaps, Ollie's mother joins them, her cheeks pink with champagne. Asha introduces her to Thomas and the stiff middle-aged woman kisses him on both his papery cheeks.

'Oh, you must come and meet Mackensie,' she says then and, linking arms with the scruffy elderly black man, she totters across the lawn towards her husband.

Asha smiles after them. Perhaps today is going to be pretty perfect after all.

The meal is surprisingly good, considering how difficult it must be to cater for a hundred and forty people, including vegans, coeliacs and the dairy intolerant. There's venison tartare to start, followed by salmon wellington, and lemon polenta cake: these are topped with an amuse bouche of truffled cauliflower soup and tailed with chocolate pralines. By the end sweat is dripping down Asha's temples and, in order to avoid fainting there on the spot, she excuses herself to go and find Zainab to try and do something about the dress.

They fiddle with it under the grand staircase in the foyer, unpicking more of the stitches of the bodice and resewing them with a kit Zainab got from the maître d'.

'How did you get on with Milo?' The dizziness is starting to subside now that Asha can breathe more easily. 'Manage to prise him from Liberty?'

The two had been talking intensely for some time under the arbour before they came in for the meal.

Zainab's hands pause.

'Well? Are you meeting him later for a quickie behind the curtains?'

'I don't think so.'

This is so different from Zainab's normal tone that Asha twists to look at her.

'Careful, you'll break the thread.'

'What, then? What happened?'

Zainab pauses. 'I think you're right, that's all. He's a bad man.'

'Ha! You always said I was just jealous!'

'Somebody's jealous but I'm not sure it's you.'

'Oh my God, what did he say?'

Another pause, though her fingers continue to work quietly, probing the flesh under Asha's armpits.

'He said that he hoped you knew what a good catch Ollie was and that you'd start behaving yourself once you were married.'

'*Behaving* myself? What a patronising cock.'

'That wasn't the worst thing, though.'

'What?' Now she does turn round. Zainab's skin is grey in the gloom.

'He said you told him to watch out because I was as desperate to bag a rich white sucker as you were.'

A moment's silence.

'I didn't . . . I would never.'

'I know.'

'I wouldn't even say that as a joke. We don't talk like that. We can't stand each other.'

'That's just it, though, right? He's clever enough not just to badmouth you, but to imply you'd been badmouthing me – to put a wedge between us.'

'I told you he was nasty.'

'Not just nasty. Dangerous.'

'Oh come on, he's just another banker wanker.'

'No, he's clever. Trying to isolate you from your friend. To weaken you. The weaker you are, the easier it will be for him to come between you and Ollie.'

Before Zainab went into criminal law she was a family lawyer specialising in abused wives. In the chill shadows of the staircase, goosebumps ping up on Asha's arms.

'You're over-reacting. He's just a prick.'

Zainab shakes her head. 'You should be careful of him.' She leans in to bite the thread. 'There. Done. Now don't eat or drink another thing, fatso.'

'If you promise not to try and fuck Milo.'

Zainab smiles and they walk back into the dining room arm

in arm. As they do so Milo glances up from the table. His gaze snags on the pair, just for a split second, before carrying on his conversation with Mackensie.

As the two women part and Asha makes her way back to the main table she feels a prick of irritation with her friend. Couldn't she have waited until another time to tell her something so unpleasant?

As she sits down she glances over at Zainab, her head now thrown back in laughter as she flirts with the teenage boy beside her.

They've been friends since university but Zainab was always tricky company. Uncompromising in her opinions, never considering that other people's feelings might be more fragile than hers.

As she adjusts the foamy skirt of her dress, she catches Milo smiling at her. This was all part of his plan to ruin her day.

She forces herself to smile back, then leans over to kiss Ollie. Milo turns away.

When the last of the plates have been taken away and the coffees come round, people start looking towards the head table.

'You can't put it off any longer,' Asha whispers to Ollie and he grimaces back at her.

'Wish me luck.'

'Say nice things about me.'

He leans in to kiss her – 'Couldn't think of any, sorry' – then folds his napkin and stands up.

She feels a rush of pride as his confident gaze sweeps the room, and the last few mutterers quiet down.

'*Well,*' he begins, blue eyes sparkling, and there's a ripple of charmed laughter. One word and the whole room is his.

His speech reduces most of the women, with the notable exceptions of Victoria and Liberty, to tears. He begins with the funny story about Asha's magazine article, leaving Victoria tight-lipped, and goes on to list her qualities: how she grounds

77

him, what a privilege it is to be by her side. How a man like him, who has been gifted all the good fortune in the world, doesn't deserve this extra blessing.

A glance at Milo then – blink and you'd have missed it.

It doesn't seem right, he concludes, that a woman doesn't get to give a speech at her own wedding, but he's glad because a list of his qualities would be considerably shorter. It could have been cheesy or toe curling but somehow Ollie manages to make it perfect.

There are cheers and applause, pats on the back from Milo and Seb. He sits down, kisses her and mutters *thank fuck that's over*.

Now it's Milo's turn.

She has to admit he's good. There are no signs of nerves, no sweating or fumbling his words. His cool self-confidence is slightly inhuman. If it weren't for his preening at the responses of the crowd, you might wonder if he had any emotions at all.

Milo was sent to boarding school at the age of seven. Ollie joined at eleven. Asha has always thought that those crucial four years made all the difference between the warm and emotionally accessible Ollie and the cool, distant Milo. Liberty's the same, smooth and polished but somehow hollow. They make a good pair.

As the speech progresses she starts to realise this is not about her and Ollie, it's about Milo and Ollie. There are school anecdotes, uni anecdotes, stories from Graveney holidays that Milo was invited to, stories from their first days in banking. She starts to twitch at the mention of women's names. These are names she has heard before: old girlfriends from whom he parted amicably, but it starts to grind her nerves. Is he doing it deliberately?

She looks at Ollie, wondering if he has noticed – probably not; he always thinks the best of his friend – but Ollie doesn't even seem to be listening. His eyes are scanning the room, his expression tense. She follows his gaze. Rapturous faces are fixed on Milo.

Now Milo is talking about a skiing holiday where he and Ollie were caught in an avalanche. Ollie pulled him to safety as his left ski shot out into thin air.

Someone heckles: 'Shouldn't it be you marrying him?'

Everyone laughs. Milo almost purrs. Asha's cheeks start to ache. Finally he's wrapping up.

'I hope that Asha and Ollie are very happy together. She's got a good 'un there.'

He raises his glass and Asha finds herself toasting her husband, rather than her marriage. To quell her rising anger she picks up one of the foil chocolate wrappers and starts making it into the shape of a dog.

'Right. Telegrams. Or rather emails. There are quite a few so you might want to talk among yourselves.'

Her attention drifts. The dog's legs are too short because she's used up too much foil on its head. She screws it into a ball and drops it with a plink into the dregs of her coffee.

Somebody wishes them well from Milan. Another sends his congratulations from Copenhagen. Names she doesn't know. Hangers-on who are hoping that success is contagious. There are hundreds of them. The news must have travelled all over the world: one of banking's most eligible bachelors is off the menu. Asha wishes they hadn't put the bloody announcements everywhere – *Tatler*, *The Times*. It sounds like crowing.

Ollie stifles a yawn. The day has taken it out of him, clearly. It's not like him to suffer from nerves, but he's definitely not been himself today. Perhaps it's lingering worry about that *work thing*, which is the most he'll say about it. She's always rolled her eyes at the banking world – boring and full of pricks – and maybe that's made him reluctant to confide in her. But she's his wife now. She should make more of an effort.

'Last one. Oh, well this is novel . . .' Milo's pause catches her attention. She looks up to see he's holding a postcard. The image facing towards the room is of a beach scene with a hot-pink slogan slashed across the front: *Albufeira!*

'Um, it doesn't seem to say any—' He turns it over and those close enough can see that the blank side has no message. There is a pause.

Beside her Ollie has gone very still.

Milo clears his throat and for the first time looks ruffled. She watches his Adam's apple bob twice, then he lays the pile of messages down on the table and continues in the same smooth tone.

'Right, in a few minutes, when everyone's ready, we'll retire to the garden for the cutting of the cake, and the party will start back here again at five.'

A cheer goes up.

A moment later, when the drinking and conversation has resumed, there's a flurry of movement next to her and Ollie lurches to his feet.

'I'm sorry,' he says. 'I think I'm going to be sick.'

12

Mango Tree Resort, Con Son Island

Sunday 25 September

They're so boring. That's the worst part. She can predict exactly how they'll respond to any given comment or suggestion: the verbal tics and clichés, the superlatives. Things are *wonderful* or *appalling*: *extraordinary* is an insult. And David's always bragging. He tells Ollie – just Ollie – about the 35% returns he made on one account, 48% on another. How his manager told him he'd never seen anything like it: it was like David had some kind of sixth sense.

'I think they genuinely thought I'd been insider trading!'

While he's talking, Asha's attention drifts to Sophie. Her head is down, the dark roots showing. The nails of the fingers gripping her glass are bitten to the quick, a little ridge of flesh marking the point where they should attach to her fingertips.

She looks up, catches Asha's eye and smiles, but the smile is grave and almost pleading. Does she know what an arse her husband is being? Even perfectly acceptable men tend to behave that way around Ollie. Showing off like they're still in the playground, or flattering and creeping like oily salesmen. David's the worst of both worlds. Now he's congratulating Ollie on some deal he did in 2015. He's not even bothering to pretend to extend the conversation to the women now; though Asha's job is far more interesting that Ollie's and she has some pretty good anecdotes involving slimy politicians that Sophie would like at least.

With a stab of horror she realises she has never bothered to find out what Sophie does. She asks the question just as David takes a break to draw breath.

'I work in a café,' Sophie says, at the very same moment David says, 'Soph does her own thing.'

'Oh?' Ollie smiles expectantly.

'Don't sell yourself short, darling. It's not really just a café, is it?'

Sophie smiles demurely. 'It's an artisan bakery. We bake thirty different types of bread every day.'

'My mum baked bread,' Asha says. 'Reckoned her grannie brought the starter yeast over from Nigeria and it was seventy years old!'

She waits for Sophie to either pooh-pooh this or confirm whether it's possible. Sophie just nods politely.

'I let it die. Isn't that terrible? I wonder if there's any way of getting hold of something similar. Would you have to go over to Nigeria and carry it home in a special refrigerated container, or could you get it sent over dry and mix it with water or something?'

Sophie's smile is glassy, until she realises the question has been directed at her.

'Oh. I don't know. Um . . .'

'How do you do it at the café? Do you keep the yeast culture for years or just mix it in powder, like with a bread machine?'

Sophie blinks. Asha starts to feel self-conscious. Is she trying too hard to involve Sophie in the conversation? Is the other woman feeling patronised?

Then David says, 'Did you hear that Janssen Hopper was going to be done for Libor fixing and then it suddenly all went quiet. A guy I know reckons . . .'

Ollie turns towards him and the two men pick up where they left off.

As the blood rises to her face Asha feels a rush of anger. Sophie has turned away from her and is apparently rapt by this discussion of currency trading. Is it a snub?

'I'm going for a wee.'

Nobody pays any attention as she gets unsteadily to her feet and wobbles across the bar. In the toilet she hisses curses into the sink as the water flows over her hands. She realises she's very drunk. Again. Another morning laid waste by hangover. Ollie will sleep, drooling onto his sun lounger, she'll take yet more painkillers and eat too much to combat the nausea. She's put on weight already. Those two boring pissheads are ruining her figure.

She takes a circuitous route back, to get some air, and finds herself passing Sean's bungalow. It's in darkness. For a single wild moment, she considers letting herself in and slipping into bed beside him.

Yup, she's *very* drunk.

As she approaches the table Ollie says: 'Here she is. She can tell you herself.'

She realises, with a rush of warmth, he has changed the subject, to *her* career.

'Tell them about the cheating MP with the crack habit.'

She laughs and recounts the scandalous anecdote involving a well-known Catholic politician and family man who preached about the *evil* of drugs and blamed the breakdown of modern society on single-parent families.

'The reporter gave him a choice. Give them an exclusive on the affair or they'd blow his crack habit. Mr Minister figured that whilst a *mea culpa* on the sexy nanny would mean the end of his marriage, at least he might still keep his job.'

Sophie likes the story and makes her tell more, and by the end of the evening she's feeling less murderous, towards her at least.

On the way back to the bungalow she and Ollie hold each other up, as a stiff breeze buffets them and the wooden path appears to be considerably more undulating than it was earlier.

▸

Ollie is humming to himself. A song that was popular around the time they got together. It makes her thinks of days in the park followed by all-nighters in bars where time spooled away, drinking themselves sober. Staggering out into the cold London dawn, stopping off for croissants at the taxi drivers' caff then making love until the rest of the city woke up.

His armpit is against her shoulder and she can smell the delicious musk of him beneath the deodorant. She squeezes him tighter and he kisses her forehead. Perhaps he's starting to relax. Slipping her hand under his t-shirt she trails her fingertips over his hipbone, down to the waistband of his shorts. He inhales and exhales. That characteristic sigh of release before they have sex. Something inside her abdomen loosens, like she's just unfastened a corset.

She was right not to make a big thing of the sex drought. He just needed a little time to unwind. Tonight they will reconnect. It doesn't matter if they're too drunk for it to be anything other than a sloppy fumble.

For a moment she considers moving her hand down inside his shorts now, as they walk, but perhaps they're a bit old for al-fresco sex. Besides, it'll be much more comfortable inside the bungalow. The night has turned chilly.

Rounding the bend at the end of the restaurant building, a blast of wind sends them staggering backwards. The sea churns with white horses and there's a low booming noise, like the bass from a gangster's car stereo. It's coming from the far end of the headland where waves are pounding the rocks. Loose sand whips across the beach, hissing like a thousand snakes. Asha is momentarily blinded as a handful of grains are thrown into her eyes and she leans on Ollie to lead her.

He stops walking.

She blinks to clear her vision. Clouds are scudding in front of the moon, throwing mobile shadows across the sand. For a moment it looks as if the beach is crowded with dancing ghosts.

Ollie is standing very still, the muscles of his arm around her waist tensed hard. His gaze is focused on the headland.

Her heart jumps into her mouth. Are they back? The couple she saw the other day, now at the other end of the resort, gradually closing in on them?

She follows his gaze. The moving shadows make it hard to see clearly. Is that a woman's profile against the rocks? For a moment she can hardly breathe.

Then the moon appears, throwing everything into clarity.

The shadowy figure was just an uneven crevice in the rock. She blows her breath out, laughs.

'I thought that was someone watching us!'

She waits for Ollie's rueful agreement or laugh, or even just a grunt of acknowledgement that she's spoken.

Nothing. He ducks his head and presses on against the wind, tense and unreachable as ever.

Her idea that they would have sex tonight takes on a certain grim determination. They need it. If necessary she will have to explain this to him in no uncertain terms. The longer they put it off the more of an issue it'll become.

God, it's starting to sound like a chore even to her.

As they let themselves into the bungalow she decides to give him time to settle down before initiating anything, conversation or otherwise.

'You know what,' she says as she makes them both tea. 'I don't think Sophie's a breadmaker at all.'

'She didn't say she was. She just said she worked in a café.'

'I know, but I just sort of assumed. Weird for a hedge fund manager's wife to work in a café.'

On the sofa Ollie shrugs.

'Are you okay?' she says carefully, pouring the milk.

'Fine.' He says it on the inhalation, so it sounds like a gasp.

'You don't sound it.'

She puts the tea down on the coffee table then sits beside him and rubs his neck to show she doesn't want a confrontation.

'Just tired.'

'Are you not sleeping well?'

'It's only been a few days. I'm sure I'll feel better soon.'

A moment's silence. Ollie's head is resting on the sofa cushion, his eyes closed: it could be exhaustion, or he could be avoiding her gaze.

She bites her lip. His chest rises and falls quickly. In anticipation? Is he waiting for her to touch him?

'I can think of something that'll relax you.'

It sounds so stilted it's all she can do not to wince, and the smile that was supposed to be sexy must look as phoney as it feels. Fortunately he doesn't open his eyes. He doesn't move at all.

Is this an invitation to continue?

This nervousness is an odd feeling: she's positively apprehensive as her hand moves to his crotch, slides inside the fabric of his shorts, meets his penis, heavy and flaccid.

'I told you,' he snaps, jerking away. 'I'm tired.'

'You're always fucking tired.'

She knows what this sounds like before he speaks, but the anger disguises her shame.

'What, so I have to *put out,* do I, whenever you feel like it?'

Is it me? she wants to scream. *Have you gone off me?* But she's too angry to expose such vulnerability.

'Fine.'

She gets up and goes to the bathroom, brushing her teeth so long she spits blood into the sink. Gradually the fury subsides and she starts crying. Hoping he will come in and see and comfort her and they will be okay again, she sits on the edge of the bath, wrapped demurely in a towel. But he doesn't come, preferring to go to bed with a sour mouth than reconnect with his wife.

Eventually the sadness turns bitter. She gets up and washes her face. Drying it she catches a glimpse of herself in the mirror. She looks hard, and older.

Hanging up the towel she walks back to the bedroom. Ollie's already asleep. She gets in beside him but it takes long minutes for her heartbeat to return to normal.

She wakes suddenly to darkness. She was in the middle of a dream. Ollie had gone to the island again and as he sat there alone, facing the open sea, a bird dropped a shell on the rock beside him. The sharp crack travelled all the way to shore where Asha was watching. It was this noise that woke her. She turns onto her back, tugging out the sheet that has twisted around her thigh. The fan revolves above her head. She feels disorientated, as if the journey from sleep to waking happened too quickly. Could her dreaming brain have been trying to make sense of a real sound?

But everything's silent. Just the murmur of the waves and the low hum of the fridge next door. Beside her Ollie breathes softly. However drunk he is when he falls asleep he never snorts or snuffles. It's a very attractive quality. The night is cool under the clear sky and she covers his bare shoulder automatically, before she remembers she's angry with him. Only she isn't any more. She just feels sad and sorry. This is their honeymoon and she's spoiling it. There's something wrong with Ollie, but rather than trying to understand she's been obsessing about her own selfish needs. She will try and be a better wife. Wrapping an arm around his waist she is gratified that he nestles into her – his subconscious still loves her. But before she can settle back to sleep she hears them.

Voices.

A glance at the clock tells her it's just past two. The bar closed when they left after their nightcap with David and Sophie, so why is anyone still out?

She sits up and listens until blood rushes in her ears.

They seem to be coming from behind the bungalow, in the jungle.

She can't make out the words, but the abruptness that seems to characterise the Vietnamese tongue is missing. She thinks they're speaking English – or at least a European language. Is it Sophie and David, out for a moonlight walk? Somehow they don't seem the type. The Americans, then? One of the voices is high enough to be a woman's, but Caspar's voice is very feminine.

She climbs out of bed and pads across to the back of the room, where the window looks straight out onto the jungle. The sky is so clear she can make out the shapes of trees outlined by moonlight through the blind. Pressing her back against the warm bamboo wall she listens again.

The man's voice is low and urgent. An argument? Did one of them storm out of the bungalow and the other followed?

If Ollie were awake he'd tell her to leave well alone, but her curiosity has been piqued. If it's not one of the other couples then who is it creeping around the bungalows after dark?

Snatching her sarong she heads for the door and then picks her way over the dried brush round to the back of the bungalow.

The jungle is a dark mass looming over their building. Ollie seems suddenly vulnerable, asleep inside that fragile wooden shack. She'll be quick. She'll find out who it is, then come straight back to him.

The moon is glaringly bright in the clear sky. Her feet are cold. She's come out without shoes. Are there insects on the forest floor that can burrow through your flesh? Coiled snakes disguised as rocks?

The air is filled with the sweet musk of tree sap, but it's not the woody medicinal scent of an English forest. She's in alien territory.

There.

She wasn't imagining them.

Two voices: one male, one female, speaking a language with European inflections. Still she can't make out the words. They're too far away from her, deeper in the trees. Her eyes strain into the blackness beyond the nearest trunks. No torches, or the cold glow of a mobile. They're out there in the pitch dark.

If they need privacy why not stay in their cabin, or go down to the beach where the waves would drown out their words? Unless they don't want to be seen.

The woman laughs. It doesn't sound like Sophie. Goosebumps rise on Asha's arms. Then the man's voice comes again: a low rumble. The words indecipherable. Then silence.

A moment later there are furtive rustles and cracks, much closer to the bungalow. Her heart jumps into her throat. Do they know she's spying on them? She backs away down the alley between the buildings, ready to bolt back inside.

Near the bungalows the trees thin out, allowing moonlight to penetrate the canopy, casting short, sharp shadows on the forest floor. In a moment whoever it is will have to step into the puddles of silver light. She will see who they are.

The rustling gets louder, then stops abruptly. She holds her breath, just able to make out a figure against the line of trees. She thinks it's a man, hard to tell who until he comes closer. But he doesn't come closer.

Suddenly she realises that her silhouette must be clearly outlined against the moonlit sea behind her.

Have they seen her? And yet it's still not a *they*. Just the one figure, the man, standing perfectly still.

And then he melts back into the darkness.

Her eyes strain for a glimpse of him, or the woman.

There. The faintest of glimmers between the trees. A face in the darkness. Watching her. And then it's gone.

Her skin crawls. She's out here, alone, and someone who did not want to be seen knows she was watching them. She hurries back down the side of the bungalow and through the door that she left ajar (didn't she?). She won't do that again, she thinks, as she checks the locks, then tiptoes through the living room to the bedroom, where Ollie lies silently, in the same position.

For a moment she's terrified someone has come in while she was outside and murdered him, but his pulse is strong and steady. He stirs a little and she covers him with the sheet, shivering in the breeze from the fan.

Sitting up on the bed, her eyes dart from window to shaded window, trying not to imagine figures creeping around the house, pushing their fingers under flimsy window frames, unpicking flimsy locks.

How stupid to have scared herself.

She won't mention this to Ollie. There's nothing to mention. David and Sophie having a nocturnal row, or the Americans indulging in some al-fresco sex. Maybe she was wrong about the language. Maybe it was a clandestine assignation between Hao and Bay. Or some other couple who didn't want to be seen. A man and a woman with a secret.

And yet where did the woman go?

She wakes up tired, even though it's past ten. Funny how a holiday does that to you. She often feels worse when she gets back than when she left. Her body must thrive on a certain level of stress and without it she's lethargic, bored. And trivial problems are taking on an unnatural significance. Like the sex thing.

She's past the point of trying now. It's humiliating. If they're ever going to fuck again he'll have to initiate it.

He doesn't stir when she gets out of bed. A sour miasma of stale alcohol seeps from his pores.

Back outside the air is already warm and the pool water's blood temperature. Sliding in she rests her head against the edge. Should she make a concerted effort to find out what's bothering him, or should she withdraw emotionally, which might force him into some kind of revelation for fear he's losing her? It seems cruel but pleading doesn't seem to be working.

It's then she remembers the Milo thing.

After their rough patch (easier to call it that) she knows he took refuge with his old schoolfriend. Apparently Milo advised him to leave her, claimed that what happened had been a timely heads-up on what would follow. She also suspects, though she doesn't like to think about it, that Ollie seriously considered following this advice. She may be wrong. Either way, the fact that they made it through, in the teeth of opposition from everybody close to him, made her respect him even more.

And then one day, not long afterwards but surely long enough for Ollie not to need the emotional crutch, she came home from work to find Milo there. It was such a cliché as to be almost comical. She was supposed to have been out at an industry awards do but had balked at putting more poisons into her fragile system, so had come home via Waitrose, armed with the ingredients for Ollie's favourite green curry.

And there was Milo's Range Rover parked behind Ollie's Merc. Ollie had left work early too. So had Milo.

Letting herself in she felt mildly sick. As if she was about to find them both naked in her bed.

The sudden silence as she took her keys from the lock made her afraid, but when she called his name he answered straight away from the kitchen. Her work heels clacked on the hall tiles – she usually slipped them off at the front door – and she pushed open the door.

The two of them were leaning nonchalantly against the counter, tumblers in hand, both smiling at her.

'You're back early,' she said.

'So are you. What happened to the party?'

It was like being in a film. 'Couldn't be bothered.' She wasn't about to tell the truth in front of Milo. 'What happened to work?'

'They were getting the juniors together to give them a bollocking about compliance so I made my excuses.'

She turned to Milo with a questioning smile.

'Just closed a deal. Thought I'd celebrate with Ols instead of the work grunts.'

'Oh.'

'G&T?'

'Okay. Just a small one. Lots of tonic.'

As Ollie went to the fridge to get the tonic she noticed their own glasses were filled with whisky. Neat by the look of it. Not Ollie's usual tipple of choice. When he handed her the glass he wouldn't meet her eyes and as she took it she saw the surface of the liquid was trembling.

They talked about the weather forecast for Suffolk where Milo and Liberty would be spending the weekend, and Ollie was considerably more animated than he would usually be about such a dull subject.

Eventually Milo said he would love them and leave them. He hugged her and Ollie walked him to the door.

Wandering to the bay window, she saw him hugging Ollie too. It seemed strange and for a moment she couldn't remember whether or not this was their usual thing. After a moment they separated and Milo laid a hand on Ollie's shoulder and said something that Asha couldn't make out from the other side of the glass. Then Milo noticed her and raised his hand. Ollie's head whipped round. Milo went to the car and Ollie came back in. He went straight to the toilet and was there for ages.

'Are you okay?' she said when he came out.

'Dicky tummy.'

'Sure it's not the whisky?'

'Could well be.' He gave a sickly grin. 'I think I'd better have a nap.'

He went off upstairs and by the time she called him down for curry he seemed a lot better.

When was that? she wonders, gazing pensively down at the ripples fanning out from the filter.

A couple of weeks before the wedding. It was at the wedding that she really started to notice something was up, but thinking about it again, was it that day when things really began to change? Did Milo say something to him? Have another go at trying to make him leave her? Had they met at other times while she was at work?

'Morning!'

Sophie's paddling in the shallows in a sarong.

'You're up early,' Asha calls down to her.

'Couldn't sleep,' she says, turning her steps in Asha's direction.

Up close she looks tired, her tan turned sallow overnight. She slumps down onto one of the loungers and rubs her face.

'Don't tell me I look like shit,' she says. 'I know.'

'Who cares? We're the only ones here.'

Sophie peers through her hair. 'Don't forget Sexy Sean. He's never going to want to fuck me like this.'

Asha snorts.

'You know what we need?'

'I know what *I* need,' Asha mutters.

'A spa day. Let's book a massage and a treatment. Just you and me, away from the boys.'

Asha hesitates before replying. After last night's row she'd really like to spend the morning making up with Ollie.

At that moment he emerges onto the terrace, yawning but fresh-faced in a towel. The morning sun turns his skin gold. She looks away.

'Morning, handsome,' Sophie says.

'Good morning. Nice weather we're having.' He stretches and groans. 'God, I was pissed last night. Can't remember much after eight.'

Is this a tacit apology? A message that he'd like to just forget about what happened?

'Me too,' she says quickly. 'This has got to stop. I blame you Peterses.'

'Guilty as charged,' Sophie says, then turns to Ollie. 'I was just asking your wife to come to the spa with me but I think she'd rather spend the day with her gorgeous husband.'

'Not at all,' Asha protests.

Ollie grins. 'Thanks very much.'

'They've got some special energy-healing expert here,' Sophie says. 'She can readjust your chakras.'

Asha laughs. 'My chakras are fine.'

'I thought you'd like that sort of thing,' Ollie says. 'That's part of the reason I booked this place instead of that other one up the coast.'

'You are kidding me? You know what I think about that bullshit.'

'Don't be so closed-minded.'

'You're the one who needs the spiritual healing.' Their eyes lock for a second, then he looks away.

'It's up to you, babe, but I'll be no fun. I'm knackered. That bed is too soft.'

He wants to get rid of her.

'Fine.' She smiles at Sophie. 'Let's do it.'

Apparently oblivious to the awkward tone of the exchange Sophie claps her hands and gets up. 'After breakfast?'

'Cool.'

Sophie heads off down the walkway. For a moment there's silence between Asha and Ollie, then Asha gets out of the pool and goes inside to shower.

The spa is a low-pillared building on the other side of reception. Three massage beds are lined up against the wall and at the back are doors that must lead to private rooms. There are dishes of flower heads, swirling patterns of black pebbles and, of course, the obligatory scented candles in hurricane lanterns to protect them from the breeze off the sea, sharper today.

As they climb the steps a woman emerges from one of the doors. She's not what Asha had expected. Short and wizened with dyed black hair, definitely Western.

'Gut morning.'

German.

'How can I help you ladies today?'

'I'd like a massage,' Sophie says. 'A really painful one. See if you can't squeeze some of this away.' She grabs a chunk of dimpled thigh flesh with an expression of disgust.

The woman nods curtly. 'And you?'

'Anything. I don't care.'

The woman regards her critically, her eyes as shiny and black as the flies that landed on the fruit salad at breakfast.

'A little reiki, perhaps. To calm you.'

'I'm perfectly calm.' She gives a brittle laugh.

'We'll start with you. You,' she points at Sophie, 'can wait on a bed. There are magazines of fashion if you wish.'

'Jolly good,' Sophie says coldly and Asha follows the woman through one of the doors.

It leads to a room lit only by candles.

'Take your clothes off.'

'All of them?'

The woman rolls her eyes.

Asha undresses, still wondering if the woman meant her bikini bottoms too. In the end she takes them off and lies down on the bed. There's warmth radiating from the soft mattress and the towel beneath her smells of lavender. It's instantly soporific.

Photographs glimmer from the bamboo walls. Pictures of the woman with various celebrities including, when obviously much younger, Princess Diana. It is signed *To Darling Carol.* Another is of Elton John, a third Gwyneth Paltrow. She's famous then. In *those* circles. The bullshit circles.

There's a rasping sound. The woman is rubbing some kind of cream on her hands. Then she closes her eyes, holds her hands straight out in front of her and starts moving her lips silently. The palms are pale and cross-hatched with soft-edged grooves, as if they've been soaking in water.

Asha feels mildly uncomfortable with her exposed breasts and dramatically waxed bikini line. Normally she doesn't approve of the prepubescent look, but she didn't want any stray hairs peeping out from her bikini bottoms. Now she feels self-conscious.

The woman's eyes open and lock on hers.

'Relax. I will not hurt you.'

'I'm not expecting you to,' Asha says.

'Close your eyes.'

She does so and almost immediately feels a cold, hard pressure on her abdomen. It's as if the woman's picked up something larger than the span of her own hand and is pressing it against Asha's stomach. She shifts position to show she doesn't like it but the pressure doesn't ease.

She opens her eyes. The woman isn't touching her. Her hands hover at least ten centimetres over her body. And yet the cold pressure remains.

When she sees Asha watching, the woman exhales sharply through her nose in irritation. She drops her hands to her sides and the pressure is instantly released. Asha is paralysed with surprise. Is it something to do with electricity or magnets? The woman was definitely not touching her and yet she could *feel* it.

'You have a blockage in your sacral chakra, your sex energies.'

'It's not my blockage. It's my husband.' It's out before she can stop herself.

'Perhaps he should come and see me, but in the meantime you need to release some of these tensions with . . .'

Sean.

'. . . meditation and yoga. Perhaps he can sense the tension in you and it's causing his own chakra to close up. Let me do some work on the area.'

'Great. Thanks.'

She closes her eyes again. This time the pressure is warm, as if the woman has poured heated syrup over the dome of her belly. It's so nice, so unbelievably comforting, that she starts to cry. Too embarrassed to admit it she lets the tears slide down her temples and into her hairline. What on earth is wrong with her? Is it really some locked-up tension finally being released? *Was* it her fault all along?

'When did it happen?' Carol says.

Her breath stops. For a moment there's absolutely silence. Even the shush of the waves seems unable to penetrate the dim hush.

'Three months ago.'

'How far along were you?'

Twenty-one weeks. Her tummy perfectly round like a cantaloupe. They had already decided on Olivia if it was a girl. It was a boy. Another Graveney to carry on the family name. Only superstition stopped her letting Ollie break the news to his parents.

Superstition and something more perhaps. Soon enough the child would belong to them and their crowing heritage. Sometimes she almost didn't like him for it. This baby. When he kicked her so violently it hurt. When the weight she put on aged her, turned her beauty homely. People patted her stomach but never offered their seat on the tube. She wasn't ready. Thirty-three was too young. Her career had barely got going. She didn't want to be one of those poor cows whose breasts leaked in meetings because they hadn't had time to express, or worse, the flint-eyed ones who had forced themselves not to care as a series of indifferent nannies brought up their children. Was there a middle path? Ollie reassured her when she dared to confide her fears: he would take his share of the burden. More of it, if she needed him to. But she still worried. How would he feel to see his sexy wife covered in baby food and shit, her vagina gaping or stitch-scarred? How would she feel about him?

Sometimes she wondered if she had driven her son out through sheer negativity. As if, like food and oxygen, her fears had passed through the umbilical cord and poisoned him.

He had given up his little life so quietly. She didn't even know until she got up from her TV dinner to stretch her cramping back. Their cream sofa looked like a murder scene.

Blood trailed after her as she walked quite calmly to the bathroom with a pressing urge to move her bowels.

When she sat down the queasiness came over her and, leaning against the wall for support, she felt him come out of her. It was so grotesque, so appalling, that she couldn't even describe this part to Ollie. What she had lifted from the toilet bowl, dripping with the blue cleaner Maria used. It was like being in a horror film. Even now the thought of it makes her head fill with white noise.

Numb with shock she carried him in her hands into the living room and called the ambulance. As she sat back down on the sofa more and more blood poured out of her until she thought she was going to die.

Ollie was away. That was the killer. That was the thing that nearly broke them. He was on a fishing weekend in Prague with Milo and the *boys*.

She called him before the ambulance came but he didn't pick up. She called him from the ambulance, from the hospital before they put her under. She called when she came round to ask if he was happy for them to go ahead and incinerate their child. And then, once they had, she stopped calling.

He didn't pick up because he was at a vodka tasting evening. An evening that developed into a rowdy singalong with the locals. He had been singing and drinking and eating line-caught bluefin tuna as their son died. She left the sofa and carpet for him to see when he got home and when he did he vomited, tuna and vodka and all.

'How was the massage?' Sophie says when she emerges.

'Like passing a kidney stone. Best of luck.'

'You won't recognise me without the cellulite.'

As Sophie heads for the little door, Asha walks quickly away, down to the sea, where she stands in the warm water and gazes out at a boat coming round the headland while her breathing slowly returns to normal.

Her abdomen, where the woman touched her – or did not touch her – feels light. Almost as if it's not even part of her body. She was the problem then. Not Ollie. That little ghost had nestled up inside her and her subconscious couldn't let go of him. But now he's gone. A new start. The fishing trip wasn't Ollie's fault. He couldn't have known. She must stop blaming him. And she will. Closing her eyes she whispers goodbye to her baby boy and imagines him drifting into the hazy blue distance.

When she opens them the boat is coming to shore. The pilot is a very old man, his face a patchwork of wrinkles, as if his skin is made from screwed-up hessian. His passengers are the Americans: Caspar's gold hair blows in the breeze like a shampoo advert. She doesn't want to have to speak to them. For some reason she's sure the older man's penetrating eyes would see right down to her soul and would find her pain amusing. But if she goes back to the spa now it will look like she's running away, and he'll enjoy that even more.

She stands her ground as the boat docks. The older one says something to the boatman, who grins and claps him on the shoulder. Caspar steps down into the water and his fisherman's trousers billow around his shins like a mermaid's tail.

'Hey, hi,' he says as he wades ashore. 'We've just been to the So Den Caves. They're amazing, truly. Aren't they, Travis?'

'Sure,' the American drawls. 'Big rock with a big hole in it.'

Caspar rolls his eyes. And then a muttered aside to Asha, 'He loved it. He only pretends to have no soul.'

Travis comes out of the sea and stands directly in front of her, grinning widely, hands on nut-brown hips. He's shamelessly topless and there are white lines under his drooping breasts where the sun hasn't reached.

'I don't believe we've been introduced. Travis Mulgrave.'

She shakes his hand. It's very dry and warm.

'Asha Graveney.'

'Ah yes, wife of the Terminator.'

'Who, Ollie?'

'Has a taste for buying up baby companies and asset-stripping them, right?'

She laughs uneasily.

'Oh, Travis, will you behave. He just can't bear to take his journo hat off even on holiday.'

She nods. Mulgrave is still looking at her.

'You're a journalist too, I understand.'

'Only a very small news mag.'

'Not *only*. Don't do yourself down.'

Suddenly her face goes very hot. *Travis Mulgrave*. Of course. Covered the Syrian war. Won a Pulitzer for it. Blinded in one eye by an ISIL sniper.

One of the eyes gazing at her so penetratingly is glass. Before she knows it she's flicking her gaze from eye to eye, trying to tell which.

Mulgrave raises a hand and taps his fingernail against his left eye. Plink plink. She cannot restrain a grimace, but neither can she look away. There's something emanating from him, some kind of magnetism or electricity. Perhaps Carol isn't so crazy. Maybe people really do have auras. If so, Mulgrave's is scarlet and spitting sparks.

The boat engine revs up.

Caspar calls, 'Thanks, Zaw.'

She tears her eyes from Mulgrave's face. Caspar is waving at the old boatman, and now Mulgrave turns too and holds up his hand. He calls out something and the old man gives a thumbs-up.

'I really should learn some Vietnamese,' she says, brightly, as if she's perfectly relaxed.

'Oh that's Burmese,' Caspar says. 'Travis knows about a hundred languages. He can talk to anyone, seriously. I've gotten so lazy!'

She has an urge to ask the usually innocuous question *how long have you been together?* but manages to stop herself.

'So. The caves. Good?'

'Oh, they were beautiful. Seriously. You can walk there through the jungle but the best way to arrive is by boat, then you can see the hole in the top. Just like a giant beehive, you know?'

She feels a moment's contempt for him, then. How could a man like Travis Mulgrave be happy with such a bimbo? Her eyes flick to the side. Mulgrave is smiling at her.

'I'd definitely recommend the boat,' Mulgrave says. 'You get past the headland and there's some actual phone signal.'

Caspar shakes his head indulgently. 'I wanted to come back through the jungle. It's only six kilometres or so, but fatso here's too lazy.'

Mulgrave says, 'The Malayan pit viper is one of the most vicious snakes in the world. It will attack for absolutely no reason if you stray into its territory.'

Caspar laughs. 'You lazy asshole. No one's ever been bitten by a snake on this island. Or a tiger, or a tarantula. I checked when we came because I was *intending*,' he glances ruefully at Travis, 'to do some hiking. But that doesn't seem to be working out.'

'Honey, you knew what you were signing up for.'

The flirtation is making Asha acutely uncomfortable and she is relieved when Sophie's plaintive wail drifts down from the spa hut.

'I can't walk!'

'Nice to meet you,' she says to Travis. He inclines his head and she feels his eyes on her back as she turns and trudges up the sand.

Once Sophie has recovered they go for lunch. Over bowls of chicken pho Sophie asks about the wedding and Asha makes it sound as magical as she possibly can. She doesn't know this woman well enough yet to share her insecurities.

'Photos!'

'Oh. Yes. Of course, I've got some on the iPad. I'd completely forgotten about electronics.'

'Yes, good, isn't it? Although David's been going to reception twice a day to check his emails.'

'Oh dear. Work trouble?'

'No no. Everything's fine. So, go and get your iPad then. Let's have a look.'

Asha heads back to the bungalow. Ollie is nowhere to be seen. Nor is he on the beach. She has the sudden irrational fear that he's gone off with another woman, though the only females here besides her are Sophie and Hao. Caspar's more attractive than both of them, but however much he might have experimented at Wellington, she's pretty sure Ollie's no longer that way inclined.

She returns to find Sophie has ordered them both cocktails. Her heart sinks at the prospect of another day of drinking followed by an evening of hazy arguments. But the combination of the happy pictures and cocktail number two turns her mood warm and fuzzy. Why did she have such a downer about the wedding? The pictures show just how perfect it really was. They look so happy and in love, gazing into each other's eyes, laughing as they cut the cake. Nothing's fake or forced. They're a young couple blissfully in love.

'Let me see your uncle Thomas.'

Asha's mood dampens a little. 'Can you believe the photographer lost the photos? The file got corrupted. I was so pissed off. I made Ollie get half our money back from the stupid cow. The only blood relation I've got left and he's really old now.'

Sophie makes a sad face. 'Oh, your dad's gone too?'

Asha waves her arm a little more wildly than if she were completely sober. 'Oh, he was never here. Some white boy who got his end away with Mum at a party. I don't even know his name. Couldn't give a fuck. His loss.'

'You go, girl!'

They cackle and clink glasses.

And then Ollie's there, and she's so grateful and happy to see him that she jumps to her feet, knocking her chair over, and flings her arms around him. He grins, delighted, and calls to the barman that he'll have whatever they're having.

They drink until past four. David joins them: both men had spent the morning at the gym. He coos politely over the photos, pointing at various people and asking if that's *so-and-so* from *so-and-so-bank*. The sun has just dipped over the roof of the bar when they call it a day – well, an afternoon – and stagger back to the bungalow, giggling, their arms around each other. The Peterses may be dreadful, but if she and Ollie are back on track it's partly thanks to them. When they get home, she might even miss them, Asha thinks as she wobbles over the threshold of the bungalow. Then again that may just be the fuzzy glow of being really drunk.

She wakes suddenly to an unfamiliar sound. Like rice spilling onto a wooden floor. It's raining. There's no sign of Ollie. He must have gone to bed.

She gets up from the sofa and watches the rain from the living room window until Ollie comes in from the bedroom and turns the lights on. He's got a headache – pressure in the air, he thinks – so has put on his glasses. She loves him in glasses. She kisses him and they move slowly in a circle to the beat of the rain. All is well. She doesn't attempt to touch him and eventually he draws away from her. A hot bath might help the tension in his head, he says.

At dinnertime they make a run for the restaurant and Asha shivers through the meal of rice and delicate tempura. She would have preferred a hot tangy soup or some tofu in a gloopy sauce. She didn't bring any warm clothes.

'What are we going to do if it's like this tomorrow?'

Ollie shrugs. 'Head into Con Dao Town? Try some street food?'

'Or we could go and see the old prison.'

Ollie makes a face. 'Sounds jolly.'

Sophie and David arrive and then, a little later, Sean. He looks tired, his skin greyed by the rain.

After the meal they gather on the sofas: she and Ollie, Sophie and David and Sean. The gang. They debate what to do in paradise on a rainy day. It turns out David and Sophie have visited the old prison before, on a previous trip to the island. Asha's surprised they haven't mentioned this trip before, but when she says she'd like to look at the place, Sophie is dismissive, pronouncing it 'too depressing.'

'Don't you think you have a duty,' she says suddenly, before she has the chance to self-censor. 'To think about depressing things?'

She smiles, trying to make out it's a joke, but Sophie's face hardens a fraction. 'I've been through plenty of difficult things. I'd rather not be reminded.'

'Sorry,' Asha says. 'Stupid thing to say.'

Sean suddenly reaches into his pocket and takes out his phone.

He looks up. 'Scuse me. It's my sister.'

There was no alert tone and for a moment Asha wonders if he's make up the text message to rescue her from the faux pas, but after walking to the partition and studying the screen, he starts tapping a reply. His shoulders are so muscular that the fabric of his grey t-shirt bags at the small of his back.

'I think there's something wrong with their rower,' David says, apparently oblivious to what's just happened between the wives. 'Normally I can do forty-five minutes on ten.'

'It felt alright to me,' Ollie says. 'Maybe a bit stiff but it warmed up after a couple of minutes.'

Sean comes back.

'Everything alright?' Sophie says.

'Yes, just checking up on me. She's always fussed over me, but I guess older sisters are like that.'

He smiles at Ollie.

'I wouldn't know, mate. Only child.'

'Apart from Milo,' Asha mutters.

'Yes, well there is him.'

'His bezzie from school,' she addresses the group, trying to sound rueful rather than jealous. 'His parents would have much rather he married Milo.'

Ollie snorts but doesn't correct her.

'They're so going to leave him half their money.'

'Good. We don't need it.'

'Nor does he!'

The silence that follows makes her realise they have been tactless. It's not often they spend time with people considerably poorer than they are, but Sean is clearly not in the banking league.

But he doesn't appear to have noticed, and is busy unwrapping the cellophane from a packet of cigarettes. She's drunk enough that the musty aroma makes her salivate immediately.

David claps. 'Ah yes, good idea!' From Sophie's sparkly bag he takes out a wooden cigar box.

'These should warm us up a bit.'

At first glance the contents of the box look like a row of thin dog turds.

'They don't let you smoke in here,' Sean says. 'I tried it when I arrived.'

'Well I don't fancy going out there.' David nods towards the rain, now coming down in bars. 'So in that case I'll just have one in bed over my excellent Winston Churchill biography.'

Asha shakes her head. 'You're such a cliché.'

David preens.

'Never in the field of human conflict,' Sean intones, 'has so much been taken from so many by so few.'

Ollie gives a bark of laughter but David doesn't get the joke.

'I think you'll find this far superior to your usual muck.' David offers Sean a cigar.

Sean shakes his head. 'They all smell like cat pee to me.'

'Oliver? A cheeky bedtime smoke?'

'Don't mind if I do,' Ollie says. 'Asha loves me smelling like cat's pee in bed.'

'Oh my God,' Asha says, widening her eyes in exaggerated outrage.

'What?' David says. 'Can't a man enjoy a good smoke now and again?'

'Not if his wife can't!'

'I do apologise. Of course, one for you, too.' He offers the tray of excrements.

'Yuck. No thanks.'

'She'd rather get her lung cancer a different way,' Ollie says mildly, tucking the cigar behind his ear.

'Oh,' Sophie says primly. 'Do you smoke?'

'Used to,' Asha says, not looking at Sean. But he leans towards her, holding out the open pack.

Asha takes a cigarette, her eyes meeting Ollie's. He's smiling but she can tell he's annoyed and that annoys her in turn. Why is a cigar allowed but not a cigarette? However much he protests *it's only because I care* she knows it's just snobbery. Fags belong on council estates.

Sean stands and turns to her. 'Coming?'

She hesitates a moment, then gets up - it would look weirder not to – and her nerve endings are singing as she follows Sean past her husband and out onto the beach.

Under the fringed roof edge Sean lights her cigarette and then his own. In the pool of light from the bar the sand is pitted, the folded sunbeds pale ghosts behind a grey veil.

Their exhaled smoke entwines and then dissipates in the rain.

'What did you tell your sister?' she says. Her voice is softer out here in the quiet.

Sean squints towards the sea, then he sighs and shakes his head. 'That I'm okay. That I'm actually quite enjoying myself. The company's pretty good. Well, some of it.'

'I take it you mean David?'

Sean chuckles.

She leans against the pillar and takes another drag. The narcotic is working straight away, like an old, dependable friend. She didn't realise how tense she was. Is it being with Sophie and David? Having to keep that natural antipathy, for their class and privilege and stupid opinions, in check? But she's been doing it for years – ever since she met Ollie – so why should it be so hard now?

Maybe it's Sean. Maybe being in the presence of her own kind is making the others seem worse. Except Ollie of course.

They smoke in a peaceable silence.

Sean eventually breaks it. 'Look.'

Arched backs are slicing through the water, just beyond the ledge where it suddenly gets deeper.

'Dolphins?' she breathes, scared to frighten them away.

'Porpoises probably.'

'How can you tell?'

'Different-shaped fin.'

'You're quite smart for a London wideboy.'

He grins. 'For an Isli'ton chav you're not too dumb yourself.' The grin fades. 'Don't you ever miss it? All that . . . *life*. You know. Now that you're in the land of the chino and Lexus.'

'I don't know,' she says wistfully. 'Maybe. But my mum died so there's nothing there for me now. Plus I didn't fancy working in a shop for the rest of my life and marrying a builder. Sorry. I know how that sounds.'

'It's okay. I'm a bar manager. Much classier.'

A burst of laughter from David makes them both wince.

'If I have to listen to him much longer I'm going to bottle him.' Sean takes a final, savage pull on his cigarette then grinds it under his trainer.

'Talk to me instead.'

'Your husband might not like that.'

'He's not my keeper.'

'If I were him I wouldn't let you out of my sight.'

She snorts. 'All the girls love a controlling man.'

Tossing her cigarette onto the pocked sand she pushes herself off the pillar but he grasps her hand. Her eyes flick back to Ollie in alarm but he's deep in conversation with David.

'What?'

He pauses, looks like he wants to say something, then drops her hand. 'Nothing. You're gorgeous and I'm drunk.'

She smiles, 'Dick,' and heads back inside.

Exactly on cue, after drink number four, David becomes loud and opinionated. He and Ollie have a disagreement over deregulation. It doesn't surprise Asha that David is on the side of total freedom for the moneymen.

'But then the actions of a few unscrupulous or incompetent individuals can have devastating consequences on ordinary people,' Ollie says.

'Not just ordinary people,' Sophie says. 'Their colleagues too.'

'You live by the sword,' David booms, 'you die by it. And if you're good enough you'll bounce back.'

Ollie is shaking his head. To be so openly disagreeing with someone he's just met he must be drunk. 'People like us – private school, rich parents – we start with an advantage. We have so much less to lose. It makes us reckless. We shouldn't be allowed to be reckless with the lives of ordinary people.'

That phrase, *ordinary people,* grates on Asha.

'Well said,' Sophie slurs, raising her glass. 'You should all tuck your dicks back into your trousers and get a proper job. Like Sean. What do you do again, Sean?'

'Barman,' Sean says.

'Oh.'

'Don't be such a poof, Graveney. We've made our country rich.'

'Careful,' Sophie giggles. 'The Yanks might be around.'

'What, *Trump and Melania*?' David brays.

'Right,' Asha says, getting up. 'On that note I think it's time for bed.'

On the way back to the bungalow she's irrationally annoyed with Ollie, who walks ahead, humming. After a moment she understands why. It's his fault she has to spend excruciating evenings with tossers like David. They're *his* people, not hers. This is supposed to be their honeymoon and it feels more like a corporate away-day with the colleague from hell. It would have been more fun if the Americans *had* turned up. Travis would have torn David to shreds.

The rain has stopped. She's only just noticed. The night is clear and fresh, the stars pin sharp. She lingers on the walkway, gazing across the sea. Even though it's shark – and God only knows what else – feeding time she experiences an urge to dive into the blackness beneath the glitter.

Approaching the bungalow she sees that Ollie has had the same urge to be in water. He's stripped to his waist, and as she watches, he peels off his shorts and boxers and walks to the edge of the infinity pool.

But there's something wrong.

It takes her a split second to realise what. An animal has bitten through the electricity cable that runs to the patio heater and the cable's dangling into the water.

At the edge of the pool Ollie pauses to brush some grit off the sole of his foot. His pale body is a ghost in the mirrored surface of the water.

It doesn't matter though because the cord is no longer attached to the heater so won't be live.

He straightens up and is about to climb into the pool.

She frowns. Drink has made her thoughts sluggish – no, but isn't it the *other* cable she should worry about – the one that goes through a hole in the wall to the electricity socket inside? *That's* the live cable. That's the one dangling into the water.

'Stop!' she says sharply.

He pauses, turning to look at her. Beautiful as a Greek statue: the muscles rippling down his flank.

'Something's eaten the flex.'

'What? Oh yeah.'

'Probably doesn't matter because we've never had it on.'

He walks round the edge of the pool and bends to pick up the cable, then tosses it away. The edges of the terrace that stretch beyond the line of the roof are spotted with puddles of rain and the cable lands in one. Immediately it leaps out again, sparks flying from the frayed end. Ollie jumps back as it kicks and spits like a cobra.

'Shit!'

He runs inside and a moment later the cord falls dead. He comes back out, running his hands through his hair.

'Jesus Christ, the water would have been live!'

Asha sits heavily on the nearest sunbed. This has got to stop, this drinking. It's getting dangerous.

He's standing away from her, breathing heavily. His skin has taken on a grey pallor. 'I'm going to bed.' His tone is weary, like he's had enough, like (or is she imagining this?) it's partially her fault.

'Okay. I'll be in in a minute.'

Her nerves are jangling. Should she wake Bay and have a go at him? If this sort of thing can happen, why aren't the cables checked regularly?

Getting up she walks to the edge of the terrace, then back again, her heart pounding. She needs to do *something*. Scream or run or hit someone. Anything to release the tension of the past few days. She won't sleep unless she does.

She will walk. A brisk walk across the sand to tire herself out and calm her down.

A light wind is making the jungle whisper: the black margin shrinking and swelling across the sand beyond the line of sunbeds. She sets off down the steps and onto the beach.

The night smells fresh and fragrant. As if the trees have waited until sundown to release their perfume. The stars are a handful of salt thrown across the sky. One falls as she watches, with an audible hiss. She was right to come out. This night is even more beautiful than the day. If she and Ollie can get back on an even keel she will insist on him coming out with her. They can make love under the stars with the wind biting their backs. Not if, *when*.

She goes down to the water's edge where the wet sand is easy to walk on. There are lights glimmering a little way out and for a moment she can't tell if it's the reflection of the stars or some kind of bioluminescence.

This is real, she thinks as she stands in the surf: this is the real Vietnam. Not the massages, the cocktails, the teak and chrome and glass: not even the *Michelin-starred local cuisine*. This silent, sublime beauty that rewards only those brave enough to stray from their warm beds.

The light moves in surging swirls. One microscopic creature following the next with only instinct to guide it, making eerily beautiful shapes, like a flock of starlings on an autumn night. A murmuration of light. Then some unfathomable urge draws the creatures out to sea and they are lost in the moon shimmer.

It's only as she's passed the spa block and reception that she remembers the voices in the night. Her back bristles and she can't help glancing behind her. The beach is a silver ribbon, unbroken by shape or shadow. The bungalows are all in darkness. Even Bay has gone to bed.

She's completely alone. And as the breeze dies away the trees fall silent.

She grew up with noise. The angry traffic on Holloway Road, the grumble of the Victoria Line beneath their basement flat, the boom of music from the bars and clubs, the shouting and fighting. It was like a lullaby. When she and Ollie first met she would have to listen to Kiss FM through earphones to get through those silent nights in Notting Hill. When they fell out she would jerk awake with a cry, the silence ringing like a smoke alarm. No, she was weaned on noise and a constant sense of threat. Now that fight-or-flight mechanism is redundant. Ollie wouldn't understand why sometimes she misses it.

A sound makes her glance up. She's covered a lot of ground. The horn of the headland is now visible as an outcrop of grey rock rising up from the sand. Beyond it the coast must curve back on itself, eventually reaching the airport. She has never seen a plane, though. They might as well be castaways.

The noise again. A rustle in the trees to her left. Closer now: the margin of the jungle has crept towards the shore without her noticing. It's only now that she remembers the figures on the headland. Silently watching the oblivious holidaymakers on the beach. But what would they be doing at this time of night? What would *anyone* be doing out here at this time of night? It must be an animal.

She stops, and stares into the blackness, straining to hear, but there's only the sea and her own breathing. Chill fingers of sand push up between her toes.

Her heart misses a beat as a tiny rodent scuttles from the undergrowth and she dances back to stop it running over her toes. She's half turned away from the jungle, deciding whether

111

to press on to the headland or turn back, when there's an explosion from the trees. A huge black figure is scrambling on its belly towards her, impossibly fast.

She blunders backwards, too shocked to scream, and the thing hurtles past, so close she can feel the movement of the air.

It's a huge monitor lizard. From nose to tail it must be the same length as Ollie. With incredible speed it races after the mouse, tail swaying, low-slung body hissing across the sand. Then, abruptly, it stops. As it throws back its blunt snout she sees, silhouetted against the moonlit sea, a spaghetti strand of mouse tail disappearing down its gullet.

She freezes as it comes crawling back up the beach towards her. But just when she's trying to decide whether to scramble up a tree or run into the sea, it makes a sharp turn and disappears into the jungle.

Fuck.

Panting, her legs trembling, it's all she can do not to break into a run and sprint all the way back to the resort. But if she does, will it just attract the thing's attention? Will it come hurtling after her, at that extraordinary speed?

She starts to walk, as quickly as she can, head bent, stumbling up hummocks and down into craters of sand. She wants to be back in the bungalow, curled up beside her warm husband.

It's only the cool glow of the bar fridges that makes her finally look up. She exhales. Almost home.

When she sees the odd shape, like a sun umbrella opening and closing on one of the sunbeds, she can't make sense of it. It can't be the wind, because the night is completely still and quiet. Then she hears noises. A high-pitched murmur followed by a gasp or grunt.

She stops, stares, then ducks behind the chrysalis sunbed, the blood rushing in her ears. After a moment she risks peering around the edge.

Two people are making love on the beach. A blonde woman kneels behind a darker male lying face down across the bed.

She frowns. The blond is not a woman, it's Caspar. But the man on the bed is definitely not Mulgrave.

She strains to make out his identity. Could it be . . . Sean? A lurch of disappointment in the pit of her stomach.

But at that moment the prone figure rears up, pressing his back into Caspar's torso to give her a clear view of his slim hairless abdomen.

It's Bay.

Caspar pushes him back down and thrusts harder, making the joints of the sunbed squeal.

Shit. Can she make a run for it, up to the bar and then along the edge of the jungle behind the bungalows?

But what if they see her? They might think she's going to tell Mulgrave. They could silence her and dump her body out to sea. *Don't be hysterical.* The dark and the shock are making her overreact. She just needs to wait here until they're done. Which surely won't be long n—

'Charming view, isn't it?'

The leg had been there, she realises now, in her peripheral vision from the moment she crouched here. Protruding from the canopy of the sunbed where its owner lay. Hairy and solid and veiny: horny yellow toenails poking from dirty flip-flops.

She doesn't move, hoping he might think she's already run away.

'You're right,' he whispers. 'We should keep quiet. Don't want to disturb them.'

So, he knows Caspar is cheating on him. What's he going to do? Make a scene? Or something worse?

She stays completely still for a moment, then slowly creeps along the back of the canopy, in the direction of the bar.

'Oh, don't go yet. You'll miss the best part.'

She makes it to the edge and is about to bolt but now she sees that Bay is resting his chin on his hands and will notice her at once if she runs. She hunkers down to wait for her chance.

'Good call. Asha Graveney, what would your husband say if he knew your secret predilections?'

'Shut up, Mulgrave,' she hisses. 'We're not all perverts.'

'It's not perverted. People have been enjoying watching each other fuck since we crawled out of the swamp.'

'Some of us are still in it.'

'Oh, don't pretend you're not still a feral street rat at heart, Little Miss Landed Gentry.'

She swears at him under her breath. For the minute she's trapped, and he knows it.

After a silence punctuated by increasingly frenzied gasping he speaks again.

'You know it's not very cool to be gay in Vietnam. One politician described it as *deviant behaviour incompatible with the morals of our great nation.* By coincidence the same politician who owns this resort.'

Asha wishes he would shut up. How the hell is she going to get past without them seeing her?

'So you see poor old Bay, if his boss were to find out, would be out on his ear. And how would he provide for his wife and kids then?'

'He has a wife?' Asha mutters. No sense trying to pretend she isn't here any more. He can probably make out her silhouette against the fridge lights.

'Check your privilege, honey,' Mulgrave murmurs. 'If you lived here you might not have the luxury of being out and proud.'

'And how do you think he'd feel if he knew you were peeping at him, given he wants to keep it hush-hush?'

'He's fine about it.'

She stares at the hairy leg. 'He knows you're here?'

'It's a *thing* for me and Caspar. Keeps it fresh, you know?'

'Don't tell him that I . . .'

'That you were getting off on it too?'

'You'd love that, wouldn't you, you creep.'

'The thought of you being turned on? Sure.'

114

'Is there *anything* you wouldn't fuck?'

He sighs and shifts on the bed, making the wicker crackle. 'Intelligence has always turned me on. Caspar's a Harvard Law School grad. He's currently representing three death row inmates.'

Asha almost bursts out laughing, especially when the moans from the bed reach their crescendo. Oddly, given the circumstances, she feels the familiar ache of arousal. She realises that Mulgrave is probably masturbating. Without another word she ducks round the chrysalis and races up the beach to the bar.

On the steps she pauses.

Caspar is standing at the water's edge, his naked body pale as pearl. A fully dressed Mulgrave is walking down the beach towards him, leaving a trail of cigarette smoke. But Bay. Bay is standing stock still, his clothes hanging from his limp grasp, his ashen face staring up at the bar. At her.

His eyes are wide with fright.

13

FV Hospital, Ho Chi Minh City

Thursday 6 October

This morning I set about trying to remember.

Closing my eyes I've pictured the resort, the bungalow, the sunbeds scattered on icing-sugar sand. The people lounging on them: David and Sophie, Caspar and Travis Mulgrave, Ollie and Sean. It's surprising what I can remember – the names, the faces, the way they spoke and moved – when I try. It's as though I've been deliberately repressing the memories. But why would I do that?

Warily I try to bring up an image of the caves, but it seems my brain won't let me see my new husband bleeding on the sand. It stops, like a horse refusing a jump, and I lurch queasily over a void.

At lunchtime I have visitors. This time Sophie is accompanied by a red-faced man in chino shorts and deck shoes.

'Hello, David,' I say, sitting up straighter.

'You remember me?' he says, in a tone that makes me wonder whether he's pleased.

'Cigars?' I say, forcing a smile. 'Far too many cocktails. A swimming race?'

'Ollie always won,' David says wanly.

'Don't,' I say softly. 'Don't turn him into a god, David. I can just about survive losing him as a human.'

'Nobody's perfect,' Sophie says. 'But Ollie was a good, good man.'

'Hear hear.'

I close my eyes. I want them to go away so I can focus on prosaic things like exercising my muscles, not how wonderful my dead husband was.

David sits in the armchair next to the bed, looking acutely uncomfortable.

'They've charged the boatman with murder,' he says. 'It'll probably be a long old process but there's a strong case against him and until the trial he'll be rotting in prison where he belongs.'

'Has he admitted it?'

'Not yet, but I expect they'll get it out of him in the end. This isn't the UK. Prisons out here don't give you Sky TV and a personal butler.'

Husband and wife glance at one another, then David reaches into his pocket.

'Sophie told me what happened with Ollie's parents, so we got in touch with your travel insurers.'

He lays out some documents on the bed.

Airline tickets: SGN to LHR. Saturday morning.

'I can check in online for you,' Sophie says. 'We got your passport from Bay, so we've got all the numbers.'

I frown and she gives a little start. Then she pulls my passport – and Ollie's – from her pocket. 'Of course you can have them here if you'd prefer.'

I take them and flick through to Ollie's photograph. Staring hungrily at his face, I take in every contour, every shadow, every curl of his hair, passing my thumb across his cheek as if I will somehow be able to feel its warmth.

'I don't know if I'm ready to leave yet. If I'm here, when I get well enough, I can go back to the caves. They might trigger a memory. I need to know what happened, Sophie. Once the drugs are out of my system, maybe everything will be clearer.'

She looks at David with anxious eyes, then someone knocks on the door.

It's Dr Sanjay and two men dressed in green uniform. Police.

David stands up, puffing out his barrel chest, the outraged Englishman. 'Now just hold on a minute. Firstly this is a very sick woman. And secondly she's not speaking to anyone without a lawyer present, so you people can just go back to wherever you came from and—'

'It's fine, David.'

'No, Asha, you are not speaking to them. How dare they—'

'Thank you, David. I can speak for myself.' I turn to Sophie. 'I'll see you both later. Thank you for the . . . stuff.' I slide the plane tickets under the fold of the sheet.

David marches out of the room, leaving a sour trail of enraged masculinity. Sophie kisses my cheek and follows him.

The younger policeman appears mesmerised by the sight of my swollen face until his superior speaks sharply to him, then, without waiting for an invitation, both of them sit.

Dr Sanjay says, 'Captain Ke Quan and Officer Linh are here to speak to you about the day of the attack.'

I stare from face to face, impassive to the point of hostility, and wonder if I've made a mistake not demanding a lawyer.

'I'll stay if you wish,' Sanjay says, 'and if you're getting tired I can let the officers know.'

It's a warning. I'm grateful to him.

'Thank you.'

The older man, Ke Quan, begins. The questions are predictable enough: timings of events, specifics of our movements, what we were wearing, what valuables we had with us. My answers are all the same: I can't remember. From the occasional twitch of his mouth I suspect this is getting on his nerves.

'Did you or your husband have any enemies?'

I open my mouth to deny this, then hesitate. Did we? Surely not Ollie. He was friendly with all his exes, kept up with everyone from university and school, even some from his prep school. The Mr Nice of banking.

Which leaves me. Do I have enemies? Plenty probably. I've upset people in my articles – politicians, businessmen, the odd celebrity – been threatened a few times, but nothing I've ever taken seriously.

'No,' I say. 'No one.'

'Did you argue with the boatman, Zaw Phyo?' the captain says. 'On the way to So Den?'

So, he has a name. Zaw Phyo. It's too alien to stir any sympathy in me.

'I can't remember.'

His eyes flash with irritation and he says something sharp to his colleague, who takes over.

'An argument about payment perhaps?' His eyes are gentler than his superior and his English is stilted.

'There was an argument,' I say slowly, 'but not with him. With the boy who brought the lobsters to the resort. Someone said it was the boatman's nephew.'

Linh starts taking notes.

'He almost hit Ollie with his boat and I got angry. Bay – the manager of the resort – told him he wouldn't be getting his bonus.'

By the speed at which he's writing, Linh clearly thinks this could be important, so I continue quickly. 'Ask Bay. They spoke. Maybe he said something. A threat. He seemed very an—'

Without warning Ke Quan breaks in: 'Is it true you and Mr Graveney argued violently the night before he died?'

I feel the colour drain from my face.

I stare at him, waiting for him to say more, but that's it. Except that it's not. The implication has fallen now, like a dead body onto the bed, and however hard I try to ignore it, I can't. They're implying I killed my husband.

'No,' I say. 'Not at all. We never fought.'

Ke Quan smiles coldly. 'All husbands and wives argue.'

'Ollie was very placid.'

'And what about you?'

I stare at them again.

'Are *you* a placid person, Mrs Graveney?'

I clear my throat, playing for time. 'Who told you we argued?'

'It was – how do you call it?' He smiles. 'An anonymous tip-off.'

'Why . . .?' *Why would anyone do that?* I want to say, but can already guess their response. There's no one out here with a grudge against us, so perhaps it's the truth.

My skin goes cold, my fingers stiffening as the blood rushes to my pounding heart.

'I . . . I don't remember any argument,' I stammer.

And then I do. I remember the night we all got drunk, when we first met Sean. *Blacks and Irish sticking together,* Ollie said. Horrible, but hardly a violent row. There were no raised voices and anyway it was just the drink talking. Not that we'd have ever come to blows, even drunk. In four years we've had some pretty heated debates but rarely even raised voices, let alone fists. Ollie wasn't capable of it.

Am I?

The hair around my injury starts to creep.

I realise then that the two policemen are watching me. I flush deeply, as if the thoughts have scrolled across my face like the information screen on a tube train.

Then Sanjay speaks. 'Could the anonymous call have been from a member of the boatman's family, say, seeking to cast doubt on his guilt?'

'It's possible.' Ke Quan raises his eyebrows, unconvinced.

They wait.

Under the sheet my left knee starts to tremble.

After what feels like several minutes Sanjay stands. 'I think that's enough for now. Mrs Graveney needs rest.'

The policemen stand too, thank me politely for my time, commiserate for my loss and allow Sanjay to lead them out of my room. He closes the door softly.

I might need rest, but I won't sleep now. The Vietnamese police clearly think I killed my husband.

14

Burney Castle, Hampshire

Saturday 3 September

Ollie doesn't return for half an hour. When he hurried off to be sick Milo went after him, and after extricating her dress from under the table Asha followed, but Milo intercepted her in the corridor, told her he'd handle it and she should get back to her guests: made her feel it was her duty. So she went back.

Now everyone's trooping down onto the lawn where the cake is displayed, bedecked in ribbons and bunting and cascades of sugar roses, the knife laid beside it, glinting in the sunlight. There are four tiers. The top one is white, the second baby pink, the third fuchsia and the lowest a vivid crimson that makes her think of skinned flesh.

Already people are gathered, phones poised, waiting for the happy couple. The photographer smiles expectantly as Asha descends the stone staircase. Then she sees that Asha is alone and lowers her camera.

'Ollie will be out in a minute,' she says calmly, as if she's in the know.

Ignoring the questioning glances she heads straight over to Zainab and gratefully takes the glass of champagne her friend offers.

'What's going on?'

'Food poisoning or something. I don't know.' She shrugs casually, but can't shake off a nameless worry. Something is definitely wrong with Ollie and it's nothing to do with what he ate.

But minutes later the two men appear, grinning. Milo's arm is round Ollie's shoulders and as they trot down the steps he gives him a playful punch in the ribs, addressing the nearest listeners. 'The silly sod stuffed his face so much he made himself sick!'

Despite the frozen smile plastered to Ollie's face he's as white as the icing on the top tier.

Eventually Asha manages to prise him away from clucking elderly relatives and Victoria.

'Are you okay?'

'Fine. Think it was the chocolates. They were so rich.'

She looks at him.

'Seriously. Didn't you think so?'

And before she can say any more he claps his hands and announces that it's time to cut the cake.

It all goes perfectly well after that. Ollie is well enough to eat at least three slices of cake so that everyone gets a shot, and by the time they announce that the party is ready to begin back in the hall, there's colour in his face again.

They go back inside and the band starts up for the first dance, the singer stepping back to let the musicians take over.

It's a funny choice. She agreed to let Ollie pick and was expecting something smoochy, like the love song that was everywhere during their first summer together: they used to get drunk to it, make love to it, eat lazy breakfasts in bed as it played on the radio. Instead he's chosen a club classic she just about remembers from her university years. It sounds even odder played in an instrumental arrangement. People start laughing and she realises Ollie's chosen this as a joke. A thumb to the nose for all the stiffs like his parents. She claps her hands, delighted.

But Ollie's not laughing. She can't tell beneath the disco lighting but he looks like he might be sick again.

Milo goes over, sits him down and pushes his head between his knees. Then he gives an exaggerated *what can you do* shrug, which banishes the concerned expressions, and before she can stop him, he grabs Asha and whirls her onto the dance floor.

Worried, she goes along nevertheless, strutting and striking poses like she hasn't done since she was a teenager. It's fun. People are laughing and filming. But she shouldn't be sharing the first dance of her wedding with Milo.

When the song ends and a more traditional tune starts up, the floor fills with other couples. She goes in search of Ollie.

Through the bodies she makes out those who are not dancing: Zainab chatting up Seb as if his scowling fiancée were nowhere in sight instead of standing next to him; Victoria, looking pink-cheeked, squiffy and almost friendly; the oldies getting bored and wondering when they can politely leave.

And finally she sees him, standing by the band talking to the singer. Not talking, arguing. Jabbing his finger at the woman's chest, while she gapes in bewilderment.

She hurries over but when Ollie sees her coming he moves away to meet her.

'What's the problem?'

'They wanted to finish early because they've got some big gig tomorrow and I said no way.'

'What a fucking cheek! We've paid to have them till eleven!' She tries to move past him, to put in her own two penn'orth, but he holds her arm.

'Exactly. That's what I told them.'

'And what did they say?'

'They agreed to stay.'

'Good. I mean . . . Well, good.'

'Come on.'

As they move away she happens to glance back. The other band members, though they're carrying on playing seamlessly, are all looking over at the singer, who is tapping her finger to her temple.

Asha scowls at the back of the woman's pale pink head but decides to ignore the insult and try to enjoy the rest of the evening.

*

123

It's so late it's early.

The band packed up hours ago, the DJ called it a night at one, and all the guests over forty have gone to bed. Even Zainab's disappeared, although Asha suspects that's because she scored with one of the chefs.

Asha, Ollie, Milo, Liberty and some of Ollie's banking friends are sitting out on the terrace, wrapped in the hotel's itchy wool blankets, passing round whisky bottles, waiting for the sun to rise. For once she doesn't care that they're talking about money, doesn't even bother to try and follow the conversation, just lies against Ollie's chest, her legs up on the bench, the skirt of the seven grand dress frayed where her heel caught it dancing, the lace spotted with mud and red wine. Globs of wax from the guttering altar candles drool through the table slats to drip onto the flagstones.

For a moment she manages to zone out the drone of voices and focus on the gurgle of water in the fountains at the bottom of the steps. Most of the flaming torches that line the path to the terrace have gone out, but the plashing water glimmers with the light from those that remain. The sound sets up a sharp ache in her bladder but she ignores it.

A single star is visible in the darkest part of the sky but directly overhead the crenellations of the castle are silhouetted against an indigo dawn.

Ollie's thumb has been moving gently across the back of her hand and now he lifts it to kiss it. She smiles at him, his face softly lit by the lamps in the room behind them. *I love you*, he mouths. *I love you*, she replies. *Are you happy?* She nods. *Are you?* He nods, his eyes glistening. Finally everything's perfect. If only she could stretch this moment out, but all too soon someone will yawn and say *that's me done*, and the day will be over.

Remarkably, though she's been drinking all day, she's completely sober. Bloated, with a bitter taste in her mouth from too much sugar and booze, but sober. Ollie's not. He's cheerily, slurringly drunk and when the conversation drifts away from him he starts humming the wedding tunes and kissing her ear.

The press of her bladder becomes increasingly insistent as his hand moves from her wrist to rest on her stomach.

'Anyone fancy a spliff?'

Beneath her Ollie stiffens. He has always been puritanically anti-drugs, and she learned very quickly not to tease him about it.

'Not tonight, mate, okay?' Milo says and the man who made the offer reddens.

The conversation doesn't resume. Liberty shifts in her seat. Seb's head lolls, his face green in the candlelight. He was doing shots of rum with Uncle Thomas and will have the hangover from hell tomorrow. Asha sighs. The evening is reaching its natural conclusion and if she puts it off any longer she'll have to add an extra few quid to the dress's dry-cleaning bill.

She gets up, making Ollie groan.

'Sorry. Don't go away.'

The lounge is deserted. The bar staff have finally given up the ghost, pulled the grille down and gone home.

Stepping into the hush of the entrance hall she sees her own reflection glimmer in the mirrors, as if there are others watching her from behind the curtains. The lights are low. The air smells strongly of the huge bouquets of white roses in their human-sized vases. Her skirt swishes as she crosses the room, and she feels momentarily like the heroine of some gothic melodrama, fleeing her demon bridegroom. A single green feather from a fascinator spirals up in an eddy of air.

The lights glare on when she pushes open the toilet door and she winces. Her eyes are dry and scratchy. She rests them as she urinates, perched on the cold toilet seat, not relishing the prospect of having to go back outside to say her goodnights and thank yous. She'd like to slip off to bed now. Wait for Ollie to snuggle up beside her. Sleep the morning away and wake up in time for a leisurely Sunday roast.

Ollie's stress seems to have entirely dissipated now that the day is drawing to a close. It's hardly surprising he was tense. Nobody can be chilled all the time.

With a pump of the moisturiser on the sink she cleans away some of the mascara from under her eyes, then uses a twist of towel to scrub the red wine stains from the inside of her lips. That helps. The blushing bride once more, well almost. She adjusts the dress so that her breasts press perkily against the corset. Nice. Maybe she isn't too drunk and tired for a wedding-day shag after all.

She goes out.

Blinded by the sudden gloom she thinks it's Ollie waiting for her in the entrance hall.

'Have they all gone up?'

'I don't know.'

She blinks. The voice is deeper and softer than Ollie's.

It's the bald man who arrived late.

He offers her his hand. His grip is refreshingly light.

'Freddie Lapozza.'

'Asha . . . Graveney.' She laughs at the hesitation. He smiles.

'Do you know my husband?'

'We were friends at school.'

'Oh, really?' She thought she'd met all his school friends and Ollie never fell out with anybody.

'It was a lovely day. Congratulations.'

'Thank you. Did you enjoy the meal?'

'Asha!'

Ollie's standing in the doorway.

'Oh, hi, I just bumped into—' She waits for the bald man to help her out but he doesn't.

'Go upstairs. I'll be up in a minute.'

'What?' She laughs.

'Go on. I'll be up.'

She stares at him. He's dismissing her like a member of staff. But his face . . . his face is ashen. For the first time in their relationship she doesn't ask any more questions, she just does as she's told, and the last thing she sees, before the curving staircase obscures her view, is Ollie's hand around Freddie Lapozza's throat.

15

Mango Tree Resort, Con Son Island
Tuesday 27 September

She wakes to find the bed empty. Ollie's not in the bungalow or out on the terrace. Perhaps he's gone to the gym.

In the shower she remembers the strange scene on the beach. Maybe Mulgrave was right about her because the memory of the two men naked under the moonlight is a turn-on. She's tempted to masturbate, but then she hears the door open. It could be Hao coming to clean the room. She gets out and dries off.

It's Ollie.

He stands awkwardly in the living room, hands behind his back as if he's been up to something.

'Hi,' she says, towelling her hair dry.

'Hi.'

A pause.

'I, er, got you something.'

He holds out something small, wrapped in tissue paper. Is this an apology?

'Thank you.' She kisses his cheek and sits down to open it.

'I wanted you to have something to remember your honeymoon by. Bay recommended a local craftsman.'

She peels back the paper. Inside is a necklace. The pendant, hanging on a silver chain, is a small case engraved with an intricate geometric pattern.

'It's called a spirit lock.'

'It's lovely.'

'It's supposed to lock your soul to your body, protect you against sickness and demonic possession, that sort of thing.' He sits down beside her. In his candy-striped shorts and pink t-shirt he looks clean and delicious. She nudges the thought out of her mind. She promised herself she wouldn't push the sex thing.

'The bigger the lock, the more protection it offers, but I . . .' He suddenly blushes. 'I was thinking that this one needs to be quite big because I want it to hold my soul too.'

His blue eyes are shining.

'You don't need a lock,' she says quietly. 'I'll never let it go.' She leans forwards to kiss him but he pulls back.

'Promise.'

'I already did, remember, at the altar?'

'Promise again. That this is for ever. Whatever happens.'

'Why?' she teases. 'What have you done?'

He smiles. 'Nothing.'

She kisses him too quickly for him to pull away. Then she holds his face and looks into his eyes so that he knows what she's about to say is the truth. 'Whatever you do in future, whatever you've done in the past – I will always love you.'

She expects him to smile but he doesn't. He kisses her, pressing his whole body against hers so that for a moment they do feel like one body and one soul.

Ollie goes for a shower and she says she'll meet him at breakfast, but when she leaves the bungalow she bypasses the restaurant and skirts round the back of the huts so as not to be seen.

It's incongruously seedy. Pieces of litter are caught in the undergrowth and black claws of mould spread across the backs of the buildings. There's a smell too: sickly sweet with the tang of fermentation, like rotten mangoes. The jungle seems to stretch its fingers out to her and she is glad when the reception hut comes into view.

He's sitting behind the desk, his elegant neck bent over a laptop. As she approaches he looks up, frowning as if trying to think of the right way to phrase something. Then he sees her.

They both start. He stands so sharply his chair falls over.

'Mrs Graveney. I hope you liked the necklace.'

'It was lovely. Thank you for helping Ollie find it.'

'My pleasure.'

'I, er, wanted . . . I wanted to have a quiet chat with you while there's no one else around.'

'Is everything in the room to your satisfaction?'

She hesitates. Is this the right thing to do?

'Last night . . .'

He stares at her, unblinking.

'Last night . . . What happened . . . I don't care about it. In our culture it doesn't matter. I have lots of friends who . . . I just didn't want you to worry that . . . I promise I won't say a word . . .' It's all coming out wrong. She's babbling patronising clichés.

'I do not know what you're talking about.'

'I understand. I just meant you don't have to worry . . .'

'I do not know what you are talking about,' he repeats sharply, the Vietnamese accent breaking through.

'No.' She holds out her hands, palms up, as if fending someone off. 'Of course you don't. It was nothing. I was confused.'

'Please,' he says, his lips curling in something like revulsion. 'I am very busy. I must carry on.'

His eyes dart from left to right and then she notices his fingers moving like crabs across the table, towards a letter opener. A rapier blade with an intricate hilt. There are letters there too, a pile of them, but can he really be thinking of opening them now?

Fear cuts through her mortification.

'I made a mistake, Bay,' she gabbles. 'I don't know what I'm talking about. Too much wine last night, ha ha!'

His face is stony, the perfect cupid's bow of his upper lip strained, as if he's trying not to let it show how much he hates her.

She backs away, towards the door, but the steps down to the walkway are nearer than she expected and she stumbles down them, going sprawling.

He moves around the desk, as if to help her up, but one hand is behind his back. Is he holding the knife? She scrabbles away from him, but her bare feet skid across the sandy wood.

He takes a step closer and any idea that he was somehow fey vanishes. Wiry muscles ripple under his shirt; he's more than capable of overpowering her.

'Bay, please, it was a mistake. I didn't see anything.'

And then there are hands under her arms, lifting her up, depositing her on her feet, wobbly-legged.

'You still drunk?'

She struggles free and spins round.

'Sean!'

'Jesus, what's the matter with you?'

She forces a breathless laugh. 'I was just asking Bay about booking a boat to the So Den Caves.'

If they were alone together she could tell him. She wouldn't tell Ollie – he would be angry with Bay for participating in something so sordid in full view of his guests – but Sean might see the funny side. She herself might, in the end, now that Bay is smiling and offering a knife-free hand to help brush the sand from her back.

'I will gather all the information and have it sent to your room, Mrs Graveney.'

'Thank you,' she gushes. 'That's great! Thank you.'

She almost runs down the walkway, sarong flapping around her hips, buttocks jiggling. Turning once, as the path bends to the right, she glances behind her. Sean is smiling after her, shaking his head in bewilderment. Behind him Bay stands perfectly still, his face devoid of expression.

True to his word, after breakfast Bay sends Hao with information about the caves. She reads it on the terrace while Ollie looks through the *Financial Times* he managed to download on his iPad at reception. Asha didn't dare ask whether Bay seemed his usual self and Ollie didn't mention anything, so perhaps it's all best left swept under the carpet.

Away from the sea breeze it's stiflingly hot and, sleep deprived from the previous night, she falls into a sticky doze. She awakes to find Ollie gone and wanders down to the beach to look for him.

Sophie and Sean lie on beds pushed close, a table between them holding some kind of board game and four empty glasses. She experiences an unpleasant stab of jealousy. Proper jealousy this time, rather than a rueful envy, and she has to force a smile when Sophie rolls her eyes behind Sean's back and lets her mouth hang open like a drooling dog. The game involves moving discs engraved with Chinese-looking symbols around a circular wooden board.

'It's got that bad, has it?' she says, flopping down between them, careful to tuck the sarong between her thighs as she crosses her legs. The sand is scalding hot but she's too self-conscious to show her discomfort. Like a silly teenager.

'Ollie and David have gone to work out again.'

'Oh my God, seriously?'

Sophie grimaces. 'Your fault, Sean. You're making them feel ashamed of themselves.'

'Good.' Sean arches an eyebrow. 'While the cat's away . . .'

The game is Chinese chess. It's fiendishly complicated and Asha soon abandons her go, but Sophie and Sean seem to be enjoying themselves. She finds herself unable to tear her gaze from Sean's face, devouring every expression as he manoeuvres his pieces. The slight frown as he thinks, the sudden softening as he realises what to do, the twitch of a smile when he knows he's caught Sophie out.

She can look more closely at his arms now, too. Close up it's hard to tell if the scars beneath the tattoos were caused by shooting up, or just plain fighting. As well as the yin symbol, on his left arm is an image of a wolf. But rather than the usual snarling pose favoured by your average meathead, this animal is slinking, watchful. It's good. It gives her a shivery frisson of lust.

After his third win Sophie surrenders and they move on to what is rapidly becoming the main focus of everyone's trip: drinking.

At some point Caspar and Travis Mulgrave appear and, unusually, agree to Sophie's bellowed invitation to join them. Travis acts as if absolutely nothing happened the night before and, speaking to him about the latest calamity in the Middle East, Asha finds herself warming to him. It's partly the drink, partly gratitude that Ollie will find a bigger group on the beach than Sean and his harem, and partly because his intelligence is breathtaking. But there's a definite spark of madness in his remaining human eye, and she gets the impression that he might be slightly psychopathic. He analyses the political situation with a curiosity so dispassionate it is almost robotic. Asha feels rather trivial for bringing up the number of babies whose lungs were burned in the attack.

The conversation is so thrillingly intense she feels a rush of disappointment when Ollie and David shamble back across the beach. The contrast between her new husband, shiny and glowing and grinning sparklingly, and the riveting debauchery of Mulgrave, the sexy menace of Sean, is stark. *I am of the devil's party*, she thinks as Ollie sits down beside her and drapes a golden, deodorant-fresh arm over her shoulder.

They sleep away the latter part of the afternoon, then wander back to the bar for another evening's drinking. Asha deliberately sits with her back to Sean's bungalow at the other end of the beach, but still the hairs on the back of her neck quiver with anticipation. When he hasn't turned up by nine and she knows he won't, the disappointment is draining. Ollie, catching her yawn, suggests an early night.

Upon leaving the bar the spell is immediately broken and she sinks against his flank, awash with a guilt that's becoming familiar. Perhaps she should admit to the crush. It would relieve the burden of guilt from her shoulders and, just maybe, the frisson of jealousy would kickstart Ollie's libido. Because it is only a crush. Like the crush she has on Tom Hardy or the one Ollie once admitted to, when pressed by Milo, on Jennifer Lawrence. Nothing really. Gone as soon as something else pops into her mind. It isn't as if her heart aches when she sees him, like it used to with Ollie.

They sit out on the terrace on loungers pushed together to lie in each other's arms, and watch the moon rise over the sea. It's getting cooler and as Ollie's nipples harden she brushes them with her lips.

'Want a drink?' he says. 'There's some whisky in the minibar.'

'No, I'm okay.'

'I think I might.' He slides off the bed.

Moodily she watches the sea, wondering if the anger rising in her gut is worth releasing, or whether she should just push it back down. It's clear the thing must be talked about, but now isn't the time. Not while her head buzzes, half aroused and half angry.

She follows him inside, gets her book and flops down on the sofa.

'Too cold?' Ollie says, coming over with his whisky and sitting down with his legs draped across her lap. She smiles, and squeezes his big toe, the anger draining.

'Will you be all right hanging out with Sophie again tomorrow? It's just that David and I are planning on heading further up the island.'

Her head jerks up from the book. 'What?'

'Yeah, David's thinking of buying this plot of land at the other end of the island, to build a resort. Like this one only more affordable, for the Center Parcs crowd. He asked if I'd like to invest in it. I thought I'd scope out the area.'

'You're kidding me.'

'What?'

The anger surges back: fuelled by sexual frustration and the bitter memory that is always a dark shadow between them.

Fishing and dancing and vodka while she bled on the sofa. She tosses the book on the table and it slides off the glass and drops to the floor with a clunk. 'This is our honeymoon.'

'We're here for three weeks. What difference does one afternoon make? Christ, at least it would break the monotony of the fucking beach.'

There's so much wrong with this outburst that for a moment she can only stare at him, open-mouthed. Firstly, he never *ever* bites that quickly. And he never gets that angry. Asha's the one who does angry: Ollie is always placating, even when he's in the right, which this time he definitely isn't.

She thrusts his legs off her lap. 'You were the one who said all the other activities were shit!'

'Well, they probably are!'

'So don't complain the beach is boring! If you'd wanted to go on some action-adventure thingy you should have said before. This was supposed to be a honeymoon, not a chance for you to expand your fucking investment portfolio.'

'It's my fucking investment portfolio that pays for it.'

'I have a job too, you know!'

'Oh yeah.' His voice drips scorn. 'If we were relying on your salary we'd be on a long weekend in Skegness.'

Not trusting herself not to say something that can't be taken back she gets up and goes inside. After yanking off the necklace and leaving it in a toothpastey puddle in the bathroom she gets into bed, her mind spinning through all the things she could say to hurt him as much as he's hurt her.

It doesn't matter where you go if you like the person you're with.
I've had better holidays than this in youth hostels.
I should never have married you.

But he doesn't come in, and as the anger ebbs away misery takes its place. This is her honeymoon. So much for the fairy-tale. Gathering the sheets into a comforting ball to cuddle, she eventually falls asleep, alone.

16

FV Hospital, Ho Chi Minh City

Friday 7 October

I'm going home tomorrow. Fortunately I still have my maiden name on my passport. Fadeyi. Never have I been more grateful to my mother's kin. If the story's out the press will be after a *Mrs Graveney*. We haven't even told the hospital. David just threw in some casual questions about when it would be safe for me to travel and Sanjay said everything was healing very well.

I force down some breakfast in the hope this will lull the nurses into believing they don't need to check on me as often. Sophie's coming to get me at one, complete with a hat and dark glasses. We've already planned our route down the emergency stairs at this end of the floor, away from the nurses' station.

After they've collected my plate I get up and go to the bathroom.

If I'm getting on a plane I don't want to smell of hospital chemicals so I run myself a lukewarm bath and step in carefully. Being upright still makes me slightly dizzy and a fall now could ruin everything. I wash perfunctorily and as my soapy hand passes between my legs it sets up a dull ache. No one will ever touch me there again. My breasts are tender and heavy, a sure sign that my period is due. No pregnancy, then: the fates couldn't even grant me that. No beautiful baby with

135

Ollie's eyes so I don't forget him. Sure enough, a few minutes later, the first tendril of blood coils out from between my legs.

I thought I had reached the depths of my misery but I was wrong. You can always go lower. My sobs echo around the sterile walls.

Eventually, after running out of energy to cry, I haul myself out of the water, dry off and open the suitcase that Sophie brought from the hotel.

The cheerful colours and patterns of my clothes disgust me. Why didn't I bring anything black?

I pull the jewellery out of the side pocket of the case and drop it into the bin under the sink. Hopefully the cleaner will find it. Some of it's worth money, but there's nothing with any sentimental value. No gift from Ollie: I left those things at home in case the luggage went missing, and the police have the spirit lock necklace.

The shiny aluminium of the bin throws my distorted reflection back at me. My black eyes are lightening to a sickly yellow colour, and I'm starting to resemble a B-movie zombie. I touch the tender part of my skull, gingerly at first, then more firmly, gritting my teeth in preparation for the grind of bone against bone. Nothing moves. Is that the titanium mesh I can feel beneath the skin?

The scrape of the main door opening. The nurse has come in. I call out that I'm in the bathroom, that I'm perfectly fine.

But there's no response. Damn it. She must be waiting to check me over. I throw the hospital gown back on, then I open the door to the bedroom.

The blinds have been pulled down and the door to the corridor is closed, so it takes a moment for my eyes to adjust.

A man is standing there.

His face provokes a flash of horrified recognition. Did he have something to do with the attack?

But he makes no move to approach me, and he isn't carrying a weapon. He's in his late teens or early twenties, hollow-eyed and thin. There's wiry strength in his arms, but surely not enough to overpower Ollie. He may have caught us by surprise.

'Need talk you.'

His voice is quiet and urgent. He glances over his shoulder and says it again. 'Need talk you.'

I see him now, against a backdrop of the sea. Hear myself shouting.

'Wh . . . what about?' I whisper.

'Need talk,' he says.

Is this the only English he knows?

'Please.'

I see him climbing out of a boat. Behind him, emerging from the water, is Ollie. He's holding his hands out to me, placatingly. *It's alright, no harm done.*

But he almost killed you!

You almost killed my husband!

The boy with the lobsters.

'W . . . what do you want?'

But he doesn't understand. Bay told us that he didn't understand English. Sent him away without his bonus. That look he gave me as the boat chugged out of the bay. Cold hatred. Ollie said he was just a stroppy teenager.

Calm down, Asha. You're not thinking straight. The boatman who attacked us is in prison.

'Please,' he says.

I slide round to the opposite side of the bed, my eyes never leaving his face. I can reach the alarm cord without lifting my hand above the level of the mattress. He won't even see me pull it.

'Need talk . . .' He throws his head back with an exasperated exhalation that makes me jump, and when he lowers it again I see his eyes are shining with tears.

My hand hesitates on the cord.

'No English,' he says. 'Please. No English. Important.'

I hesitate. If he were going to kill me surely he'd have done it by now. My hand is on the cord. The nurses will be here in seconds.

His eyes are burning into mine, waiting for permission. 'Okay.'

He takes a deep breath and I see he too is trembling. For the first time I'm aware of the fact that this poor Asian boy is alone in the bedroom of a half-naked Western woman. If I pulled that cord I could ruin his life.

'Sit down,' I say, pointing to the chair. Then I gesture for him to drink: 'Water?'

He shakes his head.

We stand opposite one another in silence, then he takes a deep breath.

He points at me. *You.*

I nod, bewildered.

Then he gestures to my left. As if to some invisible companion. Is there a ghost beside me? Is that what this is about? Some spiritual bullshit to try and make me feel better, or so Ollie's spirit can communicate the 'true identity' of the murderer? If so he can fuck off. Ollie's dead. Nowhere. Forever.

My heart is pounding but I keep my expression blank.

He huffs in exasperation. *You. The ghost beside you.*

Then I get it. 'My husband? Ollie. Mr Graveney?'

'Vang!' He nods vigorously and points again. *You and Ollie.*

'Okay.'

Now he brings up his left hand and moves it up and down like a snake winding its way through grass.

'Snake?' I say, then hiss, mimicking the motion.

He shakes his head.

'Oh. You mean the sea.'

I'm right. Now his right hand carves a path through the sea. *Boat.* He means a boat. Me and Ollie on a boat.

Goosebumps rise on my arms, forcing the hairs against the thin cotton of my gown.

He draws the outline of the cave.

'No,' I say, my voice rising in pitch. 'How do you know? You weren't there. You don't know what happened.'

He doesn't understand me but can read the fear in my eyes. 'Bac trai cua toi,' he says.

We stare at each other. Outside, the bustle of the hospital seems to be getting louder. It must be nearly lunchtime. The nurse will be in soon with my slop tray.

He lunges across the mattress and I start back with a cry, but he's only trying to reach the book Sophie lent me.

He flicks to the blank pages at the back and tears one out.

'Hey!'

He holds up a hand – wait – then strides to the bathroom door and yanks off the pen that's attached by a string to the check sheet.

Leaning on the book, he starts to draw. I ease myself around the bed until I'm close enough to see what he's doing.

There are the two stick men that are supposed to be me and Ollie, but we're no longer on the boat. We're standing under an arc which I assume represents the cave. A circle at the top forms some kind of skylight and I experience a flash of memory.

A brown and red splodge surrounded by a wash of blue.

He's looking at me expectantly, like a boy waiting for the teacher's approval.

'Me and Ollie in the cave,' I say, though I'm not sure he understands me.

He makes a *puh puh puh* sound and traces a line with his finger out of one of the entrances. I think he's trying to say that the boat has gone away, leaving Ollie and me there alone.

Another flash of memory: *the pitter patter of rain from a clear sky.*

He's drawing something else now and I move closer until I can see the smattering of soft stubble on his jaw. His BO has a young, fresh tang. A vein pulses in his neck and his breaths come quick and shallow.

He clearly wasn't happy with the first attempt because he's drawn the same thing again.

'Me and Ollie,' I say. 'Yes.'

He gives a sharp exhalation and stabs the pencil into the paper. I don't understand.

He draws a heavy cross through the first image, pressing so hard that the paper tears on the female figure's face, then looks up at me urgently. Another wave of dizziness and nausea engulfs me. Dark stars are bursting in front of my eyes. The room slides away.

Coils of black coral. A white star.

I must have been unconscious for no more than a second or so because I come round to the sound of an alarm and footsteps pounding up the corridor. I'm slumped on the bed. As my vision clears I see him, frozen by the door, staring at me in horror. He must have thought he'd killed me. I try to sit up, to reassure him that I'm alright, but can only groan and slither across the mattress.

The door bursts open.

Two nurses: the male one comes immediately to my aid, hauling me onto my back and snapping an oxygen mask over my mouth. This he does with some difficulty as my head is turned towards the boy, who is now being aggressively questioned in Vietnamese by the female nurse.

When he doesn't respond she snatches up the phone and barks, in English, 'Security!'

The boy turns and runs.

She's about to set off in pursuit so, with the man distracted, I roll over and fall out of bed. The jar of the impact sends pain scything across my head and for a moment I can only lie there moaning, as if I really have collapsed. Now the female nurse must stay and help her colleague lift me back up onto the bed, then check my vital signs. After a while I'm able to answer their questions: the shock of the intruder made me faint. No, I've never seen him before. No, he didn't attack me or take anything.

On the contrary, it's what he's left me that's occupying my whole attention, making me short with the nurses, who are only trying to help.

The book is lying on the chair by the door. Poking from its leaves is the corner of a folded page.

Eventually, satisfied that I'm okay, they open the blinds and the windows to let in some of that fresh, gridlocked-city air, then reassure me that my meal will be along very soon. Finally, after tucking my sheets in so tight I can barely expand my lungs, they leave.

I wait until their footsteps recede into the hubbub of the hospital, then climb out of bed and get the book.

Standing on the cold lino in just my cotton gown I frown at the image. He didn't have the chance to draw anything else before we were interrupted. There's just me and Ollie in the cave: the two versions, one crossed out. Then I notice a difference between the sets of figures. The female of the crossed-out pair has her face shaded in. A black woman. Me. But the female of the other pair doesn't. Did he not have time to do it? And yet he had time to cross out the first pair, as if they weren't important: as if it was the other pair he wanted me to focus on.

And then I understand.

Somewhere down the corridor a door has opened and a sudden breeze rushes up behind me, racing for the open window. It snatches at my gown and tugs at my hair, making the wound ache dully.

I don't move. I can't. I finally know what he's trying to tell me.

In that cave, on the day we were attacked, we weren't alone. There was another couple.

PART TWO

17

London

Grief is so predictable. I knew what to expect, I'd experienced it before. And yet still I wake up with that childish euphoria of another sunrise, a split second before the sledgehammer strikes.

Some days I think I'm going to be alright. I sit in the garden square and feel pleasure at the wind in my hair and the sun on my eyelids. And then suddenly I'm poleaxed by a pregnant woman, or a couple walking along hand in hand.

Sophie and Zainab have phoned twice a day without fail, morning and evening. They want to come round but I've asked them to stay away. Much more considerate to fall apart in the privacy of my own home. They keep telling me I should get out of the house, that *being around people* will distract me. I don't want to be distracted. Each crying jag feels like poison leaving my system, and yet, like a leaking stopcock, the poison seeps back in as soon as the tears stop.

The few conversations I've had with Ollie's parents have been awful. I've tried not to rise to Victoria's insinuations that it's my fault. Were there any unsavoury characters from my childhood . . .? My mother's boyfriends? . . . Someone who was after his money? . . . They mean me, of course. The grubby little gold-digger from the council estate. I hate them so much then, but we must stay in touch, at least until the funeral.

They've taken over the arrangements, ostensibly out of consideration for my fragile state, but I know that they just want to pretend I never existed. They've even suggested that attending might be 'too much' for me, but I managed to stay civil. I said that I wanted input *as his wife* and so they reluctantly allowed me to choose the hymns (no pop music, please) and the images for the memorial order of service.

It's taken me three days to prepare myself for the ordeal of going through our old photographs.

The worst thing is that I keep coming across shots I don't remember taking. Close-ups of Ollie's face, or him laughing in a bar: snatched glimpses I must have caught when drunk, or on a quickly forgotten whim, not realising they would ever have any value. My amnesiac heart skips at each one, looking forward to sharing them with Ollie, before my brain delivers the hammer blow of reality.

By the time I've chosen five that are well-lit and framed and capture something of Ollie's spirit, I feel like I've been beaten up. I crawl to the sofa and lie there staring at the ceiling that has become so familiar over the past few days.

Then I get up and go for a cigarette. Sitting on the windowsill looking out across the back garden, blowing the smoke through the gap in the sash, I think of Sean. He hasn't tried to get in touch. I don't have the emotional energy to hurt, I'm just dully disappointed. More than anyone, he would understand how I'm feeling.

As I'm emailing the photos to Mackensie, I suddenly remember a fancy dress garden party Ollie and I went to the year we got together. I'd found an Edwardian ballgown in a vintage shop and Ollie wore his grandfather's Oxford rowing gear, complete with the original straw boater. There was an old-fashioned photo booth and in the sepia shot we'd looked so happy, wrapped in each other's arms. I hadn't wanted to frame it because it was so contrived but Ollie had kept it in his 'special box' – the trunk he'd been packed off to boarding school with at eleven. Now, I want everyone to see how in love we were, the fun we had.

I trudge back upstairs and open Ollie's wardrobe. It always seemed so extravagant to have separate walk-in wardrobes, but sometimes now I will sit on the floor in the dark, breathing in the last wisps of his scent on his clothes.

Slipping inside quickly to stop the precious air escaping, I turn on the light.

There are the rows of pastel work shirts, jeans folded over A-frame hangers, much more neatly than mine, a sheepskin coat, a leather jacket, a parka with a half-eaten Snickers in the pocket that I will never throw away. The bottom of my wardrobe is a jumble of shoes but Ollie's are stacked neatly in their boxes. Looking at it all now I sense a certain OCDness. A desire for control, perhaps, or the fear of losing it.

From the shelf above the rail I pull down a sweatshirt he wore out jogging the day before we left for Vietnam, and bury my face in it. But it has the cut-grass scent of clean cotton. *Why did you have to be so fucking clean?*

I will never smell him again, never see him, hear his voice, touch him, taste him.

The thought of it makes me too weak to raise my arms above my head to replace the sweatshirt and I pull it on instead, over the multiple layers of clothing I've taken to wearing to keep out the cold that never seems to leave my bones, however high I turn the heating up.

Eventually I find the trunk, pushed up against the wall behind a stack of shoeboxes and beneath a line of long coats, as if it hasn't been touched for a very long time. This makes me sad. Was there nothing worth remembering recently?

Dragging it out into the bedroom I go to flick the catch and find that the wheels of the ancient combination have been spun. I click them to the numbers Ollie uses for all his luggage locks – his birthday – but it won't open. He must have changed the combination.

Sitting back on my haunches I wonder whether to bother. I could easily find another shot for the last page of the service.

Then suddenly I need to see all the things he considered special. Are there other mementos from our time together? From holidays and nights out? First dates? Anniversaries? All those precious moments. I can relive them here, alone in the gloom, an echoing carousel of happiness encircling my head. A moment's respite.

The catches look flimsy enough. I go down to the kitchen and pull a knife steel from the block in the kitchen. Jabbing the metal prong through the gap, I jerk it up and down, backwards and forwards until, with a snap, the left lock gives, then the right.

The case opens.

Half smiling, half crying, I rifle through programmes for plays, restaurant receipts, foreign bus tickets, magazine articles with my byline, dried flowers, shells we gathered on nameless beaches. It is all us, all of it. I wish Victoria could be here now to see this. To see how much her son loved me.

I retrieve the sepia photograph and sit there staring at it for a long time. How could I ever have considered it contrived? It's just two people, as beautiful as we ever were or will be, obviously in love. I can remember the musty smell of the blazer and the little bits of rotted straw from the boater that kept catching in my hair. We made love under a willow tree of lanterns as partygoers chatted a few feet away on the other side of the fronds.

I'm about to shut the case when I see another photograph poking out from between the leaves of a programme. It catches my eye because there are so few in here – most are on the computer – and I pull it out.

A blurry yellowed print clearly from the time before digital cameras, when even an out-of-focus shot was worth keeping. It's in remarkably good condition, as if someone's been taking care of it. Unless it's a copy. Five people stand on the side of a dusty road, their arms draped around each other.

The man on the far right is Ollie, his much younger face blurred but still recognisable. His hair is all nineties public schoolboy, floppy and very fair, as if he's been in the sun for a long time. His bare chest is tanned and his whole body is longer and leaner. I feel a twinge of desire for this boy I could never meet.

His head is turned towards the figure next to him. A curvy girl in a dark red dress with a halo of black curls. The man on the other side of her is, I'm sure, a slimmer, tanned version of Milo. I've met all Ollie's exes so the woman must be a fling of Milo's.

Next to Ollie is Seb, but I don't recognise the man standing on the far left. I take the photograph to the window but it's infuriatingly out of focus and only two things are clear. First, he is a good half-foot shorter than Ollie, second, his hair is already receding.

The shot may have been taken on a timer because there's a sliver of something that might be a wall at the base: it and the road sign beyond the group are the only parts in focus. The sign reads *Faro 46km*. Faro is in Portugal.

So is Albufeira. From the postcard at the wedding.

Something makes me turn the photo over.

There is just a date. 21.8.98

I've never seen this shot and I've been through this case once before. At the beginning of our relationship, still carrying baggage from the previous one, I waited till Ollie was at the gym and I looked through all this stuff. For letters, photographs anything that would fuel the hunger of my insecurity. There was nothing. A few medals, some schoolbooks, programmes for the first play he was in.

This picture wasn't there.

A horrible thought strikes me. Was Ollie having an affair? Of course the shot was taken years ago but what if they got back in touch, he and the girl I took to be Milo's? What if they started an affair and she sent him this to remind him of when they met?

Queasily I get to my feet and go back downstairs, still clutching the photograph.

Ollie told me his computer password years ago and for a nasty moment as the laptop starts up I wonder if he changed it, for the same reason he changed the combination on the trunk. But it lets me in straightaway. The wallpaper shot is of us cutting our wedding cake on the castle lawn – all overblown grins and glittering eyes and great blotches of colour. It makes my head pound.

I open his photos folder.

His phone always uploaded photographs directly to his computer. If he's changed something, it must be because he has something to hide.

The application opens to the most recent shot and there I am, flat out on a sofa in the Emirates lounge at Heathrow, raising a glass of champagne to camera. On our way to Saigon.

I scroll back through the pictures. A couple of shots seem to have been uploaded every day, from the day we left for our honeymoon, back to the wedding and the stag do and beyond.

There are no strange women, in fact not a single woman apart from me and the wedding guests, even at the stag do where you might have expected a little flirtation.

I wince as I glance through those shots, remembering how pleased I was that Ollie had decided on a simple pub crawl through the City, rather than agreeing to Milo organising a 'surprise' which would probably have involved strippers, and worse. From the first shot Ollie is clearly off his face, red and sweating, his arm around Milo, who has his mouth wide open, mid-bellow. Seb is there, a few of Ollie's work colleagues and a couple of cousins. In one particularly awful shot Milo is waving a toilet brush – presumably taken from the bathroom of the bar and still dripping – over his head whilst the bar staff look on stonily. They must have loathed them. I always did. I hated banker parties or 'quick drinks' that turned into full-on sessions. But the banker I hated most was Milo and I always knew the feeling was mutual. I tried to talk to Ollie about it at the beginning. Tried to work out what it was that Ollie so liked about him, so I could see it for myself, but Ollie just said they *went back a long way*.

In another shot Milo is sticking his tongue out lewdly as Ollie bends over the bar.

I scroll back down to the wedding. The images are already so familiar. We pored over the photographs in the days afterwards, looking for the best ones to frame. The photographer stayed right till the end, snapping away while we staggered around with smeared makeup, lost ties, stained shirts.

And then, to my surprise, I see one of the shots Ollie told me had been corrupted.

It was taken late in the evening and most of us are pink-cheeked with drink. Uncle Thomas is talking to Zainab and I'm standing between them laughing, the pearls on my dress glimmering. It's such a beautiful shot that Helen the photographer showed me straight afterwards and I made a mental note to look out for it when the stick came through. Except that when Ollie gave it to me the shot was gone. And yet it would seem that he managed to download it, and others.

There's one of Zainab and Ollie dancing that I've never seen, another of the bankers doing shots on the terrace, Seb and Milo gurning in matching fascinators, Thomas lindy dancing while people clap in time to the music.

I was particularly disappointed to lose the ones of Thomas, Ollie knew that. So why were the pictures on his computer all along?

When the photographer answers she's laughing at something. In the background I can hear the bustle of a party or a family meal. A child's toy plays a scratchy electronic tune.

'Helen, it's Asha Graveney.'

'Asha . . . shit . . . how are you? Oh my God, I'm so sorry.'

That instant curtailment of happiness that the sound of my voice can produce these days.

'I'm okay. I, I just had a question, really. Just wanted to check something with you.'

'Of course, of course, just give me a minute.' The bustle recedes. She must have walked into another room.

'I just wanted to ask you about the files that got corrupted.'

There's a silence.

'Sorry, I . . . files?'

'Ollie said that some shots had been lost because the files got corrupted but I'm looking at them now and they seem fine so I was wondering if it was still okay to blow them up and print them out or whether these were just thumbnails or . . .' I tail off.

'Umm. Sorry, Asha, I'm an idiot. Remind me which files got corrupted. Did you have a computer meltdown? It's no problem for me to send them again.'

'*You* did,' I say. 'You had a computer problem. Some of the files got corrupted your end.'

A longer silence.

'I'm really sorry,' she says gently, 'but I think there's been a bit of confusion. All the photos came out fine and I sent them on a stick to Ollie.'

I stare at the screen, then I click on one of the photographs Ollie said was lost. I blow it up, moving in so close I can see the gold filling on one of Uncle Thomas's back teeth. It isn't corrupted.

'Sorry,' I say. 'I must have misunderstood him. They seem fine. Sorry for bothering you.'

'No, please, it's absolutely f—'

I put the phone down before she can finish, then light another cigarette. This time I don't even bother to sit by the window and when the first column of ash falls onto the carpet I grind it into the cream-coloured pile. Standards are slipping but there's no one left to care.

How could he have lied to me when he knew I loved those photos? Unless he was going to frame one as a surprise. Maybe he was going to put together one of those special books . . .

And yet, while some of them have sentimental value because of Uncle Thomas, most of them aren't the sort of shots you'd want to frame. It was too late in the evening for any of us to look particularly fresh and there are too many people in the background. Most of them are chatting or dancing but one of them is looking over Uncle Thomas's shoulder, straight at the camera.

I realise with a jolt that it's the man Ollie had up against the wall.

I zoom in on his shadowed figure until it starts to pixelate but that doesn't tell me anything. A thick-set, shaven-headed white man around our age, there's nothing to distinguish him from the other guests. And yet there's something familiar about him.

I pick up the Portugal photograph. The stranger on the left is shorter than the others, with broader shoulders and womanly fat about the hips. The male pattern baldness that's already in evidence would surely only have got worse. He'd have been nearly bald by his thirties, and these days when that happens you only have one option.

You shave it off.

I stare at the picture until the cigarette burns down to my fingertips.

This young man and the one Ollie had up against the wall at the wedding, they're the same person.

The morning after, I asked Ollie about him. His reply was abrupt. They had been friends years ago, he said, but this man had fucked up his career and was now always trying to tap his old friends for contacts or loans. He hadn't been invited to the wedding, he'd just turned up to try and schmooze people. Ollie had had enough of it and lost his rag. And that was the end of the conversation.

I open the pictures file again and find the one of Ollie and Zainab dancing.

There he is, the bald man, at the far end of the room, a still statue amidst the coloured smears of the dancers. I click on one of the other supposedly corrupted shots. In the lindy one the bald man is standing in the middle of the semicircle, but instead of watching Thomas, once again he seems to be looking directly at the camera. He's standing on the edge of the terrace as the banker boys knock back their shots, his face a pixelated mask.

153

But it's the one of me, Zainab and Thomas that is the most unsettling. At first I didn't see him, but when I finally make sense of the shot I gasp. He's so close to the camera that his pallid cheek seems to be part of the wall. You have to look closely to see the shadow of the eye socket. He's looking directly down the camera lens. In each of the shots he's getting closer and closer and closer until . . .

Instinctively I look behind me, but see only my frightened reflection in the window. It reminds me of the look on Ollie's face as I walked up the aisle. The bald man had just gone into the church, late, and was standing at the back.

Ollie said he was angry, but he didn't look angry, he looked scared.

18

Mango Tree Resort, Con Son Island

Wednesday 28 September

Ollie apologises so profusely about the row over David's 'investment opportunity', and she's so relieved, that in the end she almost insists on his going to visit the plot of land.

'Shall I come with you?'

He looks up from his bowl of coconut and chia porridge. 'I'd love you to. But it'll be pretty boring. Are you sure?'

'If it's something you want to invest in, for us, then I should be there too. It's our future, right? I don't want you making a cock-up. Buying some malarial swamp, or sacred ground with a curse on it.'

He laughs and squeezes her hand.

They arrive in reception to find David and Sophie have hired quad bikes for the trip across country.

Asha clings to Ollie's back as they bounce down rutted tracks through rice fields and along the edge of the jungle. By the time they arrive at the bottom of a scrubby slope her vertebrae are clacking like dice.

They climb up to a plateau looking out over the sea. The remains of a grand house stand proudly in the middle of a patch of rough ground which was once paved. The flowerbeds on either side have been entirely taken over by waist-high weeds. The view is quite something, out across a small azure bay with its own crescent of beach. It's a great spot for a resort.

David and Ollie walk around to the front of the house. As Asha waits for Sophie to puff up the hill she glimpses the men passing across the gaping windows and huge crevasses in the walls. Sophie takes her arm and they follow, picking their way through knife-sharp brown grass. A lizard scuttles down a ruined wall and into the brush. Through the empty windows she glimpses scorched wallpaper, the remains of a stone fireplace scored with deep gashes. Broken bottles and rusted cans are strewn across the floor. The wind whines through the rents in the stonework.

'Idyllic, isn't it?'

Asha murmurs her assent but she's starting to find the place eerie. To be up this high feels exposed somehow and her back starts to prickle. Remembering the figures on the headland she glances over her shoulder.

'What's that?'

In an area of flat ground at the bottom of the slope is a high grey wall with what look like round towers at each corner. From up here you can see over the wall to a grid of low buildings. People seem to be milling about the open areas, but after a few moments they still haven't moved.

David comes over and hands her his binoculars. 'Only the biggest tourist attraction in South Vietnam.'

Now she can make out the figures more clearly. They are a strange greyish blue, like frozen corpses. Many are half naked, their rib cages graphically shadowed, heads hanging, arms shackled. She moves the binoculars to a group of men in uniform looming over a figure on the ground, sticks raised above their heads, frozen. She moves them again. A skeletal grey figure hangs from a post in the centre of a dusty square. In front of him five men are posed with rifles at their shoulders. It's impossible to tell whether the tableau is supposed to be pre- – the man cringing or fainting – or post-execution. Either way it makes her skin crawl.

'What is it?' She hands the binoculars back to David.

'The old prison,' he says. 'Set up by the French. Housed various enemies of the state until the 1950s. It's quite a draw. The Yanks love it.' He loops the binocular cord over his head and scratches his stomach.

Ollie has wandered into the shell of the house. 'This must have been amazing once,' he calls.

David follows him. 'The old governor's house. Built by French colonialists in the early eighteen hundreds. Shame it burnt down. You could try and rebuild but it would be cheaper to start again. Something modern, glass, with three-hundred-and-sixty-degree views of the countryside and the bay.' He sweeps his arm through the still air.

Asha's eyes drift back to the prison.

'You can't buy the land though, right?' Ollie says. 'It's a fifty-year lease or something, isn't it?'

'Correct. But you can buy the property and if you go into partnership with a local company it's all much easier. There are several that work with foreign investors. One of them – my preferred one – has a couple of hotels on the mainland, all with UK owners. Their turnover's around . . .'

Asha's attention slides away.

She walks to the edge of the slope and gazes down at the prison. How awful to be behind those walls and yet be able to hear the sea lapping at the shore, the breeze through the jungle. To know that the warm white sand is just a few steps away. It's a horrible thought and she's about to shake it off and suggest to Sophie that they go down for a swim while the boys are talking business. Then she remembers her barbed comment to Sophie about having a duty to think about horrible things. And here she is, about to run away from a stark and difficult truth.

'I'm going down to look at the prison,' she calls over her shoulder. She doesn't think anyone has heard her but halfway down the slope Sophie comes panting after her.

'I'll join you.'

It's a museum. At least there's a booth with a sign quoting ticket prices in dollars, but no one to take your money. The two women wander through the ornate gateway into a yard.

At first she thinks the place is busy, but a second glance reveals that the figures apparently milling about the enclosure are more of the mannequins she saw from the hill. Close up she sees they are made of plaster. The effect is powerful, creepy too. The layers of paint on their skin are flaking off in leprous strips.

She approaches one and tries to get into its eyeline, but the way the eyes have been painted, whether deliberately or not, it's always looking away, off into the distance, lost in its own suffering. She wishes she had gone for a swim instead.

Sophie comes up beside her. 'Spooky, huh?'

'Effective though,' she says, trying to mitigate her own simplistic gut response.

They wander around the yard, looking at each pathetic or horrific tableau in turn, pointing out the poignant details, discussing their scant knowledge of Vietnam's history, trying not to be bored or jaded.

All the while Asha feels as if someone is watching her, but perhaps it's only the dull, flaking eyes of the statues.

They're peering through the bars of a cell crowded with plaster dummies when a loud bang, like a gunshot, makes them cry out and clutch each other.

In the silence that follows, a stab of dread makes Asha glance up the hill towards the governor's house. Ollie and David are standing on the edge of the slope, still chatting obliviously. She feels a rush of relief.

'Maybe it's part of the show,' Sophie says dubiously.

'What show? It's hardly Disneyland.'

'Well, what was it then?'

'Who knows. Come on, let's go in there.'

They enter a one-storey building. On first glance the interior is entirely featureless: a single long room, its floors, walls and ceiling all the same uniform grey of bare concrete. The high windows don't let in much light and it takes Asha a moment to notice the grey squares studding the floor on each side. She goes over to one then starts back. A wan face gazes mournfully up at her through a rusted grille.

'They're called tiger cages,' Sophie says. 'They used to throw people down here, people who protested against the Communist regime. When they came out they'd lost their minds.'

Asha stares at her. The other woman looks deflated, as if the plump healthy flesh was just a bag of air that now has a puncture.

'It still smells, doesn't it?'

Asha inhales, catches the foul whiff of diarrhoea, or perhaps it's just her imagination.

'Come on, let's go.'

They pass into more depressing buildings filled with rotted statues, and even though the day is hot Asha starts to feel the dank atmosphere of the cells seeping into her. The occasional English sign describes torture methods, lime in the eyes to blind, beatings, dismemberings, gang rapes, tens of thousands dead.

When they get to the far end of the enclosure she feels as if she's completed a penance. There's only one building left. A small latrine or pump house. It doesn't look of much interest and she's about to suggest leaving but something stops her: some sense of responsibility still, to bear witness. She thinks fleetingly of Travis Mulgrave, that mad glitter in his remaining eye. The other lost to this compulsion to observe. *Is* it social responsibility, or just voyeurism?

She enters the building and is again blinded by the sudden dark. She steps forward into the gloom but her foot doesn't land. She's tipping forward, outstretched arms wheeling through nothing.

Sophie grabs her, hauls her back to safety.

It takes a moment for her eyes to adjust enough to see the black circle in the middle of the floor. An open well. Another half second and she would have fallen into it. Sophie tosses a piece of grit and seconds later there is a dry skitter.

'Sounds like concrete down there,' she says.

'Shitting hell.' Asha laughs nervously. 'I'd have broken my neck.'

'Look, there's the cover.'

A metal grille is leaning against the wall behind the door.

'That is so dangerous,' Asha snaps, anger replacing her shock.

Sophie picks up the grille. 'Looks like someone's broken off the lock.'

'What makes you think there was a lock?' Asha says.

Sophie straightens.

'Oh yes, you were here before.'

But Sophie's looking at her oddly. Asha becomes acutely aware of the chasm between them. If Sophie were to reach out and grab her arm . . .

A foetid breeze is coming up from the well, damp and chill. Asha shivers.

'Come on,' Sophie says brightly, 'let's get back to the boys,' and they walk out of the building and back into the sun.

At the top of the slope Ollie and David are sprawled on the scrubby grass, smoking cigars.

Asha sits down beside her husband, nuzzling into his warmth. The smell takes her back to dark London bars. She experiences a sudden desire to be there, amongst the grey streets and glowing windows, already lit up by now as the nights draw in. London's history is too rich and deep and outrageous for one area to be any more tainted than the next. It's easy to forget, to live your life only in the present.

'Beautiful, isn't it?' Ollie says, sweeping the glowing cigar tip around the curve of the bay.

Asha murmurs her agreement, but even as she gazes across the sparkling sea the prison is there, a dark blotch at the edge of her vision.

*

She tells Ollie about it over cocktails on the terrace, ordered from room service to allow them a break from the Peterses.

Asha ordered a simple mojito, but she saw from the menu that the damned thing cost thirty-two dollars. Christ knows what their bar bill will be at the end of the stay.

It's good though. Perfectly balanced, refreshing, thirst- and spirit-quenching. She's got to that dangerous point in a holiday where the first drink can't come early enough. If they were staying any longer, she'd be an alcoholic by the end of it. As the cold liquid passes through her chest and into her stomach she closes her eyes and leans back on the bed.

'God, I needed that. A bit of light relief.'

'I would have joined you down there but bloody David just banged on and on.'

'It wasn't much fun. I know you have to be reminded of these things, but sometimes I'd rather pretend the world is a pleasant, happy place.'

'Oh, no. Did it ruin your day?'

'No, no, it's fine.' She reaches across the gap between the beds and squeezes his hand, grateful that they are friends again.

'What was he after?'

'A fairly major wad to get the place up and running.'

'Can you afford it?'

'We, sweetcakes.' He looks at her pointedly. 'It's *we* now, or would you rather forget?'

'Forget what? Fnar.' His insecurity is touching.

'We can afford it. I mean there's plenty of money sloshing around.'

A moment's silence.

'Well, then?'

He blows his fringe. 'His business model seems sound. With all the trouble in the Middle East and North Africa there's a gap in the market for reasonably priced resorts in this area. I just don't know if I'd trust David in a business venture. He's too competitive. I think he'd make rash decisions to try and prove himself. But, well, it should be a joint decision. What do you think? It's a beautiful spot.'

'No, it's not.'

He raises his eyebrows.

'When I went round that prison and saw those *tiger cages*, people sloshing about in their own shit, dying, going mad . . . Even if you screened it off with trees or whatever, it would still be there in the back of your mind.'

'There's nothing wrong with making a decision based on principles, Ash, whatever the City thinks.'

'Yes, but I don't have to come here. It's only an investment. We just sit at home and wait for the cash to roll in, right?'

He smiles. 'Unless David blows it all on cigars.'

He's looking at her expectantly. Is it silly to make an important financial decision based on a gut reaction? Besides, it all happened in the past, and they'd be doing the locals a favour, creating jobs.

'Okay then, yes, if you want to, go for it.'

He carries on looking at her steadily.

She smiles and wrinkles her nose at him. 'Okay, no then. Tell him no.'

'Done.' He leans over and kisses her forehead, then knocks back his cocktail and gets up to order another.

Asha hopes David won't be too upset.

19

London

When the doorbell rings I ignore it – they can leave the flowers on the step with the others – and carry on staring at the flickering images on the TV.

It rings again, then a moment later there is a bang on the window. This makes me jump but I still don't have to get up. The shutters are pulled so they can't see me in here.

'Asha! It's me.'

Zainab.

'I know you're in there. If you don't answer I'm calling the police.'

With a sigh I get up from the sofa and pad down the hall.

'I'm fine. Please. I just want to be on my own.'

'Open the door.'

'Please, Zai. Just leave me alone.'

'Open the door.'

I weigh it up: the pain of speaking to her versus the pain of her making a huge fuss, then open the door.

'Shouldn't you be at work?'

She's dressed in sports gear and has a rucksack on her back.

'No crime at all in London today so they sent me home.'

As she barges past me I catch a glimpse of men with cameras gathered by the railing of the square.

Zainab goes to the kitchen and fills the kettle.

'Where's your coffee?'

163

'Cupboard above the hob.'

'Have you eaten?'

'I'm not hungry.'

She stops what she's doing and looks at me.

'You've lost, what, a stone?'

I shrug.

'Look, I don't know much about this but—'

'No, you don't.'

'But I know you're never going to feel better if you don't start taking care of yourself.'

'I don't want to feel better. Why should I feel good when Ollie's—' the sentence finishes in a wrenching sob.

Her tone softens. 'Would Ollie want you to make yourself ill?' She comes over and leads me to the armchair by the window, opening the shutters a crack to let in a shaft of dusty sunlight. A band of warmth falls across my legs. It's a nice sensation but brings with it another wash of guilt. I shouldn't be allowed to feel pleasure.

'Now, I'm going to make you some lunch, and you're going to rest.'

She takes a supermarket bag from her rucksack and begins to unload it onto the kitchen counter.

Despite myself I must find her presence soothing because I fall into a dreamless doze and wake to the smell of onions cooking. Suddenly I'm ravenously hungry. Until now I've been living on cream crackers, rice cakes and ice cream, but I polish off my omelette before she's even brought hers over to the table.

Miraculously, she was right. The calorie hit lifts my mood. I feel the tension drain from my shoulders and as I lean back in the chair the muscles in my chest give an audible creak. It's short-lived of course, because then there comes the inevitable:

'So, how are you?'

I take my plate to the kitchen and wash it in the sink.

'Fine.'

'Have the police been in touch?'

'The Vietnamese police? Why should they?'

'Because of that "other couple" thing.'

I told her about the hospital encounter when I got back to London.

'Look, I probably completely misunderstood him. Even if that's what he was trying to say, maybe they were innocent passers-by—'

'If they were they would have come forward.'

I sigh. 'Well anyway, he was probably making it all up to try and deflect attention from the boatman. I think they're related.'

'So you think the boat guy did it?'

'How should I know? I can't remember.'

'What, nothing at all?'

Whorls of dark coral in a blue sea.

'Nothing that's any fucking use.'

I put the plate and fork on the draining board and dry my hands on a tea towel that makes my skin smell musty. I've been putting the chain across so Maria can't let herself in and the house is deteriorating by the day. The urge to pour myself a glass of wine is strong, but it's only two o'clock so I reboil the kettle, watching the steam curl up to the plaster cornices.

'Are those reporters bothering you?'

'Not really. I only go out to the corner shop and if I wait until five they've usually gone.'

A pause. I don't want to know but I have to ask. 'What are they saying about it all?'

Zainab sighs. 'Pretty much what you'd expect.'

'That I did it? To get my hands on all that lovely money?'

'Not all of them.' She hesitates. 'I wasn't sure whether to show you, but this guy is a pretty well-respected journalist.'

She takes out the current affairs magazine and puts it down carefully on the table. In the byline is a picture of a considerably younger Travis Mulgrave.

'That fucking arsehole.' I thrust it back across the table. 'He was at the same resort. He's a total creep. Probably making out

I'm some depraved nympho who killed Ollie in a sex game.'

'Just read it.' With a curled lip I pick it up.

The headline of the article is *Another Forgotten Victim of the Far East Tourist Trade*. But the accompanying picture is not of Ollie, it's a shot of a wrinkled brown-skinned old man. It takes a moment, but then recognition dawns. Zaw Phyo. I skim the first paragraph.

They are used as cheap labour, fishing for scallops and lobsters to satiate the appetites of rich travellers, but when something goes wrong, as it did for honeymooning banker Oliver Graveney, there's no easier target for Vietnamese authorities desperate to preserve their hard-won reputation as the honeymoon destination of choice for the wealthy and in-the-know. Rather than accept that crimes might have been committed by locals the police here and in many other Far Eastern destinations prefer to lay the blame on the easiest target: Burmese migrants. I've seen for myself the precarious lives these people lead, watched as their daily wage is slashed for a minor misdemeanour, for which they have no redress as they are undocumented and lacking the most basic workers' rights.

The article goes on to list violent crimes against Westerners that have resulted in the conviction and sometimes execution of Burmese men, then it moves out to the broader picture. My attention wanders as he details the statistics and geopolitical influences, the machinations of big business and corrupt politicians with their fingers in the pies of hotel and land corporations. Then I get to the final paragraph.

But we mustn't forget the human story here. A man has been killed. A very wealthy man who, like all very wealthy men, will have made enemies along the way. Were there, among the hundreds made jobless by his brutally effective corporate style, those whose bitterness turned murderous? Victims of his hostile takeovers perhaps? The boards of BBKV, or Greenhill Brothers, let go when the market was at its most challenging? Could this be a hit?

We may never find out but the sad truth is, if we ever do, it will probably be too late for Zaw Phyo.

I close the magazine and breathe deeply.

'Ollie didn't have enemies,' I say finally. 'I would have known about them.'

'Maybe *he* didn't know about them.'

I stare at her as the silence stretches between us.

She stays for an hour or so then, once she's extracted a promise that I will cook one of the ready meals she's brought for me, says goodbye. Thankfully the reporters have packed up and gone so we can linger on the doorstep. The air is fresh with rain and the scent of rosemary. The gardeners are in the square again, always planting, whatever the season, so that we locals can pretend that every day is summer.

'Thanks for coming. It was really nice.'

I don't want to say more in case she feels obliged to make it a regular thing – looking after her bereaved friend. She looks tired, I realise. As much as she rolled her eyes about banker wankers, she liked Ollie. They made each other laugh. I think of the photo of her dancing with him, the twinge of regret that is almost jealousy, that I let someone else occupy his arms that night, when I should have held him tight and never let him go.

'Call me whenever, okay? Middle of the night, whatever, even if you just want to cry. Just remember, whatever you're feeling, it's perfectly natural. Sorry.' She presses her lips together. 'You already know that.'

I smile and nod, but what I'm experiencing isn't perfectly natural. Yes, I'm angry, like I was when Mum died, with the doctors who failed her, and the way she just stopped fighting, but these other feelings aren't normal. This creeping dread that something isn't right, that there's more to the story than a robbery gone wrong.

I want to go back inside, curl up in a ball on my bed, but Zainab is lingering on the doorstep.

'Listen, I've been umming and ahhing about showing this one to you.'

'What?'

She reaches into her bag and pulls out a rolled-up newspaper with the scarlet banner of a tabloid.

I take it. 'That's not your usual taste.'

'There's a piece with quotes supposedly from an *anonymous friend*. I just wanted you to know that it wasn't me and . . .' She tails off.

'. . . And what?'

'Well, just . . . be careful who you trust.'

With a sudden dart forwards she kisses me on the cheek, then turns and jogs down the steps.

I shiver at the sly wind snaking up from the road. Autumn is turning to winter already.

I thought I wanted to be alone, but when her head disappears behind the hedge and the birdsong resumes I feel bereft. And more than that: uneasy. I glance up and down the empty road before closing the door.

I take the newspaper straight to the bin in the kitchen. I don't need to read whatever sensationalist bullshit some former colleague's sold for a few grand, but the bag is overflowing, so I leave it on the counter.

Something has to be done about the state of the house. The place is starting to smell.

Maria weeps inconsolably for the first five minutes of our telephone conversation and I find myself offering clichéd words of comfort just to make her stop. When I tell her I'd like her to start coming in again she sounds relieved. Perhaps she thought I would let her go. Unable to face seeing her in person I say I have to go out but I'll leave the chain off and she can let herself in.

Half an hour before she's due to arrive I get dressed and leave the house. I sit in the square, on the bench under the cherry tree. I have lost so much weight that the bench slats press uncomfortably against my sit bones. On a last-minute impulse

I've brought the paper Zainab left. I'd like to know what this *friend* has been saying about me: it might help me identify them. Flipping through the pages I come to a grainy long-range photo of myself, standing at the kitchen window in my pyjamas, my hair a wild black halo, my eyes clearly dark-rimmed even at a distance. The headline reads FEARS FOR TRAGIC HONEYMOON BRIDE.

Well, at least they're not saying I did it.

A close friend who wished to remain anonymous told *The Sun* that they feared for Asha's health. 'She's talked about suicide, about not being able to go on without Ollie. She doesn't eat or sleep, hardly leaves the house.' Psychiatrist Keith Holder confirmed that the days and weeks following a sudden death are often the most dangerous for those left behind. 'Family and friends should keep a close eye on—'

I close the paper.

Could it be Sophie? I'm tempted to call and ask, but what if she says yes? Perhaps she did it for me, so that people would know I wasn't sitting at home rubbing my hands with glee. If so, I wish she hadn't. The story is intrusive and salacious and Victoria and Mackensie are bound to think it came from me.

Hurling the paper into the nearest bin I set off along the gravel path that skirts the perimeter of the square.

I'd hoped that sleep would give me a clearer perspective but I'm just as confused as I was last night: the missing photos, the bald man, mementos of a holiday Ollie never mentioned, the girl with dark hair.

Perhaps every early death leaves a mess like this. The discovery of secret relationships, of bad blood, things they never told you for fear of hurting you. I try to think what Ollie would discover about me if it had been the other way round.

I never went in for discussing past relationships with a new partner and I wonder if any of my exes would feel the need to attend my funeral. Gary, who I never found out was bisexual until we were about to move in together. Brady, who used to check my text messages. The usual grubby detritus of youthful affairs. Nothing that would give Ollie the sense of disquiet I'm feeling now.

Two things are bothering me and I'm not sure if they're related.

Firstly, it could be that the 'other couple' story was cooked up to try and make Zaw Phyo look innocent, but I have to consider the possibility that it might be true. If so, could Officer Linh be right about us having enemies?

The second thing is, was Ollie was being threatened at the wedding? I thought it was stress, he said he was angry, but in the church at least it looked like fear. What was he afraid of? Of me finding out something that might have made me reassess our relationship? Something about his past? Or – worse – his present?

The last sliver of sun sinks below the buildings opposite and the garden is plunged into shadow. I shiver and glance into the impenetrable gloom between the trees. Travis said it could be a hit. If so, is the hitman still out there? Was I just collateral damage, or a deliberate target?

I jump as my phone trills loudly. It's Maria telling me she's finished and will see me again at the weekend.

Suddenly I want to be at home, barricaded behind our triple-locked front door.

Letting myself out of the square I hurry across the road, too scared to look around in case someone is watching me. I scramble through the front gate and up the steps then have to stand for a few seconds, fumbling for the keys. Finally I'm in.

Maria has left the lights on and turned the heating up and crossing the threshold is like being enclosed in an embrace. The scent of Ollie has been woken by the warm air and I pause for a moment on the step, breathing him in. Then the hairs on the back of my neck rise.

Now that I'm home safe, I risk turning round and glancing up and down the street.

My heart stands still.

From the shadow of the plane tree that leans over the railing at the end of the square, someone is watching me.

A more dedicated reporter? He makes no move to approach or call out to me and there's no sign of a camera.

But when I blink he's gone. Gone or never there?

I go inside and shut the door, checking the locks three times before I'm satisfied I'm safe.

The kitchen is spotless. The fruit bowl is overflowing, there's a fresh loaf on the breadboard, and a vase of cheerful yellow flowers on the worktop, accompanied by a card signed by Maria and her elderly boyfriend, Jack.

I manage not to dissolve into tears.

Instead I sit down at the island and stare at my reflection in the black marble. It's only six but I want to go to bed. And I'm going to break my promise to Zainab. The less I eat the more tired I am, the longer I can sleep. If only I could sleep away the next few months or years and wake up healed, with just memories instead of this unbearable ache of loss.

Fears for tragic honeymoon bride . . .

Suddenly the thought of oblivion is very appealing. Clearly this 'friend' knew me better that I know myself. I trudge upstairs.

The door to Ollie's study is always kept shut, and the sight of it wide open makes me start, until I remember that Maria has been in. Now he's gone I suppose she thought she could finally tackle the room she'd always been banned from touching.

There's a strong smell of spray polish and I feel a twinge of regret that this part of Ollie is now gone for ever.

I walk in and turn in a slow circle. I'd forgotten we had furniture here; it was always covered up with tottering piles of papers. Maria's found some boxes and piled all the papers in.

I pick up one of the stapled documents from the first box. It's filled with endless rows of dense figures. There's no way of knowing what they relate to. How, in this modern world where

171

everything's on computer, did Ollie end up with all this? I want to get rid of it, but then again there might be some legal stuff here that impacts the will.

Is that how a gold-digger thinks?

I experience a sudden rush of anger, that the Graveneys have done this to me. Have made me think of myself as they think of me. Made me doubt my love for my husband. I loved Ollie. We got married for love, not money, and now that he's dead, this is my house. I don't care what happens to the money but I can't leave this place with all its memories.

Then a horrible thought strikes me. What if Ollie never had the chance to change his will? He probably had some complicated clause to protect it from inheritance tax, so maybe it won't be as simple as everything going straight to his wife. Maybe he'd arranged for his money to go to his parents.

Could they try and take the house away from me?

Jittery with panic I search through the boxes until I find the letterhead of our lawyer, then I pick up the landline.

When I tell his PA my name, her voice tightens a notch. 'Putting you through.'

'Asha. I'm so, so . . .'

I let the platitudes wash over me, not even bothering to murmur any of my own. He's not my friend, I don't owe him any consolation.

'I haven't been in touch because I wanted to wait until you felt ready to start going over things.'

'I just wanted to make sure that . . . that everything will be okay, Lewis.'

I sound like a child.

'That I won't lose my home.'

When he speaks again his voice is as smooth as chocolate. He must be used to reassuring hysterical widows or divorcees. 'It's a fairly protracted process. There are various protocols we need to make sure of before we start distributing assets to the beneficiaries.'

'Beneficiaries? Isn't it just me? I'm his wife.'

'Don't worry, it's just the process we have to follow. With an estate this size it may take longer, but if you're in any financial difficulty you must let me know straight away and we'll sort it out.'

'They can't take it away from me, can they, Lewis? The Graveneys?'

A pause. 'No. No parents, secret brothers and sisters, cousins, or anyone that comes out of the woodwork except where there's definite proof of paternity have any claim on the estate. You concentrate on yourself and let me worry about the nuts and bolts.'

'Thank you.'

'I'll see you tomorrow.'

Another pause, this time my end.

'At the funeral.'

'Oh. Yes.'

After the phonecall I sit and stare. Who'd have thought it would take such a short snatch of time for concern about my own material needs to overcome my sense of loss? The Graveneys were right about me. I wonder if Lewis will tell them about my call.

I must have been staring at the box for minutes before my eye finally registers the contents. Then I frown. The name on the glossy brochure seems familiar.

I take it from the top of the pile.

Greenhill Brothers.

Where have I heard that name before?

I begin flicking through the pages. It looks like a small fund. The portfolio seems pretty bog-standard to me, not that I know much about that sort of thing, but their growth stats are amazing. A neat little place on the up, the board members only in their thirties by the looks of them. All shiny-faced and grinning with excitement at the prospect of selling the company in a couple of years and being set up for life. Maybe Ollie was thinking of

173

buying it.

Then I remember where I've seen the name. In Travis's article. Right at the end when he talked about the idea of us being attacked by someone Ollie had upset in his professional life. Travis mentioned a hostile takeover. All the men on this board would have been let go, and when I glance at the dates it confirms that the brochure was produced just before the last big crash. They'd have found it very difficult to get jobs again in that market.

I'm about to turn the page when my fingers freeze.

I take the brochure to the window and frown at the picture of one of the senior fund managers.

Brown hair, bushy eyebrows, the face almost unrecognisably slimmer and framed in a neat brown beard.

It's David.

20

Mango Tree Resort, Con Son Island

Thursday 29 September

'It's gone.'

'What has?' Ollie looks up from the TV. He's been checking the financial markets.

'The necklace you gave me. I left it by the sink and it's not there. I wanted to wear it today.'

'Have you checked the cases?'

'Of course I have.' The response is snappier than it should be. Though she's only owned it a couple of days the necklace is important to her.

With a sigh he turns off the TV. 'I'll help you look.'

Over the next half hour they turn the bungalow over. There aren't many places it could have got to, the bungalow is so sparsely furnished.

'Did you wear it to the bar or swimming or something?'

'No.' She's on the verge of tears now.

'You didn't lend it to Sophie?'

'Christ, Ollie, I'm not an idiot. I'd have remembered that!'

'You were pretty pissed last night.'

'Not that pissed.'

They stand opposite one another, the bed between them.

'I left the window open last night,' he says. 'So I guess someone could have climbed in while we were at the bar.'

'You left the window open? All night?' She hadn't noticed because the blind was down. A chill crawls across her chin. 'Why would you do that?'

'To get some fresh air.'

'You had the fan. Oh my God, Ollie. Anything could have got in. Or anyone.'

'If it was a break-in, don't you think they'd have made more of a mess? Taken more stuff?'

'So where is it?'

'How should I know?' His voice is rising. 'It's your necklace, you tell me.'

Asha shrugs. 'What if it was the maid? She's the only one who has a key apart from us, right? She's here every day. She's probably pretty poor. We should talk to Bay.'

'Hey, hang on, you can't just go round accusing the staff. I'll get you another one.'

'I don't want another one. I want that one.'

He laughs. 'You sound like a spoiled brat.'

'Says the man who's so rich that it doesn't matter if *the staff* steal from him?'

Ollie sighs and turns away. He looks tired and even though he's the one being an arsehole, she feels guilty.

'Maybe it'll turn up.'

He waves a hand. 'It doesn't matter.'

This hurts more than anything. It was a special moment when he gave it to her; now it's as if those feelings never existed.

'It does matter.'

He turns back and when his eyes meet hers she can see the kindled spark of anger. It makes her heart quicken but she won't back down. If she sets up a pattern of being afraid to stand up to him, things will only get worse.

'What do you want me to do about it?' he says coldly.

'Speak to Bay. Get him to talk to the maid.'

'No. I'm not doing that. You can't just go around accusing people.'

'So, you're going to let her get away with it?'

'Asha.' He raises his palm as if warding her off. 'If you want to speak to Bay, you go and do it.'

Stalking out of the bedroom she lets herself out of the bungalow.

But a few paces from the terrace she stops, her feet buried deep in the already hot sand. She can't speak to Bay, not alone, after what she saw on the beach. The idea is mortifying and not a little frightening.

Then she hears the sound of a hoover coming from further up the beach. One of the bungalows is being cleaned.

She sets off in the direction of the sound.

The door of the bungalow is open and she can see Hao, not hoovering but using a machine to polish the wooden floorboards. This bungalow is normally unoccupied so perhaps she's preparing it for the arrival of new guests. Asha hopes so. It would be a relief to have a break from David and Sophie.

She knocks but the woman doesn't hear, so she steps inside and finally, as Hao turns to make a return sweep with the polisher, she sees her, straightens up and kills the power.

'Good morning,' Asha says loudly and slowly.

The woman just looks at her.

'I was wondering if you'd seen a necklace my husband bought for me. It's gone missing from our bungalow.'

No response.

'It's silver.'

The woman blinks.

'Besides us you're the only one who has a key.'

Nothing.

'Just give it back and we'll say no more about it.'

Silence.

'Can't you speak English?'

She's not moving a muscle; it's as if she switched her own power off with the machine's. It's so unbelievably rude. She's just waiting for Asha to give up and go. But she won't. Why should she?

'I know you can. You take our orders at breakfast.'

'I no see your necklace.'

Asha jumps and it takes a moment to collect herself.

'It's er . . . it's very important to me. If you find it I'll give you a reward. Money.'

'No see necklace.'

'A hundred dollars if you give it back.'

'No see necklace.'

'Please stop saying that. It's traditional Vietnamese. It's called a spirit lock—'

'I know what it's called.'

Ah, so now they're getting somewhere.

'I left it in the bathroom. Perhaps you moved it while you were cleaning.'

'You should not have it.'

Asha stares at her. 'What?'

'It is holy thing, not tourist trinket. Tell your husband.'

'Tell my *husband*?' She laughs sharply. 'He doesn't make decisions for me.'

'Perhaps he no look so unhappy if he make them.'

It happens without warning. Perhaps because of the stress, or the argument or the lack of sex, she just snaps. The slap rings out like a rifle shot. The small woman's head snaps round and it's then that Asha sees it, the flash of silver under the collar of her starched white shirt. With a cry of triumph she grasps it and yanks. The chain snaps and the pendant thuds onto the floor.

It's a spirit lock, but it's not her spirit lock.

Hao picks it up and looks down at the broken ends of the chain.

'I'm sorry,' Asha says stiffly. 'I've obviously made a mistake.'

But the lack of contrition in her tone must be obvious to Hao because when the older woman looks up her brown eyes finally have a spark. It is the spark of hatred.

'No, I no take your necklace. Perhaps the goddess take it back because you not deserve it. You think it okay to treat others like

178

this. As if we your slaves. As if we nothing. The goddess will teach you. It will be a hard lesson.'

Asha stares at her, remembering the round-cheeked woman smiling at her from the margins of the jungle when they first arrived. She gives an involuntary shiver.

'Are you threatening me?'

'I tell you the universe is watching. You will learn.'

Pocketing the broken amulet, the woman turns her back on Asha and starts up the polisher again. Asha stands for a moment, her lips parted, then she turns and runs back to the bungalow, wishing that she had listened to her husband. That she had never have come.

When she tells Ollie what happened, that she broke Hao's necklace by mistake, he is furious and actually throws a glass across the room to shatter on the coffee table. It's impossible now to ask for Hao to come and clear it up, so they do it together in strained silence. They don't speak for the rest of the day.

21

London and Hampshire

What do you wear to your husband's funeral?

Do I dress up, as a *celebration* of his life – in the iridescent blue dress I wore on our first anniversary, a feather in my hair? I think Ollie would have liked that. But then this will confirm to his parents that I'm just a brazen strumpet.

Drab, then? Head-to-toe black, no makeup, the picture of self-neglect and distress? Victoria will be disgusted by my lack of effort. Letting myself go when I should be keeping a stiff upper lip.

Classic widow's weeds? A smart black suit, a hat with a veil à la Jackie O?

Does the fact that I even care, that it's even occupying a square inch of my head space, mean that I didn't love him enough?

The hours tick by and soon it's too late for deliberation. I pull on a black cocktail dress, the barely-there black tights I reserve for job interviews, a suit jacket and flat black pumps. My hair is awful, patchy and lumpy where they shaved it for the operation, so I tie it up in a dark green headscarf, then apply a lick of brown lipstick before going down to meet the cab.

I've no idea how much it will cost to get all the way to Hampshire, I just booked it on Ollie's account, still trotting along happily like everything else, waiting for him to come home.

It's mid morning and the winter sun has warmed the cab's interior. I tug my skirt down as I slide across the leather seats, already regretting my choice as the cabbie glances at me in the rear-view mirror. We pull away so silently the outside world might be a film projected on the windows.

The heat, the burble of the radio and the smooth motion of the car is soporific and my depleted body yearns to sleep but my mind won't let it. It's like one of those fluffy worms on a string children run between their fingers, squirming and knotting, doubling back on itself, never getting anywhere, in and out of the same old questions, as if questions are the only thing it can bear.

After I found the brochure with David's picture I googled Greenhill Brothers. From Ollie's point of view the takeover was very successful, the shareholders were delighted, and with much more financial clout trading profits went from strength to strength. It was handled solely by the acquisitions side of Ollie's company, so he may never even have met David, let alone have made the connection between the young, ambitious banker and the bloated drunk we met at the resort.

Next I googled David.

His CV on LinkedIn was predictable enough. Radley then Cambridge, then the London Business School. Cut his teeth at J.P. Morgan, headhunted to the Man Group then poached by Greenhill. Made redundant after the takeover and then: nothing. Vague phrases about freelance consultancy. Words that could only mean professional death.

Was it just a coincidence their being at the resort, or did he come out to Vietnam to try and persuade Ollie to do the decent thing and help him out? The man whose career he had ruined?

And Ollie would have done – if I hadn't told him to say no.

How did that make him feel?

Is it remotely conceivable that he and Sophie were so incensed by Ollie's refusal that they followed us to the caves and smashed our brains in?

No. That's ridiculous. David isn't the violent type, and Sophie was so kind to me after it happened. She would have to be a psychopath. They both would.

I'd got so obsessed with the idea that I almost forgot to put the photograph of Ollie and the dark-haired girl in my bag. I'm going to ask Seb about it after the service. Did something happen in Albufeira and, if so, was it serious enough to end in blackmail?

Enough.

Resting my head against the seat back I try to empty my brain. I don't want to undermine Ollie's memory with these convoluted theories.

Halfway across the Hammersmith flyover I catch a glimpse of a broad colourless sky above the jumbled grey building blocks of the city. Who would choose to live in London? What were we thinking? Why didn't we move to some Dorset farmhouse, have babies and puppies and chickens? Ollie could have brewed artisan cider while I made cakes and jam and cheese and got bracelets of fat around my wrists. There would have been no time for holidays, no desire to lie on some foreign beach. We'd have tumbled gratefully into bed at the end of every noisy, chaotic day, smelling of hay and baby milk and fermenting apples.

Oh God, Ollie, why didn't we do it?

I slip the invitation from my shoulder bag. Gold-edged with embossed black lettering.

Oliver De Montfort Graveney
Beloved son
Gone from our sight, that is all

The tone is so placid, as if Ollie's death fitted into the natural order of things. I hate them then, for their calm acceptance when my grief is so raw.

The address of the church means nothing to me but maybe it has some Graveney significance. The scene of Ollie's baptism perhaps. Or did he light the candles there every Sunday as a boy, dressed in a long white robe and a ruff, scarlet with embarrassment?

182

The thought makes me smile. I wish I could have been there, smirking at him.

As we fly down the motorway I mouth the poem I plan to read, but falter at the last verse.

The stars are not wanted now: put out every one;
Pack up the moon and dismantle the sun.

My throat swells.

Pour away the ocean and sweep up the wood.
For nothing now can ever come to any good.

I don't think I can get through it. But if I don't, what will they think of me? Ollie's voice drifts to me from a long way away: *it doesn't matter what they think.*

But maybe it does, Ollie. Maybe if I don't display the appropriate level of grief they'll think I had something to do with your death. Maybe I'll go to prison. But then maybe that doesn't really matter. You've gone: the worst thing has happened to me. Compared to this everything will be easy.

Finally I sleep.

I wake to find we're parked directly outside the church. Mourners stream around us, peering through the blue-tinted windows as I gape and blink.

'No hurry, love,' the driver says. 'Whenever you're ready.'

I wait for them to pass through the wicket gate, but more arrive. Unrecognisable faces, some of them weeping, as if they've lost someone close to them, but I don't know these people, so how can they have meant anything to Ollie?

Milo comes out of the church to shake the mourners' hands.

A sobbing middle-aged woman, trim as a twenty-year-old, approaches and he folds her into an embrace. Then Liberty is there, smiling and hugging too, as if they are Ollie's brother and sister: his true family. When she pulls away she says something to Milo. He looks up and his eyes catch mine. There's a beat when the true animosity he feels for me is nakedly on view, then he smiles and raises a hand.

I get out of the car and smooth down my dress.

In the few moments it takes me to walk to the lych-gate Victoria Graveney has joined them on the porch, standing between them, her arm linked through Liberty's. Even as I watch, the fake smile she has plastered to her face to greet the mourners slides away.

We stare at each other. Someone pushes past me.

Victoria goes back into the church, then Milo and Liberty follow and the door closes. I'm alone out here. The cab engine starts and I turn to run back to the road and beg him to take me home. *I can't face this. I can't—*

Zainab is walking up the slope towards the church, dressed in a black suit of almost aggressive sharpness, her lips plum-dark, her kohl-rimmed eyes flashing like a warrior queen. I fall into her arms and sob. She allows me this indulgence for a minute or so, then pushes me away and holds my face with both her hands.

'Ollie loved you a million times more than any of this shit-shower. This is nothing, just a pantomime. He was yours, Ash. You had his heart and his soul. That's all that matters. Now, come on. You can do this.'

She kisses my cheek and then, as the soft, sad notes of the first hymn begin, we walk arm in arm up the path that leads to the church.

I grip her hand throughout the ordeal that follows. At one point my chest is shuddering as if some crazed animal is trying to burst out. I can't do the poem and nobody asks me to. The Graveneys have engaged Ollie's childhood friends and teachers and even one former girlfriend to eulogise for him, and whilst I recognise the portrait they're drawing, they've missed out the essence of him. I realise then that I have that on all of them. Zainab's right, I knew the deep-down heart of Ollie. He was an attentive son, a delightful nephew, a charming friend and colleague, but he reserved the real him for me. Those nights

184

when we whispered our secrets, our fears and our truths to one another: things we'd never told anyone else. The times we laughed ourselves sick while other people looked on, mystified. The soul-peace of knowing you'd found the other half of you.

I close my eyes and the tears flow like a river.

They mention my name once. A dry-eyed Mackensie stands up from the front pew before the last hymn and pronounces that, on behalf of Oliver's friends and family and his new wife Asha, they thank everyone for coming and invite us all to raise a glass to their darling son at the Eastbury Hotel.

Zainab's car is an ancient gold BMW, bought cheap at an auction. Its former owner, a Battersea drug dealer now serving twelve years, had ostentatious taste in accessories and as Zainab turns the ignition key the engine roars like its exhaust pipes have fallen off. An elderly woman passing us almost collapses with fright and I catch a glimpse in the rear-view mirror of disapproving scowls.

'If you'd picked up your bloody phone, I could have come down with you,' Zainab complains as we pull away.

'I turned it off,' I say. 'Didn't feel much like talking this morning. Sorry.' But I'm not sorry. I'm glad to have put the wind up the stiffs, with their perfectly appropriate condolences and immaculate funeral attire. It would have made Ollie laugh like a drain.

The hotel is grimly middle-class. We're the first to arrive and the maître d's attempts not to bat an eyelid when he sees us emerge from the gangsta wheels are almost amusing. He directs us down a corridor leading to a large, entirely characterless function room. There's a bar at the back and a buffet running down the right-hand side. It's heaving with platters of nasty-looking quiches and dried-out sausages. The sight and smell of them make me feel sick.

We walk past the girl with the tray of wine glasses and straight to the bar where Zainab purchases a bottle of Glenmorangie, then we retire to a corner with two tumblers and a bucketful of ice, and set about the serious business of getting off our faces.

So many people have come to mourn him, more than were in the church. They circle me and Zainab like vultures, hungry-eyed, their mealy-mouthed commiserations barely concealing what they really want to say. Their faces twitch, as if even they are not sure whether they can choke back the words. *Was it you was it you was it you?*

I thank them, unable to stop my lips quivering or fresh tears spilling down over my stiffening collar, and they go away satisfied.

When we get a moment to ourselves I tell Zainab about the photographs. The shot from Portugal and the supposedly corrupted ones I found on Ollie's computer, the strange bald man appearing in both sets. She's too pissed to offer anything constructive other than that *all men are bastards and pervs deep down*.

I can't complain though, I'm as drunk as she is. If Victoria comes over something will be said. Something bad.

She's talking to someone I don't recognise and as I watch they turn in my direction. The new person, an ancient woman in velvet and pearls, eyes me pityingly, while Victoria's expression twists into a grimacing smile. The old woman says something and Victoria visibly sighs, then takes her arm and begins shuffling towards us.

'No fucking way,' I mutter. 'I'm not your pet any more,' and excusing myself from Zainab – who's now too busy chatting up the waiter to notice – I start picking my way across the room to the toilets.

A bald man is talking to our lawyer, Lewis Downing. I stop.

Could it be the one in the photo? The man Ollie grabbed by the throat?

Feeling my attention Lewis Downing looks in my direction and nods. The bald man turns to follow his gaze. Our eyes meet for a second, then he turns back to the conversation.

It's not him.

I turn in a slow circle, scanning the other bald heads in

the room. The noise of conversation is becoming unbearable, a hollow booming in my ears like bombs exploding underwater. My head is spinning with too much alcohol on an empty stomach. I lose track of how many times I have revolved, whether I'm looking at men I've already scrutinised.

He's not here.

But Seb is. He's working the room like a pro, his smile serious, his eyebrows compassionately tilted, but unlike Milo, I get the feeling that his words will be genuine.

I needed to talk to him. What about?

The sun comes out, lancing through the windows, lighting an invisible path for the dust motes to dance along. Seb's hair glows gold, like Ollie's when he was on holiday.

Our holiday.

Their holiday.

Portugal.

As I set off across the room Lewis Downing excuses himself and goes through the double doors that lead into the hotel corridor. Does he want to speak to me?

A couple stands in my way and I push past, sensing their surprise, to the little group surrounding Seb.

'. . . always the best at everything. I bloody hated him.'

Ho ho ho, sigh.

The same 'perfect Ollie' routine I've been hearing various permutations of throughout the day.

'Can I talk to you?'

'Asha!' His grey eyes widen. 'Of course. Excuse me.'

With a gentle hand at my back he guides me through the crush of people, which miraculously parts for him, like Moses. There are sad smiles and nods, like a mini Mexican wave, but I'm not sure if they're for Seb, who mourns like a pro, or me.

The corridor is cool and dark and my head starts to clear.

'You look like you need to sit down. Let's go through to the lounge.'

This room is as bland as the function room, its faux-antique furniture just the wrong shade of wood, the pattern on the upholstery cheap and ugly.

We sit down opposite one another before the dead fire and Seb leans in earnestly. He thinks he's here to listen to me vent my grief, or perhaps discuss my latest theory of who attacked us. What he's clearly not expecting is this:

'I want you to tell me about Portugal.'

He blinks. 'What?'

'That holiday the three – no, four – of you took in 1998. Something happened. I want you to tell me what.'

His mouth opens. His lips are too full to be truly attractive. There's just too much loose pink flesh. His tongue creeps out to moisten them.

'Uh . . .'

'When they were reading the telegrams there was a post-card from Albufeira. I could tell from Milo's expression there was something wrong. Then I was looking through some old photographs and found this.' From my handbag I draw out the yellowed shot taken by the roadside.

Seb takes it, then covers his mouth with his hand, as if worried what he might let slip.

In the silence the carriage clock on the mantelpiece ticks.

'That's me,' he says finally, 'Milo, Ollie, some girl he was seeing and Freddie Lapozza.'

I exhale softly. 'Freddie Lapozza?' Of course, that was his name.

'Just a friend,' Seb says, his eyes sliding away from mine. 'At the time. We were all at school together.'

'You don't see him any more?'

'We drifted apart, you know how it is.'

I do, but he's lying.

'So why did Ollie have him up against a wall at the wedding?'

He sighs, shaking his head before I've even finished speaking. 'I don't know, Asha, I'm really sorry.' He tries to give me back the picture. 'I guess there are just some things we'll never kn—'

'If you can't tell me, Seb, I'm going to the police. It's totally out of character for Ollie to launch himself at someone, so there must have been something serious going on. Maybe this guy was involved in what happened in—'

'No!'

Silence rings in my ears.

'Don't go to the police. Please.'

'My husband was murdered. If what happened in Albufeira has any connection with what happened in Vietnam you need to tell me.'

'It doesn't, I swear.'

'How do you know?'

He closes his eyes and leans back in the chair.

It was a last blow-out before they started their jobs in the City that September. Three of them had something lined up. It was only Freddie who was struggling. Tutored all the way through school just to keep up, he managed to scrape a third. The others got firsts and seconds. This might not have been a problem – plenty of bright kids piss away their student years – but it didn't take long for interviewers to spot that Freddie wasn't one of the bright kids. For Ollie, Milo and Seb the holiday was a celebration. For Freddie it was just an interlude before another bout of exhausting, ego-sapping job hunting.

He was anxious, but not so anxious that they couldn't all enjoy themselves. They'd booked the villa for a month and from day one set about the serious business of partying.

They frequented all the clubs along the Strip, drinking until two or three in the morning, then carrying on at home with whatever drugs they could get their hands on. All of them except Ollie brought a different girl home every night (sometimes more than one).

Ollie started seeing a local waitress, but the relationship went sour. She wouldn't leave him alone. Hung around the clubs like the spectre at the feast, waiting for him to leave the group so she could get him alone and bleat that she loved him. At least that's what Seb guessed was going on. Unlike Milo, Ollie kept the more salacious details of his relationship to himself.

He started staying in to avoid her, drinking alone, moody and sullen, but on the last night of the holiday they persuaded him to come out for one last blast. They began with a few lines of coke in one of the Irish bars, then moved on to speed and spirits at their favourite sports bar. Milo had had his eye on one of the barmaids there ever since they first arrived but she'd been playing hard to get.

It was a windy night and Seb remembers the swirling dust getting into his eyes and throat as they moved from bar to bar, grit stinging his bare calves. At some point the party got separated. He can't remember how or why. He and Freddie went back to the villa around two in the morning expecting to find the others, but there was no sign of them, so they drank a bit more and fell asleep on the terrace.

The next morning they were awoken by the arrival of the police.

The barmaid at the sports bar had accused Milo of raping her. Milo said it was consensual but Seb could tell he was worried. What would happen if his new boss caught a whiff of the scandal? The City was just waking up to its endemic sexism. Harassment cases were big news.

At this point there was still no sign of Ollie, though they knew he was there because he kept throwing up in the toilet. Only after the police had left did he emerge, white and shivering with hangover, to find out what happened.

Immediately he took control, sitting Milo down and grilling him about the timescale and location and any witnesses to the alleged rape. Apparently there was no DNA evidence because the girl had been dragged into the sea, and no reliable witnesses as all the people in the bar were off their faces. All Milo needed was an alibi.

So they gave him one.

'I didn't really think about it at the time,' Seb said. 'The fact that we were covering up a crime. We were just helping out a mate.'

They went to the police station and gave sworn statements that Milo had accompanied them back to the villa at midnight, where they had all carried on drinking until around four in the morning, when they'd fallen asleep. Ollie told the police that earlier in the evening the same girl had threatened to cry rape against him unless he gave her money. He'd handed over five thousand escudo. Milo said she had pulled the same trick with him but he'd given her nothing.

'My God, Seb.'

'I know.' He looks at his hands, limp in his lap.

'What happened to her?'

There's a long silence.

'I think she was charged by the police with making a false allegation. She lost her job.' He looks up at me. 'Look, I'm not proud of what we did out there, but Albufeira had nothing to do with what happened to you. I'm sorry, Asha. I wish I could help.'

He hands back the picture.

'Is that her?' I point at the curly-haired young woman in the picture. 'The one who accused him.'

'No, she was Ollie's.' I wince at the expression. 'A local. The other one was English.'

The other one.

He runs a hand through his hair and I notice it's just beginning to grey at the temples. The golden boys are tarnishing.

As he starts to get up I speak quietly. 'Do you think he did it?'

'Did what?'

But before he can reply, the air in the room becomes unbreathable.

Milo is standing in the doorway. 'Asha, darling. Are you alright?'

The flesh of Seb's face seems to undulate and he looks for a moment like he's going to be sick.

'I just felt a bit faint,' I say. 'Seb was helping me. Actually, Seb, *could* you get me that water after all?'

'And maybe a bite of something,' Seb says, rising quickly. 'It might make you feel stronger.'

'Good plan,' Milo says. He moves aside to let Seb out of the room just a beat too late, making Seb wait, then fills the threshold again. I've always found his eyes disconcerting. They're too small and deeply set. You can't see the whites until you're standing very close to him.

'How are you getting along?'

I nod, and keep nodding, my mouth frozen into a smile. There was a time when I would have spoken up, railed at him, threatened him, but now I'm scared.

Milo raped someone.

His eyes bore into me and for a moment I wonder if he can read my mind.

Then, over his shoulder, I see Lewis Downing striding down the corridor towards the foyer.

'Excuse me,' I say, jumping up. 'I must catch my lawyer.'

'Really?' he says as he moves aside to let me pass, and something tells me that my haste will get straight back to the Graveneys.

Though I almost run down the corridor, by the time I get to the foyer there's no sign of him. I wait for a few moments, catching my breath, in case he's gone to the toilet or outside to make a call, but he doesn't come back, so I return to the function room. The crowd is thinning out. Zainab is staring moodily into her glass. She'll be spoiling for a fight so I should extricate her soon. Would it be a mistake to go now, to leave the Graveneys and Milo to conspire in my absence? But what can they do to me?

Steeling myself I approach Victoria and Mackensie and wait while they take their leave of a group of particularly obsequious mourners.

Then it's my turn.

'Asha.'

'Victoria. Mackensie.'

And then Milo is there too, with Liberty on his arm. She's holding a glass of what looks like iced water and I feel instantly vulnerable. I am drunk and they are sober. I must be careful.

'Going so soon?' Milo says.

'I'm not feeling well,' I say.

He looks at Mackensie.

'Well, in that case, you must go and rest,' Mackensie says. 'Have you seen a doctor?'

'No, but I may do. Perhaps for something to help me sleep.'

'And you don't look like you've been eating properly,' Liberty says sweetly.

'No, well, I don't feel like eating, and it's hard to sleep. As you must be finding too.' I nod to Victoria but her expression is stony.

'Sounds like depression,' Liberty says. 'You must be careful, darling. Maybe ask the doctor for antidepressants.'

'Of course I'm depressed.' I try to keep my tone even. 'Wouldn't you be?'

Liberty's eyes glitter.

'Of course,' Mackensie echoes.

'Well, thank you. The service was lovely. Ollie would have—' My voice breaks.

'Oh, Ollie would have loathed the whole damned circus,' Milo says.

'He was always so modest,' Liberty agrees.

'Always,' Victoria says. 'Even as a child . . .'

The conversation carries on without me so I move away, retrieve Zainab and make for the exit. Her waiter, Elvis, has agreed to drive the BMW back to London the following day for fifty quid, so we go outside and sit on the hotel steps, waiting for the account car. Zainab rests her head on my shoulder and we sway to the lullaby of the fountain in the middle of the drive.

By the time the car arrives, circling the fountain and pulling up in front of us, she's asleep and I have to haul her inside, clipping her into her seat belt as if she's a child.

As the countryside scrolls by I think about what Seb told me. Albufeira may have had nothing to do with what happened to us in Vietnam, but it has showed me two things. That Ollie was prepared to do something very bad to protect what he valued. And that Milo is more dangerous than I could possibly have imagined.

22

Mango Tree Resort, Con Son Island

Friday 30 September

'I'm sorry.'

She's sitting out on the terrace in sunglasses, gazing moodily at the sea. 'I want to go home.'

He kneels beside the bed and takes her hand. 'Don't say that.'

'This is shit, Ollie. I've had enough. Whatever needs to be sorted out between us we can sort out in London. It's just too depressing arguing here.'

'I know. I agree. And it's my fault.'

'Yes it is. We haven't had sex in weeks.'

'I know I haven't been myself.' He sighs, then inhales. Something . . . something happened, back in London.'

She straightens in her seat.

'Nothing for you to worry about, but it's been on my mind. It shouldn't have been. I should have let it go, dealt with it when we got back, but I couldn't. I'm sorry.'

She makes herself look at him, and the inevitable happens: her resolve wavers at the sight of his lovely anguish.

'What? What happened?' Her tone is hard but it can't hide the fact that she's melting.

'It was . . . money. To do with money.'

'The Hadsley-Kirkwood thing?'

'Yes. It fell through.'

'Oka-a-y. Deals fall through all the time though, right?'

'We lost a lot of money this time.'

'How much?'

'I don't know yet. I'm waiting to hear if the accountants can offset anything.'

'Are we going to lose the house?'

'No.' He gives a grim chuckle. 'It's not that bad. Don't worry, you won't be supporting me.'

She turns in the chair, swinging her legs over his head so he's sitting between her thighs, like a supplicant.

'Do you promise me that's all it is? That you haven't . . .' Her voice cracks. 'That you haven't met someone else.'

'Oh, Ash . . .' He takes her in his arms. 'My darling. You're the only person I could ever want in the whole world. I'm just so scared of losing you.'

'I don't give a fuck about the money, Ollie,' she sniffles into his shoulder. 'Even if you lost every penny. You do understand that, don't you?'

'I couldn't lose you, Ash. I couldn't survive it.'

'You're not going to, you fuckwit,' she murmurs. 'You're stuck with me – spoiled brat that I am.'

'Don't. Please. Don't remind me of anything I said. I wasn't—'

She kisses him to stop him talking. His response is immediate, hard and desperate. They fuck like animals there on the terrace. It's grunting, urgent, selfish and over within a couple of minutes. But as far as she's concerned it's the best lay she's ever had.

'So,' he says, over the mango porridge that has become his favourite. 'Your choice. Anything you like. I'll trek up a mountain, hike through the jungle. Crawl over burning coals. Whatever you fancy.'

His boyish grin is back. She reaches across the table and links her fingers into his. The sense of relief is overwhelming.

'Anything, as long as it doesn't involve you and David comparing biceps.'

'You're bored of admiring my masculine prowess?'

'No. Only David's.'

'Okay. Something without David and Sophie.'

'Shhhh.' They've just walked into the restaurant. Sophie looks more tired than ever but David is bouncing in his deck shoes.

'Morning, morning!'

Sean's behind them but Asha glances away so quickly it could look as if she hasn't seen him. The Peterses head for their usual table and Sean wanders over to the partition and gazes out across the sea.

'What about those caves?' she says. 'We could go the land route, through the jungle, or by boat. The boat's supposed to be prettier.'

'Great. Then maybe we can get the guy to take us on somewhere. There's that other resort up north a bit. I only didn't book it because it's bigger. It's another six-starrer. Probably a good restaurant.'

'Perfect.' She leans over and kisses him.

'I'll go and ask Bay about it. See you back at the bungalow.'

Changing into her bikini she thinks about what he said. She's always taken it for granted that they would be rich forever but of course, if the money's going to keep coming in, someone has to work for it. But why should it have to be Ollie? This Hadsley-Kirkwood thing has affected him far more than she would have expected. He's had enough, it's obvious. He's getting burned out. Maybe it's her turn to bring home the bacon. Go and work for some big tabloid, instead of the magazine. Ethics and incisive journalism are all very well but it's tales of shagging soap stars that make the big bucks. It wouldn't have to be forever, just until the babies came. But then again, maybe he should be the stay-at-home parent. He's the patient one, after all, affectionate and understanding. The stressed-out argumentativeness was totally out of character. Shame on her for not realising earlier that there was something seriously wrong.

Yes, when she gets back she'll look into a change of scene. It would be unethical to get Ollie involved – he knows some big newspaper names – but maybe she could call one of her contacts. Maybe even Mulgrave. Haha. Well, they did spend that intimate evening together.

Ollie comes into the bedroom. 'Sorted. You ready?'

She thinks about taking him to bed again, but the morning is too gorgeous to miss, so she wraps a sarong round her waist and follows him out into the brilliant sunshine.

As they head down to the shore she glances longingly at the sunbeds. The irony is that, after her trip to the prison, she could do with a day lounging on the beach, reading a book she actually enjoys. Plus, despite the fact that it's now late morning, there's still no one else here so they'd have the place – and the chrysalis sunbed – to themselves. For a moment she thinks of calling after Ollie's retreating back to tell him she wants to reschedule, but the boat is already puttering into the shallows and Ollie is raising his hand in greeting.

It's the same boatman Casper and Mulgrave used. Small and wrinkled, naked to the waist of his faded blue twill shorts. For some reason, though his pecs sag, and the skin of his arms hangs loose, he has a certain attractiveness. With his full head of dark hair and athleticism he's the type to be fathering children into his nineties. As he helps her aboard his vivid blue eyes shine from his face like sapphires.

Ollie climbs in after her and the narrow vessel rocks as he sits down, all pale, awkward, outsize Englishman. He reaches to shake the boatman's hand, introducing himself with his usual formality, which makes her squirm a bit.

'I'm Asha,' she says, enjoying the papery smoothness of the boatman's grasp.

'Zaw,' says the boatman, shaking and grinning.

Once the serious business of powering out of the bay is done, he slows the engine and pulls on a red sunhat as faded and threadbare as his shorts.

'I want a hat like that,' Ollie mutters.

'You can't buy authenticity. In fifty years your Vilebrequin one will look like that.'

He raises his eyebrows and takes off the white straw trilby that cost over two hundred pounds. Asha has always hated it.

'Swap,' he calls across to the boatman, gesturing to the red rag.

The man pouts and shakes his head. 'Sister's son. Gift. Many years.'

'Do you think he means the lobster boy?' Asha mutters but Ollie is now taking out his wallet.

He offers the boatman a 200,000-dong note. She ought to know how much this is worth but she doesn't.

Zaw shakes his head, eyes narrowed against the sun.

Ollie offers 500,000.

There's the ghost of a smile on the man's lips as he shakes his head once more.

Without taking his eyes off Zaw's face, Ollie tips his entire wallet onto the bench, slamming his hand over the notes before they're whipped away by the wind. He grins triumphantly. 'Gimme that hat!'

'Hahaha,' roars the boatman. 'You crazy English. More to life than money. That boy, he love me. I love him. Is good! No hat for crazy English!' He tugs it comically down over his eyes.

Ollie puts the money away, then reaches forward and shakes the man's brown hand.

'Love not money,' he says.

'Ah yes yes. Love no money!'

Their laughter is snatched away by the wind.

The headland comes parallel and then drops behind them. Asha remembers the figures that stood there watching them, and now she sees a glimpse of mud track leading away from the tip of land, presumably to join the road somewhere inland. Perhaps it wasn't so strange after all. They'd driven up, or walked, to look at the view and their attention just happened to be drawn to the resort. Perhaps they were looking out for celebrities.

Beyond the shelter of the headland the sea is darker and the wind blows cold from the open water.

A chime from her bag makes her frown, then she realises: it's her long-forgotten phone, just come into signal past the headland, as Mulgrave promised. A message from Zainab. **Are you shagging yet?**

She smiles and deletes it. Fortunately Ollie hasn't seen. He's looking back at the resort, now a straggle of doll's-house huts dwarfed by the jungle behind.

The beach is completely deserted.

23

London

I wake with the cry that has become habitual, not that it matters
now that there's no one beside me to jolt from sleep.

I dreamed I was drowning. Dark weed curled around my
face, green scuttling crabs trying to take bites out of my cheek.

Padding downstairs I make myself a strong coffee and drink
it by the window that overlooks the square. In the fragile dawn
light the shrubs are starting to turn from black to green.

Somehow the hours pass. I'm not sure I'll ever have a use
for them again. Maybe Liberty's right and I should get some
antidepressants. I turn on my phone and call the doctor. He
can fit me in at ten: an emergency appointment. His PA must
think I'm suicidal too.

When I end the call I find there's a text from Sophie.

**Hope it went well yesterday. We were both thinking of you.
Will try to call later. Lots of love xxxxxx**

I stare at it for a long time.

Since the attack she has been so supportive. But what if it
was all just to mask some darker motive? Yesterday's revelation
about Ollie demonstrated pretty clearly that people are capable
of more than you could ever imagine.

My mind is so preoccupied I almost miss my appointment.
The doctor is solicitous, calm, matter of fact as he prescribes a

short course of Prozac and some Diazepam to help me sleep. We discuss counselling options and he gives me the details of various charities and helplines. Finally he says I must try to eat properly, however poor my appetite, and take some light exercise: physical health will aid my emotional recovery.

To make some gesture towards following his advice, on the way home I let myself into the garden and walk the circuit of the path while I read the information in the packets of pills. It hasn't changed much since I last took them, after Mum died. I remember the sensation of tranquillity seeping down over my mind like syrup half an hour after popping the first Diazepam. But I also remember what it was like coming off them. Not just the physical symptoms – the anxiety, the shakes, the foul taste in my mouth – but the crushing realisation that I'd just put my grief on hold. That it had been a short hiatus, and now I had to pick up the process where I left off.

They're pointless. I throw them in the dog-shit bin.

The phone rings as I'm letting myself back into the house. Sophie. I try to keep the suspicion out of my voice.

She wants to come over.

I'm not sure I want her in the house but I do need to speak to her. About Greenhill Brothers. About David.

'Why don't I come to you? The doctor says I should take some exercise so the walk to the tube will do me good. What's your address?'

'Oh, come to my local café. I'll buy you lunch.'

'Can't I just come to yours? I've had photographers outside my house. I'd rather not give them an opportunity.'

She hesitates and then says, 'The café's quite dark at the back, no one will see you from the street. It would be good for you to be out and about.'

Too tired to argue, I write down the address and tell her I'll be there as soon as I can.

We live near a school – I've never been able to work out exactly where it is – and the children are out to play as I walk to the tube. I pause a moment to listen to their shouts and screams – they're like music – then move on.

Nobody pays me much attention. My hood hides my hair, which is surely my most distinguishing feature. With the toggles pulled tight, in boring jeans and ankle boots, I look like any other woman trudging the streets. Although perhaps I needn't worry. The road was clear of photographers this morning. They've moved onto a bigger story. Ollie and I are ancient history.

It's been such a long time since I took the tube and I almost wish I had popped a Diazepam before coming out. There are so many people, all of them moving at top speed in smooth flows that seem to be more akin to physics than human endeavour. I insert myself into one of the slipstreams and am carried down into the depths of the station. Even at this time the platform is crowded. As I lean against the grimy tiles, trying to catch my breath in the stuffy air, I sense I'm being watched and raise my head.

No eyes catch mine. Everyone has something more pressing to do than connect with their fellow humans. They stare at phones, nod to music, or just hide beneath hoodies. Did someone take my photo, I wonder, or just have a good stare at the woman who may or may not have murdered her husband? I'm glad then of the *friend* who said I was suicidal. I'll take pity over hatred.

The train roaring down the tunnel towards us makes my heart pound. I'm like an awed country mouse, in London for the first time. I join the throngs boarding and find a spot between backpacks and sweaty armpits.

It's a short journey but I'm relieved to emerge into natural light again. Even though the street is a main artery out of London, thanks to the rain the air is fresh and clean. I tilt my head back to let it cool my face, then set off in the direction Sophie told me.

My first emotion, as I spot her waving through the window, is anger. She has lied to me. This is not the secluded sanctuary she promised, it's a small, bright artisan café with large shared tables and a counter that faces the street.

I hesitate on the pavement, wondering whether to head straight back to the tube, but then she's coming to the door and opening her arms and I'm drawn by the force of social convention.

A blast of warm air that smells of fresh bread hits me as I open the door. One glance at the open MacBooks and foreign-language newspapers scattered around the communal table makes me unwind a notch. This is not the place for the tabloid-reading or gossip-hungry. I step over a folded Brompton bike owned by a bearded man in a tartan shirt and hug her.

She leads me to the back of the café, where there is indeed a more private ante-room looking out over a courtyard that would be nice in the summer, but the vintage wrought-iron furniture just looks shabby in the rain.

As soon as we sit down she gets up again to order me a latte, and I gaze through the streaked glass at a pigeon that has landed on one of the rusting tables. It gazes mournfully back.

Sophie returns with the drinks and two almond croissants. I take a small bite, for the sake of politeness, but there's something so comforting about the sweet paste filling my mouth, perhaps really doing something to my endorphins, that I finish the whole thing in a minute.

'Good?' she says, like a plump matron.

'Gorgeous, thank you.' Already the sugar is hitting my blood-stream, waking up my brain.

'They should be at that price. Now. The truth. How have you been?'

'Same as everyone who loses their husband, I suppose.' I'm proud of the lack of shake in my voice. If I'm not getting stronger, at least I'm getting better at hiding my weakness.

As she dips her head to sip her coffee I notice that the dark roots are longer. And the pink cashmere jumper she's wearing has moth holes.

'Have you heard from the police?'

'I'm not really expecting to. I guess if they need me for the trial they'll call me.'

She nods and silence falls. Now that our common ground has been dealt with, we have little to say to one another. I'm not sure how to bring up what I wanted to discuss.

'How's David?'

'Good, yes. He sends his love.'

'What's he up to? Back at work?' I've said it before I can stop myself.

'Yes,' she says breezily, pushing hair from her eyes. A raw patch of eczema runs down the side of her face. 'Have you seen Ollie's parents?'

'We talked at the f . . . funeral.'

Just when I thought I was starting to feel better, it's like the air has been punched from my chest. It takes me a moment to recover, though Sophie can't have noticed because next she says, 'And how's it all going with the will? When will that side of things be sorted out?'

'I'm not sure.'

'Listen.' She places her hand over mine. 'If you need any help at all, David's more than happy to look things over with you.'

'I have a lawyer.'

'You never know whether you can trust them, though, do you?'

'No, but . . .'

'If you got him through Ollie he might be working for the Graveneys too. Just be careful. Talk to David first.'

Her voice hollows as nausea floods over me. After so long in famine mode my body can't take the sudden hit of sugar. I stagger to my feet.

'Asha?'

'I'm sorry. I have to . . .'

'Darling—'

Ignoring her outstretched arm I stumble back through the café and out into the rain. As I ricochet down the pavement, people I bump into ask if I'm alright, but I pull away, the flood of nausea rising. Everyone's looking at me. I need to hide before I'm recognised. An alley opens up on my left. I stumble down it and throw up on some discarded fast-food cartons.

Afterwards I lean back against the damp wall, wondering if this time my beleaguered heart will give out for good. I had so many questions for her, but my body let me down. I must start taking better care of myself or I won't have the strength to find out the truth. If there's any truth to find.

I don't know how long I've been leaning there, my hair slowly filling with raindrops like the pearls on my wedding day, when I hear her voice. My first thought is that she's come to find me. I'm relieved. I want to be taken home, put to bed, plied with hot tea, have my hair stroked like my mother used to when I was small.

'No, she's definitely not coming back.'

I shrink into the shadows.

'Of course I tried,' Sophie goes on, 'but it's not the right time . . . Well can't you get them to wait a bit longer? A week, maybe two?'

She walks past the end of the alley but doesn't even glance in my direction.

'You're welcome to try yourself.'

She's moving away now, heading towards the seedier end of town, and I can no longer make out her words. Is she talking about me?

Legs shaking, I walk unsteadily to the top of the alley and follow her.

It's funny the assumptions we make. PLUs I called them, because of the way they spoke and dressed, their attitude, their mannerisms, but as I approach the terrace of run-down townhouses opposite the council estate, I realise that in one very important way Sophie and David are nothing like us.

They are not well off.

The tall houses are divided into flats, greying net curtains across the windows, the front gardens concreted over and strewn with rubbish and broken glass. The odd car parked along the street is a rusty Ford or Vauxhall.

As she walks down the road she seems to shrink and hunch. An overweight drudge returning from a poorly paid service job. Coming level with one of the houses she gets out her keys and glances up to the top floor. Is that where she lives? A top floor flat on this run-down street?

Then I step on a shard of glass and in the momentary silence between cars passing there is an audible plink.

She turns sharply.

For a moment we just stare at each other.

Her look of shock subsides into a sort of furtive horror, and then she plasters a sickly smile onto her face.

'Asha! Are you following me?'

'Is this where you live?'

She glances up at the flat, her eye catching on something at the window, then back at me. 'For now. David's between jobs. We sold our house to free up the equity for investments.'

'Like the hotel.'

'Yes.' She's still smiling.

We're ten or even twenty paces apart and I have to raise my voice as a car starts up nearby, but I have no desire to move closer to her.

'You said David would help me look after my money. Why would he do that?'

A beat of silence.

'Because we're friends. Aren't we? I thought we were.'

'You were kind to me in Vietnam. You did all that someone I'd just met could have done in a crisis, and more.'

Her eyes don't leave my face. A grubby wind lifts the hair at the side of her head, revealing the black roots.

'And now you still want to help me. Why?'

'Because we're friends.' Her voice is harder now, the smile gone.

The front door of the block opens and a man comes out. Scruffy and overweight in sweatpants and a t-shirt, two days' stubble shadowing his broad jaw.

'Hello, Asha. How are you?'

'Hello, David.' I keep looking at Sophie. 'You're not my friends. You were never Ollie's. And now you just want to keep me sweet so that I'll invest in your hotel because,' I pass my gaze up and down the shabby building, 'you're desperate.'

'We are not,' Sophie says. 'We're here because—'

I cut her off. 'Because David's *between jobs*? And has been since Greenhill was taken over? I know what desperate looks like, Sophie.'

'Oh yes, of course you do.' David's tone is bitter. 'You were lucky you got the clean end of the stick with Oliver Graveney. We got the shitty end, me and Sophie and hundreds of others.'

'I'm sorry about that, but—'

'But it's not your responsibility? You're enjoying the money though, money that was creamed off my company, aren't you? Dirty money. *Our* money.'

I open my mouth then close it again.

'It would be peanuts to you. A couple of mill. I bet you don't even know how much you're worth now, do you? You don't ask questions, you just live the life.'

'David—'

'Forty million at the last count.'

I swallow hard. 'But the Hadsley-Kirkwood deal falling through cost Ollie a fortune. He's going to have to make people redund—'

David gives a bitter laugh. 'Don't treat me like an idiot. I may be down and out but I can still afford the *FT*. Hadsley-Kirkwood went through fine. Ollie would have made a killing on it. And now it'll all come to you.'

I stare at him. Why would Ollie lie to me about a banking deal?

'We're not asking you to pour your money into some hare-brained scheme,' Sophie cries, the desperation in her voice now plain. 'It's not a lame duck. David's a genius. He'll make this work. You'll get your money back and more! Like we told Ollie!'

208

'And what did Ollie say?'

They stare at me. The rain has slicked Sophie's hair to her putty-coloured cheeks and drawn dark lines down David's sweatpants. How did they even afford the flights? Two weeks at Mango Tree just on the off-chance that we would come through?

'He said no, didn't he?'

'Because of *ghosts*!' David roars. 'Because your husband has the luxury to worry about stupid bullshit like an *atmosphere*! Lucky him! I've lost my house, my career, everything!'

I'm glad, for a moment, that Ollie didn't betray me, didn't tell David that it was me who said no, who said it was depressing, who was afraid of ghosts. David's face is bone white, his lip twisted in hatred.

'Jesus fucking Christ!' He kicks the green plastic wheelie bin, overturning it. Sophie cringes as rubbish flies everywhere.

'Get off my property!'

'David . . .' Sophie's voice is thin.

'I said,' he marches up to me, 'get off my property!'

Before I can react he grabs the hood of my jacket, twisting it in his fist, and throws me backwards. I stumble across the pavement, and then at the edge of the kerb I teeter into the road, just as a car is passing. The driver swerves, sounds his horn, slows for a moment, and then drives on, unwilling to get involved.

David stalks towards me, then Sophie is tugging at his arm. 'No, David! Come inside.'

I run then, back the way I've come, towards the lights and life of the main street.

On the way back to the tube I shiver under my damp clothes, my clavicles aching from the strain of being sick.

It seems like everyone wants a piece of Ollie, even now he's dead. Especially now he's dead.

Once he'd said no to investing, David and Sophie had so little to lose. They'd gambled their last few grand and lost. There was nothing to come home to.

Another couple, that was what the boy said.

I remember looking back towards the beach and seeing that it was empty. No Sean, no Americans, though they were often absent, and no David and Sophie.

This last fact is the most surprising. In hindsight they were always there, always waiting for the right moment to tap us, but as we left for the caves the beach was empty.

And I know now that David is more than capable of violence.

Under the shelter of the tube entrance I take out my phone, and call Zainab. To my relief she answers straight away.

'You okay?'

I turn to the tiled wall, holding the phone close to my mouth. 'I think I know who attacked us.'

24

London

I have to wait until 2 a.m. London time to make the call to Saigon. The contrast between the silence of my bedroom and the bustle of the Vietnamese police station is stark. It makes me feel more alone than ever.

Ke Quan will call me back, says a call handler stiffly, as if she's reading from an instruction sheet and has no idea what the words say.

An hour later nobody's called. The orange sky is lightening to milky grey.

I call again but before I do I google the name of the British ambassador to Hanoi and find a biography listing his wife's details. This has more of an effect on the call handler and about three seconds later the inspector comes on the line.

'Mrs Lever? How can I be of service?'

'Oh, hello, Mr Quan. This is Asha Graveney.'

A long silence, then, 'I was told a different name.'

'Oh, sorry, your colleague must have misunderstood me. The ambassador's wife is a friend, and she advised me to call you. I wanted to ask you something.'

Silence. He doesn't even have the courtesy to ask me what.

'Have you checked the alibis of the other couple staying at the resort, Sophie and David Peters?'

'No.'

More silence.

'I would like you to do this, please.'

'We have your attacker. We are not looking for anyone else in relation to the crime.'

'But—'

'I will call you if anything else comes up.'

He puts the phone down.

I'm so furious I can hardly breathe. I ring again, and this time the call is dropped as soon as I ask to be put through, so I just keep calling, again and again and again, until finally a man's voice answers.

'Mr Quan?'

'No. This is Officer Linh. Mr Quan is busy and thought I might be of service to you.'

'It was you who came to the hospital.'

'Yes, madam.'

'Do you remember,' my heart's beating faster, 'do you remember asking if I had any enemies?'

'Yes, madam.'

'Well, I think I do.'

In the silence that follows I can hear the low-frequency hiss of a million other conversations passing through the same lines.

'Please, go on.'

I tell him about the demise of Greenhill Brothers, about the way David lost his temper and had to be pulled off me.

'And didn't Zaw Phyo claim there was another couple at the caves?'

'This is very interesting,' he says.

'Will you interview them, check their alibis?'

'We have the correct suspect, Mrs Graveney. The motive was, as it usually is, money. The necklace is worth more than Zaw Phyo's monthly salary. Please concentrate on getting better and do not worry any more. This man will not get away with what he has done to you.'

He's about to get me off the phone. I search desperately for some way to convince him. And then I remember.

'But the necklace went missing *before* that trip.'

The line goes silent. 'Hello? Officer Linh?'

'What did you say?'

'My necklace, the spirit lock, it went missing before we took the boat trip. The one you found at the boatman's home couldn't have been mine unless it was planted there by someone else. Who told you it was mine?'

A pause, and then he says quietly, 'Mrs Peters identified the necklace. She said you showed it to her – a gift from your husband.'

My blood runs cold. 'What if she lied?'

Another silence. In the background I hear someone laughing, a burst of siren.

When Linh comes back on the line, his voice is quieter, less official. 'I have a contact in the Metropolitan Police. I will ask him to interview Mr and Mrs Peters and then liaise with me. I can check with the hotel and local CCTV footage, although I'm afraid we are less well served out here than you are in London.'

If he were standing in front of me I'd hug him. Instead I just thank him.

But after the call ends the sense of triumph seeps away. Do I seriously want it to have been David and Sophie who attacked us?

By the time I get to bed it's gone four and the birds are chittering in the square. I'm not expecting to sleep but miraculously, as soon as I climb under the bunched-up duvet, darkness slams across my mind like a security grille.

My dreams are heavy. Images converge and coalesce, evolving into something I think I understand before collapsing into randomness again. A coiled ammonite unravelling into the spinal column of a human foetus then back to a curled fern leaf. The pitter patter of rain that becomes the tapping of crab claws across a rock. The tapping gets louder, becoming a boom, and then an alarm clock shrieks through the silence, waking me. Groaning I grope around the bedside table, trying to thump it into quiet, then I realise it's not the alarm clock. It's the front door.

By the time I get downstairs I'm expecting my visitor to have given up and gone away, but there's a figure behind the glass.

A reporter?

I keep to the shadows by the stairs.

'Asha? It's Lewis. Lewis Downing. Are you there?'

'Yes.' I pat down my hair and hurry to the door and open it. This is my chance to find out why our lawyer was avoiding me at the funeral.

He looks pale and slightly sweaty, although that might be the moisture in the air. The atmosphere outside is oppressive. The remaining leaves on the trees in the square cling limply to the naked branches. The ones that have fallen are black and rotten.

'Hi.'

'I hope you don't mind my calling in person. There was something I wanted to talk to you about that I'd rather not discuss over the phone . . .'

'Of course. Come in.' I open the door wider, with a rush of relief that Maria's been. 'Go on through.' By the time I've closed it and joined him in the dining room he's already unloading papers from his bag.

'It seems like a lot but I've marked the bits you need to sign.' He doesn't look up as I sit down at the table and pick up the first wedge of papers. As I turn to the page marked by a fluorescent sticky he passes me a pen and I place it on the line where he has scrawled an X.

As I do so I become aware that he's stopped moving. His warm breath travels across the table to my hands.

I raise my head. 'What are they?'

'Legal stuff. To allow us to access the estate. Could I have a glass of water?'

'Sure, help yourself.'

While he's in the kitchen I flick through the pages of dense prose, most of it incomprehensible. 'I guess I ought to read it.'

He comes back to the table, and puts the glass down, the water already drunk. 'It's not necessary.' He slides a second document across. They're stacking up.

'What happens if I don't?'

'My recommendation would be just to sign them.'

I pick up the pen again. Then I hesitate. 'No, I'm sorry, I really need to read them.'

'Really, Asha, I must advise you, as your legal representative . . .'

His eyes slide away from mine.

'Why were you avoiding me at the funeral?'

He doesn't reply, doesn't even seem to be preparing the words. The silence expands. Then I hear the buzz of a phone set to vibrate.

'Excuse me.'

He takes the call but doesn't say hello, just listens for a moment before replying with a single yes.

When the call ends he stands opposite me, as if waiting for something to happen.

Then it does.

There's the rattle of a key in the front door. With a sob I leap up from my chair and run out to the hall in time to see the door swing open. *Ollie.*

A broad figure is silhouetted against the daylight.

Of course. Milo has our spare key.

He comes into the hall, followed by Mackensie and Victoria, and closes the door. We stand, a frozen tableau in the gloom.

'What are you doing here?'

'We're just here to support you,' Milo says gently. 'To help you make the right decision.'

'What decision? What are you talking about?'

I back into the dining room where Lewis is waiting with the papers.

'What is this, Lewis? What the hell's going on?'

The Graveneys come in and stand on the other side of the table. Milo comes very close to me and snakes an arm across my shoulder.

215

'You poor thing. It's been so tough for you and I know this is all you need. That's why we're here, so you don't have to face things alone. Let other people take some of the burden.'

Lewis's left eye flickers.

I shake Milo off and address the lawyer. 'Please tell me what's going on. What are these papers for?'

Lewis holds his breath a moment, then appears to make a decision. 'It's power of attorney to allow for control of the estate to pass to Mr and Mrs Graveney,' he says. Victoria's head snaps round and she fixes him with a malevolent stare.

'You've been behaving so erratically, Asha,' Mackensie says eventually. 'We don't want you to make any poor financial decisions.'

'I haven't been behaving erratically.'

'You're depressed,' Milo says. 'You admitted it yourself. You've been taking antidepressants.'

'I . . . I got some from the doctor but I threw them away. I never took them.'

'So you say,' murmurs Victoria.

'You've been telling your friends you're suicidal.'

'I never told anyone. Papers make up any old rubbish.'

'It's not the first time. Ollie said you were on pills when your mother died. It's clearly a predisposition.'

'I . . . But . . .' I pause, take a breath. 'You know what? Just get out of my house.'

'We will as soon as you sign the papers.'

'Fuck the papers.'

Victoria gives a little whimper. 'You see, Lewis? Unstable.'

'Either you sign them, my girl, or we go to court,' Mackensie says. 'They'll agree you're not mentally fit.'

'No they won't,' I say with false confidence. 'Grief isn't mental illness.'

He glances at Milo. *Round three.*

'Other people can speak to reporters too, you know,' Milo says. He hasn't moved from the end of the table. Not a single dark, oily hair is out of place. '*Cui bono*, Asha?'

'What?'

'Who benefits?'

'I know what it fucking means.'

'Well, it's you, darling, isn't it? You're the one who had most to gain from Ollie's death. And if even his family thinks you did it, well . . .'

Victoria and Mackensie are watching me, and though their mouths are straight lines, a smile flickers behind Victoria's eyes.

Tremors run down from my neck, through my chest, and loosen my bladder.

'You know full well I had nothing to do with what happened to us.'

'Do we?' Victoria says.

'Do you really think I could overpower Ollie? If anything it would be the other way round.'

Now she gasps. 'You're accusing *Ollie* of attacking you?'

'Scum,' Mackensie says, then – quietly – 'always were, always will be. Ollie would have come to his senses sooner or later.'

My breath doesn't seem to be filling my lungs properly. I'm starting to hyperventilate.

'Sign the papers,' Milo says. 'And we can be out of each other's hair for ever.'

'Go fuck yourself, Milo. And the rest of you.'

'I think it might be time to call the police, Mackensie. She's becoming aggressive.'

And then Lewis is between us. 'Enough.'

From the corner of my eye I see the cooker clock flick to the hour. The numbers tremble in my vision. Everyone's attention is on Milo, waiting to see what he will do. I remember then what he did in Portugal. Why did you lie for him, Ollie? You helped make this monster who thinks he's entitled to get whatever he wants, by any means.

I can feel the heat coming off Lewis in waves. He's afraid of this man, and yet he stares him out now, a vein in his neck pulsing.

217

'I won't have anything more to do with this,' the lawyer says, his voice thin. 'Asha, read those papers thoroughly before you even think about signing them. I'll leave them with her, but that's all I'm prepared to do.'

'Lewis, don't go!' I can't stop myself. I'm terrified of these people. I don't know what they're capable of.

'We're all going,' Lewis says. 'Aren't we?'

It's Milo who moves first, stepping back and smiling benevolently.

'Do the right thing, Asha. The money doesn't belong to you. Ollie earned it, it should be divided equally between the people he cared about.'

'It should be given back!' Victoria says shrilly.

'It was never yours to begin with,' Lewis says. 'Ollie earned it through his own efforts.'

'Don't forget who pays your fucking salary,' Mackensie snarls.

'I have many clients,' Lewis says evenly. 'Though of course I'd be sorry to lose you.'

He gestures towards the door and after a beat they take his cue, moving around the table and out into the hall. As he passes me, at the back of the line, I see he's shaking.

'Thank you,' I whisper, but he doesn't reply. His white face is fixed forward.

A moment later the front door slams and is followed by the angry roar of Milo's Range Rover. It snarls up the road and around the corner, followed by another vehicle, presumably Lewis's. The whine of the receding engines is finally replaced by birdsong.

They're gone.

I sink down into a chair.

For the next hour I'm in shock, chaining cigarettes at the kitchen table. How could you have left me alone like this, Ollie? At the mercy of those monsters? What if they take me to court? Will I have to try and prove my sanity to a judge?

Fuck fuck fuck.

A rattle of thunder outside makes me upend the mug I've been using as an ashtray and filthy liquid bobbing with orange butts spills across the table. As I'm clearing it up, to the comforting patter of rain against the window, my phone rings.

Automatically I go to answer it but then I see the caller.

Milo.

Holding the phone at arm's length from my body I wait for it to go to voicemail, then wait again while the message comes through.

'Asha, sweetheart. I am so sorry. We all are. It got completely out of hand and things were said that nobody meant. I guess we're all still stressed and upset. I'd like to apologise properly.'

He's coming back.

'We'll be able to talk better without Vic and Mack there. Vic's a nightmare sometimes, isn't she? But we've all been friends for years: you and me and Ols. I'd hate for us to fall ou—'

I delete the message and hurl the phone into the tote bag hanging on the chair.

He's coming back. I need to get out. But what if he lets himself in with his key while I'm away and starts snooping through the house, or worse, plants something that will make people think I'm crazy? Or even that I killed Ollie?

A bulky black car passes the kitchen window and I freeze.

It carries on to the corner and I can move again. The next few minutes are a blur. Grabbing the bag I run to the front door, deadlock and chain it then set the alarm, before scrambling down the stairs to the basement. I'm sure Milo doesn't have a key for the basement door. This is where Ollie keeps – kept – all his tech equipment so the door is sturdy enough that he won't be able to shoulder-barge his way in. I let myself out and stand in the rain, double- and triple-checking the locks before finally scrabbling up the basement steps, slipping on the wet metal, expecting at any moment to see Milo's dark head come into view. But the garden is empty and no rumble of Range Rover disturbs the patter of rain on the pavement. After peering around the hedge I dart out into the street. It's empty. The few pedestrians hurry by with their heads bent against the rain.

I take the long way, round the other side of the square, keeping to the shadows of the dripping trees. There is no silent watcher tonight. Was it Milo all along?

I'll go to Zainab's. She'll put me up for the night. And maybe she's found something out. When we last spoke she didn't seem very convinced by my David and Sophie suspicions, but she was interested when I mentioned the rape. She said she'd do some digging. If I can find something to use against Milo, something that might put the Graveneys off him . . . With him out of the picture I might be able to handle them alone.

Zainab doesn't answer her phone, and the disappointment is enough to punch the wind out of me. I realise then that in losing Ollie I've lost everyone. I have no family and all our friends were his, his and Milo's: their loyalties will lie with him now. In that relentless march up the career ladder I left people behind on every rung. My Islington friends fell by the wayside well before that. Sophie and David were never more than graspers. There's only Zainab left.

And Sean. The only person who can truly understand what I'm going through.

My departure from Vietnam was so hurried I never got his number but I know he manages a bar in the city, near Tower Hill. It shouldn't be too hard to find.

The impetus to *do* something is bracing. My heart pounds as I stride through the rain, but for once it's just adrenaline, not fear or grief. I tip my head back and let the water stream down my face. My body needs this. I've neglected it so long.

The lights from the tube station are a welcoming beacon in the rain. Behind it the setting sun has turned the sky the colour of roses. I duck my head and make for the barriers. I'm lucky, it must be rush hour and the commuters crushing through the gates take no interest in me.

I end up in the only free millimetre of space on the platform, wedged between two overweight Asian girls just behind the yellow line.

The atmosphere is tense. There's jostling and complaints, requests to move up with their unspoken postscripts, *you idiot.*

It's a relief when the approaching train's glare fills the tunnel. People surge forward and suddenly I'm over the yellow line. The pressure wave of air is followed by a hot blast of exhaust fumes and now the train is close enough for me to make out the driver. I register brief surprise that it's a woman.

And then someone pushes me.

I stumble forward with outstretched arms, as if that will somehow save me. The train's a third of the way along the platform, still travelling so fast.

There's a shrill scream. Is it mine?

A black coffin opens up below me, the live rail indistinguishable from the others, but all directly where I will fall before the train hacks me to pieces.

Ollie.

Mum.

The train's brakes scream. The driver's eyes bulge in horror.

Then I'm being hauled back into a cushion of people. I clutch the woman next to me as the train roars to a halt. There is a moment's stillness, and then the doors rumble open, as if nothing has happened. The disgorging passengers grumble as they push past me and my saviour.

'Are you alright?'

Now the people on the platform stream around us into the brightly lit carriage.

'Yes, yes, I'm fine.'

'Are you sure?' She's in a hurry. The platform is emptying rapidly. Soon the doors will close.

'Yes, yes. Thank you. You saved my life.' I laugh, as if it's funny.

The door alarm sounds and we stumble onto the train. We

separate then, and I find a spot in the open section, clinging to the red bar above my head.

I could have been killed. This fucking city. These fucking people in such a hurry to get back to their poky little flats to stare at their crappy soaps almost killed me. And whatever the Graveneys think – or pretend to – I'm not ready to die. Not just yet.

The doors close.

On the other side of the glass the platform is slowly emptying. At the back of the queue of people shuffling towards the stairs is a man dressed in black, a hood pulled low over his face. Unlike the others, who stare straight ahead, he's looking at a poster on the wall. But as he moves forward he doesn't turn his head back to the poster. It's as if all he wants to do is face away from the train.

As we move away I start pushing my way down the carriage, my eyes fixed on his head, waiting for it to turn, or for the hood to go down and reveal – what? The bald head of Freddie Lapozza? David's square jowls? Isn't this man a little slimmer than either? Impossible to tell from this distance.

But he doesn't turn, and as we hurtle into the tunnel, all I can see is my own scared reflection.

25

London

I get out at Tower Hill and for a moment the view takes my breath away. The Square Mile lost its charm for me the more jaded I became with Ollie's work functions, but now it brings back memories of all those first dates: stumbling around in a glow of love, oblivious to the drunks falling out of the bars, sharing kebabs, throwing coins into the river for wishes. We thought nothing could touch us.

My nerves are still on edge so I pause for a cigarette on a bench on the hill. It's the last one of the pack of twenty I bought the day before yesterday. Ollie would be disappointed in me. I smoke it watching the traffic stream across the bridge. Only the red lights of the cars break the monotonous grey of the drizzle.

Was the shove on the tube platform a deliberate attempt to kill me, or just an accident? Did the guy hide his face because he was so embarrassed that in his haste he'd almost knocked me in front of a train? Or was it a *hit*?

.That's the word Travis Mulgrave used.

For the first time I think about the electrical cable in the pool of our bungalow. Surely the resort was too slick to have allowed that sort of poor maintenance. What if someone cut it? Then there was the open well at the prison: I'd have broken my neck if Sophie hadn't pulled me back.

Was somebody trying to kill us from the moment we arrived? If so, surely that discounts opportunistic robbery?

The Peterses were there all along and had the opportunity. But Sophie pulled me back. Plus, at that point Ollie hadn't said no to the investment.

None of it makes sense to me. Perhaps my injured brain just isn't working properly any more. I tip my head back and let the rain cool my eyelids.

As rush hour passes, the flow of commuters coming out of the station becomes a trickle and for a moment I'm alone up here. My heart starts to beat faster. In the corner of my vision the old Roman Wall is a slab of shadow, and I can't shake the feeling there's someone behind it, watching me.

Then a group of people tumble out of the station, laughing and shouting. Getting up from the bench I tag along behind them and we head down into the dark maze of the City.

Sean said his bar was near Tower Hill, so with Fenchurch Street to the west, Whitechapel to the east and the river at my back there are only a handful of streets I need to cover. But each of them contains two or three bars so this could still take all night.

I begin with one of the first places Ollie and I ever went together. Hollowed out of the arches under The Minories, the bar is dark as a crypt and smells of spilled beer. God, I could do with a beer. I could do with getting quietly lost in one of these booths, having to be poured into a taxi home by barmen who've seen it all before. But what would I find when I got there? Milo waiting for me: my drunkenness just more evidence of my unstable state of mind.

I ask for Sean at the bar, and after the shaking of heads I leave.

As the evening segues to night I try bar after bar, getting wetter and colder and more exhausted. My trainers squelch at every step and the eyes of the bar staff become more concerned. I can feel my thoughts starting to slacken. Perhaps I should eat something.

My hopes lift as I draw near to Ollie's office on Fenchurch Street, but while some of the people in these places recognise me and make stiff conversation – their customers must have recounted the lurid details of our case – none of them knows Sean.

I trudge north and for a while there's nothing but darkened office blocks and closed shops, rough sleepers foetal in doorways.

We're too far from Tower Hill now, I suspect, as I push open the heavy door of The Gavel. This far east would surely count as Aldgate, so I must have missed somewhere. But as I enter the warm fug of beer and body odour I decide to have a break. A bowl of chips and a pint of something sugary to give me energy for the disappointed slog back to the tube.

It's crowded, but as I stand by the door a group gets up from a booth at the back and, the first to spot the few inches of space, I slide in.

Taking off my jacket I lean back against the wood. The bar is so busy I might just rest my eyes before I fight my way to the front to order. The noise is a wave breaking over me, submerging me. I go under.

Dark weeds in a blue sea.

The pitter patter of rain.

Ollie looking down at a fossil – no, a tiny baby curled in his palm. Its black eyes open. There are whorls in the centre, spiralling like a galaxy.

I jerk awake to the sound of laughter and for a moment imagine I'm back at one of Ollie's work dos, sandwiched between traders and fund managers talking over my head about money.

Then I realise I don't know the men sharing the booth with me.

There are three of them seated, plus one standing at the head of the table, blocking my view of the rest of the bar. They're drunk. I can smell it on them, see it in the lazy way their eyes follow the conversation. On the table are many glasses. How long have I been here?

'Ah, she wakes!' cries the one sitting beside me. His features display the bland handsomeness of privileged English boys, but his hair is coarse as pig bristle.

'You don't mind bunking up with us, do you?'

225

'Excuse me.'

'Why, what have you done?'

I stand, but instead of shuffling out of the booth to let me pass, he just leans back against the cushion, legs spread, so that I'll have to clamber over his crotch to get out.

Once I would have done something. Slapped him, stamped on his foot, called him a prick; now I just duck my head, grip the edge of the table and try to pick my way over. He lifts his knee deliberately so that my foot can't clear it and as I fall forward, throwing out my arm instinctively, he catches it and places my hand on his crotch. Immediately I feel the flabby bunch of gristle start to firm. His friends laugh.

'I know it isn't as big as a black one,' he says. 'But I've had no complaints.'

'Like fuck you haven't, Barney!'

More laughter, as if all that's happening is a bit of pleasant banter. I try to pull my hand away but his grip on my wrist tightens. Our eyes meet. There's a glint of cruel pleasure in his.

A little spark of the old fire returns and I squeeze with all my strength. He gives a scream and pushes me away with such force I tumble over the edge of the table and land on my back on the floor. A cheer goes up from the rest of the bar.

There are no women here.

No one attempts to help me up, they just stand over me like giants, their faces stony.

'Fucking bitch,' Barney snarls.

One of them nudges me with his foot. The man who was standing at the end of the table takes a mouthful of his drink and then spits on me.

It happens so quickly. One moment he's laughing, lager drooling down his chin, the next he's pirouetting across the bar to slam into the edge of another booth. He folds in two like a flatpack table, blood like a bright paint splat in the centre of his face.

The bar goes quiet. And then conversation resumes as if nothing's happened.

226

A hand reaches down and hauls me to my feet.

I stare.

'Sean?'

He doesn't smile. 'Are you alright?'

'I'm fine.'

He turns, the tendons connecting his neck to his shoulder bulging. 'I think you lot owe this lady an apology.'

Barney is standing up, oblivious to the groans of his bloodied friend trying to pull himself up on a table.

'Sorry, mate, we were out of order. Too much sherbert at lunch and—'

'I'm not your mate and it's not me you should be apologising to.'

'I'm sorry. We all are, aren't we, boys?'

And the men do look, suddenly, like plump schoolboys who have scrumped apples from the headmaster's garden. This is why they're so dangerous. They think they mean no harm.

'We'll pay for any dry cleaning.'

'*Dry cleaning?* Asha, do you want to have this lot arrested for sexual assault?'

Barney pales. I pause just long enough to make him suffer.

'No. Just fuck off.'

They do, rapidly crossing the bar and thrusting open the door to disappear into the night. I catch a glimpse of lamplights glinting in puddles.

Sean's chest is rising and falling rapidly under his t-shirt and his cheeks are flushed with the adrenaline of the fight. I feel my own cheeks reddening. I'm not tired any more.

'Wow,' he says finally. 'It's so good to see you. How did you find me?'

'I . . . I just went looking. Sorry.'

'No, no, I'm glad. Let me get you a drink.'

I ask him for wine and crisps and when he brings them he slides into the booth opposite me. Briefly his knee touches mine, then he moves it away.

'So, how have you been?'

227

'Pretty shit actually.'

'It's early days.'

'Yeah.' Feeling the prick of tears I lower my gaze and sip my drink.

'Once the trial's over and everything's done and dusted, you can start rebuilding.'

'What if I don't want to rebuild?'

'I said it's early days.' His eyes are soft. I've missed him. I remember how comfortable I felt in his company in Vietnam, how refreshing it was to be with someone I could relate to again after years of bankers. But perhaps that connection is just shared loss.

With a jolt I realise I've been looking into his eyes too long.

'Anyway, I don't know if the trial's going to resolve anything,' I say quickly. 'I'm not sure Zaw Phyo's guilty.'

His eyes widen. 'Seriously?'

I tell him about the boy who came to the hospital claiming there was another couple at the caves, my fears about Sophie and David.

Sean shakes his head. 'You know that's all bullshit, right? He's just saying that to get his uncle off the hook.'

'Probably.' Under his direct gaze I'm embarrassed at my gullibility.

'And Sophie and David?' He blows out his breath. 'They're wankers but I'm not sure they're murderers.'

'Yeah, I suppose.' It all sounds so outlandish now. Perhaps I've just needed someone to ground me.

I open the crisps. As soon as the salt touches my tongue my appetite surges and I devour them greedily. My body seems to have woken up in his company.

I tell him about the Graveneys' attempts to make me sign away Ollie's estate. The vehemence of his reaction surprises me. He slams his pint down, slopping beer over the table.

'Those fucking lowlifes.'

'I know—'

'They can't do that, can they? Just leave you with nothing? You need to get a lawyer. You're his fucking wife!'

This concern for my wellbeing takes my breath away and suddenly I burst into tears.

'I'm sorry,' he says. 'I should keep my mouth shut. It's nothing to do with me.'

I reach across the table and close my fingers round his tense fist.

'No, it's nice. To feel that somebody cares. I've got no one left, Sean.'

He places his other hand over mine but doesn't look up to catch my eye. 'You've got me.'

'We hardly know each other.'

'What happened in Vietnam. We'll never forget that. And besides,' now he does look up, 'when you meet someone you have a connection with . . .'

Our eyes lock for a moment, then I draw my hand away.

'Sorry,' he says.

I open my mouth then close it again, confused by the feelings coursing through me. Am I mistaking desire for gratitude? I need to be careful that I don't start something I can't get out of. Better to have a friend than a bitter ex-lover.

'Thank you,' I say finally. 'It's good to know I have your friendship.'

'Whenever you need me.' He understands.

The bar is emptying now. The clientele were only here for post-work drinks and when Sean's phone starts to ring we both hear it. He takes it out of his pocket and glances at the screen, then kills the call.

'Take it if you want,' I say.

'Nothing important. Just one of our suppliers'

It was a double zero three number. A European brewery perhaps.

Afterwards the conversation resumes along safer lines. How I've been sleeping, the things that helped Sean cope after Emily's death. Then a barman comes over and says there's a blockage in one of the pipes in the cellar. Sean excuses himself and I watch him cross the bar with that slightly rolling gait familiar to me from my childhood. All the tough guys walked like that, partly to be threatening, and partly because their upper bodies were so bulky. The drunk traders were clearly frightened of him and there's no mistaking the tremor that runs through me as he reaches up for one of the pint glasses on the top shelf of the bar, revealing a strip of muscular stomach – physical desire. I really must be careful. I'm not ready. Perhaps I never will be.

While I wait for his return I cast my eyes around the room. The dark wooden bar runs all the way along the back wall, rough stone arches behind containing rows of bottles, backlit so they gleam like jewels. The bar is supported by carved panels interspersed with bearded Atlas-type figures, their torsos straining to support their load. It looks familiar. Perhaps Ollie and I have been here after all.

Sean comes back. The problem is not as simple as he thought and he might be a bit longer. He'll get them to make me some food while I wait. I tell him I'd rather go home. He protests but I reassure him I'm okay. It's the truth: I really am feeling better for seeing him.

This time he does give me his number and assiduously taps mine into his phone then sends me a text to check it's working. Finally we kiss, chastely on the cheek. Friends.

It's dark outside and still raining, but somehow that adds a touch of glamour to the night. Puddles shiver with light, water droplets glitter on the edges of parapets and bus shelters. Under the feet of the commuters is another city, a mirror image breaking up and reforming as they march through.

I walk quickly past the Roman wall and am mounting the steps to the tube station when my phone rings.

Zainab.

'Sorry about earlier. I'm a shit friend.'

In the background I hear a man's voice.

'Ooh, you've got company.'

'It's fine. Hang on, Elvis.'

'Elvis? The waiter from the funeral?'

'It was late by the time he got the car back so I invited him to stay. For a while.'

I laugh. 'You dirty bitch. Sounds like he wants you to get back to him.'

'I just wanted to tell you what my Met guy said.'

I move away from the lights of the station, into the shadows of Trinity Square Gardens. 'Go on.' The hedges drip quietly as I walk towards the monument to the dead.

'I got him to trace that girl who was raped in Portugal. He came back to me with some interesting news. She killed herself a couple of months after Ollie and Milo left. Afterwards her brother went to the police and tried to get them interested in charging Milo again but they didn't want to know. Case closed. Masters of the Universe win again. I don't mean Ollie – of course I don't, but you could say, if it's true, that Milo got away with murder.'

I stand under the stone pillars looking out at the glimmering river.

'Ash? You there?'

For a moment I consider walking halfway across Tower Bridge and then simply climbing over the barricade. I'm not sure I have the energy to keep going.

'Asha?' Her tone is sharp.

'Yes, sorry. I heard. I was just thinking.'

'Well don't. Just concentrate on looking after yourself, okay?'

'Okay.'

'Promise me.'

'I promise.'

We say goodbye and I end the call. It must be closing time because people in various stages of drunkenness are stumbling through the gardens in the direction of the tube. I stop one of them and ask for a cigarette, then smoke it gazing out at the brutal silhouette of the Tower.

The rape charge could have ruined Milo's career and it sounds like the girl and her brother weren't prepared to just let it drop. What if Milo decided to silence her for good? He could have paid a local to do it. What if he really did get away with murder?

And look at him now, acting like the Graveneys' long-lost son. If they manage to wrest Ollie's estate from me, they'd be a very rich old couple. With no one to leave it to except their son's best friend, who stayed by their side as they grieved for him. Their rock.

Cui bono, Milo?

Maybe you do.

26

London

The call from Officer Linh wakes me from my doze on the sofa.

'At ten thirty on the 30th of September Mr and Mrs Peters took a taxi to a local visitor attraction, Con Dao prison, and there they met a representative of HSBC bank. After an hour touring the site of the old governor's house they drove with him in his car to Con Son town where they dined at the Thu Ba Seafood Restaurant. CCTV footage and a statement from the bank representative confirms they arrived at 12.40 p.m. and stayed until 5.15 p.m., when the restaurant called them a taxi back to Mango Tree. They arrived at 5.50 p.m. where they were told by the manager, Mr Bay Nguyen, what had happened at the caves.'

There's a pause as I take the news in, unsure whether to be disappointed or relieved.

'We also checked the alibis of the staff and additional guests of the Mango Tree, and they were satisfactory. The two Mr Mulgraves trekked along the Lo Voi mountain range for two hours with a local guide, until the elder man became ill. An ambulance was called and the paramedics diagnosed overexertion and recommended rest. The ambulance brought them back to Mango Tree at 3 p.m. where they stayed in their bungalow for the remainder of the day, receiving two room service deliveries, during which the maid saw both men.'

I think of Travis Mulgrave lying in the back of a foreign ambulance, perhaps on oxygen, all sense of his own invincibility evaporating with every chest spasm.

'And Sean Kearney.'

My attention snaps back to Officer Linh and my heart jumps into my mouth. I've never even considered Sean.

'At ten in the morning he took a taxi from Mango Tree to Con Son town, after telling Mr Nguyen he wanted to explore the town. During the period in question he was at a small bar called Fat Baby's. The owner confirmed that Mr Kearney was there for the critical hour during which you were attacked.'

I exhale quietly. In the background I can hear the bustle of the police station, the sing-song Vietnamese voices with that edge of sharpness that makes it sound as if an argument is going on. Outside my own window the trees murmur in a wind that occasionally makes the sash clunk.

'Officer Linh, did the boatman do it?'

There's a pause.

'That is where all the evidence points. These people come from Myanmar with nothing. They are desperate.'

Money. If he did it, it was for money. I think of Milo.

'What if someone, someone who had something to gain from our deaths, sent someone to kill us? A hit.'

'In my experience, if one can be obtained – which is not so hard in Vietnam – a hired killer will use a gun. They do not wish to get close to their victim, just to carry out their job and get away. This attack had the feel to me of panic – at a robbery gone wrong perhaps, in which case Phyo may well be guilty – or . . .'

'Or what?'

'Or hate.'

The line hisses with silence.

'Whoever did this, in my opinion, was filled with rage and hatred.'

Goosebumps creep up my arms.

'What could we possibly have done,' my voice is high, as if I'm about to cry, 'to deserve this?'

'Can you think,' he says gently, 'of anything? Of anyone?'

Suddenly smarmy Milo doesn't seem to fit the bill. He might be greedy and sly and doing his best to worm his way into the Graveneys' affections, but he didn't hate Ollie. He loved him. And Ollie loved him back. Enough to lie for him about the rape.

What if someone else knew about that lie, and thought they could use it to their advantage? Someone as desperate as the Peterses, with as little to lose. Someone who sent the photograph to Ollie.

'There is something . . .'

Linh waits patiently for me to go on, but I don't.

'Mrs Graveney? Tell me what is on your mind.'

'Not yet,' I say quietly. 'I need to speak to someone first.'

As if echoing my own thoughts he says, 'Be careful.'

'Thank you.'

I'd put the Albufeira photograph back in Ollie's case and, as I trudge back upstairs to fetch it, my legs heavy as lead, I realise I haven't eaten since the crisps at Sean's bar last night. I must have something. To stay strong, to keep my mind sharp.

I study the photograph over a bowl of over-salty packet noodles. The girl in the red dress holds my attention again, as if she's gazing at me down the years, imploring me to see something that I just can't.

After the meal I feel better. I turn on Ollie's computer and look through his email contacts. Nothing. I switch to Google. The name is unusual enough that he's pretty easy to trace. His profile picture is a younger, more hirsute version of the man I saw at the wedding. He's holding a bottle of champagne and laughing, friendly arms draped about his shoulders. The image he wants to project is of success and popularity.

I type a message. **We haven't met but I believe you knew my husband Ollie Graveney. As you may know Ollie died recently and amongst his papers I discovered a cheque made out to** you that he clearly didn't get round to posting. Is there an address I can send it to?

Just how greedy or desperate are you, Freddie?

Hitting *send* I settle down for a long wait.

To pass the time I scroll through the photos again. The raw agony from before has dulled to a wistful ache. The scenes seem so distant, so removed from my life as it is now that they might have happened to someone else. The beautiful couple dancing by candlelight are another couple entirely. I can't imagine what thought was making her smile, can't read the expression in the man's eyes.

Eventually I come upon the shots Ollie told me were corrupted. I squint at them, trying to make out the features of the bald man, but the closer I look the more the images pixelate. There's too much information; the pieces cannot hold together. They've become a series of discrete packages of code. Unreadable. Like everything else I've discovered.

There was another couple.

The raped girl killed herself.

They all lied for Milo.

Ollie was in love with the girl in red.

Somebody sent him that photograph.

Nothing holds together. Everything is pixelated.

I get to the pictures of the stag do and am about to scroll straight past when something catches my eye. Behind Ollie's head is the wooden torso of a man holding up the bar. When this photo was taken they were drinking in Sean's bar. I frown. Did Sean know any of them before Vietnam?

Another pixel.

The computer bleeps. A message has come through.

Freddie Lapozza has sent his address, along with a simple *thanks*. No question as to what the money was for, and no word of commiseration. I smile grimly. I'm going to enjoy this.

*

236

I was worried I'd stand out in Archway, an obvious target for knife-wielding muggers, but I realise as I trudge out of the station in my dark rain jacket and jeans, I look like everyone else: my head bent with exhaustion, my skin sallow, my clothes drab and in need of a wash. I walk quickly and purposefully, like I used to on the way back from a club in Islington – *leave me alone, I don't want any trouble.* It's too early for trouble anyway. I'll be gone before it gets dark.

In the unforgiving cheer of morning sunlight the place somehow looks worse. The piles of rubbish have been stripped of any gritty urban glamour, the stench of piss from every doorway is nauseating and even the fresh produce they're laying out on Astroturfed tables is filmed with grime.

I've memorised the route so I don't have to take out my phone.

I pass betting shops and fried chicken joints, charity shops and community help centres, phone boxes full of prostitute cards, run-down pubs, their windows plastered with match schedules. Nobody gives me a second glance. Perhaps I'm not a tourist here after all, perhaps it's *there* that I was the stranger passing through.

The door numbers scroll up and up, and soon I'm well into the hundreds. This street must go on forever. Perhaps if you followed it the shops and fast food joints would gradually peter out to green fields and trees. I'm tempted just to keep walking. What possible happiness will I find at my destination?

I pass an empty property, grilles across the window and a scorched front door, and then I'm there. Number 157. A flaking blue door squashed up beside the window of a phone-unlocking shop.

I raise my hand then hesitate.

I survived. Isn't that enough?

No.

I press the button of Flat 5, not expecting him to be in at this time on a Tuesday morning. Surely he has some kind of job.

The speakerphone scratches into life. 'Yeah?'

Not only unemployable by the City that embraced his peers, but actually unemployed. Living – no, surviving – in a flat above a shop. Abandoned by his so-called friends when he could no longer grip the rung they perched on so comfortably. He must have loathed them.

'Post,' I say.

There's a buzz. I push the door open and step into a dark hall that smells of damp.

Passing a table piled with leaflets I start up the stairs to the fourth floor. I'm tired by the second and pause for breath by a door with a splintered base, as if someone's tried to kick it in.

The sound of sirens and car stereos is muffled in here, like I'm inside a padded cell.

As I carry on up, the building becomes narrower: the walls, with their flock patterns of leering faces, close in. It gets colder, too, as if I'm climbing a mountain.

His door is a blank white rectangle with a single Yale lock, easy to force open, a message to burglars that there's nothing here worth stealing.

There's a sudden stillness when I knock, as if some imperceptible noise has ceased, then footsteps snick across lino. The door opens.

He looks worse than he did at the wedding. The weight that has settled on him has stripped him of the youth that clung to Ollie and the rest. His tracksuit bottoms make me think of David. Two lots of failed dreams. Two pairs of bitter eyes fixed on Ollie and me.

I shiver involuntarily.

'Next time,' he says, 'just leave it on the table downstairs, yeah?' There's no hint of public school any more.

I reach out a hand. 'I'm Asha Graveney. We met at my wedding.'

'Fuck,' he says, then runs a hand across his stubbly head. 'Of course, sorry, I thought you were just going to send it.' He plasters on a smile. One of his incisors is brown.

'I thought I'd pay a personal visit. As you knew Ollie so well. Can I come in?'

'The flat's a bit of a mess, erm . . .'

I push past him.

He's right, it is a mess. Shabby, dirty and unloved. There's a smell like a teenager's bedroom but without the fresh pungency of youth. This is ingrained: dirty clothes, food rotting in bins, something wrong with the drainage. It's also so cold I can see my breath.

I'm standing in a small living room, the single grimed window looking out over the high-rise opposite. The fabric of the patterned sofa has frayed to reveal the bulging yellow foam beneath. There are scorch marks on the coffee table.

'Do you want a cup of tea or something?'

'Yes, thanks.' He blinks. He wasn't expecting this. Presumably very few women who enter want to stay long.

'I haven't got any milk.'

'That's fine.'

'Or teabags actually.'

A glass of water will do.'

'Why not just give me the, er, cheque?'

I don't move. In the silence the sounds of a couple arguing seep through the walls.

'What's this about?' He shifts slightly to the left, until he's standing between me and the front door. Too late I remember the menacing presence in those photographs.

'My friends know I'm here,' I say softly. 'They're waiting for me in a bar by the station. If I don't meet them in an hour they'll call the police.'

'So, go,' he says. 'Keep the money, I don't give a shit.'

I snort. 'I'd say a blackmailer usually does give a shit about money. That's generally the point.'

I sound braver than I am. It's all I can do to keep my voice steady. If he knows I'm bluffing he'll know he can do whatever he likes to me. Thanks to the 'friend' saying I was suicidal, people will just assume I jumped off Beachy Head.

I take out the picture and throw it down onto the sofa between us.

It must be familiar. He doesn't even try to pick it up.

'Seb told me what happened in Albufeira, and you were the only one desperate enough to stoop that low for money.'

He winces as if I've physically struck him.

'You went along with it all and then they just cut you off. Ollie was the richest. Is that why you went for him and not Milo? Did you . . .' I take a deep breath. 'Did you kill him because he wouldn't give you the money you thought you deserved for all those years of loyalty?'

'*Kill* him?' His eyes widen. 'What are you talking about? I had nothing to do with that. Okay, so I asked for money, but I didn't kill him. For fuck's sake, what would be the point?'

'Because you hated him for having everything when you had nothing.'

'Jesus Christ, I wanted money, that was all. Do you seriously think I followed you out to Vietnam to beat you to fucking death? It was me who should have been worried about being killed. I'm surprised they didn't arrange for me to have a *little accident*. Your husband was the psycho, not me.'

'I'll let the police decide that.'

'Be my guest. Blackmail's one thing, but I suspect they'll be more interested in murder.'

I stare at him, confused. 'But . . . Ollie had nothing to do with the death of the girl in the bar. She committed suicide long after you all got back to London. '

'I'm not talking about the girl in the bar.'

'Then . . . who?'

We seem to be in a brief hush with no sirens or music or screaming. Without them it's eerie. His look of triumph dies, becomes something nearer to a grimace. His face has a waxy, yellow pallor that speaks of fast food and alcohol. He sinks down on the sofa.

'You should go. Just go. Remember Ollie the way you want to.'

'I need to find out the truth. About what happened to us in Vietnam.'

'I don't know what happened.'

'But you know something about Ollie. Tell me. It might be relevant.'

'It isn't.'

'Tell me anyway.'

'I might have been wrong about the whole thing.' He sighs and presses his thumbs into his eye sockets.

'If you were wrong,' I say softly, 'then why was Ollie so upset at the wedding? Why did he attack you?'

Finally he drops his hands into his lap and looks up at me with haunted eyes. 'What did you think I was blackmailing him about?'

'The rape. You and him and Seb covered up the fact that Milo raped the girl. You were threatening to go to the police.'

'What and shaft myself too?'

He picks up the photograph and gazes at it, running a thumb across his own youthful face, unrecognisable as the man he is now.

Then he moves it across to the girl in the red dress with the halo of dark curls. He looks up at me. 'Do you really want to know?'

27

Albufeira, 1998

They began at the Irish bar. It was Freddie who got hold of the drugs, some uppers to boost his mood, and Ollie's. He'd barely left the house for the past week, for fear of being cornered by the increasingly fanatical Estela. Of the group, Ollie had always been the one Freddie felt closest to and he was pathetically grateful to have a partner in his misery, someone to distract him from his own despair.

But the speed didn't help Ollie. He just became agitated and snappy, stalking out of the bar when he didn't get served quickly enough. The rest of them followed, pushing down the main street against the wind, and Milo steered their steps towards the sports bar at the end of the Strip where the pubs and clubs petered out, to be replaced by scrubland and half-built hotels. Freddie didn't like coming here and he felt the tension as soon as they walked in. The waitresses noticed them straight away and their closed faces turned to the English one with the bleach-blonde crop.

Milo had fancied her the first time he saw her, but as the holiday went on and he made no progress, his desire turned darker. She didn't seem to know how to brush him off politely, so instead brazened it out with sneers and insults, *in your dreams, sweetheart, go home and have a wank,* which made the rest of the bar guffaw. The other customers were sick and tired of these privileged English boys. Freddie watched uneasily as the slights to his overblown ego riled Milo more and more. His laughter became wolfish, his lip curled at the corner. Freddie had known Milo long enough to be able to hear what he was thinking. He was going to teach that bitch a lesson.

Tonight was as bad as ever. Milo would brush her breasts as she leaned across the table to collect their glasses, then spread his hands innocently if she reacted. Freddie wished she would just summon the manager but she had guts; she thought she could handle him herself. Ollie, the only one of them who might have had an influence over Milo's behaviour, just stared into his drink. In the end, Freddie decided to drag the nearly comatose Seb back to the villa. The other two were welcome to each other.

Outside the bar they saw Estela leaning against the railing of the boardwalk. She would wait all night to try and talk to Ollie. Freddie's insides ached at the sight of her. She was wearing the red dress that had so charmed his friend the night they met her handing out club fliers and it whipped in the wind coming off the sea, like flames. Occasionally a blast of wind would make it cling to the contours of her body, her full breasts and neat round belly. How could Ollie not want this girl? Freddie wondered whether you lost your appetite when everything was handed to you on a plate. It was a small comfort.

'Go home,' he called across the road, Seb hanging off him, hiccupping. 'He's not worth it.'

Her head moved towards the sound of his voice but she didn't speak. Her eyes were black and hollow, her white fingers gripping the railing.

'He's not interested, Estela.'

Her head swivelled back to the door of the bar, the dark coils of her hair rising like snakes around her head. The pumping bass of that summer's club tune carried across the wind, like the pounding of a tormented heart.

He knew then that she would never give up. She was a beautiful, graceful, charming stalker, and if Ollie was really unlucky she'd follow him back to London.

When they arrived back at the villa Freddie poured Seb onto a lounger by the pool and went to make himself a drink. If only they'd drunk here every night before hitting the clubs he wouldn't be so horribly overdrawn. The others had overdrafts too, but they didn't give them a second thought, knowing the measly few thousand pounds would be wiped off by their first pay cheque. Freddie wondered, as he sat by Seb's hunched and grunting form, why it was so easy for some. What had he done wrong?

He wanted to get drunk, to forget everything for this one last evening, but found that he had drunk himself sober.

He was still lying there, staring morosely into the still water of the pool – they were sheltered from the wind up here in the hills – wondering whether it was true that drowning didn't hurt, when Milo came back. He pretended to be asleep when Milo walked out onto the terrace, and could feel his friend standing over him before finally going back inside. He heard the shower pump begin, but then he must really have fallen asleep because he woke to frantic whispering coming from the villa. Seb was still out cold beside him so Freddie eased himself off the lounger and tiptoed across the terrace to the villa. If they came outside he would pretend he was just having a pee.

Milo sounded calm but Ollie was violently agitated. All Freddie heard was Milo saying, 'Show me,' then soft footsteps padding down the steps that led to the road.

Freddie waited until he was sure they were gone, then went inside. His room had the best view of the looping route into the town and from the window he could make out two figures moving quickly under the moonlight.

He smoked a cigarette, had a piss, and after an hour or so saw the two figures coming back. They were moving slower now and at one point stopped for one of them to bend double over the verge.

Freddie pulled the curtains across and quietly closed his door. Then he stood behind it and pressed his ear to the warm wood to listen.

They came back into the villa and he heard the pop and clink of beer bottles opening. The whispering was hard to make out but occasionally there would be a storm of breaths that could be someone crying.

He started violently when, on the other side of the door, Milo spoke his name.

Wide-eyed, he stared at the flimsy barrier of MDF between them, willing Milo not to twist the handle. There was no way he could be back in bed by the time Milo entered the room. His friend would know he had been listening. For some reason the thought made his flesh crawl.

'Asleep,' Milo murmured, slightly louder. 'Seb too. Out on the patio.' The voices receded into one of the bedrooms and after that there was silence.

Minutes passed, then half an hour.

Freddie listened intently, until the silence rang in his head and he wondered if he'd simply gone deaf, then eventually, desperate for a piss, he ventured out into the hall.

He stood in the gloom, breathing shallowly, trying to make no sound.

The villa was in darkness but for the light under the bathroom door which they always left on, to avoid walking into the wall when staggering out for drunken pees. No light pollution out here to guide the way.

Checking in both directions, he saw through the patio window that the sky had begun to lighten with a pink and yellow dawn. It was a sight to fill a person with hope, expectation of what tomorrow might bring, but it only gave Freddie a sense of dread. He had the feeling that he was on the brink; that the best of his days had passed. That tomorrow was the start of an inexorable slide into failure and despair.

Crossing the corridor he pushed open the bathroom door, fumbling at his flies.

He almost pissed his pants there and then.

A man was crouched on the floor by the bath.

'Jesus Christ, Milo!'

His friend pulled the shower curtain across then unhurriedly

245

got to his feet, all the while holding Freddie's gaze. He stood very close, nose to nose with Freddie, filling his whole sphere of vision. It was intimidating. Like a rugby player trying to psych out a weaker opponent, and yet Milo was smiling. 'What you up at this time for?'

'Needed a piss.'

His tone was casual but it had been an effort to keep the stammer from his voice.

'Go on then.'

Freddie turned to the toilet, laid a hand against the wall and tried to urinate.

He couldn't.

Behind him Milo was breathing evenly.

Freddie had just begun to panic when a thin stream of liquid started to sputter into the toilet. He stared fixedly down at the skidmark on the bowl, as behind him there came the quiet plink of water dripping onto the tiled floor. The stream tailed off.

'Finished?'

'Yup.'

He zipped up.

'Back to bed then, sleepy-head.'

'Night.'

'Goodnight.'

He walked out of the bathroom, crossed the corridor, opened his bedroom door, went inside and closed it behind him.

It was then that the press to urinate surged back.

He wet himself there on the rug.

It wasn't the spot of colour that had caught his eye as it dropped onto the tile from Milo's wet fingers. It was what he saw when, not daring to move his head, he swivelled his eyeballs to peer through the gap where the shower curtain met the wall. At first he thought it was a man. He thought Ollie had tried to cut his wrists in the bath. But it wasn't a man, it was just a set of clothes – dark jeans, a striped rugby-shirt – all drifting in a sea of scarlet.

Milo was washing blood out of Ollie's clothes.

28

London

I knew the rest of the story from Seb. The arrival of the police, the conspiracy to get Milo off the hook with the rape, but that was the first I'd heard of Ollie being in any trouble.

Freddie told me they stayed two more nights, until the police had dropped the case against Milo, and soon started to hear rumours that Estela was missing. People knew she was infatuated with Ollie and that he had rejected her: they said it might be suicide. But Ollie was never called in for questioning.

They went home, parting ways at the airport and wishing each other luck. Freddie watched Milo and Ollie get into a cab together, their heads close. He waved them off, but they only looked up at him at the last minute. Ollie's face was pale but Milo was grinning. The untouchables had done it again.

Freddie didn't even know we were getting married until he saw the ads the Graveneys insisted on placing in the papers. That final insult, added to the injury of his finances, made him decide to call in a debt.

'Go to the police if you want,' he said as he escorted me back down the dank staircase. 'A criminal record couldn't make my life any worse, could it?' He smiled grimly and opened the door.

We stood a moment by the rush and roar of the main road. I wondered if he felt as I did: that in a way we were kindred spirits. Both rejects from the club. Both of us damned.

'How much?' I asked him as I turned to leave. How much had he demanded from Ollie?

'A hundred thousand.'

Less than we spent on our wedding.

Between breaks in the traffic on the way back to the tube I glimpsed him, a balding, ageing man in cheap clothes: overweight and yet somehow diminished, fading like an old photograph, slowly being written out of his own life story.

There's a little over two hundred grand in our joint account. Pin money. If the Graveneys are going to get their hands on it then what does it matter what I do with it? And even if they aren't it doesn't matter. There's too much of it. Great choking swathes. Why didn't we ever do any good with it, Ollie? We were too wrapped up in ourselves and our tiny difficulties. Well, there's nothing wrapping me up any more. I'm stripped bare, blinking into the light, finally seeing all the suffering I knew was there but had chosen to forget.

I write Freddie a cheque for a hundred and fifty thousand pounds, address it and leave it on the table to post in the morning.

Then I sit down by the window and smoke.

Freddie implied that Ollie and Milo had something to do with Estela's disappearance, and clearly something bad happened out there for Ollie to be so freaked out by the blackmail attempt. But Milo had already proved himself capable of violence against women. In his devotion to my husband did he decide to rid Ollie of the inconvenience (and the competition) of Estela? Is Milo a killer as well as a rapist?

There's only one way to find out.

The prospect should frighten me, but my eyes start to droop almost immediately I've finished the phone call, the strings of thought breaking and drifting. Perhaps I'm approaching some kind of an ending. I sleep away the rest of the afternoon.

Milo agreed to meet me at his office, for privacy. I told him I wanted to talk about money. Presumably he's expecting me

248

to capitulate. He'll be delighted at the thought that his little bullying taster worked so well, without even having to get the big-gun lawyers involved.

But of course I have no intention of giving up my claim to Ollie's money. I was his wife, even if only for a few weeks, so it's mine by rights, but more importantly I now have plans for it.

After I've spoken to Milo I call Lewis Downing and say I'd like him to look into setting up an Oliver Graveney foundation to help underprivileged children. The enthusiasm with which he accepts this task suggests that he feels pretty bad for colluding with the Graveneys. Perhaps he's a good man, after all. Someone I can trust. Apart from Zainab and Sean, perhaps the only one.

I post Freddie's cheque on the way to the tube. The act of divesting myself of money helps me breathe more easily. If it *was* the boatman who attacked us, he did it for money. Money allowed Milo and his friends to get away with rape and . . .

And murder?

I'm too preoccupied to be watchful and we're halfway to the City before I raise my head and realise that I'm almost alone in the carriage. It's a Circle Line train, one long bendy tube, and as we round a curve in the line I see that, at the other end of the train, a man is sitting. A man in a black hoodie, black jeans and trainers.

I'm certain, at that moment, that this is the same man who tried to push me in front of the train.

'Hey!'

I get to my feet.

If I let him follow me into the dark courts and alleys of the City I'll be in real danger but here, under the bright lights and CCTV, he won't dare. I can confront him, find out who he is, what he wants. Who sent him.

The train lurches as I stagger towards him, ricocheting off the seats and rubbery concertinas connecting the carriages. He raises his head a fraction. He knows I'm coming.

The tracks clatter beneath us and for no apparent reason the wheels start to scream. Wires like huge underground worms appear on the other side of the glass as we swing close to the walls of the tunnel. My reflection is wild-eyed.

'What do you want?'

I'm two carriages away now but he hasn't moved. His hands hang in his lap. White hands.

The clatter of the tracks becomes louder and suddenly we burst out into Temple station. People get on and I must pause for them to move out of my way, keeping him in sight all the time.

The door-closing alarm sounds and I take the opportunity while the train is stationary to run through the next carriage. He's waiting for me in the one beyond, head bent, moving images on the advert screen behind him throwing his flickering shadow across the carriage floor.

The doors start to close. I'm almost on him. But at the last minute he bolts from his seat and slips through. It's too late for me to follow and as the doors shut I can't see beyond my own reflection. He's gone.

By the time I reach Mansion House my heartbeat has almost slowed to normal. I feel deflated. Have I missed an opportunity to discover the truth about what happened to us in Vietnam? Or was this man simply spooked at being accosted by an apparently unhinged stranger? I should have just taken his picture on my phone.

As I trudge up the steps of the station and out onto Queen Victoria Street I realise I was lucky. Fog as thick as a Victorian pea-souper makes it impossible to see across the road. It would have been so easy for him to grab me from behind, even on this busy thoroughfare.

A thought occurs to me. If Milo sent him he'll know where I'm heading.

Fortunately I know the route well enough to take a back way. We used to meet Milo and Liberty at his office and head off to one of their favourite restaurants: a white-tiled place that smelled like a butcher's and specialised in offal. I think Milo thought eating something's marrow made him more of a man.

I walk quickly, occasionally stumbling down the kerb or jerking back from near misses with lampposts. Huge splodges of red mist resolve themselves into silent buses. It's the only sign I'm still in modern London.

The solid glass doors of Milo's bank reassure me that the normal world hasn't simply dissolved.

I push through and the security guard looks up at me with dead eyes. We used to be on good terms with those guards, Ollie and I, back when I could still stomach Milo.

I say the name of his company, fill in a pass, and am waved through the barriers to the lift.

I wonder, as it shoots me silently upwards, whether I have made a gross miscalculation, walking into the wolf's den. Milo is the one with the power and connections. People are prepared to lie for him: perhaps more so than ever now that his favour carries so much financial clout. If he hasn't set me up already I must be prepared for him to do something that makes me look bad – or mad. Call security and say I've attacked him, perhaps? That I've been stalking and threatening him? In Victorian London a man like Milo could have had an inconvenient woman like me confined to an asylum for the rest of her life. Who's to say he can't now?

The lift comes to a hushed standstill and the doors open just as I tuck my phone back into my bag.

It's eerie walking through the deserted offices, past unmanned reception desks, deserted cubicles and empty sofas. I think briefly and nostalgically about my own office in Soho, with its knotty wooden floors and peeling paint from where the brothel upstairs had a water leak. Will I ever go back there, I wonder, or will my compassionate leave simply stretch on for ever? I always belittled the magazine in company. And yet there was something real about that place, something human that echoed our sense of endeavour: that we were striving for the truth. This glass labyrinth is all about hiding the truth. *Don't think, don't question, just trust us.*

And like a fool, I did.

'Keen as ever.'

The voice makes me jump.

'You're five minutes early. Lovely to see you, Darling.'

He steps out from a dimly lit meeting room and embraces me, holding me a split second too long, until my pulse quickens.

'Hello, Milo. Thanks for agreeing to meet me.'

The formal tone makes him flash me a quizzical look, but he dismisses it quickly. 'Come through. I've got wine. I know you like Chardonnay.'

I follow him into a meeting room dominated by a huge glass table that looks like it might slice you in two if you leant on it. There are no windows and no CCTV. I'm guessing that meetings here are strictly off the record. It would be my word, the suicidal widow, against his, the international financier.

Laying my bag carefully on the seat beside me I wait while he pours me a large glass. I have no intention of drinking it. *She was drunk when she got here.* A visceral sense of danger closes my throat as he smiles and hands me the glass. The cushion on his chair whispers as he sits down, as though it's in on the conspiracy.

'Well,' he grins. 'Good to see you. How are you?'

I nod and smile. *None of your fucking business.*

'It didn't go so well the other day, did it? I was going to apologise in person but thought I'd better let the dust settle. I think Mack and Vic knew they'd been over-hasty.'

'Over-hasty?'

'Yes. Well, you need some time to think things through, without the pressure of anything legal.'

'What do you mean?'

'Lawyers, contracts, blah blah. Proof of mental capacity, that kind of thing.'

'Are you threatening me?'

'Not at all.' He sips his wine, holding my gaze.

'I was Ollie's wife—'

'For four weeks.'

'I was Ollie's wife, which means I'm entitled to everything we owned.'

He opens his mouth but I speak over him. 'However . . .'

His jaw twitches. The silence hisses between us.

'I'm prepared to consider my position.'

He raises an eyebrow.

'In exchange for some information.'

'What kind of *information*?'

'I want you to tell me the truth about what happened in Albufeira.'

For a moment he is perfectly still. When he finally speaks his voice is so soft that I fear it won't carry. 'What's that got to do with anything?'

'Everything. If it's true, what I've been told, then this money is blood money and I want nothing to do with it. Tell me about the girl in the sports bar.'

His forefinger rising from the table is the only sign that he might be perturbed. 'Now, that's my business, don't you think?'

'Did you plan to rape her, or was it a spur-of-the-moment thing when she wasn't interested?'

He flinches, then his smile seeps back. 'They're always interested in men like me and Ollie, you should know that more than anyone.'

I hold his gaze but feel the strain like physical pain.

'I decided to call her bluff, waited for her after work. She seemed perfectly willing at the time. Afterwards, she tried to get money out of me. I said no, she went to the police. That's it.'

His chair creaks as he leans back, legs spread, palms on the table, taking up far more than his share of the space in the room.

'I said the truth, Milo.'

'It's nothing to do with what Ollie did.'

'Yes it is. You helped him so he lied for you. Said you'd been at the villa all evening. That was a lie, right?'

There's a moment's silence and then he chuckles. 'You got me. Not just a pretty face, eh? It's a dirty business, money, Asha. When you've got it everyone's trying to wrestle it off you. That's why you don't stray out of your class. You know I didn't really approve of you and him, right?'

He sips his drink, his eyes never leaving my face.

'That miscarriage business was a lucky escape.'

It's my turn to flinch.

'I told him to get out while he still could, before he was well and truly up shit creek. *Look at what happened last time*, I said.'

'What did happen?' I breathe.

A slow smile breaks across his face. He's been keeping this quiet for two decades to protect Ollie, but now I can see his glee at the prospect of finally telling me. He's rolling the words around his tongue, imagining how they will taste when he utters them to me: the money is one thing, but now there'll be the added bonus of shattering my image of my husband.

'The silly bitch got herself pregnant.'

Seb and Freddie had already gone back to the villa. Ollie had drunk himself into a deep depression and wanted to go back too but Milo was determined to wait for the blonde waitress to finish her shift. Ollie told him what happened next.

When he left the bar Estela was waiting for him on the promenade. Without his friends to protect him it was harder to fob her off. She hung onto him, slapping him, crying, hurling abuse in Portuguese. Drunk male Brits with tattoos had started emerging from the bars on their way to clubs. If he wasn't careful he'd get his head kicked in. He dragged her away, along the road to where cordoned-off steps led to crumbling cliff. You could sunbathe there if the beaches were too crowded, but it was treacherous, and tonight the sea was rough.

She told him about the baby, asked him to take her back to the UK. Horrified, he refused. The baby was bad enough, but her instability was now plain. She'd be a liability to the life he planned to build in London. She begged. Her Catholic parents would disown her, the baby would be taken away, she would be ruined. He told her to have an abortion.

She hit him again and then she pulled out a knife. It all happened so quickly. First she held it to her own throat, then, when he tried to stop her, she slashed at him. The knife missed, he pushed her and she fell back, her head cracking against a razor of rock. Then she went still.

He scrabbled over to where she lay. It was too dark to see clearly but as he lifted her head he could feel the sticky injury at her temple. She was making horrible grunting noises and twitching her legs. He tried to pick her up, intending to carry her back up to the road and raise the alarm, but the drink and the drugs and the buffeting of the wind made it impossible, so, reassuring her that he would go for help, he left her.

The Strip was busy now, the atmosphere wild and slightly dangerous, in a biting wind that whipped dust into whirling demons, the same club tune pounding from every bar, all out of sync, like the soundtrack to a nightmare. Two Portuguese policemen were scrutinising the groups of young men stalking down the street with looks of distaste on their faces, their thumbs hooked over the handguns in their belts. Suddenly Ollie was scared. During their stay they had done little to ingratiate themselves with the locals and he was sure there had been complaints about criminal damage, nuisance, noise, sexual harassment. And now he had murdered one of their own. Somebody's beautiful daughter. Killed her and left her like the rubbish they all left on the beach.

Digging his bloodied hands into his pockets he ducked his head and hurried past them.

Back at the villa Milo calmed him down, said it was alright, that they would sort it. Together they retraced Ollie's steps back to the cliff, bullied by wind, half blinded by grit from the road. The streets were now deserted. Even the policemen had been driven inside. They could hear the waves crashing all the way along the promenade and Milo said this might do them a favour. Sure enough, when they climbed over the tatty cordon they found that Estela's body was gone. The sea had washed it, and the blood, away.

Ollie was distraught. If he had stayed with her, if he had spoken to the police, she might have lived. Milo comforted him, led him home, got the blood out of his clothes. They were both in the same boat, Milo told his friend. After all, he'd got a little carried away with the barmaid. Fucking Freddie and his pills, mixed with all the booze: they'd all behaved out of character. It was Freddie's fault.

He stayed with Ollie until he had finished throwing up, and they worked out their stories. The bond that had been there since their first rugby match was infinitely strengthened that night. They were brothers now, until the end.

'And now the end has come, and we never betrayed one another. He was a good man, your husband. Solid.'

I breathe slowly and steadily, thinking of my husband's soft hands covered in blood and brain matter.

'What would you have done if her body was still there?' I say evenly.

He takes a sip of wine before answering, then lays the glass down with a quiet tink. 'Pushed it into the sea, of course.'

This time I don't bother asking if he's threatening me. Of course he is. Milo is more than capable of murder and for a split second I wonder if he really did have something to do with Ollie's death, but I quickly dismiss it. He hates me but he didn't hate Ollie. They were blood brothers. Until the end.

I stand up and pick up my bag carefully.

'Is that it?'

'Yes.'

'So the Graveneys can expect to hear from your lawyer?'

'Yes.'

'A woman of her word.'

'A man of his.'

We smile at one another. He thinks he's won. Let's hope he'll carry on thinking it long enough for me to get out of the building.

The lift seems to take an inordinate amount of time to rumble up and, as I stand on the balls of my feet, hands stiff at my sides, I can feel his dark presence behind me. Finally it arrives and the doors slowly part, but even as I step inside, I'm waiting for his fingers to close around my throat. His misshapen reflection in the beaten brass walls of the lift is like the true image of the monster beneath his skin. The doors finally close, the lift begins to thrum, and a few long seconds later I emerge into the foyer. The security guard's phone is ringing. I don't wait to find out who's on the other end, just stride out into the night.

Then I run. Not looking back, barely breathing, zigzagging left and right through alleys and squares until I'm sure I'm safe.

In a shop doorway I take my phone out of my bag and touch the screen. An image of a microphone appears, the red bar at the bottom jumping at the rustling of my sleeve. I listen to the entire fifteen-minute recording, then save the file. Afterwards I call Zainab and ask her for the number of her guy in the Met. She wants to know what's going on but I haven't got time. Not yet.

The call takes several minutes to be put through and as I wait I stare anxiously up and down the street. Passers-by seem to take on Milo's appearance, his gait. The air smells of his aftershave. My name is called at the edge of my hearing.

Then a man answers. 'Mrs Graveney? How can I help you?'

It's too late, Milo. Too late. 'I'd like to report a rape and murder. I have a taped confession.'

29

London

I've spent all this time chasing Ollie's phantom, as though finding answers to the Albufeira mystery would somehow lead me to the truth of what happened in Vietnam. All I've learned is that my husband was a liar and a killer.

The days drift by. I'm a ghost in my own house, occasionally fielding calls from Lewis Downing and the police, crying to Zainab, avoiding those from the Graveneys. The hatred drips from my phone like acid when I play back their messages, but I don't care. I don't care about much at all, in fact, which is a relief. Hours pass leaving no impression: I'm sleepless, appetiteless, my emotions and physical needs dulled. The only thing of note that happens is that one morning I faint while running a bath.

One moment I'm bending down to adjust the temperature, the next I'm slumped over the edge, my cheek resting on the enamel by the plughole, water creeping into my left nostril. Another minute and I would have drowned. The shock surprises me. Once I've righted myself I have to sit down on the floor with my head between my knees until my heart stops pounding. I wonder, as I crouch there, whether this reaction is simply instinctive, or whether I actively don't want to die.

That evening I make myself a proper meal, of pasta and pesto with one of the ready-to-bake baguettes Zainab stacked in my cupboard. My diminished appetite means I have to throw most of it away, but afterwards I feel stronger: more connected to the world. For the first time since meeting Milo I cry. For the poor girl with Ollie's baby in her belly, left broken on a rock to be washed away by the tide. For the first time since the miscarriage I hate my husband. I wish he were still alive so that I could punch and slap and kick and scratch my rage out on him.

The next morning I go out to the big supermarket on the other side of the tube station. It's been such a long time. We used to eat out so much that the little local stores were adequate for our emergency bottles of booze or packets of crisps. I'd forgotten these places existed.

I shuffle up and down the aisles, loading my basket with whatever comes to hand – bread, chocolate, ready meals, cans of soup, more wine – then I head for the cigarette counter.

Standing in the queue something catches my eye. A headline in a red-top on the counter.

HONEYMOON KILLER FACES FIRING SQUAD

Suddenly the lights are too bright. The shelves close in on me, the glaring colours of the shouting products assault my brain.

An old man gazes out at me from the paper, his face a mask of wrinkles, no red cap to shield his frightened eyes. He didn't do it. I've always known it, but it was so easy to believe, the voices assuring me of his guilt so soothing. And now he's going to die. His wiry little body ripped apart by bullets, for something he didn't do.

And it's my fault.

I knew he was innocent and I did nothing.

I drop my basket with a clatter and run out of the shop.

At home I call the paper Travis Mulgrave works for and finally get through to him.

'Can't you do something?'

'What do you suggest?'

'I don't know, some kind of diplomatic pressure or—'

'I'm a journalist, not a president.'

'But he didn't do it!'

'Oh, *now* she tells us.'

'Don't. Don't fucking tell me you told me so. He's going to die and I can't do anything about it.'

'Honey, you're the only one who *can* do something.'

'What?'

'Give them the real guy.'

'I can't! I don't fucking remember!'

'I've seen battle wounds, sweetie. Yours was a bump, that's all. Those memories are there somewhere, you just need to access them.'

'How?'

'Drugs. Hypnosis.'

'There isn't time! Travis, he's going to get shot!'

'You need to remember.'

And with that he ends the call. I stare at the phone, my eyes wide with panic. I don't know what to do. Somebody has to help me.

I call Zainab, but just get her answerphone.

With no one else left I call Sean. It rings for ages. He's not going to pick up: he's at work. But the rhythmic tone starts to calm me, the roiling tangle of my thoughts stretches and straightens.

I think of the photograph of Ollie, Seb, Milo, Freddie and Estela. That image, so much more powerful than words. That's why Freddie sent it. He knew it would trigger something in Ollie: it would take him back, to that holiday, make him relive all those thoughts and feelings. If a picture can do that, imagine how much more powerful if he was actually back there? The crash of the sea on the rocks the softness of his hand in hers, the smell of her blood. The reality of what happened would be inescapable. The memories would surge back.

Suddenly I know what I need to do.

Finally Sean answers.

'Asha. Are you okay?'

'Yes. I . . . I think I am.'

'You sound funny. What's the matter? You haven't taken something?'

'No. No. I just . . . Did you see the paper? About the boatman.'

A moment's silence. 'Yes.'

'I can't let that happen.'

'He knew the score when he attacked you.'

'But he didn't. He didn't attack us. I'm sure of it. It doesn't make sense.'

'We've gone over this.'

'I know that's what everyone thinks. But there's only one way to be sure. I need to remember.'

Sean sighs. 'We all want that, but you can't beat yourself up about it forever. You've had a brain injury. The memories just aren't there.'

'What if they are? What if they are and they just need a trigger?'

'What sort of . . . trigger, what are you talking about?'

I take a deep breath. I feel perfectly calm and alert, my thoughts ringing like a tapped wine glass.

'I have to go back to the caves.'

30

Con Son Island

I arrive at the airport early. To kill time before going through to departures I head to WHSmith and flick through the magazines. The usual stuff. A reality star addicted to painkillers, the child of a famous singer drowned in a swimming pool, a soap actress with cancer. There are divorces, eating disorders, surgeries gone wrong. All these A-listers who thought nothing could touch them ever again: desperate and suffering. It should be a comfort to find that I'm not alone, but it isn't.

I replace the depressing mag and pick up one of the tourist guides to Vietnam, flicking to the page about the islands. There's a section on the resort I've booked into, slightly cheaper than Mango Tree but still eye-wateringly expensive. I pass my gaze across the images, hoping that something will come to me, even now, so that I don't have to go through with this, but there's nothing. The fire curtain falls as we motor out of the bay. And yet, those fleeting images and feelings – the ghosts of memory fluttering at the edges of my conscious thought – make me think maybe there is something there, waiting to float centre stage with the right stimulus.

My phone rings and I leave the shop to answer. It's Zainab. When I tell her where I am, what I'm planning, she's riven with guilt and apologies. She'll get in a cab right now and come with me. I tell her I don't need her, but only because Elvis is there. I can hear him having his own conversation in the background.

I ask how it's going with him and catch the forced restraint in her response. She doesn't want to tell me in case hearing about other people's happiness breaks my heart. Perhaps she's finally fallen in love.

'Oh, listen, I did a bit of digging and I've found out some more about that girl in Portugal. Shall I email it to you?'

There's a desperate brightness to her voice, she's trying to assuage her guilt at being a less than attentive friend, and I can't bring myself to burst her bubble.

'Sure, great. I won't get much signal but I'll look at it when I can.'

Neither can I bring myself to tell her that Milo's crime was nothing to what my husband did.

After she's extracted promises for me to call her from Vietnam whenever I can, we say goodbye. Afterwards I feel like crying.

I wander round the tiny Boots, the strip of boutiques, even the luggage shop, but have soon exhausted all the possibilities this side of the gate. I'm not hungry but perhaps I should force down a sandwich.

Walking out of the shop I stop dead. Standing at the end of the strip, a holdall slung over his shoulder, is Sean.

In my bewilderment I wonder if it's coincidence, but then he's striding towards me, his expression strained.

We kiss on both cheeks, then I brace myself for what's bound to be a concerted attempt to talk me out of going back. For a moment he doesn't speak, then he lets his breath out in a rush and rubs his eyes.

'Let's go for a coffee.'

He takes my hand. No one's done this since Ollie and the sensation is exquisitely pleasurable. As we walk along hand in hand the blood rushes in my ears, and I wonder if given time I might actually fall in love with him. But when I look down at his stubby, rough fingers with their bitten nails, I think of Ollie's; of his baby-smooth skin – *never done a day's work in your life* – the perfect pink and white crescents of his nails. With tears

263

blurring my vision I slip my hand from Sean's on the pretext of hooking my bag up on my shoulder, and we pass into the railed-off area of the coffee bar.

For a while we just sit in silence, him staring down into his drink, swilling the black liquid around the cup. Americano. A grown-up's drink. Ollie's tastes were childlike. Sweet, milky lattes. Gingerbread syrup at Halloween. Strawberry frappuccinos in the summer, with mountains of squirty cream.

The tears start to prick again so I take a castigatory mouthful of scalding coffee and close my eyes as it sears the roof of my mouth, savouring the physical pain.

'I know why you want to do this,' he begins quietly. 'And I respect you for it. To go out there all alone and face this thing. That's brave. But . . .' He fixes me with those dark blue eyes. '. . . I'm scared for you.'

'Scared of what?' Cold fingers walk up my spine.

'I just . . . I think you're underestimating how you'll feel when you see the place again.'

'It can't make me feel any worse, can it?' But even as I say it I know it's not true. There have been moments over the past week when I've felt almost human again. 'My mind's made up so please don't say any more. Thanks for trying, though.'

Getting up I lean in to kiss his cheek but he moves unexpectedly and our mouths connect. I pull away sharply.

There's a beat in which neither of us can speak. Sean collects himself first.

'I'm not letting you go alone.'

The old-fashioned turn of phrase makes me smile. I'm about to say that he doesn't have a choice when I register the holdall lying under our table. He's packed and ready.

'I want to be there to support you.'

'No, Sean, it's . . .' The roof of my mouth is burnt raw. The pain makes it hard to concentrate.

'I booked my tickets when I got off the phone to you.'

'But . . . I couldn't ask you to do that . . .'

264

'Would Ollie want you to go on your own?'

I notice how dark his eyes are. An angry sea where Ollie's were the colour of tropical shallows.

If I say no I'm out there alone. Aside from the emotional crutch of his company, what if there really was another couple? What if they're still out there and I'm walking into a trap? I could ask for a police escort but that would be stressful and distracting. I need to be relaxed for the memories to surface.

He's still watching me with those petrol-blue eyes.

I swallow. 'Thanks, I'd love you to come.'

We sit on welded-together chairs waiting for the flight to board. The departures lounge is crowded and too hot, the chair backs far too narrow for Sean's broad shoulders. Even if I shuffle to the edge of my own seat our upper arms are touching. I've stripped down to my t-shirt but he keeps his arms covered. I remember those track marks and wonder again when and how he managed to straighten himself out. It must have taken some willpower not to slide back into that easy oblivion after Emily died.

He's booked himself onto the same plane as me. Maybe with the last of the cash from his and Emily's honeymoon pot.

Eventually the flight is called and we join the slouching crocodile of people at the gate. Standard class this time. Ollie's money can be put to far better uses than turning left.

On the plane Sean is several rows in front of me, and after we've stashed our bags in the overhead lockers we part to take our seats. When the others in my row arrive I ask if they'd mind my taking the aisle. The wheedling, the charming and inveigling you have to do when you haven't got the money to get things just how you like them.

It's dusk by the time we taxi to the runway, a tequila-sunrise smear across the horizon promising holiday delights. By the time we take off it's drained away, leaving London dishwater dark.

There's no one to hold my hand any more, so as the engine howls I grip the arms of the seat and press my head into the cushion until the tendons of my neck strain. My eyes are squeezed shut so I can't see the tarmac screaming past, or the pitying amusement of my fellow passengers.

There's a deep whir as the wheels come back up, and a shudder as we pass through the low clouds. And then stillness. I open my eyes.

Most people around me are staring at screens. Some are already asleep, or trying to be. There are no personal TVs here. No Dom Perignon, no amuse-bouches or goody bags. Just tired, cramped people wishing the next few hours away. I stare at them, the couples ignoring each other as they pore over magazine articles about some other couple in the first flush of love or the last twist of hatred, and I think, *look up!* Look up at the man beside you. Look into his face, memorise the lines, the creases of his smile, the texture of his skin. This might be the last hour you have with him.

I open the in-flight magazine and stare blindly at perfume and watch ads until the meal comes round, announcing itself with the smell of damp socks.

After I've eaten, a few mouthfuls of beef bourguignon and a pot of mandarin jelly, I try to look out of the window, but the fat man in the window seat has pulled the blind halfway down. God knows why as he's now asleep, a brown gravy-stain in the corner of his open mouth. In the sliver of sky I make out a few stars and the faint glow of moonlight. I should have kept my original seat. I'd like to have seen the moon shining off the tops of the clouds. Ollie would always nudge me on night flights like this. 'Look, Asha, it's magical.' But my face would always be buried in a book.

An hour passes, maybe two, and the cabin lights dim. Spotlights start going on all around me. It seems there are plenty of us unable to sleep. Guilty consciences and regrets, or just insomnia?

As the dry air in the cabin dehydrates me, the burned roof of my mouth starts to sting again. The pain gets steadily worse until

266

it's all I can think about. I press my call button and after ten minutes a stewardess appears. She tells me they can't distribute any kind of drug onboard.

The prospect of another six hours with this is unbearable so I get up and set about extricating my case from the crush of the overhead locker.

The paracetamol packet in my washbag is empty, shreds of foil laid teasingly over rounded but empty blisters. I swear under my breath and walk up the aisle to Sean.

In the pressurised air my feet feel oddly heavy, like I'm walking on the moon in weighted boots.

He's asleep. Crouching beside him I lay my hand gently on his arm, but he doesn't wake. I try again, a little more firmly, but still he doesn't stir. Then I remember. He doesn't like flying: always takes a pill before take-off. Given the circumstances I'm sure he wouldn't mind me looking for myself. Besides, the chances are he won't even know about it.

His holdall is near the front of the locker. I pull it out and crouch to unzip it. Beside me his breaths are regular and heavy, his fingers motionless on the armrest by my cheek.

The zip makes a low buzz and his forefinger twitches. I glance around guiltily. Perhaps this isn't acceptable behaviour. Would I do it to a girlfriend? No, but I might a sister. Or a lover.

Rifling through the folded clothes my hand strikes something firm. But it's only his electric shaver bag. I carry on, delving through underpants and t-shirts, the blood rushing to my face making my mouth hurt even more.

Here's his tablet, his electric toothbrush, his phone, his—

I pause. That's not his phone. Sean has an iPhone. This is some cheap knock-off brick, the sort of thing you pick up in a Bangkok market for a dollar.

My heart lurches. Has someone slipped something into his luggage? Then I remember that the holdall was never out of his sight.

He packed this phone himself.

Beside my ear comes the soft rasp of Sean's hand moving against the fabric of the armrest. It has bunched into a fist and his breathing is shallower. Is he about to wake up? If he opens his eyes now this looks bad.

I re-zip the bag, pressing the pad of my thumb against the closing teeth, which pinches the flesh but muffles the buzzing sound. Standing up I find that it's much harder to get the bag back in than it was to get it out. The rubber feet catch on the edge of the locker with a sharp clack.

Sean inhales.

Panic gives me strength. With one last shove the bag slides in and I close the catch. Then, with a final glance at Sean's apparently still slumbering face, I flee back to my seat.

After a draining stopover in Hong Kong, where we make the mistake of sharing two bottles of wine, we're on our way to Saigon. This time we're delayed for an hour on the runway and they try to keep us quiet with more booze, so that by the time we touch down at Con Son the pain in my mouth has been replaced by a full-blown hangover. On the way to the resort I hang out of the taxi window, gulping down the dusty air, unable to take in the beauty of the indigo dusk, or the driver's friendly chatter. Sean, by contrast, managed to kick off any residual drowsiness from the sleeping pill with two cans of Coke from a vending machine in the airport, and his eyes are bright as he gazes out of the window at the gathering darkness.

When we arrive I let the driver and Sean unload the cases while I walk up the decking to reception. A tiny woman is waiting for me with a pert smile.

They've put me by the sea. I don't want to be by the sea. I don't care about the view. I want to be at the back, by the road. I'll pay extra if necessary.

Sean joins us, solicitous, concerned. She thinks there's been a mistake with the rooms – they've booked us into two when really we only want one. I correct her sharply and she flushes, finally giving me my key and mumbling about showing me to my cabin. I say I'll find it, then walk away from them, towards the murmur of the sea.

I lie on the bed for hours staring up at the bamboo roof of the hut. This one isn't just *by* the sea, it's *in* the sea, on stilts, reached by a rope-handled wooden walkway. When I close my eyes it's like I'm floating on a dark ocean, a starless sky pressing down on me.

Nausea forces me up and I go out onto the veranda that looks seawards. The night is cold and clear, the moon bright enough that I can make out the rocks just below the surface of the water, hanks of seaweed drifting around the struts of the hut.

The boat sliding over a coral reef.

I freeze. That's a new memory.

There was a coral reef. Dead white and sharp as a razor, just below the surface as Zaw Phyo's boat drew us nearer to the cave.

I can see it.

Oh, Christ. I can see the cave. A swollen grey belly: a gap like spread legs for a boat to enter and dock. Neither of us said what it looked like. *Pregnant.* The wind was making an eerie noise, crying round the empty dome as if it wanted to be let out. We're almost there. The boat engine dies, and then . . .

Nothing.

That's it. There's nothing more.

Deflated, I squat onto my haunches and trail my fingers in the water. The memories won't come if I force them. I need to let my subconscious do the work.

Clouds draw slowly across the moon until I'm standing in darkness. No bioluminescence here, just the plash of the water. I think of sharks cruising beneath my feet.

It's early when I wake. My sleep was fitful and full of menacing dreams.

I hate being marooned out here and though it's too early for breakfast I walk the gangplank back to the shore and read on the cold sand until the sun is fully up and the restaurant starts to fill.

It's a glass box with sliding doors that open onto the beach and reminds me a little of an English holiday camp. I drink green tea, trying to muster an appetite, but by the time Sean surfaces at eight, I still can't face any food.

'Hungover?' he says, smiling.

I don't tell him that I've remembered the cave. I'm sure he'll just say I'm imagining it. Maybe he's right.

'Are you going to eat something?'

'I'm not hungry.' It's my stock response these days and he just nods.

'So, when do you want to go?'

'I need to book a boat. Should have done it last night.'

Sean stands up. 'Let me do it. You just relax.'

Eyes of both sexes follow him as he passes through the restaurant. This resort is busier than Mango Tree, and not as chichi, the sort of place favoured by reality TV stars or footballers. I wonder if the oglers think Sean is famous.

'Sean!' I call after him, but he doesn't seem to hear. I wanted him to ask reception to put me in a different cabin, one on land. It occurs to me that perhaps I could ask him to stay with me tonight. I'm scared of being alone on that raft, tethered to the shore by that most fragile thread. Just to hold him, to listen to him breathing, would be bliss. But of course it's impossible.

A woman passes me with a plate of Danish pastries. The sight of the sweet glaze over an egg-yolk-yellow apricot makes my tongue prick. I realise, as I pick up my water glass with a shaking hand, that it's foolish not eating. Under the burning sun I'll be more spaced out than ever. I go up to the bar and am about to sweep some pastries into my napkin when I think about the sugar low that's bound to follow. I turn my attention to the fruit bowl. Papaya, mango and cactus fruit. I wrap them in the napkin and slip them in my bag, then, as I am about to return to the table, I remember each fruit will need to be peeled.

Most people appear to have finished their breakfasts so I'm sure they won't miss the stubby little fruit knife on the chopping board. This I wrap more carefully, then I transport the whole lot back to the table.

After I sit back down there's a repetitive buzzing sensation against my foot, as if a wasp is trapped beneath the decking. It's coming from Sean's rucksack.

A phone. On vibrate.

Perhaps the burner phone is for business calls. This might be important.

I retrieve the brick from his bag and glimpse the beginning of a text before the screen goes dark.

This must stop now please do not—

There's something foreign in the tone. I lay the phone on the table ready for him to check but as I sip my tea it occurs to me that going through his bag is inappropriately intimate. I don't want to give him the wrong signals. I snatch it up again and have just tucked it back into the rucksack when he comes back.

I'm being picked up at midday.

Three hours.

31

Midday

'Can you believe my fucking shower doesn't work? A place like this and they can't even get their plumbing straight.'

I sit up on the sun lounger and shield my eyes. His towel is still slung over his shoulder and his jaw is tight with anger. The tension of the trip is taking its toll on him too.

'Hey, don't stress about it, use mine.'

I hand him my key card. 'I'll trust you not to go through my underwear drawer.'

He grins and I go back to my book. But the words might as well be in a different language. I can't fix my eyes to a page for more than a couple of seconds before glancing up and scanning the horizon for the boat.

It doesn't help that the staff seem to be constantly milling about in my peripheral vision. Despite the price difference they are more in evidence than at Mango Tree. After a while I begin to notice that their attention seems fixed on me. When one goes inside, another takes up his position on the steps to the restaurant. Finally I call one over.

'Are you watching me?'

An older person might have fronted it out, but this boy is barely out of his teens, his skin smooth and glistening.

'Your friend said you were sick.'

'Not at all. I'm fine.'

His gaze is guileless. He taps his head. 'Sad sick.'

Shit, I mutter and look away. They're obviously worried I'll try and drown myself in Sean's absence. As long as they don't insist on accompanying me to the caves. I want to go alone. Sean understands. He didn't even offer to come with me, but said he'll be waiting when I get back.

I decide not to confront him about what he said to the staff. He's only caring for me.

The minutes crawl by. Ten thirty, eleven fifteen.

When the boat finally appears around the headland, twenty minutes late, I leap up and run down to the water. It takes a few minutes to come in and as it drifts through the shallows Sean joins me.

'I got you a fresh water.'

I thank him. The bottle is deliciously cold.

'Make sure you keep hydrated. Drink it on the boat.'

'I will.'

We look at each another and then he smiles, but it doesn't stretch to his eyes.

'Don't worry.' I touch his bare shoulder. 'I'll be fine.'

'I'll be in my cabin, okay? Come and find me when you get back.'

I lean in and kiss his cheek, then turn to the boatman. He extends a hand to help me aboard. Sitting down in the stern I settle my bag onto my lap to protect it from the water. In it is my phone, and a pen and paper to make notes.

The engine coughs into life and the boat swings away from the shore. I look back to see Sean walking up the sand towards a gaggle of resort staff, who watch silently as we pick up speed. They clearly think I'm never coming back.

The engine noise becomes a whine, then a roar, and within a minute we're bumping along through the dark waves, the line of white sand receding behind us.

I realise I haven't even glanced at the boatman.

He doesn't look at me, though he must know my story, but gazes diligently out beyond the prow. If I were him I'd have brought someone with me, just in case the English woman goes mad again and accuses him of murder.

As we clear the headland I reach into the bag for my phone. Nothing yet. I suppose it might take a minute or so for any messages to come through. The fruit has partially unwrapped and is now a pulpy mess at the bottom of the bag. It doesn't look appetising and I almost toss the whole lot over the side, but I decide to try and force something down. Already the heat and the motion of the boat are getting to me. I start to peel the papaya with the knife, tossing the parings over the side. The flesh is sweet and warm, and juice bleeds all over the front of my vest. When I'm finished I wash my hands and the knife, leaving a trail of crimson in the waves.

The sun is a laser beam on the back of my head. Why on earth didn't I think to bring a hat? Thank God Sean remembered I would need water. After the fruit I open the bottle he gave me and guzzle it down in one.

He's been such a good friend to me. I know I should disabuse him of the idea that we could ever be together. It's too soon, yes, but that aside, whatever he thinks, we are so different. It was refreshing having him around when we were with David and Sophie: he made me laugh. But Ollie made me laugh more. And whatever he did all those years ago to that poor girl and her baby, it was an accident. An accident he covered up because he was shocked and scared and too young to know better. Ollie was a good man at heart. I'm not sure that Sean is such a good man. He has secrets.

My phone vibrates in my bag – a message has come through. I'm about to reach for it when the boatman's body becomes suddenly alert.

I look up and my heart trips. We're in sight of the cave.

Though we must be approaching from the opposite direction the dome is just as I remembered, a grey belly with a gap like spread legs, just wide enough for a boat to enter. The engine dies down and I can hear the wind sighing round that empty belly.

We're drifting over glassy water. Pink jellyfish float over rocks and banks of coral, most of it white and dead. A shoal of silver fish changes direction and vanishes.

Five green crabs.

My breath catches. The memories are there, just waiting for me to pass through those stone legs and into the womb of the cave.

We slide over the coral reef and come under the shadow of the rock face. A moment later we're inside the dome: a neat crescent of white sand enclosed by the walls and lit by a shaft of sun through the skylight. There are some very large rocks and a scattering of smaller ones.

Was one of them used on me?

The boat bumps against a sand bank and the engine putters to a stop.

'I take boat,' he says, jabbing his finger up the coast a little. 'Go fish. You call me when want go.'

A brown and red splodge, standing in the water with his fishing rod.

'Thank you.'

He holds his hand out and I step down into the water. Even here, in this tropical heat, there is the shock of the cold.

'Careful,' he says.

I look up at him. His eyes are such a pale brown they're almost gold.

Then he revs the engine and a moment later the boat passes between the rock stacks into the open water, banks to the left and vanishes.

I wade out until I'm directly under the shaft of light. The soft sand moulds itself to the shape of my feet. If I close my eyes I can feel the world revolving around me.

A white star. The pitter patter of rain.

Breathing quietly, I sink deeper and deeper into my subconscious.

A curling leaf fern, tiny green crabs all in a line, black coral. Except that now she sees that it's not coral after all, but clumps of dark, curling hair.

There. That's new.

My breath quickens.

The crabs dance in the water. Five of them, ranging in size from big to small. The sand billows then settles around them. In the shape of . . . in the shape of toes. They are not baby crabs, they are green-painted toenails. A foot beside her cheek. Her face is in the water. She can feel it lapping almost up to her nostril, but not quite. If the foot were to push down on her head her nose would go under and then she would drown.

The memories are tumbling too quickly, into a great loose pile that will not hold together.

The pitter patter of rain. Then, from nowhere, a blow. Heavy and shocking. Not rain. Footsteps. Footsteps running along the sand towards her.

I open my eyes.

My God.

There was no warning. No confrontation, no smiling pretence at befriending the tourists in order to rob them. Just that sudden, devastating violence. Planned. Not opportunistic. Not Zaw Phyo.

The waves plash at my ankles. My mind delves deeper and I can feel the buds of memory begin to open.

Bending to look at a rock with a tiny fossil curled like a foetus.

No. I squeeze my eyes tighter. The flowers are opening randomly. Where does this fossil memory come in?

The pitter-pattering makes her think it's raining. She turns round to tell Ollie. There's a woman running towards her. Dark brown curls like writhing snakes. A white star-shaped scar on her right temple. She holds a rock. Something is happening in Asha's peripheral vision but she can't tear her eyes from the rock. It's the size of a cantaloupe. It must be so heavy to lift. And now the woman is bringing it down, its own weight giving it momentum.

And then, a moment's respite in the flow of this gush of memory. I should . . . I should write it down. With numb fingers I fumble around in my bag, almost dropping my phone into the water in the process. But now—

'Look, it looks like a baby.' She traces the tiny coil of million-year-old spine with her fingertip. He comes over and puts his arms around her. 'There'll be babies, Ash. I promise.' A flash of irritation. She extricates herself. 'I didn't mean like that. I was just showing you.' They move away from one another to let the moment's discomfort pass. She walks into the water while he wanders up the sand, towards the opening that leads to the jungle. The land route, if you were walking here instead of coming by boat. Zaw Phyo has gone fishing up the beach. He's told them to call for him when they're ready to go. If she peers through the legs of the cave she can see him, a little brown and red splodge, standing in the water with his fishing rod, perfectly still.

The world spins queasily. My blood is so hot, beating against the thin walls of my veins, threatening to burst out at my temples and behind my eyes.

As the woman brings the rock down, its own weight giving it momentum, Asha's eyes lock with those of her attacker. They are jet black and filled with hatred, but her colouring is not Vietnamese. It's Mediterranean.

I stare blindly at the glittering sea.

I was attacked by a dead woman.

My hands feel like they're encased in ski gloves as I take out my phone and tap in the word: *Estela.*

I need to go back to the resort and call Officer Linh. But when I try to stand I find that I can't get up. It must be shock. I'll have to wait a while for my strength to return.

I see then that two messages have come through from Zainab. I open the first and blink to clear my hazy vision.

It's a picture of a young woman, cropped blonde hair and a nose ring, fire dancing in her dark blue irises as she raises a flaming sambuca to her lips. She's wearing a t-shirt emblazoned with the words *Paddy's Bar, Albufeira*. From the right sleeve peeps a tattoo. The lower half of a black semicircle with a white dot at its centre. The yang symbol. This was the girl Milo raped. The girl who killed herself.

I frown. Something nudges at the boundaries of my mind. What? I can't seem to be able to think straight. The heat, the lack of food is getting to me.

But, wait, I did eat. So why do I feel so strange? My thoughts unmoored, drifting. All I want to do is sleep.

Lazily I open Zainab's other message.

Her name was Emily.

I blink, trying to clear my head. Emily was . . . Emily was Sean's wife.

32

Afternoon

What a beautiful place. The spread legs and arcing belly of the cave, with its neat sapphire bellybutton open to the sky. The grey walls, shimmering with mica and feldspar, sweeping down to the sand where scattered rocks and pebbles warn that this won't be here for ever, that all beauty must decay. One day, thousands of years from now, this shell of stone will crash down into the sea. Or perhaps it will fall in the next storm.

The sun sparking off the waves blinds me. It has all the glitter of glamour magic: that sleight of hand that has you looking one way, while the real trickery is happening elsewhere, in the dark beneath the surface. When we came here I was afraid of the sharks, the stonefish, the stingrays that could drive a barb into your heart. But it was you I should have been afraid of all along.

In nature, beauty is a warning. The multicoloured bands on a coral snake, the rich pigments of a poison dart frog, the rainbow frills of a cuttlefish that tell you it's death to touch. Why shouldn't it be the same in humans? Your perfect face is nothing but a mask. I thought I could read your thoughts in those blue eyes, but they were just mirrors reflecting my own desires.

It's so peaceful, with the murmur of the sea and the light breeze singing through the skylight. The water laps at my toes, skin-warm. The sun is directly overhead. If it wasn't, if we had tipped over into afternoon, I would see your shadow growing in front of me, dulling the glimmer of the sea. You're coming up behind me. I can hear the

whisper of your feet sinking into the wet sand. But I can't get up.
You've made sure of that.

I fumble for the opening of the bag, the mouth of it pulsing in
my vision, as if it's trying to tell me something. That you are a liar
and a killer and I must save myself. All I can do is try, but you
have taken so much from me already, and now even my strength is
gone, my co-ordination. I cannot tell whether my fingers have closed
around the knife or my pen or even the empty water bottle. They
are thick and numb: sausages on a butcher's slab. But there's no
more time. I have just slipped the thing that might be the knife into
the pocket of my shorts when your hand descends on my shoulder.

I turn my head and am just able to make out your familiar shape.
My vision may be blurred but my eyes are open. At last.

It was Sean who stole the necklace and planted it in Zaw Phyo's
home, who cut the cord of the patio heater to make it look like
an accident. Him following me in London.

Now he sits down beside me, his arms crossed over his legs.
The fine hairs gold in the sunlight. And then he smiles. That
heartbreaking smile that almost convinced me I could love him.
Now it makes my blood run cold. I thought he understood me.
That we had *chemistry*. He befriended me for one reason: to kill
me, and now he's going to finish the job.

But they were wrong about me, the papers, all those concerned
hotel staff, I'm not quite done with life yet. I'll try to fight him,
to live, but I don't have much of a chance. He's strong and
clear-headed – and maybe he's not alone.

I try to turn my head and the beach blurs greasily. When it
comes back into focus I'm looking at the jungle. That's where
they must have come from that day Ollie and I came here. But
today no figure breaks the line of the trees.

'Estela?' he says mildly. 'She went home after I killed Ollie. I
told her I'd sort things. And look how easy you made it for me!'

Finally everything makes sense. He was the *anonymous friend*
who spoke to the papers, preparing the ground for when I threw

myself in front of a train, or drowned myself in the spot where I lost my precious husband. That's clearly what he has planned for me. The drug was to weaken me, so I couldn't fight him off, but it's also the perfect alibi. I gave him the keys to my hut. Has he planted empty pill packets there for the police to find when I don't come back? No one's expecting me to come back. It's in everyone's interests – Sophie and David, Milo, the Graveneys – that I don't.

We've made it easy for him all along. The crowing ads in the papers and *Tatler*. The stag do that just happened to blunder into his bar, no doubt braying about our twenty-grand honeymoon. Did he recognise Ollie and Milo from all those years ago: still the same arrogant arseholes who thought they owned the world and everybody in it? But it was Milo who raped Emily.

I turn back to him, but this time the beach stays in focus. 'Why . . . Ollie?'

'Em was my sister. The rape really fucked her up. She got back into drugs again and then sort of lost hope. I should have killed that bastard. But what Ollie did to Estela was worse.'

'You knew Estela?' The fog in my head is dissipating. Could it be the food I ate? He didn't expect me to eat anything and perhaps adjusted the dose accordingly, so that I'd make it here without falling unconscious.

'We were all working in Albufeira. Trying to make something of ourselves, leave our pasts behind and start again. And then your husband and his friends came along.'

He's drawing a picture in the sand. A lazy spiral like a revolving galaxy. What kind of a life must they have had, him and Emily, to need to leave it all behind in a beach resort in Portugal? The track lines peep from the sleeve of his hoodie, ugly welts beneath the golden hair. To think I was impressed by them. Back then I saw only beguiling danger, not despair. What a fool. A privileged fool who somewhere along the way lost her compass. Perhaps I deserve this.

'I always thought they'd get some kind of karma,' Sean continues quietly. From a distance we must look like lovers sharing intimacies. 'And then they came to the bar that night, and I saw that they were rich and successful and worst of all, they were happy. It was then that I realised we'd have to be their karma. Me and Estela.'

He sighs, brushes the sand from his fingertips and clambers to his feet. I'm running out of time, but my muscles are still too weak to support me, let alone fight him off. Reaching down, he hauls me upright and swings me into his arms, like a bridegroom about to carry his wife across the threshold.

'Why Ollie and not Milo?' This time I exaggerate the slurring. The drug is slowly leaching from my brain but I don't want him to know that. I need more time.

He steps into the water.

'You haven't worked it out yet?'

He pauses and looks down at me with a kind of benevolent pity. The slow child who just can't work out how to finish the jigsaw.

I blink into the glitter of the water, following the frazzled strands of thought, back, back . . .

The way she was standing made it cling to the contours of her body, her full breasts and neat round belly. How could Ollie not want this girl?

The silly bitch got herself pregnant.

A moan escapes my lips. Estela had Ollie's child. The child we could never make.

He sees the realisation dawn. It makes him smile.

'With you dead, Nico's the sole heir.'

Nico. The boy I saw on the headland, standing beside his mother. Sean deleted the photograph I took. Otherwise Ollie might have recognised her, even after all these years. Might have felt that burning obsession still radiating from her black eyes.

'I wish it didn't have to be this way, Asha.' He bends and kisses me lightly on the lips. 'I'm not evil. It was your husband and his friends that were evil. They did this to you.'

'Sean, please,' I whisper. 'Don't.'

My toes are dangling in the water now and as he moves forward my buttocks and hips are submerged. Suddenly I'm lighter in his arms.

'I could . . . love you.'

He smiles sadly. 'Nice try. I could love you too but sometimes things just don't work out.'

He steps out deeper, into the shaft of light coming down from the skylight. It makes his hair burn gold.

'You're not this person.'

'It won't hurt, I promise. It'll be like going to sleep.'

We go deeper, and now the water is supporting us both, blood warm between our bodies. He turns me in his arms, until I'm facing him, my thighs interlinking with his, my arms around his neck. The glitter of the water on his face makes him look like an angel. An avenging angel acting on behalf of a God who wouldn't step in for his sister and Estela. And I am on the side of the demons.

Then I remember, he's doing this for hate and money. There's nothing noble about that.

He closes his eyes and moves in to kiss me.

As if it's been dislodged by the motion of the water I let my arm slip from his neck and drop to my side. My fingers drift to my pocket. If it was the pen I put in there, it's all over.

As our lips touch I raise my curled fist to the triangle of space where his left arm is wrapped around my body, where I can feel his heartbeat against my breast.

Can I do this? Have I got the strength, the stomach for it? But it turns out that just like Milo, I'm capable of anything.

Sean's eyes snap open. He must have felt the sudden purposefulness of my movements, the unexpected control. His mouth hardens beneath mine, his muscles tense: the prelude to pushing me away, to thrusting me under the water and holding me there. This is it. This split second. My only chance.

I drive the knife into his body as hard as my drugged muscles will allow, but the blade is sharp. I feel his flesh and sinew yield beneath me, and then a sudden rush of heat across my wrist.

His lips part and then, quite gently, his arms slip from my waist. In slow motion he falls backwards, until the sea takes the weight of him, turning him slowly until he's wrapped in a ribbon of blood.

Long seconds pass as I watch him, almost willing him to surface, to gasp for air, to beg me to help him, but his only movements are with the gentle ebb and flow of the reddening waves.

Finally I turn away and wade to the shore. All I want to do is sleep and never wake up.

Without the support of the water my legs give out, so on hands and knees I crawl up the beach to where the cave wall slopes down to the dry sand. Now I can see him, standing peacefully in the water, one hand resting on his fishing rod. Like Zaw Phyo was the day Ollie and I came to this place.

My cry is so feeble it is lost among the calls of the jungle birds, but somehow he hears me. He hears and turns, and the last image I see, before unconsciousness takes me, is the boat man running towards me, his rod forgotten, blue cap sailing out behind him like a bird.

Five Months Later

The café is around the corner from Lewis's office. A bland chain with lines of laptops like riot shields, paper sugar packs dissolving in pools of coffee on tables strewn with muffin crumbs. There's the usual inoffensive background music, designed to stupefy bankers and lawyers. A girl with a guitar singing a ballad that was once a rock song.

My eyes dart from one spot to another then back to my watch as I sip my coffee. My mind is veering from blank terror, to a grandiose sense of my own magnanimity, to the certainty that I'm a complete fool and that if Ollie knew what I was doing he'd have me sectioned.

There's still time to leave. To call the police.

She must know this is a possibility. She probably won't even come. She's half an hour late already.

Outside the plate-glass window the traffic is nose-to-tail. Like the people. Suits and skirts and heels and mobiles. Moving quickly against the sharp spring breeze. On office errands or early lunch runs. No steps slow, no eyes lock onto mine. I am invisible, trapped on the other side of the glass like Alice.

The coffee is gone, as if someone else drank it. I press my fingertip onto a muffin crumb then flick it to the floor. The man beside me starts watching a loud YouTube clip featuring men jumping off the roofs of trains. The barista drops a glass on the way back to the counter and people cheer. I look at the window again.

My breath stops.

The picture that had formed in my mind – of a twitching and dilapidated Mrs Rochester, with bristling facial hair and odd shoes – is entirely off the mark. The woman crossing the road from Blackfriars tube looks perfectly sane and respectable, and yet I know at once that it's her. Thick-waisted, her coarse dark hair shot with grey, she's clutching a pink tote bag and anxiously scanning the shop fronts for the universal beacon of the Starbucks logo.

The afternoon sun whitewashing the window gives me a few minutes' advantage. Minutes during which I'm tempted to scramble up from my seat and dive through the staff-only door to the urine-smelling alley beyond and then away to freedom. But then her face clears in brief surprise and her steps falter. She has found me.

I get up from the low armchair and stand stiffly as she pushes the pull door, then waits for a couple to come out, then thanks them, and finally enters.

I thought *I* was scared.

She's visibly trembling as she moves her gaze around the room, blindly at first – it passes over me once without registering my presence.

She must be the same age as Ollie but looks older, her eyes pouched, deep grooves running from her nose to her mouth. The scar on her temple is hidden by dark curls, the last vestiges of her youthful beauty. It shouldn't matter. There should be a paunchy Iberian fisherman to cook for and bicker with, but there was no mention of a husband in the conversations with Lewis Downing. No one to be shocked or protective, or to hold her hand as she made this journey into folly or peril. If there was, perhaps she would never have done what she did.

Her gaze finally catches mine and for a moment the hiss of the coffee machine, the lilting music and the buzz of conversation all recede.

Our eyes are the same colour. Staring into them as she brought the rock down onto my head must have been like looking in a mirror.

She swallows, brings the tote bag into her stomach, then crosses the room.

I hold out my hand, the businesslike gesture intended to establish me in the position of power. It works. She dips her head, gabbles something in Portuguese, corrects herself and says in careful English, 'Hello, I am Estela Pereira.'

'I'm Asha Graveney. Would you like a coffee?'

'Si. Yes. Thank you.'

From the length of my exhalation as I walk to the counter I might have been holding my breath for an hour. My hands are shaking as I take the paper cup and the over-zealous barista fusses at the spill with a blue cloth until I snarl at him. When I get back to the table Estela is still standing.

'Please, sit down.'

She does so, arranging herself carefully, back straight, wincing slightly as if waiting for a blow. I glimpse a silver cross at her throat.

'Thank you for coming.'

She nods.

And then it's gone. My whole prepared speech, complete with its demands and bargains and threats, pops like a soap bubble. And there are just the two of us. Two wounded women, staring at one another in silence.

To my surprise she is the one who breaks it.

'Forgive me.'

At first I think it's just a turn of phrase, the start of a sentence: *forgive me if I –* but for a moment she says no more.

Mustering some degree of self-control I manage the first part of my speech. 'I asked you here so that we might talk about Nico.'

'I am so sorry,' she says. 'For what we did. To you and Oliver.'

Oh-lee-ver. I flinch at his name.

'I want to explain. Before the police come.'

I don't correct her.

'I did it for Nico.' She looks down at her open palms and then up again, defiantly. 'And for what they did to me. Afterwards,

287

because of this,' she moves aside her hair and I see the scar, 'I could no longer read or write. It was so hard anyway without my family. But because of the injury I could not work. Not respectable work, anyway.'

'Why without your family? Where were they?'

'My father is,' she corrects herself, 'was a Catholic priest. A good man to those that knew him, but a harsh father. He would beat us for any small thing he disapproved of. If he found out what I had done, he would never have forgiven me for the shame I brought on the family.'

Her English is accented but fluent. She must have been bright, once.

'How did you know Sean Kearney?'

The spark in her eyes dims.

'His sister, Emily, and me, we were friends.'

'Please, tell me everything that happened that night.'

She tells me that Ollie pushed her. Not that she fell, as Milo put it, whilst attacking him. I suppose I will never know which version is true, and perhaps it doesn't matter.

She says that she managed to crawl back up to the road and made it to the flat above one of the bars that Emily shared with her brother. Sean found her collapsed in the stairwell. By the time he took her to hospital she was drifting in and out of consciousness. There had been a bleed on her brain, but before they took her through to the theatre she made Sean promise not to tell anyone what had happened. Better let them all think she was dead.

The café has started to empty and soon hers is the only voice. She's speaking so quietly I can hardly hear her over my own laboured breathing.

The baby, they told her when she came round, was fine, but she would need to stay for more tests. Terrified her parents might search the hospitals for her, she checked herself out the next day.

Emily and Sean gave her money and helped her find a flat in Lisbon, where she worked for a while in bars and restaurants. A charity helped her when the time came for her to give birth. There were no messages of congratulation, no visitors to the little convent hospital, except Sean. To tell her that Emily had killed herself.

They wept in each other's arms and swore, on the life of the new baby slumbering at her breast, that they would take revenge on those English men.

As she looks up and meets my eyes I see, for the first time, the fire that must have driven her obsession with Ollie.

'For a long time,' she goes on softly, 'I was so angry, but then, as Nico grew, I saw what I had been given. A gift not a curse. Nico was so clever. He could read so well. He loved books, adventure stories. He told me when he was old enough he would make his fortune and save us both.'

The fingers of the hands twisting in her lap are stained yellow from nicotine. I need a cigarette so badly I could cry.

'Sean and me,' she goes on, 'we kept in touch. Sometimes he sent money. I thought, like me, that he had started to get over what happened. I did not realise he had spent all the years looking for them.'

Our eyes meet again and, despite the hot air blasting from the ceiling vent above us, I shiver.

'Sean called me last summer and said he had found a way to get the money to send Nico to college. He said he had found the men that hurt us. They were all very rich, he said, and so happy with themselves. They did not care what they had done to us. They had received no punishment, by God, the law or their own consciences.'

With a sick, hollow feeling in my belly, I realise I have some sympathy for the people who killed my beloved husband.

'At the time Nico and I were living with a man, but he was not a good man. Nico and he would fight when he hit me. I drank. I was desperate. I let Sean persuade me.'

I look away, out of the window at the roaring traffic, and think of the girls I went to school with who were pregnant by sixteen. My mother always kept me informed about the grim trajectories of their lives. Cautionary tales to show me how right she had been to push me so hard through school, to keep such tight reins on my social life: the church youth club then straight home for bath and bed. So I didn't end up like them, with their violent partners, their soul-destroying jobs, their bleak futures. I had always felt so superior. That they had made their choices and I had made mine.

Estela could have chosen not to sleep with Ollie. But in her place I wouldn't have made that choice. I would have fallen in love with him as she did. But because of timing, of circumstance and location, it all worked out for me. That's not choice, that's luck. I have nothing to feel superior about.

I hand her a paper napkin from my saucer and she dabs at her eyelashes, clumped together with tears. Now I can see the beauty that must once have been so striking. Like the green-eyed Afghan girl from the photograph it has been lost, coarsened and crushed through bitter experience. Her waist is thick, her clothes are cheap, her handbag a designer knockoff from a Portuguese market. Ollie wouldn't have given her a second glance now.

And yet, the first time I saw it, the image of the girl in the red dress had sparked a little flame of jealousy. The only time I'd felt it about one of Ollie's conquests. All the others, groomed and pampered like dressage ponies, were trivial, but in Estela I saw a rival, an equal. It could have been me. What happened to Estela could have happened to me.

One of the waitresses leans between us and takes our dirty cups, oblivious or perhaps just indifferent to the emotional charge thrumming in the air.

Estela takes a deep breath and continues. 'Sean knew where you were going on your honeymoon. We agreed to meet there, on the island, and wait for an opportunity. He said you had to die also, so that Nico would be the sole heir, but when the time came . . .' her voice becomes a whisper, 'I could not. My hands would not let me strike hard enough.'

I raise my fingers to my own matching scar.

'I let Sean think I had killed you and then I fled back home. I was so scared and so sorry. When I saw you on the television I wanted to hand myself in but I couldn't do it to him, not after all he had been through.'

Outside the window a bus stops and disgorges tourists. We are close to the Thames here. Sometimes Ollie and I would catch a boat to one of the gentrified wharves. Dine on lobster as the setting sun turned the river into a red snake, then hail a taxi back home. I wonder what Estela and Nico were doing when we were eating those meals.

When she speaks again her voice is stronger. 'I was glad when I received the letter from your lawyer. Now that Sean is dead I am ready to take whatever punishment is decided for me.'

There is a certain dignity in her weather-beaten face as she sits upright in the chair. Only the trembling of her hands gives her away.

I take a deep breath. My turn.

'I asked you here for an explanation, which you have given. But there was another reason.'

She nods, her nostrils flaring like a cow scenting the abattoir.

'In a moment I'd like you to come with me to my lawyer's office, just a few streets from here.'

She swallows and her grip tightens on the pink bag, shielding her chest. 'Will the police be waiting for us there? I must speak to my son before they take me. He does not know what we did, what *I* did.'

'Taking part in the murder of his father?'

She bows her head, absorbing the blows like a martyr. I make her wait, just for a moment, but her distress doesn't bring me the sort of satisfaction I had anticipated when I pictured this scene.

'The police won't be there.'

She looks up.

'Nico is Ollie's son. Ollie was a rich man. If he'd lived, if he'd known he had a son, he would have wanted that son to be provided for.'

I pause to swallow. It should have been our son, mine and Ollie's.

'My lawyer and I have drafted some paperwork gifting a legacy to Nico. I'd like you to read it before we sign, to make sure you're happy with the terms. There will be enough to see him through college and beyond.'

She closes her eyes. Her face has turned the colour of the spilled milk on the table. 'I cannot take your money,' she breathes. 'It is blood money.'

'The money isn't for you, it's for Nico,' I say, then add with forced harshness, 'The only reason I'm not telling the police everything is to protect him.' For her to allow this we must be enemies.

She straightens and, sure enough, a look of defiance crosses her face, but only for a moment, then it's gone. And suddenly, before I can react, she is leaning across the table and pulling me into her arms.

Her hair is in my face, smelling of pine needles, her body has a mother's softness but her heart is beating against mine with such violence. The violence of love. I think of Ollie, born to sweet delight. Nothing was ever taken from him, only given. He didn't understand, he could never know what love and loss can drive us to.

The ballad drifting down from the speakers above our heads reaches its climax and the last guitar chord dies away to silence. I will see him again soon, in Lewis's dim office. I will see him in Nico's eyes, or his smile, some whisper of Ollie. As young as the boy in the photograph: Ollie redeemed.

There's a flurry of spring rain against the window pane. But when I open my eyes the sky is blue.

Acknowledgements

Thanks, as ever, to Eve White, for just about everything.

To Sam Eades, the best editor a feisty heroine could wish for and a joy to work with.

To the charming Ben Willis, publicity hot shot and quote reaper.

Thanks to Sophie Buchan for her pitch-perfect copy-edit, Loulou Clark for the cover, Claire Keep in production, and marketing whizz, Jen Breslin. To Hannah Goodman and the rest of the rights team, and all those working so hard for the book in other markets. Thank you. I love seeing all the brilliant covers.

To Paul Stark and the audio team. There's nothing like hearing your book being read out by a professional to make you feel Proper.

Thanks to my mum, who loves thrillers, especially other people's.

To my husband Vince, for his constant love and support, and for never questioning why I make my living dreaming up ways to kill husbands.

And finally to my lovely sons, who I suspect, despite the muttering and eye-rolling, are quite proud to have a writer for a mum, which makes me very happy.

Reading Group Guide

Topics for discussion

1. What is the effect of shifting locations and timeframes in the novel? Could you keep track?

2. What are your first impressions of Asha and Ollie? Are they really happy together, or are there cracks in their love story?

3. How do Asha and Ollie's family backgrounds differ? Does this cause tension in the relationship?

4. How does the author heighten the tension when Asha and Ollie arrive in Vietnam? Were there particular moments when you were fearful for their safety?

5. The Mango Tree Resort feels like an extra character in the novel. Discuss how the setting is used in the story.

6. Can Sophie and David be trusted? Do they have ulterior motives?

7. Did you suspect who was the murderer? What clues did the author leave?

8. The ending is left ambiguous: what does life hold in store for Asha? Do you think it was the right ending?

Q and A

Alison Belsham interviews Sarah J Naughton

Q: The island setting in Vietnam with the caves is distinctive and absolutely intrinsic to the story. Have you been to Vietnam? And did the setting suggest the story or did you come up with the story first, then pick a honeymoon dream setting for it?
A: The church in *Tattletale* was such an effective element of the book that I knew the setting of *The Other Couple* would be important. The more glamorous it was, the more effective the juxtaposition between that heaven and Asha's hellish experiences. I've never been to Vietnam but I have visited caves like So Den in Thailand, and as a child I loved Durdle Door in Dorset. There's something eerie and slightly menacing about these huge rock formations.

Q: The real tension in the book is between Asha and Ollie's family and friends, who don't think she's good enough for him. Where does Asha find the strength of character to stand up to them all, both before and after the wedding?
A: With such a deprived background, Asha had to be a fighter to get where she did. She also had great parenting (I've never bought into the idea that single parent families are in any way inferior to dual ones), and the worst thing that could happen to her has happened: she no longer has anything to lose. That tends to make someone braver, or just reckless.

Q: At the start, Ollie seems like the perfect husband, but at the same time we know right from the beginning that something's not right in their relationship. This makes the relationship between them seem much more realistic and less saccharine than it might have been in the hands of a less skilled writer. In writing it, was it hard to strike the balance between the positive sides to his character and the negatives?

A: To be honest, I consider their relationship a very good one. Ollie *is* pretty perfect – I was in love with him as I wrote, and to have that effect he had to be human, not a dull Disney prince spouting platitudes. He made a mistake as a young man that he was too immature to deal with at the time. This doesn't make him bad. And he was too scared to tell Asha in case he lost her, which seems pretty reasonable. I try to empathise with all my characters' choices, so I didn't have to balance any specific characteristics for Ollie, just spend time in his head.

Q: The sense of rising menace in this book starts from the very first page and builds beautifully to a crescendo at the end. Is this something you had to plan very carefully, or did it just develop naturally as the story unfolded?

A: I do plan my books. If you know where the plot's going you can really enjoy the writing, but the build up of tension should happen naturally as the reader becomes more involved with the characters and their fates. If it doesn't then you haven't written them properly.

Q: All of your characters seem very real and accurately drawn. Are they completely imaginary or do you cherry pick different characteristics from people you've known?

A: My heroines are, of course, made up of facets of my own character, and Mags and Asha are quite similar in many ways. Once you've got some basic character traits down you can predict how they'll respond to a situation. Many of my characters are

296

based on friends and colleagues, others on actors. Could you guess who Ollie was? Travis is pretty easy too.

Q: The group dynamic between Ollie and his wealthy male friends seems very familiar! Have you known or observed packs of men like this in real life?
A: I've encountered a few entitled, boorish arseholes who consider the rest of us contemptible because of our class / income. Many of them, like Milo, display genuinely psychopathic traits (no empathy or remorse, utter selfishness) and I'm afraid they crop up very often in positions of power. Until we stop valuing the old fashioned alpha-male traits that they pick up at sports-obsessed boarding schools, society will carry on being callous and unequal.

Q: I found Asha's inner conflict over how to handle her problems with Ollie fascinating. Do you think things could have played out differently if she'd been more confrontational with him from the start over the state of their relationship?
A: At the start of a relationship we're all desperate to please this person who seems so perfect to our rose-tinted gaze, so we overlook warning signs and allow patterns to develop that are very difficult to unlearn. Like I said, I think Ollie and Asha's relationship is pretty good and I can understand why she didn't try to stop him from seeing Milo – that sort of controlling behaviour is never good practice in a relationship, however worthy the motives. Yes, Ollie does some pretty unpalatable things, but we are all shades of grey and under pressure our worst traits reveal themselves.

Q: Everybody loves a wedding – and Asha and Ollie's was no exception. How did you use this as a device to tell us more about Asha and Ollie's relationship?

A: Weddings are such cauldrons of emotion and family tensions. Characters are boiled down to their essence, conversations take on great significance, and the day seems to send ripples out across the past and future. Fortunately they're also great plot devices, gathering all your protagonists together in one emotional pressure cooker. With Ollie and Asha it enabled me to highlight her alienation and the tensions between herself and Ollie's family and friends that would become significant later on.

Q: The settings and scenarios in the story come across as totally realistic and very well researched. What were the most interesting parts of your research and did you come across anything interesting that you weren't able to include in the book?
A: Research is really just a springboard for action. Settings and description should be evocative and believable but not intrusive or laborious and there's plenty of rich material you have to leave out in the interests of pace. The presence of the real-life prison on Con Son with its infamous 'tiger cages' was a stroke of luck that enabled me to give paradise a dark heart. The treatment of these prisoners by their colonial oppressors echoes Asha's own racial heritage, and links to the racist treatment of the Burmese migrants: an uncomfortable truth she'd rather ignore but that Travis forces her to confront.

Q: Psychological thrillers, like The Other Couple and Tattletale, are generally stand-alone stories. Would you ever consider writing a series, such as a police procedural?
A: I would absolutely love to write a series. My current work in progress, *The Mothers Club*, features a DI I've taken rather a shine to, but I know so little about the police world, and it's been done so well in the past by so many amazing writers, I'm not sure there's a niche left for me. Saying that, my dad used to tell us bedtime stories featuring a giant, crime-busting wolf called Badolfo (consider that copyrighted), so maybe that's an avenue I could explore.

Alison Belsham is the author of *The Tattoo Thief*, published by Trapeze.